THE HEIGHTS OF ZERVOS

April 1941 – a few days before the German invasion of Greece, a Greek ferry leaves Istanbul on its usual run to the Gulf of Zervos. The passenger list reveals the presence of four Germans and two Englishmen. The situation is tense and dangerous as the enemies, on neutral territory, try to avoid a flashpoint. Then, as the port of Istanbul disappears astern and the weather worsens the ship becomes a battleground and the quiet monastery standing on the heights of Zervos takes on a crucial significance in the war that is about to break.

COLIN FORBES

The Heights
of Zervos

COLLINS
London · 1990

William Collins Sons & Co Ltd
London · Glasgow · Sydney · Auckland
Toronto · Johannesburg

AUTHOR'S NOTE

I wish to record my thanks to Mr Michael
Willis of the Imperial War Museum for his
invaluable technical assistance.

TO JANE

0002 213 222 2488

ISBN 0 00 221322 2

© Colin Forbes 1970
The reprint 1990
Printed and bound in Great Britain by
Billings Book Plan Ltd, Worcester

1 · Saturday April 5, 1941

Dietrich.

The name on the identity card immediately caught the attention of the Turkish passport control officer. *Dr Richard Dietrich, German national, born Flensburg. Profession: archaeologist. Age: thirty-two.* Officer Sarajoglu buttoned up his collar against the cold and studied the card thoughtfully. Behind him in the harbour of the Golden Horn a tugboat siren shrieked non-stop, a piercing sound which the raw, early morning wind from the Black Sea carried clear across Istanbul. Sarajoglu, a man sensitive to atmospheres, was unable to define the feeling of suspense which hung over the waterfront. At half-past six on a morning when winter still gripped the straits the worst always seemed likely to happen.

'You are travelling on business?' the Turk enquired.

'I am leaving Turkey.' Dietrich took a small cigar out of his mouth and flicked ash which fell on the counter separating them. He was a very large man, dressed in a belted, leather coat and a dark, soft hat. His reply had been arrogant in manner and wording, implying that since he was leaving the country his activities were of no concern to this bureaucrat. Sarajoglu concealed his annoyance but proceeded to make a gesture of independence, conveying that although German troops had recently marched into Bulgaria, his country was still neutral territory: using a gloved finger, he poked the German's ash off the counter. It fell off the edge and landed on Dietrich's highly-polished boot. Sarajoglu, who had watched the fall of the ash, looked up and stared at the German. No reaction. Dietrich had clasped his hands behind his back and was staring through a frost-coated window at the harbour.

He was a man whose sheer physical presence was formidable – a man over six feet tall who must weigh at least fourteen stone, Sarajoglu estimated. Even so, the head seemed a little large for the body, a squarish head with a short nose, the mouth wide and firm-lipped, the jaw-line suggesting great energy and enormous determination. But it was the eyes which the Turk found most arresting, large brown eyes which moved slowly and deliberately as though assessing everything. He might be on the list of known German agents, Sarajoglu was thinking. Without much hope, he held on to the card and asked Dietrich to wait a moment.

'I have to catch that boat, the *Hydra*,' Dietrich informed him roughly, 'so hurry it up,' he rumbled as the Turk moved away into a small room behind the counter. Pretending not to have heard, Sarajoglu closed the door, opened a filing cabinet, took out the confidential list of German agents and ran his eye down it. No, his memory had not deceived him: Dietrich was not on the list. It wouldn't have helped much if he had been there; unless caught committing an act of espionage against the Turkish state any German national was at liberty to travel through the country in civilian clothes. But had the name been there he could have asked some awkward questions. He turned to a youth who was typing at a desk close to the wall.

'The *Hydra* – she hasn't changed her sailing schedule so far as you know?'

'No, she's sailing at 7.30 a.m. and making the normal ferry run – Istanbul to Zervos. Why, sir?'

'Nothing really. But there are three Germans aboard the vessel already and now I've got a fourth outside. It's just unusual – Germans travelling to Greece at this stage of the war.'

'Greece isn't at war with Germany – only with Italy.'

'Yes, and that's a curious situation.' Sarajoglu bit the edge of the identity card lightly between gold-filled teeth. He was in no hurry: there was an hour yet before the ferry sailed, so Dietrich could cool his heels. 'Curious,' he repeated. 'The

Greeks have been fighting Italy, Germany's ally, for over six months, but the Germans still remain neutral. I heard a rumour yesterday that British forces have been landing in Greece – one of our captains saw their transports in the Piraeus. They must anticipate a German attack.'

'They probably hope to prevent one.' The typist peered through the window towards the counter beyond. 'Who is the big brute out there?'

Ah, so you don't like the look of him either, Sarajoglu thought. 'He is a Dr Richard Dietrich. He is thirty-two years old – so why is he not in the German army, I wonder?'

'Better ask him.' As the typist resumed work Sarajoglu's lips tightened. He flicked the cutting edge of the card sharply across the youth's ear, noted with satisfaction that he had flinched, then went outside to the counter. The German was standing in exactly the same position as when he had left him, hands behind his back, staring out at the harbour, his manner outwardly unruffled by the deliberate delay. Sarajoglu felt even more irritated as he laid the card on the counter and spoke with exaggerated courtesy. 'You may go now, Dr Dietrich. A pleasant trip.'

The German picked up the card without haste, put it away inside his wallet, his eyes on Sarajoglu all the time. He stood with that typically German stance, his legs splayed well apart, his body like a human tree trunk. The Turk began to feel uncomfortable: there had been precise instructions from above as to how to deal with German tourists – don't play them up and treat them with every courtesy so there can be no cause for complaint from Berlin. He felt relieved when Dietrich turned away, nodding curtly to the porter who hastily picked up his single bag and followed him out of the shed and up the ice-sheathed gangway.

Inside his cabin Dietrich gave the porter a modest tip, a sum which normally would have provoked a sarcastic response, but as the German stared at him, clearly inviting his speedy departure, the porter thought better of it and left the cabin with a polite mumble. Locking the door, Dietrich

kept his coat on: it was bitter on deck and that was where he
had to go in a minute. The single button of his coat carefully
left undone enabled him to slip his hand inside with ease and
he withdrew a Luger 9-mm. pistol, holding it in his hand for
a moment while he wondered whether to hide it in the cabin.
No, there was still a risk and he had carried this weapon on
his person all the way down through the Balkans. It was in
just such a place as this – in a neutral port at the point of
departure – that an attempt might be made on his life.
Replacing the gun inside his coat, he left the cabin to carry
out an important precaution – a swift tour of inspection of
the five thousand ton Greek ferry.

The bitter wind raked his face as soon as he reached the
deck, a wind unpleasant enough, he soon found, to keep the
handful of fellow-passengers below decks. Half an hour later,
his tour of the vessel completed, he stood near the stern
where he could keep an eye on the gangway for late arrivals.
It was just possible that they might send someone on board
at the last moment. Standing by the rail, Dietrich seemed
impervious to the weather as he quietly smoked his cigar.
The lifeboat covers were still crusted with last night's snow-
fall, the masthead rigging still encased with glassy ice, but
the battered yellow funnel was dripping as the ship began to
get up steam. To all outward appearances Dietrich had
wandered round the vessel with the idle curiosity of the
newly-arrived passenger who is vaguely interested in his
temporary home. But now, as he smoked his cigar, he was
cataloguing his discoveries in his mind.

From the chief steward, a voluble soul, he had learned
that the *Hydra* carried a crew of six, that the captain's name
was Nopagos and that he had plied this regular passage
between Istanbul and Zervos for the past fourteen years.
Dietrich also knew that so far, in addition to himself, there
were six passengers aboard: two British civilians who were
sitting in the saloon, one man in his late twenties while his
companion was probably a few years beyond thirty. Which
was interesting, since both men were of military age. He

turned as the chief steward arrived at his elbow, speaking to him in Greek.

'Looks as though we've got our full complement of passengers aboard, sir.'

Dietrich nodded, guessing that the man was getting to know him as much as possible in the hope of a decent tip before the ship docked at Zervos. He checked his watch. 'There's still time for last-minute arrivals.' Again he was probing for information.

'Doubt that, sir. I was talking to the ticket office manager a few minutes ago on the phone – he sold seven tickets for this trip so it looks as though that's the lot.'

Dietrich nodded again and the steward glanced curiously up at the huge German. Sensing that he was no longer in a talkative mood, he excused himself. Left alone once more, Dietrich continued his mental itinerary. Two British civilians, one Greek civilian who lived on Zervos and apparently had something to do with the monastic order who owned the ferry – again a man of military age, but Dietrich presumed that his slight limp must have kept him out of the Greek army now fighting the Italians in Albania. And, finally, three Germans. He had seen two of them briefly, both men in their early forties who had the appearance of businessmen, but the third, a man called Schnell, had apparently come on board very early in the morning and locked himself away in his cabin. 'With his cabin trunk,' as the voluble steward had explained earlier when he was chattering away to Dietrich who had listened without comment as he smoked his cigar. But on this point the large German had detected an uncertain note in the steward's voice and he had asked a question.

'You find that odd – that he should keep a cabin trunk in his cabin?'

'Well, sir, it takes up a lot of space and I offered to have it put in the hold when he came aboard. After all, we shall be docking at Zervos in twenty-four hours. He was quite abrupt with me, the way some . . .' He had paused and

Dietrich, knowing he had been about to say 'the way some Germans are,' had smiled grimly to himself. But the steward had changed his wording in time. '. . . the way some people are when they arrive early. He insisted it stayed with him in his cabin so he must be carrying something valuable.'

Dietrich frowned as he recalled the steward's words – it was this cabin trunk and its unknown contents which occupied his thoughts as he gazed out over the muddle of decrepit-looking tramps and coasters which congested the Golden Horn harbour. A typical oriental port, he told himself sourly – no organisation, no real control. Now, if this had been Hamburg or Emden . . . He heard a sound behind him and remained motionless. Was it likely that an attempt would be made to assassinate him at this late hour – a few minutes before departure? If someone had been put on board to do the job surely they'd wait for darkness to fall when the *Hydra* was well out in the Aegean? On the other hand, a knife in the back on deck and a quick dash to escape down the waiting gangway couldn't be entirely ruled out. And the passenger list was suggestive, too.

Out of the corner of his eye he watched the Greek approaching, hearing the faint slur of his limping step. The man's name was Grapos and even with that slight limp Dietrich thought he would be an asset to any army: of only medium height, there was, nevertheless, a suggestion of tremendous physical strength in those broad shoulders and that powerful chest which swelled the coloured, checked shirt. Not a prosperous individual, Dietrich decided: his grey jacket and trousers were of poor quality, the red tie round his neck was faded and his boots were shabby. The German was turned sideways now, one large foot resting on the lower rail, and he noticed something else which conflicted with the man's general appearance. A paperback novel with an English title protruded from one pocket. The Greek was very close now, stopping almost behind him, and his eyes were shrewd and alert.

'Always it seems so long before the boat sails,' he began. 'You have been to Zervos before?'

'Once.' Dietrich spoke the single Greek word and then turned his head away to gaze out over the harbour. Grapos might have been surprised had he known how much Dietrich had registered in that brief glance. The Greek's face was strong-featured, the jaw-line formidable, and the long straggle of dark moustache which curved round the corners of his wide, firm mouth gave him the look of a bandit or guerrilla. But the point which had instantly alerted Dietrich was the fact that Grapos had spoken to him in Greek. Which could only mean that he had sharp ears, that he had heard Dietrich conversing in that language with the steward, unless that talkative character had already informed Grapos that they had a Greek-speaking German aboard.

Dietrich could still see Grapos out of the corner of his eye, could still have detected any sudden movement, and he had not forgotten that assassins can be hired in any country. Standing by the rail, he had the feeling that the Greek was examining him, was checking on his probable strength in any hand-to-hand encounter.

'There is bad weather on the way,' Grapos remarked and looked upwards.

'Why do you say that?' Dietrich's tone was brusque, un-encouraging, but the Greek seemed not to notice.

'Because of the birds.' Grapos lifted a hand and pointed to where a cloud of seagulls wheeled and floated in erratic circles high above the white-coated domes and minarets on shore.

'Don't you always get birds over a harbour?' Dietrich sounded bored with the company which had thrust itself upon him, but now he was observing the large, hairy-backed hands which gripped the rail as though they might pull a section loose bodily.

'Yes, but not so many, and they are uneasy – you can tell by the way they fly. I have seen them fly like that over Zervos before the great storms. This will be a bad voyage,' he went

on cheerfully. 'We shall run into a storm before we land at
Katyra. Let us hope it does not strike us off Cape Zervos.
You see,' he continued with relish, his eyes on the German's,
'the entrance to the gulf is very narrow and the cape has been
the graveyard of a hundred ships or more . . .' He broke off,
grinning savagely as he displayed a row of perfect white
teeth. 'But, of course, you know – you have been there
before.'

Dietrich said nothing as he hunched his broad shoulders
and threw the smoked cigar butt into the water below. Two
ships away along the wharf another vessel was preparing to
leave, her white funnel belching out clouds of murky smoke
which the wind dispersed in chaotic trails. Behind him he
heard footsteps retreating, one of them out of step. Grapos
had taken the hint and was on his way to find someone else
who would listen to his chatter. Or was he? Dietrich turned
and saw the steward, available for more conversation, standing further along the deck. But Grapos had opened a door
and disappeared inside the ship as though he had found out
what he wanted to know.

Extracting a Zeiss Monokular glass, a single-lens field-
glass, from his pocket Dietrich focused it on the other
vessel getting up a head of steam. The Roumanian flag
whipped in the wind from her masthead and she was, he
knew, the *Rupescu*. Her decks were strangely deserted for a
ship on the point of departure and at the head of the gang-
plank two seamen stood as though on guard. It was quite
clear that shortly she would follow the *Hydra* across the Sea
of Marmara and into the Dardanelles, which he found
interesting. The *Rupescu*, a fast motor vessel, was twelve
hours out of the Bulgarian port of Varna and the situation
could be a little tricky since she was bound for the Aegean.
German troops now occupied the whole of Roumania and
Bulgaria, so technically the Allies might regard the *Rupescu*
as an enemy vessel, a prize to be sought out by the British
Navy. Certainly the British Legation at Istanbul would
already have wirelessed Egypt of her presence in the straits.

But Dietrich doubted whether she would be seized – the British Government had broken off diplomatic relations with Roumania but had not yet declared war on that unhappy country. Satisfied with what he had seen – nothing out of the ordinary – Dietrich put away his glass and then stiffened as a shabbily-dressed man dashed up the gangway. Under his arm he carried a batch of newspapers and he flourished one in the German's face when he came along the deck. Dietrich bought a copy, glancing at the banner headline before he went below. *German Army Poised To Attack?*

The engines were throbbing steadily as he made his way along the narrow companionway and walked calmly into the saloon, a small cramped room with panelled walls which was already reeking of acrid cigar smoke. Pulling out his copy of the *Frankfurter Zeitung*, Dietrich sighed and sank heavily into an ancient arm-chair in a corner which allowed him to see the whole room while he pretended to read. Hahnemann, a thin-faced German in his early forties and dressed like a commercial traveller in a cheap suit, sat in the diagonally-opposite corner smoking one of the cigars responsible for the bad air. In another corner, a heavily-built German of medium height, his clothes well-cut and dark, sat reading some typed sheets, also smoking a cigar. That would be Volber. The fourth corner was occupied by a small bar where a man in off-white uniform was polishing a glass. Thank God, Dietrich was thinking, those two don't look sociable types. I could do without useless conversation at this moment. The thought had hardly passed through his head when two men opened the doors and stood as though hesitating whether to come in. Their first few words warned Dietrich. They were British.

*

'Go on in, for God's sake,' Prentice said impatiently to Ford, who was standing in the doorway. 'Don't just stand gawping. We've paid our fares just like the rest of these johnnies.'

Ford's face was expressionless as he carefully made his

way through the smoke to a table close to the bar. As they settled behind a low table the steward took Dietrich's order and a minute later placed a glass of beer in front of him. Ford kept his voice low as he made the remark. 'That chap who's just got his beer looks like another bleedin' Jerry.'

'I think they all are,' Prentice murmured nonchalantly. 'This is a funny, funny war at times.' Unlike Ford, who sat stiffly and kept an eye on the other three men without appearing to do so, Prentice was outwardly the soul of relaxation. When the steward arrived for their order he deliberately raised his voice so the whole room could hear. 'A beer and a glass of *ouzo*, laddie.'

'Beg, please?' The steward looked at a loss. Prentice leaned round him and stabbed a finger in the direction of Dietrich's table, his voice louder still. 'One *ouzo* and a beer – beer – like that chap over there ordered.' The other two Germans glanced in his direction and then looked away, but Dietrich, who had lowered his paper, stared hard across the room with an unpleasantly enquiring expression.

'Tough-looking basket, that big one,' Ford remarked, keeping his own voice quiet. 'If I met him in Libya I'd let him have two in the pump. Yes, two – just to be sure.'

The drinks were served and Ford sipped at his palely coloured beer cautiously, then grimaced. 'They've got the washing-up water mixed in with the beer.' He eyed Prentice's glass with even more distaste. 'You're not really drinking that, are you?' But his question was purely rhetorical – Prentice would drink anything, smoke anything, eat anything. Some of the dishes he'd consumed during their brief stay in Turkey had astounded and appalled the conservative Ford. Prentice pushed the glass of colourless liquid towards him.

'Go on, it tastes just like whisky.' He watched with amusement while his companion took a gulp and then almost dropped the glass, looking round suddenly to make sure his experience hadn't been observed. Dietrich was still watching him over his paper.

'Lovely!' Ford choked. 'A delicate mixture of nail varnish and turpentine. If that's the Greek national drink no wonder the Romans licked them. It still seems odd travelling with a bunch of Jerries for company.' He looked round the saloon as he heard a distant rattle. The gangway being hauled up probably. In one corner the thin-faced German was absorbed in a book while the man crouched over some typed sheets made notes with a pencil. They might have been aboard a normal peacetime boat and the war seemed a long way from Istanbul.

'It really is damned funny,' Prentice began, his lean, humorous face serious for a change. 'Here we are on a Greek ferry just leaving for Zervos – in the middle of a life-and-death war with Adolf Hitler's Reich – and because the Greeks are fighting the Italians but not the Germans, we can travel with three Jerries we mustn't even bump into if we meet them in the corridor. I must remember this trip when I write me memoirs, Ford.'

'Yes, sir,' said Ford automatically, and received a sharp dig in the ribs for his pains. He understood the hint and swore inwardly. He'd be glad when this ferry trip was over and they could get back to normal service life, to being Lieutenant Prentice and Staff-Sergeant Ford. Before they had boarded the *Hydra* Prentice had given him a stern lecture in their Istanbul hotel bedroom and he had tripped up already.

'Ford,' Prentice had begun, 'for the purposes of this sea trip back to Greece and while we're on board the ferry, I want you to forget I'm a lieutenant and, what's more important still, forget that you're a staff-sergeant. We're sporting civvies, but if you keep on calling me "sir" it's a dead giveaway. There may even be a German tourist on that broken-down old Greek ferry.' Prentice hadn't really believed that this would happen but he was dramatising the situation to try and make Ford forget his years of professional training for a few hours.

'I'll watch it, sir,' Ford had replied and had then watched

Prentice throw his trilby on the bed with a despairing cry.

'Ford!' he had bellowed. 'You've just done it again! Look, I know we're at the fag-end of our trip with the military mission to carry out liaison with the Turks in case Jerry attacks them, but we really have got to watch it . . .'

The trouble really had been the Turks themselves. Anxious to keep out of the war if they could – and who could blame them for that? – they had invited the British to send a military mission to discuss possible defence measures if the worst happened. But to avoid provoking the attack they feared, or rather, to avoid giving Berlin an excuse for launching that attack, they had insisted that the mission should travel in civilian clothes. A Signal Corps man, Prentice had found plenty to discuss with his Turkish opposite numbers in the way of a plan for setting up communications, and Staff-Sergeant Ford, ex-Royal Artillery, was now one of that rare breed, an ammunition examiner, an expert on explosives, both British and foreign. In this role he had also finished his work late when he had been taken to see a Turkish dam it was proposed to blow up in the event of a German invasion. So both of them had returned to Istanbul to find the plane with the military mission aboard had already left for Athens.

'When's the next one,' Prentice had light-heartedly asked the chap at the legation.

'There isn't one,' the legation official had informed him coldly. 'You'll have to catch a boat out of here. The very first available boat,' he had added. 'I've already looked it up for you – it's a ship called the *Hydra*. Sailing for Greece tomorrow morning. Just after dawn,' he had concluded with a twinge of waspish humour which Prentice, who hated rising early, had not fully appreciated.

Later, Prentice had discovered that normally there was a regular service operating between Istanbul and Athens, but the Turks had just cancelled this because of rumours of German troop movements along their northern borders. So, that left the ferry to the peninsula of Zervos, which was in

northern Greece, much closer to Salonika than Athens, but
at least it would land them on Greek soil. The legation, of
course, had been in the devil of a hurry to see the last of
them. Prentice had a shrewd idea that the Ambassador was
having kittens at the thought of British soldiers disguised as
civilians wandering the streets of Istanbul. A downright un-
neutral posture, His Excellency must have thought. As he
expressed it quietly to Ford in the saloon of the *Hydra* while
he swallowed the *ouzo* in two gulps. 'I really think if there'd
been a boat leaving for Russia they'd have pushed us on
that.'

'Maybe. I still think it's queer there should be three
Jerries all on the same trip on this leaky old tub,' Ford
persisted. He could hear the rattle of a chain somewhere.
They'd be off any minute now.

Prentice grinned. 'They may be embassy staff transferred
from Istanbul to their place in Salonika.' He studied Ford,
noted again the stocky build, the neatly-cut black hair and
the alert eyes which watched the room constantly. Always
wanting to have a go, was Ford. An aggressive, controlled
chap who carried an air of competence and energetic ability.
As for Prentice, he never went out of his way to have a go,
but if the necessity arose he was more than able to cope with
his leisured, laconic manner. The difference was that for
Ford, the army was a way of life, whereas for Prentice it was
a necessary but time-wasting interval which kept him from
his advertising job in the West End of London.

'But if they're embassy staff,' Ford went on obstinately, his
hands cupped to hide his mouth, 'why are they travelling
separately? They don't know each other, that's obvious
enough.'

Prentice felt the ship moving away from the quayside and
checked his watch. 7.30 a.m. Ford had a point there, he was
thinking. And if they were embassy staff going to Salonika
why the devil hadn't they taken the train from Istanbul along
that line through Macedonia? By all accounts it was a nightmare trip, stopping at every little out-of-the-way village and

taking anything up to a couple of days, but at least it would have got them there direct. So why were they in such a rush to reach Greece by the earliest possible hour? Why, Prentice kept asking himself? Why?

*

Field-Marshal von List stood up from behind the desk at his G.H.Q. in southern Bulgaria and walked to the window, still holding the meteorological report. Beside the desk his staff officer, Colonel Wilhelm Genke, waited patiently. The field-marshal was worried and from long experience Genke knew that this was not the moment to speak. The clock on the desk registered 7.30 a.m.

His face seasoned and grim, List gazed out at the view, and this didn't please him either because it was a reminder of the piece of paper he held in his hands. It was an hour after dawn and beyond the stone houses of the village he could make out where the mountains rose to meet the clouds which hung low over Bulgaria, clouds which promised more snow on the way. Which the met. report also promised. He could vaguely see the snow from where he stood – great drifts of it piled up on the lower slopes under the cloud ceiling. His voice was harsh when he spoke.

'It's foul, unspeakably foul weather. They could be wrong, I suppose. They're wrong half the time, these so-called weather experts. Look at what happened in Norway.'

Genke coughed, timing his intervention carefully. 'Spring is late all over Europe, sir. There is still deep snow across the Russian steppes and no sign of a thaw . . .'

'Don't let's talk about Russia yet. We have to settle this business first.' List turned round, a tinge of sarcasm in his voice. 'Berlin, of course, is quite confident.'

'Berlin is always confident when other people have to do the work, sir. But you have exceptionally powerful forces under your command.'

On that point, at least, the field-marshal agreed. The

Twelfth Army comprised two motorised, three mountain Alpenkorps and light infantry divisions, three regiments of the Liebstandarte Adolf Hitler Division – and five Panzer divisions, the spearhead of the coming onslaught on Greece and Jugoslavia. A force of enormous strength and great mobility – theoretically powerful enough to overwhelm everything which stood in their path. But there was deep snow on the Greek mountains, deep snow on Olympus and Zervos. Could the machines overcome the hazards of this damnably prolonged winter? The question was never far from his mind – and zero hour was almost here.

Gazing out of the window, he thought that Bulgaria was the most Godforsaken spot he had encountered in his life, and even as he watched, white flakes drifted down outside the window, several clinging to the glass and beginning to build up opaque areas. Would spring never come? Yes, zero hour was very close indeed. Beyond the window he heard a familiar sound – the grind and clatter of tank tracks moving over cobbled streets. The supporting Panzers were rolling towards the border and would be in position before nightfall. The timetable had been set in motion and the operation was under way. Now no power on earth except Berlin could stop it. And within hours even Berlin would have forfeited that prerogative. From outside the house came the sound of a vehicle stopping, its engine still left running. Genke shuffled his feet.

'The car has arrived, sir.'

List buttoned up his coat to the neck, put the peaked cap on his head and started for the door. But on the way he paused to glance at the wall map which an orderly would take down as soon as they had left, a map of the southern Balkans and eastern Mediterranean zones. Then Genke opened the door and Field-Marshal von List strode out with his assistant following. Genke had noted that pause to glance at the map and he knew which area had attracted List's attention. He had looked first at Istanbul, then his eye had followed the sea route through the Dardanelles and across the Aegean where it had finally alighted on a certain peninsula.

Zervos.

*

'The *Rupescu?*' The Senior Naval Intelligence Officer at Alexandria looked up at his assistant, Lieutenant-Commander Browne. 'Is that the Roumanian ship the Legation people at Istanbul sent the message about?'

'Yes, sir. It left the Bulgarian port of Varna yesterday and arrived at the Golden Horn a few hours ago. There's some mystery as to her ultimate destination.'

'What mystery?'

'It's a bit vague, sir. Apparently she's bound for Beirut – but it's her first trip out of the Black Sea for months and I suppose the Legation's bothered because the Germans control Roumania now.'

'I see. That's rather delicate – we still haven't declared war on Roumania. You're suggesting we keep an eye on her? To make sure she is heading for the Lebanon?'

Browne looked out of the window where a white jetty sparkled in the early morning sunshine, its arm enclosing a basin of brilliant blue water where warships lay at anchor. A transport bound for Greece was just beyond the jetty wall, sailing north-west and leaving behind a clear wake of white on the blue. 'It's the only vessel in the area which has the remotest connection with the Axis powers – and so far we have no idea what she's carrying.'

'Probably collecting rather than carrying – trying to pick up a final cargo before war is eventually declared and we can pounce on her. We're very stretched, you know that, Browne.'

'I was thinking of the *Daring*, sir. She's patrolling off the Turkish coast and could intercept the *Rupescu* soon after dark. I'm not thinking of boarding her – but it might be interesting to get her reaction when a British destroyer comes in close.'

'Send Willoughby a message, then. And radio another one to Istanbul. We've had two requests already from those querulous diplomats.' The senior officer looked at the wall clock. 7.30 a.m. Yes, it would be after nightfall before Willoughby arrived.

*

The tension had slowly risen aboard the *Hydra*, a tension which seemed reproduced by the steady beat of her throbbing engines as she left the Dardanelles and proceeded far out into the open Aegean. By nightfall she was midway between the Turkish and Greek coasts, steaming through seas which were beginning to curdle. The tension rose from small, meaningless incidents. The meeting at a doorway between Prentice and the squat, dark-haired German, Volber, when the latter had started to push his way through first and had then changed his mind, offering prior entry to Prentice. The episode at dinner when a cork came out of a bottle like a pistol shot and for several seconds the company had frozen. The careful way in which passengers of different nationalities turned to go in another direction when they saw someone coming towards them.

'It's not frightfully funny any more,' Prentice had remarked over dinner irritably. 'Look at the way they're sitting – like pall-bearers at a funeral.'

'They'd have more fun at a funeral – afterwards, anyway,' Ford had pointed out. 'It's almost as though they're waiting for something to happen.' All the others occupied a table to themselves. Dietrich, Hahnemann, Volber and Grapos – all sitting in splendid isolation with empty tables between them while each ate and drank as though he were the only person in the room, taking care to make no sound except for the occasional clink of cutlery. Even the captain, Nopagos, who came in later, was unable to help. He had explained this briefly to Prentice in his careful English while visiting each table in turn before taking a table of his own.

'It is difficult, Mr Prentice – British and Germans on board, you understand.'

'Frightened there'll be a rumpus?' Prentice had enquired genially.

'Rum . . . pus?'

'A battle, a fight.' Prentice had play-acted with his fists, glad of the chance to pull someone's leg, then had relented when he saw the Greek's doleful expression. 'Don't worry, we'll be good. But I bet you'll be damned glad to drop this lot off at Katyra in the morning.'

'The safe arrival in port is always the happy time,' Nopagos replied ambiguously and went away to his solitary table.

When dinner was over one passenger, Dietrich, lingered in the room long after the others had left, smoking his cigar and drinking coffee from the pot the steward had provided after clearing his table. Like the saloon, the dining-room was panelled and small gold curtains were still drawn back from the porthole windows. Occasionally, he glanced out of the nearest window which gave him a view across the moonlit sea to the north-east, a sea which had now ceased to tremble with small waves and was already developing massive undulations which heaved towards the vessel with foam-topped crests. The dining-room was beginning to sway ponderously and Dietrich shifted his feet wider apart to counter the movement as the woodwork creaked ominously, the horizon beyond the porthole dipped out of sight and then climbed into view again. The fourth German, Schnell, had still not appeared, and Dietrich had mentioned this to the steward when he had brought the extra pot of coffee. 'Perhaps he's dead,' he had said with rough humour, 'he could be for all we've seen of him.'

'He had dinner served in his cabin,' the steward had remarked, 'and he wanted a Thermos of coffee made up for the night. Probably he doesn't sleep well at sea.'

'He won't if he drinks a whole Thermos of this,' Dietrich had replied. The coffee was Turkish and the prospect of consuming it in such quantities suggested a steel-plated stomach and an inability to sleep at all.

'We get passengers like that occasionally,' the steward had prattled on. 'They just don't seem to like mixing with strangers. This man is like that – he was in the toilet when the dinner was taken in, as though he didn't even wish to see the steward. He's Austrian, I think,' he had added.

'Indeed? Why do you say that?'

'His big cabin trunk has labels on it from the Hotel Sacher in Vienna. The steward thinks he spends a lot of time sitting by his porthole gazing out to sea – there was a pair of field-glasses opened by the table next to his wrist-watch. Call me if you want anything else, sir.' Left alone by himself Dietrich had drunk two cups of the strong-tasting liquid while he thought about the invisible Herr Schnell. It was ten o'clock when he walked out of the deserted dining-room to take a final tour of the vessel, and at this hour the *Hydra* had the feel of a ghost ship, one of those phantom vessels which drift round the seaways of the world and are only seen as a mirage in the night. There was no one about as he descended a creaking staircase and began to walk along the empty companionway on the deck containing the passenger cabins. He had chosen this staircase deliberately and his rubber-soled boots made no sound as he paused by the first cabin which the Austrian occupied. Cabin One was silent but there were narrow streaks of light in the louvred upper half of the closed door. He made no attempt to see through the louvres – he had tested that possibility with his own cabin door earlier in the evening – but clearly the mysterious Schnell was still secreted inside his own quarters. He might not be awake, Dietrich was thinking as he stood quite still, since a man who spends hours inside one small room is likely to get drowsy and fall asleep with the lights still on.

The next cabin was the wireless room. Here, instead of pausing, Dietrich walked past slowly, seeing through the half-open door the Greek wireless operator reading a news-paper as one hand reached out for a sandwich. So far everything seemed normal, perfectly normal, but Dietrich could not rid himself of a feeling of growing unease. The next cabin was in darkness. Volber's. The German who looked like the owner of a small business – or a member of the Gestapo. Often the two types could easily be confused. Cabin Three still had the lights on and from behind the closed door came the faint sounds of dance music. Herr Hahnemann was tuned in to Radio Deutschland, perhaps feeling a little homesick aboard this swaying ferry in the middle of the Aegean. There was just the possibility, of course, that he was waiting for a signal innocuously inserted into the regular programme, the playing of a certain tune, but Dietrich told himself that this was fanciful. The strained atmosphere aboard the ferry was beginning to affect his judgement. There were lights in the next cabin, too, the temporary home of the two Britishers. Dietrich paused outside and then walked steadily on as the mumble of voices died suddenly. When a cabin door opened behind him he was careful not to turn round. An interesting thought had struck him: was Volber really asleep inside that darkened cabin or was he somewhere else, having deliberately given the impression that he had gone down for the night? Silently he passed his own darkened cabin and began to mount the staircase at the other end of the companionway. The vessel was steaming steadily westward and as he opened the door at the top he faced the stern, consciously bracing himself and squaring his shoulders as the moan of the wind took on a higher note, rasping his face with its icy blast. Dietrich had experienced the wind from the plains of Hungary, a wind which swept straight in from the depths of faraway Siberia, but as he slammed the door shut he thought he had never felt a more penetrating chill.

The deck was deserted. No sign of Volber. But the boat was still there, the vessel he had seen through the porthole from his dining-room table. She was moving along a course parallel to the *Hydra*'s, ploughing through the rising seas perhaps three kilometres to starboard. The deck was lifting sufficiently for him to hold on to the rail as he made his way to the stern, his face muscles drawn tight and not from the bitter wind which froze his skin. Taking out his Monokular glass, which was small enough to conceal inside the palm of one hand, he looked back along the deck. Lifeboats, the snow melted and gone during the day, swung slowly on their davits, reproducing the movement of the sea. A thin trail of smoke floated from the *Hydra*'s funnel, was caught up by the wind and thrown into a spiral. There was no sign of life anywhere. He aimed his glass, saw the other ship as a blur which merged in one long glow-worm of light, focused, brought the lights forward as separate portholes, noted the white funnel and the unidentifiable flag which whipped from the masthead. For perhaps a minute he stood motionless, one part of his mind on the lens, the other part alert for the slightest sound which might warn him that he was no longer alone on that empty deck, a sound which might warn him of the attempt on his life he had feared ever since coming aboard. Then he closed the glass, pocketed it, and checked his watch once more. 10.10 p.m. Yes, it was the *Rupescu*, the vessel which had got up steam as soon as the *Hydra* had made preparations to leave the Golden Horn. Shoulders hunched against the wind, he made his way back along the unstable deck and went down into the warmth which met him as soon as he opened the door. Inside his own cabin he took off his hat and coat, lit a fresh cigar, put the Luger within easy reach and settled down to wait.

*

'It was the big German,' Ford said as he closed the cabin door and re-locked it. 'I caught him on the staircase at the far end – he still had his coat and hat on and he was going up on deck. I don't like it.'

'Don't like what?' Prentice withdrew his hand from where it had rested near the pillow which concealed his Webley .455 revolver and began studying the patience cards spread out over his bunk.

'The feel of this old tub – those Jerries being aboard and not talking to each other. They come from the same country and they haven't said a blasted word to each other from what I've seen.'

'Perhaps they're English and in disguise – that would explain the non-fraternisation.' He picked up a card, placed it over another. 'Not been formally introduced, you see.'

Ford lit the last of his army issue cigarettes, the ones he could only smoke when they were alone, and started thudding a heel against the woodwork as he sat down on his bunk. Prentice looked up and stared pointedly at the thudding heel until Ford stopped the noise, then went back to his game. 'You could always get some kip,' he suggested hopefully.

'Couldn't sleep a wink,' the staff-sergeant told him emphatically. 'Not with those Jerries aboard creeping all over the shop when it's long past their bedtime.' He got up and went over to the porthole, pulling the curtain aside with a jerk. 'That ship's still there, too. Wonder why it's keeping so close to us?'

Prentice slammed down a card and lit a Turkish cigarette quickly while he watched the sergeant who continued staring out of the porthole in his shirt-sleeves. 'Ford, there are things called sea-lanes. Ships are liable to follow them. If you've ever crossed the Channel you'll see quite a few ships not far from each other the whole way across. I really think that Turkish food must have done you a power of harm – you're not normally as jittery as this.'

Ford turned away from the porthole, closing the curtain again. 'And I'm not normally travelling on a boat with a load of Jerries for company. There's something strange going on – I can feel it.'

'Three Jerries . . .' Prentice started to point out.

'Four! There's that other one the captain mentioned to us earlier in the day – the one that never comes out of his cabin at the end of the companionway.'

'All right, four! But hardly a load of Jerries – you make it sound as though there's a division of them aboard. What can four of them do aboard a Greek ferry in the middle of the Aegean which – when I last heard of it – is controlled by the Royal Navy? If you go on like this, Ford,' he continued with a mischievous grin, 'you'll end up in sick bay with some M.O. asking you what scared you in your cradle! Now, how do you expect me to get this game out if you persist in banging your foot and peering through portholes as though you anticipated a whole German army arriving at any moment?'

'Sorry. It's probably that last meal we had in Istanbul. What was that dish again?'

'Fried octrangel,' said Prentice absent-mindedly as he turned his attention to the cards. 'It's a baby octopus. A great delicacy.' He didn't look up to see Ford's face, but a few minutes later he became aware again of the restless sergeant's movements and glanced up to see him putting on his coat over his jacket.

'Feel like a breath of fresh air,' Ford explained. 'Don't mind, do you?'

'Yes, I think I do!' The lieutenant spoke sharply. 'Going out on your own isn't really a very good idea.'

Ford's eyes gleamed as he dropped the coat on to his bunk. 'You don't much like it either, then?'

'I just don't think it's too clever for us to separate at this time of night. There!' He dropped a card on a small pile. 'You see, it's coming out.' Prentice smiled grimly to himself as he went on playing: Ford had smoked him out there. No, he wasn't entirely happy about the situation aboard this ferry, but he saw no point in alarming the staff-sergeant at this stage. Prentice was a man who, despite his outwardly extrovert air, preferred to keep his fears to himself. Those Germans who were worrying Ford could, of course, be spies, and if they were they had chosen the right place to come – the strategically important peninsula of Zervos. As he played out his game Prentice was thinking of a military conference he had attended in Athens just before departing for Turkey, a conference he had attended because a question

of communications had been involved. He could hear
Colonel Wilson's clipped voice speaking now as he automatically placed a fresh card.

'It's the very devil,' Wilson had said, 'getting permission
to send some of our chaps to Mount Zervos. The official in
the Greek War Ministry who's responsible says Zervos is
seventy miles from the Bulgarian frontier and in any case the
peninsula comes under the command of the Greek army in
Macedonia. He just won't have us there.'

'Not even to send a small unit to set up an observation
post?' Prentice had ventured. 'From what I gather the
monastery under the summit looks clear across the gulf to
the coast road taking our supplies up to the Alkiamon Line.'

'You gather correctly,' Wilson had told him crisply. 'But
the monastery seems to be the stumbling-block. Apparently
for many years the whole peninsula has been a monastic
sanctuary and you need a government permit even to land
there. They won't grant one of those to a woman – the only
women allowed in the area are the wives and relatives of
fishermen who live there . . .' He had paused, his expression
icy until the ripple of laughter had died. Perhaps he had
sounded unnecessarily indignant on that score. 'The guts of
the thing is that this Greek official practically suggests we'd
be violating something sacred by sending in a few troops . . .'

'You believe him?' Prentice had interjected quietly, never
backward in speaking up when his interest was aroused.
There had been an awkward pause before Wilson had
answered that one. Only a tiny fraction of the Greek popula-
tion was believed to hold secret Nazi sympathies, but it was
feared that one or two of these undesirable gentry might
occupy key positions inside the Greek government.

'We can only take his word,' Wilson had replied eventually.
'But the thing that sends shivers up the spines of our planning
staff is the idea of German troops capturing that monastery.
It's perched nearly three thousand feet up at the southern tip
of the peninsula and has a clear view across to that vital
coast road. And that's not all. There's some freak in the

weather up there which means the summit of Mount Zervos is nearly always cloud-free – so you get an uninterrupted view of that road even when visibility's nil a few miles away. A Jerry observation post stuck up there would put us in a proper pickle.'

'Can't we just send a few troops across the gulf and then tell Athens afterwards?' enquired the enthusiastic Prentice. 'Fait accomplis are difficult to argue against.'

That suggestion, as Prentice well remembered, had brought down the wrath of God, in the person of Colonel Wilson, on his head. The whole conference had listened in silence while he had been treated to a lecture on Allied relations with the Greek government, and Wilson had concluded by saying they were continuing to make representations to Athens to allow them to send troops. Afterwards, a Royal Artillery major had further enlightened Prentice: beyond the head of the gulf a range of hills formed a natural defence line, but if the Wehrmacht attacked and were able to emplace heavy guns on the lower slopes they could bring down an annihilating fire on the coast road from behind these hill crests – *providing they had an observation post on Mount Zervos which could guide the fall of the bombardment.* The major ended up by saying that if the Germans ever did get the Allies in such a position it would be little short of a massacre.*

Prentice dropped another card in place and sighed as the *Hydra* tilted again, a slow, deliberate roll as though revolving on an axis. While in Turkey he'd almost forgotten that conference, never believing for one instant that he would ever set eyes on Zervos, and here he was less than eight hours' sailing time from that benighted peninsula. And why the hell did ships always have to leave almost at dawn and arrive somewhere else at that same God-forsaken hour? Finishing the game, he started shuffling the cards, uncertain whether to continue playing. Then he paused. Ford was again standing

*Later in the war the same threat materialised at Monte Cassino where a German observation post reported to the gunners every movement of Allied troops.

by the porthole, the curtain drawn back, and there was something in his manner which caught Prentice's attention. 'What's up?' he asked.

'It's this ship – she's coming in damned close, whatever you say about sea-lanes.'

Prentice stood up quickly and went over to the porthole. The unknown vessel was now sailing on a parallel course less than a quarter of a mile from the *Hydra*'s hull and even as he watched the gap seemed to be narrowing. 'She is damned close,' he agreed, and felt a faint prickling of the short hairs at the back of his neck. He watched for a little while longer to be sure the ship wasn't simply passing them, then took a decision. 'I think we'd better pay our friend, Captain Nopagos, a little visit . . .' He broke off in mid-sentence. 'What was that?'

'Sounded like someone falling over in the passage – I think he hit our door . . .'

'Better see – and watch it!' Prentice dropped the pack of cards on to his bunk, sat down and idly let his hand rest close to the pillow which concealed the Webley. He looked half-asleep as he watched Ford, who had now reached the locked door. Ford hesitated, listened for a moment, then heard a groan and a shuffling sound. He unlocked the door, opening it cautiously.

The Greek steward who looked after the cabins was lying face down in the companionway, his body wriggling as a slight moan escaped him. Ford looked both ways along the passage and saw that it was deserted. The *Hydra* was moving in a heavy swell, rocking slowly as the sea lifted and lowered it. He bent down quickly and noted that the man's hands were underneath him as though clasped to his stomach. There was no sign of injury so far as he could see – the poor devil must have been taken sick while walking down the companionway. He looked back inside the cabin and called out to Prentice.

'It's the steward. I think he's had an attack or something. I'd better go along and find someone . . .'

'Hold it a minute!' Prentice's nerves were on edge and his mind raced as he took in the implications of this unexpected incident. Ford going off to seek help would mean they were separated, a situation which he felt could be dangerous. There was something queer going on, very queer indeed. 'No, don't do that,' he told Ford quickly. 'Can we get him in here? Let's have a look at him first.' He stepped into the companionway to give Ford a hand, stooping down to hoist the steward by the shoulders while the sergeant took the legs. They were standing in this position, still in the companionway with their hands encumbered, when the cabin door next to them was thrown open and Hahnemann came out. At waist-height he held a German machine-pistol, the weapon aimed at Ford's chest as he spoke in English.

'Put the Greek down and lift your hands. Be careful! If I shoot, the Greek dies, too.'

They put the steward down gently and as he reached the floor his hands and feet began to scrabble about in a more life-like fashion. His face turned and Prentice saw that he was scared stiff, his complexion whiter than the jacket he wore. With Ford, he raised his hands, turning slowly as he stood up so that he could look down the passage where he caught a glimpse through the half-closed door of the wireless-room. The radio operator still sat in front of his set but now his hands were tied behind the back of his neck and then the view closed off as Volber came out holding a Luger pistol.

'Look at the wall!' snapped Hahnemann. 'And keep still.'

They faced the wall and Prentice felt Volber's quick hands pat his clothes and explore his body for hidden weapons. The shock of the hold-up was going now and Prentice's mind coldly searched for a way of upsetting the enemy who had decided to continue the war on neutral territory. The Greek steward was standing up, had faced the wall when Hahnemann gave the order. The German issued his instructions in a crisp, controlled manner which interested Prentice and warned him that any counter-action would have to be swift, unexpected and totally effective. The voice spoke again at Prentice's back.

'And now you go inside the cabin. Quickly!'

Prentice obeyed the order without hesitation. In fact, he went inside so quickly that Hahnemann was caught off balance as the lieutenant tore through the open doorway, hooked his right heel behind the panel and slammed it in the German's face. His instinct was to dive for the revolver under the pillow, but knowing he hadn't the time, he jumped close to the wall as the door was thrown open again. Hahnemann jumped into the room, literally leapt through the doorway, turning as he saw Prentice a fraction of a second too late. The lieutenant grasped the machine-pistol by the barrel and swung the muzzle viciously to one side, still holding on, then jerked it backwards beyond the German who had expected him to pull it away from him. The muzzle was still aimed futilely at the outer wall. Continuing the rearward jerk, Prentice felt the weapon come free and in the same second felt his feet slip under him. He went over on the back of his head, still gripping the weapon as clouds of dizziness addled his brain and he saw only shadows through a mist. He was still struggling through the mists, seeing them clear gradually, when something hard and heavy hit him in the side. Hahnemann had just kicked him. When he recovered some sort of a grip on himself the German was standing over him with the machine-pistol aimed at the centre of his chest. In the doorway Ford stood grimly silent with Volber's Luger pointed at his stomach.

'Get up!' said Hahnemann savagely, backing away as Prentice, wondering why the hell he was still alive, clambered painfully to his feet. That hadn't been too clever. The back of his head felt to be split in two and an iron hammer was banging down the split. He gulped in several breaths of air, trying to hear what Hahnemann was saying. 'Over by the wall. Quick!' Everything had to be so damned quick for this chap. Tottering a little, Prentice went over to the outer wall and leant against it where Ford joined him a moment later.

Volber went out of the cabin, closing the door behind him. He had other things to do, Prentice assumed. Like knocking the captain unconscious. It had all happened so swiftly that he was still wondering what the hell they hoped to achieve, was still suffering from a partial sense of shock. Alongside him Ford stared at the German with an intent look, waiting for him to make that one small mistake. The trouble was he didn't look like a man who repeated his mistakes – letting Prentice break loose had put him in a state of total alertness, and although he was guarding two men on his own he stood back far enough to give his gun a good field of fire. One quite brief burst would kill both of them: Ford, as a weapons and explosives expert, was under no illusions on this point.

'Why are you aboard this ship, Lieutenant Prentice?' demanded Hahnemann.

Prentice glanced at the table where Volber had left the papers and paybook he had extracted from their pockets while searching them for weapons. Hahnemann must have looked at these while he was coming up out of the mists. He wasn't in any hurry to reply – time was a factor the German clearly valued, as though he were following a carefully worked out timetable. And Prentice had detected a note of anxiety behind the question, so his reply was deliberately non-informative. If only his head would stop pounding he might be able to out-think this basket. 'To travel from Istanbul to Zervos,' he said. For a horrible second he thought he had made a fatal mistake. Hahnemann's finger tightened on the trigger and Prentice braced himself for the lacerating burst of bullets, but the German regained control and smiled unpleasantly.

'That I understood! Now, Lieutenant Prentice, before I shoot Sergeant Ford in the stomach I will ask the question again. Why are you travelling on this particular ship on this particular night? You understand? Good.'

Prentice found he was sweating badly on the palms of his hands and under his armpits. He hadn't the least idea of what Hahnemann was talking about but he doubted whether he could convince the German of this. His brain reeled as he sought desperately for words which might half-satisfy their interrogator, and with a tremendous effort he managed a ghastly smile in an endeavour to lower the temperature before it was too late. 'I take it you're in the German army?' For the first time Hahnemann showed a trace of uncertainty and Prentice followed up his tiny advantage quickly. 'Then you'll know that according to the Geneva Convention all we have to give you is name, rank and number. You've got those there on that table already.'

It was a hair-line gamble, switching the conversation to this topic, but Prentice was counting on the German's training to make him pause, to cool his anger, to gain control again. To his great relief he saw the machine-pistol muzzle swing to a point between himself and Ford where it could fire in either direction. The German had, at least temporarily, recovered his balance. Prentice had now assessed Hahnemann as a highly-trained individual who normally kept an ice-cold grip on his emotions, but who also, occasionally, in a state of fury, lost that grip and went berserk. They had just witnessed such an occasion when their lives had trembled on the brink. In short, he was an extremely dangerous man to be near at any time, but rather more dangerous when he held a gun in his hands.

'What were you doing in Turkey?' Hahnemann asked suddenly.

'Trying to get a berth home to Athens.' Prentice's quick tongue rattled on. 'And the civilian clothes were loaned to us by the Turks. Our ship struck a mine off the Turkish coast two days ago and we were dragged out of the sea more dead than alive. We were the only survivors – and don't ask me the name of the ship or how many she was carrying because you wouldn't answer that either if I were holding the gun. And don't ask me why the Turks didn't intern us because I don't know – except that they seemed damned glad to get rid of us at the earliest possible moment. They'd have put us on the normal Istanbul – Athens service, but that was cancelled at the last minute so we were hustled aboard this ferry. The first available ship out, they said – and this was it.'

It had been a long speech and he hoped to God that it had satisfied Hahnemann on the one question which seemed to bother him – why were they aboard the *Hydra*? There was a hint of respect in the German's eyes now and Prentice decided to press a point home, forgetting that it's always a mistake to overdo a good thing.

'So we're your prisoners-of-war at the moment,' Prentice continued, 'but don't forget that the Royal Navy controls the Aegean. If there's a British destroyer in the area you may find me holding that gun within a few hours, so let's drop the threats.'

'There is a British destroyer near here?' The gun muzzle was aimed straight at Prentice's chest and the note of cold fury had come back into the German's voice. 'You know this?' The words were an accusation and Hahnemann's jaw muscles were rigid with tension, a tension which instantly communicated itself to the two men with their backs to the wall. The tip of the gun muzzle quivered, the outward sign of the nervous vibration bottled up inside the man holding the weapon. Christ! Prentice was thinking, we're a nervous twitch away from a fusillade. Where the devil did I go wrong? He spoke carefully but quickly, his eyes fixed on Hahnemann's as he struggled to gauge the effect of his words while he was talking. 'I'm not thinking of any particular destroyer – I'm in the army, not the navy – you know that. But these seas are constantly patrolled so it's just a matter of luck – yours or ours.' He shut up, hoping for the best and determined not to overdo it a second time. His shirt was clinging to his wet back and he daren't look at Ford in case Hahnemann thought he was passing a signal. It was becoming a nightmare and he had a grisly feeling they might not live through it.

'Turn round and lie on the floor – stretch out your hands to the fullest extent.'

The unexpected order threw Prentice off balance; it was

impossible to follow this German through his swift changes of mood, but at least there weren't going to be any more of those trigger-loaded questions. Knowing what was coming and unable to do a thing about it, he joined Ford on the floor. Hahnemann was going to put them out of action temporarily while he attended to other matters. Out of the corner of his eye he saw the machine-pistol butt descend on Ford's head and then the sergeant was slumping unconscious as Prentice turned his head. The muzzle was aimed at his face. 'Flat on the floor,' Hahnemann commanded. Prentice was turning his head away when a ton-weight landed on his tender scalp. A brilliant burst of white light flashed before his eyes and then vanished in the flood of darkness which overwhelmed him.

The rifle muzzle which pressed into Dietrich's face when he opened the cabin door in response to the urgent knocking was accompanied by an apology. 'You must remain in your cabin until further orders, Herr Dietrich. I am sorry . . .'

'Whose orders?' Dietrich had stood with his hand behind his back, his voice harsh and unintimidated by the sight of the weapon. For a moment it seemed as though he would push Volber out of the way by walking straight into him. The German had paused, uncertain how to handle this aggressive reaction, but Hahnemann, who stood close behind with the machine-pistol in his hands, had not been taken aback.

'By order of the Wehrmacht!'

Dietrich had stared past Volber, ignoring the squat man as he stared clear over his head, his eyes fixed bleakly on Hahnemann. Again it seemed as though he would push the rifle barrel out of his way and Hahnemann had instinctively raised his own weapon, wondering even then if he were committing some error. 'That is not enough,' Dietrich had rumbled. 'The officer's name if you please.'

'Lieutenant Hahnemann, Alpenkorps.' The sergeant had replied automatically and had felt the reflex of snapping his heels to attention, but he had desisted in time. Now he was furious with his own reply, but there was something about Dietrich which he found disturbing, almost intimidating. 'You will stay in your cabin,' he barked. 'Do you understand? Anyone found outside their cabin without permission will be shot!' Immediately he had spoken the final words he felt he would regret them. Dietrich continued to stand in the doorway and now Volber didn't exist as the huge German's brown eyes gazed with cold detachment at the lieutenant, an unblinking gaze which he found difficult to hold. 'Lieutenant

Hahnemann?' Dietrich repeated slowly, and there was an ironic, uncomfortably mocking note in his voice. 'I think I can remember that!'

Hahnemann persisted, but more quietly. He had his orders and he was carrying them out, whoever this might be. 'Please give my sergeant the key of your cabin so it can be locked from the outside.'

Dietrich gazed thoughtfully at Hahnemann a moment longer, then turning on his heel so that the door hid part of his body, he slipped the concealed Luger he had been holding inside his coat pocket and went back into the cabin. With a muttered expression of annoyance Hahnemann walked forward, extracted the key himself, put it in the outside of the door, closed and locked it. He had kept an eye on Dietrich's broad back while he had completed this action but all he had seen was a spiral of cigar smoke rising from the large head bent over some papers on the table. With a vague feeling of misgiving, he hurried away to attend to the next stage of the operation.

When the cabin door had been closed and locked, Dietrich waited a moment, then straightened up, his head cocked to one side. Yes, he had been right – the *Hydra*'s engines were slowing. For the mid-sea rendezvous, of course. They must have taken control of the engine-room at an earlier stage and by now they would command the bridge. An efficient operation planned with the usual meticulous care and attention to detail, including the bringing aboard of Herr Schnell and his outsize cabin trunk containing the weapons. Switching off the light, he used his pocket torch to make his way across the cabin and looked out of the porthole. The *Hydra*'s engines had almost stopped now and the *Rupescu* had come so close that a collision seemed inevitable, but distance was deceptive across water and especially at night. Standing by the porthole window, his cigar glowing for anyone who cared to see, he watched the transfer of the German troops from the Roumanian vessel to the Greek ferry. The soldiers, wearing life-jackets, were coping with the heavy swell, but had they arrived later, or had the sea worsened earlier, they might have found the operation impossible. German luck again – like the luck of the marvellous weather over France in May, 1940, like the luck of Hitler when he marched into the Rhineland unopposed in 1936. You can't get far in this world without luck, Dietrich was thinking, as he watched a boatload of troops being lowered to the sea. There must have been over twenty men aboard and the craft very nearly capsized as the sea heaved up to meet it, but at the last moment someone released the ropes and the boat followed the natural curvature of the sea's fall. The uniformed soldiers wore soft, large-peaked caps and were heavily loaded with equipment. Alpenkorps. A unit of the élite German mountain troops who had conquered Norway, men trained to fight in appalling terrain such as the peninsula of Zervos.

He remained standing there for some time, his body by now fully accustomed to the steady sway of the floor under his widespread feet, and while he waited he counted the transfer of over two hundred men to the Greek ferry. More than enough to take Zervos, providing they received heavy reinforcements in the near future. After all, the only people who stood in their way were a handful of monks at the monastery and two policemen at Katyra. Unless the British had managed to put their own troops ashore on the peninsula and had had time to dig in. Even after the transfer had been completed, when a boat containing, so far as Dietrich could see, the crew of the *Rupescu*, had made the narrow crossing, he still waited as the engines of the *Hydra* began to throb with power.

The ferry had resumed its interrupted voyage, was moving away and leaving behind the Roumanian vessel like an empty carcase when Dietrich opened the porthole and thrust his head into the elements, ignoring the growing force of the knife-edged wind which chilled his face, froze his neck and penetrated inside his clothes as he watched the *Rupescu* slowly settling in the growing turbulence of the sea. They

had switched off all the lights before they had left her but by
the light of the moon he saw her bows awash. The sea-cocks
had been opened before the final party had crossed to the
Hydra, of course. He was still leaning out of the porthole when
her superstructure sank below the billowing waves, leaving
for a brief moment only the white funnel showing like some
strange lighthouse moored in mid-Aegean. Then that, too,
submerged and there was no trace left that the *Rupescu* had
ever existed. Withdrawing his head, he rammed the porthole
shut, switched on the light and sat down at the small table
close to his bunk. The breath of night air had woken him up,
had put a sharper edge on his brain. All of which helped,
because they came for him close to midnight.

When Lieutenant Hahnemann unlocked the door, turned
the handle, then pressed it open with his foot, his machine-
pistol under his arm, he found Dietrich sitting at the little
table, still wearing his coat with his legs stretched out before
him and crossed at the ankles. He was smoking a fresh cigar.
He regarded Hahnemann as he might have looked at a piece
of badly-cooked meat, then transferred his attention to the
tall, beak-nosed man who had walked briskly in behind
Hahnemann, a striking-looking German in his early forties
who held himself very erect as his cold blue eyes studied the
seated man. Under his civilian coat, which he wore open at
the front, Dietrich saw the boots and uniform of the Alpenkorps.

'This is Colonel Burckhardt,' Hahnemann informed him
harshly. He paused as though expecting some reaction.
'People normally stand in the colonel's presence,' he went on
bleakly.

'Tell this man to go away so we can talk.' Dietrich addressed the suggestion to Burckhardt who was looking down
at him with interest. He hadn't moved since they had
entered the cabin.

'You can talk with the two of us,' Burckhardt began
tersely. 'Unless you have a very good reason for wishing to
speak to me alone.' Rather like Hahnemann earlier, Burck-

hardt wondered why he had replied in a way he had hardly intended. And yet . . .

'What I have to say is not for junior officers.' Dietrich's brief mood of amiability was rapidly vanishing and he looked grimly at the colonel. 'I would have thought you hadn't a great deal of time to waste, so shall we get on with it?'

Burckhardt's expression showed no reaction, buti nwardly he felt a trifle off-balance – he had been going to say almost precisely the same thing and now this strange passenger had forestalled him. He had the odd feeling that he was losing ground in some way. He spoke decisively. 'Hahnemann, you have duties to attend to – leave me with this man until I call you.'

'He may be armed,' Hahnemann protested.

'Of course I am armed.' Dietrich had spoken quickly, off-handedly, but again he had anticipated Burckhardt's question. A lesser man than Colonel Heinz Burckhardt might have felt annoyed, but the colonel was a man who had risen to command an élite arm of the Wehrmacht and his reaction was one of amusement.

'I am going to take out a Luger pistol,' Dietrich explained, and this time he stared at Hahnemann as though he might not grasp plain German, 'so kindly keep a hold on yourself – and your weapon!' Producing the pistol from inside his coat, he remarked that it was loaded, and while he was saying this he turned the Luger so that for a moment it pointed directly at Burckhardt. 'I could have held up your colonel,' he told Hahnemann grimly, 'and forced you to surrender that weapon on threat of shooting him. You should have relieved me of the pistol yourself.' As he spoke, the Luger lay harmlessly on the table. For a moment Hahnemann wondered whether to pick it up, but Dietrich's attention was so clearly concentrated on the colonel, was so clearly no longer aware of his presence, that he felt at a loss and glanced at Burckhardt for instructions.

'Leave us for a while. I shall be up on the bridge in a few minutes.'

They waited until the cabin door had closed and when the colonel began to pace up and down without speaking, slapping his gloves lightly on his thighs, Dietrich stood up. The action startled Burckhardt, who was six feet tall. He had realised that Dietrich was a tall man but only now was he able to see that the German stood two to three inches above him. Rarely impressed by another man's physical presence, Burckhardt found himself a little overawed by the formidable civilian who stood before him with his shoulders hunched and his hands clasped behind his back. Dietrich waited a moment and then put a hand inside his coat and extracted something which he dropped on to the table. 'My papers, Colonel Burckhardt.'

With a sense of growing disappointment, Burckhardt looked at the papers carefully, glancing up to find Dietrich watching him without any particular expression. 'You're an archaeologist, I see, Dr Dietrich?' He couldn't keep the flatness out of his voice.

'Look at them carefully,' Dietrich urged him patiently. 'See anything unusual about them?'

'No!' Burckhardt replied after a second perusal. There was a snap in his voice now.

'Good!' Dietrich lifted his shoulders and towered over the colonel as he went on with withering sarcasm. 'I was travelling aboard a Greek ferry across the Aegean – aboard a ferry which might at any moment be stopped and searched by a British destroyer. Under those conditions you really expect me to carry papers showing that I am an officer of the Abwehr?'

Burckhardt stood quite still and his heart sank. God, the Abwehr! That damned Intelligence organisation of the incredibly influential Admiral Canaris. They never told anyone what they were going to do – not until they had done it. And they never told anyone where they were going until they had been there and arrived back in Berlin. They were responsible to no one except the wily old admiral who had started his career with naval Intelligence, and the admiral was answerable only to the Führer himself. The Abwehr was disliked – feared might be a better word – by all the regular Intelligence services because it lived a life of its own, but even more because of its legendary record of coups. In some uncanny way the admiral managed to be right every time in his forecast of enemy intentions, which doubtless explained the esteem in which he was held by Hitler. Oh yes, Burckhardt had heard about the Abwehr, but this was the first time he had met one of them.

He glanced briefly at Dietrich and then resumed his pacing. Had this devil been put on the ferry to check up on the operation because it involved a naval phase – the seizure of the *Hydra* and its subsequent voyage to their objective? He would have preferred Dietrich to go on talking but in the absence of a single word from the huge German his imagination roamed over a dozen possibilities, not all of them pleasant to him personally. They had as near as dammit botched the transfer of the troops to the *Hydra*, he was only too well aware of that. By the skin of their teeth they had avoided over twenty men going into the sea when they had lowered the first boat from the *Rupescu*. All of which, Burckhardt had no doubt, Dietrich had witnessed from his porthole. And that rough-tongued Hahnemann hadn't made things any easier.

'I shall require proof of your identity as soon as possible,' he said eventually.

'Naturally.' Dietrich was smoking his cigar while he watched the colonel steadily as though weighing up his ability. 'You had better send a wireless message to Berlin – I can give you the address.'

'Not yet – we must maintain radio silence at all costs. May I ask the reason for your being aboard the ferry during this crucial operation?'

'You knew there would be two British soldiers aboard?' demanded Dietrich.

'Knew?' Burckhardt was startled again, immediately suspecting that there had been some awful slip-up.

'Yes, "knew", I said. Did you know?' Dietrich was talking with the cigar in his mouth, his legs well-splayed as his powerful personality began to dominate their conversation.

'No,' the colonel admitted. 'I was worried when I heard about them, but we are only concerned with a lieutenant and a sergeant . . .'

'Papers can be easily forged or doctored, including army pay-books. These two men could be far more important for all we know. Like so many people, Colonel, you place too much reliance on the printed word. My own papers never came out of the state printing house.' He watched the officer's reaction with grim amusement.

'I don't think I quite understand,' Burckhardt replied slowly. He would have liked to examine the Abwehr man's documents again but he had already scrutinised them twice without detecting any flaw.

'You think that the papers describing me as an archaeologist were run off in the normal way?' Dietrich's tone again verged on icy sarcasm. 'So that any clerk could see them? If the army security operates in that fashion it perhaps explains several things which have gone badly wrong. No, they were produced by the Abwehr's own documents section. Naturally! So don't feel too confident about the real identity of those two Englanders who just happen to be aboard!'

'It could still be a coincidence,' the colonel insisted stiffly, putting a bold front on a situation which disturbed him. If the Englanders had been put on board for a secret purpose then this might come within the Abwehr sphere, and already he felt that Dietrich was beginning to assert his authority in an unpleasantly effective manner.

'No!' The Abwehr man contradicted him bluntly. 'We knew they were coming aboard. They have been in Turkey for several days so why should they choose this particular vessel on this particular trip?'

'For several days? They were supposed to have been saved from a ship which sank off the Turkish coast . . .'

'What ship?' Dietrich pounced on the statement. 'Is this what they have told you?'

'Yes. Lieutenant Hahnemann questioned them . . .'

'He has Intelligence training, this Hahnemann?'

'No, but he is shrewd and he said their story rang true – the lieutenant, Prentice, told him this . . .'

'I have seen that British lieutenant and I would say he not only has his wits about him – he is also capable of making up a convincing story on the spur of the moment.' Dietrich paused, the cigar clenched between his teeth, going over what he had just said. 'But, of course, if they have been planted on this ship they would have a story ready beforehand – in case anything happened.'

Burckhardt's expression was controlled and remote. The Abwehr man had interrupted him three times and he wasn't prepared to put up with his overbearing attitude any longer. Politely, but firmly, he would confine him to this cabin while the operation proceeded, and to hell with the consequences later. He opened his mouth to say the words, but Dietrich spoke first. 'You are, of course, in command of the expedition, so you must take your own decision. I merely advise further questioning of the prisoners.' He paused, again having forestalled Burckhardt, and it seemed almost as though he could read the colonel's thoughts. Certainly his last remark had decided Burckhardt that perhaps it might be wiser to wait a little longer before he took such drastic action.

'I'll get Hahnemann to have another word with them,' he said quietly.

'This Prentice, he speaks German, then?' Dietrich was off on a fresh tack, his agile mind always seeking further information which might point in a significant direction. Without waiting for a reply he frowned suddenly and walked behind Burckhardt to the porthole.

'Not so far as I know – but Hahnemann speaks excellent English.' He was talking to Dietrich's back now as the German bent down to look out to sea. The Abwehr man used his hand to smear a hole in the steamed-up glass.

'Does he now? Hahnemann speaks English? I find that interesting, very interesting.' Without explaining the remark, Dietrich continued to peer through the porthole intently as he took out his handkerchief and rubbed the glass clearer. He spoke without turning round. 'Did Hahnemann find out anything else when he was interrogating our prisoners?'

Burckhardt had turned to leave the cabin but something in the Abwehr man's voice made him wait a little longer. He looked down at the broad back which stretched the coat's seams tautly; Dietrich would have a little trouble getting clothes which fitted him. 'I believe there was some mention of a British destroyer in the area but I'm convinced he was bluffing,' the colonel replied.

'Bluffing?' Dietrich had straightened up and his expression was forbidding. 'First you talk about a coincidence and now you hope he was bluffing. Life is rarely as kind as that – especially in wartime.' The sarcasm had gone but the grimness remained as he regarded Burckhardt with something like anxiety. 'There is a strange vessel approaching at speed from the north-east. I thought I noticed its lights through the porthole. Unless I'm very much mistaken it is a British destroyer.'

*

Burckhardt was leaving the cabin when he very nearly collided with Hahnemann, now in uniform, who was rushing down the companionway. Halting abruptly, the soldier saluted and spoke breathlessly. 'There's an emergency, sir. Lieutenant Schnell would like to see you on the bridge – it's very urgent . . .'

'I know!' Burckhardt had already pushed past him, heading for the staircase rapidly. Hard-faced young men of the Alpenkorps, fully uniformed, pressed themselves against the companionway wall with their rifles at their sides to let him pass. One man hastily extinguished a cigarette under his boot. The doorways to the three cabins recently occupied by

the German passengers were open and inside more men of
the Alpenkorps sat on the floors and leaned against the walls,
their faces tense as they watched their colonel pass. The
grapevine had worked already, reporting the rumour that a
British destroyer was approaching fast. The whole atmosphere of the Greek ferry had changed, had become more akin
to that of a troopship. Dodging round kit piled in the
passage, Burckhardt made a mental note to get that shifted
and then leapt up the staircase. Pushing open the door at the
top he received a blast of cold wind and a douche of icy spray
full in the face. Without even bothering to wipe himself he
glanced quickly along the deserted, wave-washed deck. All
the troops were under strict instructions to remain below
decks and he was satisfied with the outward appearance of
normality. Strange how the sea seemed far worse up here
than down below. The thought flashed through his mind as
he went into the wheelhouse.

Inside the enclosed area everything was quiet and there
was a feeling of disciplined control, but under the silence
Burckhardt sensed an atmosphere of nerves tautly strained as
the *Hydra* ploughed on through mounting seas. Lieutenant
Schnell of the German Navy, wearing inconspicuous dark
trousers and a dark woollen sweater, was holding the wheel
while the ferry's captain, Nopagos, stood a few feet away
with a signalling lamp in his hands. Behind him, crouched
on his knees out of sight, an Alpenkorps soldier held a
machine-pistol trained on the captain's back.

'Over there. To starboard.' It was the helmsman who had
spoken, nodding his head towards the north-east. Schnell
was a typical German naval officer, round-faced, his dark
hair neatly trimmed, a man of thirty with watchful eyes and
a steady manner. Taking in the situation at a glance, Burckhardt accepted a pair of field-glasses from another soldier
whose uniform was covered with a civilian raincoat. To
starboard a slim grey silhouette was bearing down on the
Hydra, a silhouette with lights at her masthead. Burckhardt
focused the glasses on the ship and his lips tightened. Yes, it

was a British destroyer sailing on an oblique course which would take her across the bows of the ferry within a mile or two. He handed back the glasses and moved into the shadows in case other glasses were aimed in his direction from that distant bridge. They wouldn't be able to pick out individuals yet, but within a few minutes they'd pick up all the detail they wanted if the destroyer maintained its present course. He spoke quickly to Schnell. 'What is Nopagos doing with that signalling-lamp in his hands?'

'He will have to use it in a minute . . .'

'I don't like that.'

'We have no alternative.' Schnell had half-turned round to stare at the oncoming warship. 'She is bound to signal us, so tell the Greek I understand the use of signals at sea.'

Burckhardt thought quickly. It was a damnable situation: the very existence of the expedition now depended on the signal-lamp in the hands of a Greek whose ship had just been shanghaied from under him. He saw the knuckles of Schnell's hands whiten under the overhead light as he gripped the wheel and steadily kept to his course. Still crouched on the floor, the Alpenkorps soldier with the machine-pistol moved gently with the sway of the ship, his face drawn with tension as he watched Burckhardt and then transferred his gaze to Nopagos' back. Burckhardt maintained his outward appearance of calm confidence, his hands thrust into his coat pockets, although inwardly his nerves were screwed up to fever pitch. He began speaking to Nopagos in his careful, Teutonic-sounding Greek.

'The British destroyer may start signalling. If that happens you only use your lamp when I gave the order. I want you to understand this clearly – the man at the wheel is a German naval officer thoroughly conversant with signalling procedures. He will be watching. If you make any attempt to send a distress signal, we shall know. If there is an emergency we shall engage the British destroyer and we shall undoubtedly be sunk. I hope you realise that it is unlikely anyone will be saved in seas like this . . .' Without putting it in so many words he managed to convey that Nopagos' crew were hostages. He had just finished speaking when the moonlit wake of the oncoming destroyer became clearly visible. A few seconds later the door to the bridge opened and Dietrich came inside. Burckhardt swung round and turned away again when he saw who it was. Completely unruffled by his reception, the Abwehr man walked across to join the colonel after glancing at the approaching destroyer.

'It's probably just a routine check,' he remarked, 'but let's hope they are not expecting a signal from their friends locked up below.'

A nerve jumped by the side of Burckhardt's neck underneath his collar. Dietrich had hardly arrived before voicing the most alarming suggestion at this critical moment. He had just quietened his mind after the Abwehr man's remark when the door burst open again and Hahnemann strode on to the bridge with a furious expression. He had hesitated to stop Dietrich following Burckhardt up to the bridge but now felt he should keep an eye on him. Burckhardt turned on him instantly. 'Hide that gun, you bloody fool – they may be watching the bridge. And while you're here – had either of those British soldiers any means of signalling in their possession?'

'No signalling lamp,' Hahnemann reassured him quickly. 'They definitely had no signalling equipment of any kind. The lieutenant, Prentice, had a revolver under his pillow. But nothing to send a message with.'

Burckhardt glanced at Dietrich with an expressionless face, but the German was still studying Hahnemann, who glared back at him defiantly. 'And no torch?' Dietrich queried in a deceptively mild tone. 'Not even a pocket torch?'

Hahnemann looked confused. He started to answer Dietrich, then his face stiffened and he addressed Burckhardt. 'One of them had a torch, yes, sir. It was inside the pocket of his coat hanging up behind the door.'

Dietrich caught Burckhardt's glance and he lifted his eyebrows in an expression of foreboding, then frowned at

Schnell who had turned to say something. 'Here it comes, sir. They've started.' Across the swelling Aegean where the waves were growing higher a light began to wink on and off from the destroyer. Schnell had half-turned to starboard, his eyes fixed on the flashing lamp which went on with its brief explosions. On the bridge no one moved or spoke as all eyes were fixed hypnotically on the signalling light and Burckhardt could feel the stillness of men suspended in a state of horrible anticipation. So much depended on the next few minutes but Burckhardt had no intention of surrendering, whatever happened. He had had some experience of the devastating fire a British destroyer could lay down; in Norway he had seen a German troop transport reduced to a burning hulk by only a few salvoes. What those four-inch guns might do to the hull of the *Hydra* was something he preferred not to contemplate. The lamp stopped flashing and Schnell spoke.

'We are asked to identify ourselves.'

Burckhardt stood up a little straighter and gave Nopagos his instructions in Greek. 'Signal that we are the Greek ship *Hydra*. Nothing more. And remember that Lieutenant Schnell is a naval officer.'

The tension on the bridge was becoming almost unbearable, like a physical affliction. Nopagos wiped his lips and glanced behind to where the Alpenkorps man gazed straight at him, the muzzle of the machine-pistol aimed at the small of his back. Burckhardt nodded confidently without speaking, as much as to say get on with it. The captain adjusted his cap and started to flash the lamp while Schnell watched him coldly, his hands still on the wheel. To the colonel it seemed to take an age to send the short message. Was marine signalling really so complicated? Was Nopagos managing to trick Schnell while he inserted a desperate S.O.S. among the jumble of flashes? A dozen appalling possibilities ran through his mind but he could do nothing but wait, hoping that his threat had struck home to the Greek. The lamp stopped flashing. Nopagos mopped the back of his neck with a coloured handkerchief as Schnell addressed Burckhardt over his shoulder.

'He has identified us simply as the *Hydra*, ownership Greek. Nothing more.'

With a supreme effort Burckhardt resisted the impulse to let his shoulders relax; both the Alpenkorps soldiers kept glancing towards him for reassurance. German soldiers, Burckhardt had noticed before, were never entirely happy at sea – the existence of the British Navy probably had something to do with their lack of enthusiasm for water-borne expeditions. He watched the destroyer still moving on her oblique course. Would her captain be satisfied with that signal? Just a routine check, Dietrich had suggested. But a moment later he had raised the unnerving suggestion that the two British soldiers might have been put on board deliberately – that the destroyer out there was expecting another flashing signal from a porthole confirming that all was well aboard the *Hydra*. Blast the Abwehr!

'They're signalling again!' Schnell spoke quietly, his eyes on the distant flashing light which was now less than a quarter of a mile away. Burckhardt stood quite still, resisting the impulse to pace up and down the bridge: it was vital at this moment to preserve an absolute outward calm. He felt that his feet had been glued to the deck for hours and God knew there were enough signs of tension on the bridge already. The signal lamp in Nopagos' hands wobbled slightly – if he had to carry on answering these bloody questions much longer he was going to crack. The soldier crouched behind the Greek captain was sweating profusely, his forehead gleaming from the light over the bridge. Hahnemann was lightly tapping a nervous fingernail on the butt of his machine-pistol and Burckhardt wanted to roar at him for God's sake stop it! Schnell, a highly experienced naval officer, was still holding the wheel tightly. All these little details Burckhardt took in automatically while the lamp on the British destroyer blandly went on flashing its message. Only Dietrich seemed undisturbed, almost at ease as he stared at the ceiling with the unlit cigar motionless in the centre of his mouth. He dropped his eyes and caught the colonel watching him.

'There is a Greek called Grapos aboard,' Dietrich commented. 'I think he could be dangerous if he isn't watched carefully.'

'I dealt with him myself,' said Hahnemann in a flat tone. 'He was sleeping in the saloon – he had no cabin – and I was able to knock him out before he knew I was there. He's tied up in one of the holds.' The endless strain of waiting had neutralised his natural dislike of the Abwehr man and he looked at Dietrich without resentment.

'I do have this ship under control,' Burckhardt added icily.

'Perhaps it might be better if I went below,' Dietrich said almost amiably. He glanced to his left and saw that Hahnemann was leaving the bridge as a cloud of spray broke over the bows of the *Hydra*. When the lieutenant had gone there was a loaded silence as the light from the destroyer continued flashing, the ferry's engines went on throbbing heavily, and the sea heaved endlessly under them. After the winking light had stopped, Schnell cleared his throat twice before speaking. 'They wish us to report where we're from, our ultimate destination and the time of arrival.'

Without hesitation Burckhardt rapped out more instructions in Greek. 'Tell them we're bound from Istanbul, that our destination is Katyra, Zervos, and our estimated time of arrival 0530 hours.' Nopagos blinked, glanced again at the sweating soldier behind him, took a firmer grip on the lamp and began signalling. The gun muzzles of the destroyer could be clearly seen in the moonlight as the vessel remorselessly continued on course without altering direction by as much as a single degree. Burckhardt found it unnerving – why was all this interest being shown in an ancient Greek ferry which spent its life plying between Istanbul and the remote peninsula of Zervos? He kept a tight grip on himself as Dietrich's rumbling voice spoke again behind his back. 'I'm wondering now whether this signalling isn't a smoke-screen put out until they get close to us. If they were expecting their own private signal from the prisoners below the course they are maintaining would make sense – they would keep on that course until they fired the first shot across our bows. Ten minutes should tell us the worst.' And having fired this last shot across the colonel's bows he quietly left the bridge and went out on deck.

Tight-lipped, Burckhardt heard him go, relieved that at long last the Abwehr man was leaving the bridge. But secretly Burckhardt agreed that Dietrich's estimate was just about right. In the next ten minutes they should know the worst.

3 · Sunday April 6

As he struggled in the darkness with the ropes which bound his wrists, Prentice was bathed in sweat from his exertions. He lay in his bunk sprawled on his side, his ankles also tightly bound together while a further length of rope joined his wrists to his ankles, a rope drawn up so tautly that his knees were permanently bent. The fact that they had thought of turning out the cabin lights didn't help him either; it meant he had to work blindly by feel and this made ten times more difficult a task which already seemed insuperable. And because his hands were tied behind his back he had soon given up the attempt to fiddle with the knots he couldn't see, and a little later, when it struck him that they had probably used Alpenkorps climbing rope, he gave up his efforts to break the cords by stretching his wrists against them – a rope which could support a man dangling from a cliff face was hardly likely to weaken under the mere pressure of two straining wrists. So it seemed hopeless: a rope which couldn't be broken and which couldn't be untied. There was, however, one other alternative. Prentice was thin-boned and he had unusually slim wrists, so now he was concentrating all his strength on compressing his hands into the smallest possible area and then trying to pull them upwards through the loops which imprisoned him. His success to date had fallen rather short of the milder achievements of Houdini and for a few minutes he stopped struggling while he rested.

He was turned on his left side, facing inwards to the cabin, and while he rested he contented himself with straining to see the time by the light of the phosphorescent numerals of his watch on the table. Almost 12.10 a.m. so far as he could make out. In that case the guard would be looking in on them shortly – he checked the cabin every quarter-hour. With typical Teutonic punctuality he had, so far, arrived at precisely the quarter-hour. He lay listening for the sound of footsteps and heard only the distant murmur of voices. Twisting his head round, he called out in a loud whisper. 'All right, Ford?'

The sergeant, similarly bound in the next bunk, was just recovering from the pounding headache which had assailed him when he regained consciousness after the blow from Hahnemann's machine-pistol. From the sound of Prentice's voice he guessed that the lieutenant had enjoyed a less painful return to the land of the living, something which didn't entirely surprise him when he recalled Prentice's speedy recovery from a hangover after a night of Turkish hospitality. He wet his lips before replying. 'Fine and dandy, sir. We'll have to sue the *Hydra*'s owners for damages when we arrive back.'

Prentice grinned in the darkness. 'We might just do that, laddie. Now, the guard'll be looking in any minute, so pretend you're still out cold.'

'Got it, sir.' The faint hammering inside his brain was sending waves of dizziness through Ford, a sensation which wasn't improved by the Aegean waves outside which regularly lifted the ship and tilted the cabin with an unpleasant rolling motion. Combined with his dizziness, Ford had the feeling that he was turning over and over and over. It cost him a certain effort to make his enquiry. 'Making any progress, sir?'

'A bit,' Prentice lied cheerfully, 'but not enough yet. I think they used steel hawser cable to truss us up.' He checked his watch again. Nearly a quarter-past twelve. Was the guard going to be late this time? The curtains were closed over the porthole so the cabin was in almost total darkness except for the light seeping in from the door which was not quite closed. He found that slightly ajar door tantalising – for all the use that unlocked door was to Prentice at the moment it might have been locked and bolted on the outside. But it did give him warning of the guard's approach as he proceeded with his unvarying patrol. After he had entered the cabin to make his quick check on the prisoners he continued his slow tread along the companionway and Prentice, who had exceptional hearing, found previously that he was able to follow the tramp of the retreating boots and their progress up the distant staircase which ended with the thud of a door closing. So his sentry-go also took in the open deck aloft, God help him. But for Prentice this made sense – the German commander, knowing there was little risk of an emergency while they were on board, was conserving his manpower, letting his troops rest as best they could before morning. Prentice lifted his head, then called out quickly. 'Here he comes!'

The Alpenkorps guard reached the door and reacted with his normal caution, switching on the light and entering the cabin with his rifle levelled. He stood there for a moment, watching the two inert bodies, then peered round the cabin to make sure that it was empty. As he left he switched off the light and closed the door firmly. Lying on his bunk, Prentice used a little army language wordlessly – now he couldn't hear the basket marching away and, more to the point, he wouldn't be able to hear him coming back again. Gritting his teeth, he renewed the struggle to free himself, pressing down his left hand to hold the rope taut while he compressed his right hand and pulled upwards, wriggling a wrist which was now moist with sweat. The moisture might help, might eventually make it a little easier to slip his wrist upwards out of that biting rope. To give himself extra leverage he pressed his bound feet against the side of the bunk, breathing heavily as he strained desperately at the rope. Five minutes later he lay limp and exhausted by his exertions, taking in great breaths of muggy air as he summoned up his strength for a renewed onslaught. The cabin seemed to be tilting more steeply now and the woodwork was groaning as though the timbers might give under the enormous pressure of the sea. The effort to free himself had been so great that his head was beginning to ache badly and he felt that he had a steel

band drawn round his temples. A light flashed briefly and
he bit his lips. God, this was no time to black-out. A second
later he lay still as a dead man, his heart pounding with
excitement. That flash of light hadn't been his eyes playing
him tricks. The light had flashed from the companionway as
someone opened and closed the door soundlessly. *Someone
had come inside the cabin.*

Fear. Uncertainty. Growing alarm. The emotions darted
across his fatigued brain as he continued to lie quite still,
straining his ears, trying to accustom his eyes to the darkness
quickly. The trouble was that damned sentry lighting up the
cabin had taken away his night sight for a few minutes and he
wished he hadn't watched him through half-closed eyes. Had
Ford also realised what had happened – that some unknown
person had crept inside their cabin with uncanny silence? He
had no idea. His ears had still provided no evidence that
there was someone else present but instinctively Prentice
knew that they were no longer alone. He found the stillness
unnerving, the creaking of the ship ominous, and the
thought that someone who moved like a ghost was approaching him terrifying. His mind was strained, his nerves strung
up to fever pitch with their recent experiences, and now a
nightmare idea flooded over him – someone had been sent in
to kill them quietly. A knife in the chest, then a swift
despatch overboard into the Aegean. Feverishly his imagination worked it out: the German commander might not want
his unit to know about an episode like this, or perhaps there
was an S.S. section aboard. Lying helpless in the darkness,
his nerves close to breaking-point, he foresaw the next step –
the hand coming out of the darkness to feel over his chest,
finding the right place, the upheld hand striking downwards
with one savage thrust. Keep a grip on yourself, for Christ's
sake, Prentice . . . His heart jumped, his throat went dry, he
felt he was choking – now he could see something, a shadow
which had interposed itself between the bunk and the
phosphorescent hands of his watch on the table. The
intruder was feet away, standing beside his bunk, looking

down at him. He tried to call out, but croaked instead, a sound like a bullfrog. A hand touched his cheek and he jerked involuntarily.

'Keep quiet! Listen!'

Prentice was stunned, lay absolutely still with sheer shock. The voice had spoken in English with a Teutonic accent. He swallowed quickly and kept his voice down to little more than a whisper.

'Who is it?'

The voice ignored the question, speaking in an urgent Morse-code fashion. 'Keep still! I have a knife . . . I will cut the ropes on your hands . . . a British destroyer is close . . .' Prentice felt cold steel between his wrists, stiffened the rope as the knife began to saw the fibres apart. '. . . at the back of the ship is a raft . . . use the knife to cut it free . . . when the raft is on the sea and you are away from the ship . . .' The knife sawed steadily, one of the ropes snapped. '. . . you send up a distress light . . . they are on the raft . . .' Another rope snapped as Prentice pulled his hands away from each other to increase the tension on the remaining rope. He spoke quickly.

'I ought to know who you are – I may be able to help you later . . .'

'Shut up!' The knife was sawing more slowly now and Prentice realised that the man who was freeing him was taking care the knife didn't jab into him as the last rope snapped. The voice went on speaking, the voice of a man using a foreign language and desperately anxious to make his meaning clear. 'The distress light will be seen . . . by the destroyer . . . but Burckhardt will dare not shoot at you since that warns the destroyer things are wrong . . .' Prentice felt the last rope part, freeing his hands, then heard the measured tramp of an Alpenkorps guard approaching along the companionway, the boots clumping dully on the wood.

He froze, his feet still tied. It wasn't time, not nearly time, for the guard to check on them. The intruder had entered the cabin soon after the guard had left – deliberately so. Prentice had grasped that. So had the guard changed his routine? He was going to enter the cabin and catch him with his hands free – and catch this unknown helper in the act. The guard's tread was closer now, was slowing down prior to switching on the light and coming inside. Another thought struck Prentice and he felt a shiver run through his body – since he could hear the guard coming the door must be slightly open. Yes, it was! A thin line of light showed round the door frame. The intruder hadn't closed the door properly and the swaying of the ship had opened it wider. Lying quite still in the darkness, Prentice realised that they were finished. The guard had closed the door last time, so when he noticed that it was open, and even if he hadn't intended coming in this time . . . He wondered what the feelings of the unknown man were who was waiting with them in the unlit cabin without making a sound. He still had the knife – would he use it on one of his own men? Would he even get the chance? That partly-opened door would alert the guard and he'd come inside prepared for anything. Lying back on the bunk, he turned himself sideways and hid his hands, hoping they would still appear to be roped up. Another huge wave hit the vessel, thudding against the hull with such force that he felt it was coming through. A second later he heard a further thud outside in the companionway and a muttered oath in German. The wave had caught the guard off-balance. Bathed in sweat, his heart pounding solidly, he waited and listened. For a moment there was a drawn-out silence, followed by a metallic click. The guard cocking his weapon? Prentice had a fierce impulse to call out a warning, but he kept his mouth closed, then heard the tread of the guard's footsteps again just beyond the cabin door. He had turned his head sideways now, his eyes almost closed as he watched the entrance for the first shaft of light which would tell him that the door was being opened. He heard more footsteps coming along the companionway, brisk footsteps which hurried. He could imagine the scene clearly – the guard noticing the door which should have been closed, his beckoning to a comrade who was hurrying along the passage to join him. Then the two of them would burst inside the cabin and it would be all over. The hurrying footsteps stopped outside the door and voices were raised in German. Prentice knew a little German, but not enough to speak it, and they were talking too rapidly for him to grasp what they were saying. Perhaps the new arrival was the sentry who normally checked their cabin? His mind was still grappling with possibilities when he heard feet hurrying away along the passage, followed by the deliberate tread of the sentry's footsteps as he also proceeded into the distance and up the staircase. A door thudded shut. Both men had gone.

'You must cut the ropes on your feet yourself . . .' The voice of the unknown man spoke quickly again. 'There is a coat and a cap on the floor . . . you turn left when you leave the cabin . . . hurry!'

The knife had already been placed on Prentice's leg and he was working on the ropes round his ankles when light flooded briefly into the cabin and then the door closed again. Prentice looked up quickly but he was too late – he saw no more than the departure of a shadow as the intruder disappeared. While he was sawing at the ropes the ship began to roll more violently, the angle of the cabin's tilt increasing steadily. They were moving into dirty weather. Behind him he heard a creak inside Ford's bunk and the sergeant's voice was a careful whisper. 'Who the devil was that?'

'God knows.' Prentice was free now and he nearly stumbled full length as the vessel rose abruptly while he was feeling his way across the darkened cabin. He'd have to risk a light – there had been a fierce urgency in the intruder's final words and in less than fifteen minutes the sentry would be back. And this time he would come inside their cabin. Switching on the light, he noted that the door was firmly closed, then ran across to Ford's bunk. He used his knife to cut the ropes as he talked. 'We've got to get on that raft and away from this ship p.d.q. Then we can loose off a signal to that destroyer . . .' Ford was rubbing the circulation back into his wrists when Prentice tried on the coat which had been dropped on the floor. An Alpenkorps greatcoat, it was a little too long and fitted loosely across the shoulders, but he thought it might serve. The soft, large-peaked cap was also ill-fitting but he settled it on his head as the sergeant looked at him.

'You're the spitting image of a Jerry,' Ford informed him. 'And your face fits, too.'

'Thanks very much . . .' Prentice was moving towards the door, the knife concealed inside his pocket. 'I'll walk on the left – you keep to my right. That way I'll try and cover you if any cabin doors are open.' Switching off the light, he paused while he listened with his ear pressed to the inner side of the door. He thought he understood now the restless wakefulness of those murmuring voices he had heard earlier – if the Alpenkorps men below decks knew of the destroyer's presence that would be more than enough to spoil their beauty sleep. It also meant that they were likely to be alert, which would make their walk along that companionway a hundred times more dangerous. He whispered to Ford quickly. 'Here we go. If anyone calls out to us we just keep moving as though we haven't heard. Now!' Opening the door quietly, he peered out. The passage was deserted in both directions. He walked straight out, closed the door behind them, and began walking down the companionway with Ford at his side.

The first cabin door was half-open and before he had reached it he heard voices speaking in German. He walked at a steady pace, not too quickly, not too slowly, staring ahead as they drew level with the doorway. Out of the corner of his eye he had a glimpse of a smoke-filled cabin, a blur of uniformed bodies, and then they had passed it. Maintaining the same pace, Prentice kept his eyes fixed on the distant staircase where a pile of army packs lay huddled near the lowest tread. The next cabin door was also open, wide open. Smoke drifted into the companionway as the vessel heeled violently and Ford had to grab at the rail to save his balance.

Prentice briefly slowed his pace while the sergeant caught up. That had been lucky – if it had happened opposite the open cabin door, Ford, dressed in British civilian clothes, would have been completely exposed to view. Prentice's mind was coldly alert as they came close to the doorway. From inside he could hear more animation, the sound of raucous laughter as a voice ended in a shout. Someone telling a story, he guessed. One Alpenkorps soldier, his fair hair cut to a stubble, lounged inside with his shoulder resting on the door frame and his back turned towards the companionway. Prentice kept walking forward and as he began to walk past the doorway another burst of laughter echoed inside the cabin. An N.C.O. stood in the middle of the room, half-turned away from the doorway, waving his hands as he pantomimed something. An energetic attempt to keep up morale, Prentice was thinking, something to take the minds of the men off that destroyer outside in the night. But he thought the laughter was a little forced and short-lived. The main thing was it concentrated attention inside the cabin as they walked past it. Only one more cabin to pass, again one with the door open.

They were close to it when a soldier started to walk out, then changed his mind and went a little way back inside, his hand holding the door frame as though he had remembered something and had paused to ask a question before he came into the passage. Prentice quickened his pace, his eyes fixed now on that hand which rested on the door frame, the hand which would move a fraction of a second before the man turned and came into the passage. The backs of the fingers were covered with dark hair and the nails were neatly trimmed; in his keyed-up state his mind automatically registered these tiny details as he moved forward without hesitating. The fingers lifted off the woodwork – the soldier was coming out. His mind tripped a reflex to halt his moving legs and the fingers settled again on the woodwork. Then they were walking past the door and within a few paces of the staircase. At the foot of the steps Ford glanced down, saw inside a German army pack which had its flap drawn back. With his interest in explosives he paused involuntarily as he saw the demolition charge and the timing mechanisms. By his side Prentice sensed the pause and grasped his arm, urging him upwards without a word. The lieutenant was mounting the steps when the bows of the *Hydra* plunged downwards, elevating the staircase in his face so suddenly that he nearly fell over backwards, tightening his grip on the rail just in time. Half-way up, he looked quickly back along the companionway as he continued climbing. It was still deserted.

When he pushed open the door at the top it was almost torn from his grasp by the force of the wind. He waited until Ford was safely on deck, then used both hands to close it without a slamming noise. With the howl of the wind and the heavy slap of heaving water it seemed a needless precaution, but the thud of a door closing is a special sound and that guard might be somewhere on deck. The water-washed deck gleamed in the moonlight and beyond the funnel to port a burst of spray exploded near the rail. With Ford motionless at his side Prentice scanned the deck which seemed to be deserted. A moment later a gust of wind whipped the ill-fitting Alpenkorps cap from his head and blew it into the sea. He had lost the most distinctive part of his disguise. He looked to starboard and was staggered to see how close the destroyer was steaming, frowning when he saw the signal lamp flashing. Was she calling on the *Hydra* to heave-to? With a very slight turn of his head he looked towards the stern and saw the raft waiting for them, its canvas cover drawn back, and by the light of the moon he could see the rescue loops hanging from its sides and bobbing with the *Hydra's* motion.

The raft had been covered with the canvas when he had last seen it and he hadn't recognised what the cover concealed. If it really carried distress lights they might just make it, might attract the destroyer's attention and be picked up. Not that he was too enthusiastic about the prospect of being aboard that tiny craft in seas like these. The whole surface of the Aegean was heaving up in a series of mountainous crests which raced towards the ferry with an insidious gliding movement as though intent on overwhelming it. He was about to make his way towards the raft, waiting for a moment when the ferry was pulling itself out of one of the great rolling dips, when he caught a brief twitch of a shadow to starboard beyond the funnel. The shadow of a huge man wearing a soft hat and standing close to a swaying lifeboat. Putting a warning hand on Ford's sleeve, Prentice kept perfectly still. It was the big German who had come aboard as a passenger at Istanbul. From the way he was standing he appeared to be talking to someone who was out of sight under the wall of the bridge. Go away, Prentice prayed. Get lost! The German began to move, to turn in his direction.

*

'Italian mines have been sown in the Gulf of Zervos.' This latest signal from the destroyer should have reassured Burckhardt but it sent a chill through him.

It should have reassured him because the destroyer's commander had sent the captain of the *Hydra* a friendly warning, but instead he was appalled. The passage from the narrow entrance to Katyra, at the head of the gulf, was a distance of twenty miles, and the prospect of sailing twenty miles at night through mine-strewn waters was not an experience he contemplated with great enthusiasm. Mechanically, he ordered Nopagos to signal a message of thanks to the destroyer while inwardly he cursed his allies. In the interests of security the Italian High Command had been given no warning of the Zervos operation, but it was the most fiendish luck that on this night of all nights they should suddenly decide to sow mines from the air in the vital gulf. This, he told himself grimly, is going to be a voyage to remember.

'Go down and have the British prisoners escorted to my cabin.'

He gave the instruction to the soldier not preoccupied with guarding Nopagos, his eyes still on the warship as the soldier left the bridge. There might be something in what that damnably arrogant Abwehr man had hinted at . . . His thought broke off as Nopagos completed signalling and stood waiting with a resigned look on his face as the destroyer sent a short series of flashes in reply. Yes, Burckhardt decided, it was a good idea to have the British prisoners questioned again, but this time he would let his second-in-command, Major Eberhay, undertake the interrogation. Like Lieutenant Hanhemann, Eberhay also spoke English.

'They wish us *bon voyage!*' Schnell was unable to keep the relief and exultation out of his voice.

Burckhardt could hardly believe it, but the feeling of salvation which flooded over him did not affect his judgement. He issued the warning swiftly to Schnell. 'Be sure to maintain exactly the same course and speed – it may be a trick to test our reaction.' He switched to speaking in Greek. 'Captain Nopagos, kindly stay exactly where you are until I give you further orders.' From the destroyer they would easily be able to see the *Hydra*'s bridge, Burckhardt was thinking as he remained in the shadows, and if the British commander were shrewd his glasses would at this moment be focused on the ferry's bridge. He watched the destroyer's course without too much hope and inside his coat pocket his hands were clenched tight. Had they really got away with it?

'She's still on course.' It was Schnell who had spoken and the note of anxiety had crept back into his voice. With an expressionless face Burckhardt continued to stare at the warship as more steam emerged from her funnel and she began to change course for the north-west. Incredibly, they had got away with it. Speaking a word of congratulation to Schnell, he left the bridge and went down the staircase in time to meet Major Eberhay who was at the foot of the steps. Behind him strolled Dietrich and behind the Abwehr man Hahnemann was running along the companionway towards them. Several Alpenkorps soldiers were moving away in the opposite direction. 'What's the matter?' he asked Eberhay.

'The British prisoners have escaped . . .'

'They were tied up!' Burckhardt immediately fastened on the salient point.

'Exactly!' It was Dietrich, standing behind the small major, who had replied, and the single word pinpointed a double emergency, a crisis, the full implications of which Burckhardt had not yet grasped, although the Abwehr man's tone was a warning.

'We are searching now,' Eberhay explained crisply, his manner quite unruffled. 'Put two more men on the bridge,' he told Hahnemann, who issued an order, summoning two soldiers from the nearby cabin and then going up the staircase as they followed him. 'And I have met Herr Dietrich,' he went on as Burckhardt appeared to be on the verge of saying something, 'we have been discussing the British destroyer . . .'

'It's turning away . . .' Burckhardt began.

'You are sure?' Dietrich interjected.

Eberhay stared up curiously at the Abwehr man as Burckhardt stood on the bottom stair and glared at Dietrich with a look of thunder. More troops were filing out of the cabins under the orders of Sergeant Volber who was instructing several to search the engine-room, to mount a double guard on the wireless operator's quarters, but not to go out on the open deck yet. Volber would take a small section to the deck himself.

Dietrich was facing the colonel bleakly, not at all disconcerted by Burckhardt's attitude. 'I heard of a similar case,' he told them. 'One of our merchant ships off Norway raised the Argentinian flag as a British destroyer approached. The warship turned away as you say this one is doing now. But it made a complete circle and came up unexpectedly on the stern of the ship and boarded her before the sea-cocks could be opened. So the danger may only be starting.' Burckhardt stood quite still on the step, his feeling of relief ebbing away;

he remembered the incident this damned Abwehr man had just recalled. Dietrich turned to Eberhay without waiting for a reply. 'So, if you don't mind, I'll come on deck with you and see what that ship is doing.'

Burckhardt said nothing as he walked past them, heading for his cabin while Dietrich followed the major up the staircase, turning up his coat collar when they reached the deck. A guard stationed permanently outside the door stood to attention as Eberhay went briskly to the bridge. Inside he noted that Hahnemann had stationed two more soldiers in the rear away from the light and he stared with keen interest at the destroyer as Dietrich joined him.

'It will be an hour before we know whether they've really gone,' Dietrich commented as he looked at Eberhay. The contrast between the two men was startling. Whereas Dietrich was easily the largest man aboard the *Hydra*, Eberhay was small and lightly-built, his face lean and alert as a fox's and his manner almost dandified. In his early thirties, he wore over his uniform a civilian raincoat belted close to his slim waist. The name sounded Hungarian in origin, Dietrich reflected, and there was certainly Balkan blood in his veins. Which probably accounted for the air of intelligence and sophistication which radiated from him.

'The escape of the prisoners is unfortunate,' Eberhay remarked, offering his cigarette case, 'but we shall soon find them.' Dietrich shook his head, noting that the contents were Turkish as he extracted his own case and took out a cigar. Eberhay lit the cigar for him as he stooped low to reach the match. 'I'm going on deck now to supervise the search.'

'It is the manner of their escape which is more than unfortunate – it could be catastrophic,' the Abwehr man observed.

Eberhay glanced sharply up at him and then, without replying, made his way on to the open deck followed by Dietrich. As they left the bridge the *Hydra* plunged its bows into a massive wave and a torrent of spray drenched them. Dodging close to the starboard side of the funnel,

Eberhay mopped his face with a silk handkerchief. Dietrich had also moved and now he was standing by a swaying life-boat where he caught the full blast of the icy wind. He had to pull his hat down tight over his large head and on another man the compressed hat might have looked absurd, but on this man, Eberhay reflected, it only emphasised an air of physical menace which seemed to emanate from him.

'Your name suggests a Balkan heritage,' Dietrich rumbled, switching unexpectedly to an entirely different topic.

'My grandfather moved from Budapest to Munich last century,' Eberhay replied stiffly and a little uncomfortably. 'The family has been entirely German since then.' Something about Dietrich suggested to the sensitive Eberhay a whiff of the Gestapo, and he was reminding himself to mention this to Burckhardt when he saw two Alpenkorps soldiers slip past on the port side, their bodies crouched low as they made their way towards the stern. Dietrich had turned and was also looking towards the stern as though something had caught his attention. Without warning he moved rapidly along the deck, his finger pointed.

'There!' he bellowed into the wind. 'By that raft!' Eberhay ran forward, surprised at the confident way Dietrich had exposed himself. Two men were standing near the raft as the Alpenkorps soldiers charged along the deck and within seconds a furious struggle had begun. Prentice found himself thrown back against the rail, temporarily winded. A clenched fist scraped his jaw as he jerked his head aside and lifted one knee. The soldier twisted to avoid the thrust, lost his balance and Prentice crashed down on top of him, his right hand reaching for the man's throat. But the German foresaw the attack again and buried his head in his chest to ward off the hand, trying to grab blindly for the lieutenant's hair. They fought ineffectually for a short time and then Prentice tore himself loose from the soldier's grasp and jumped up as though fleeing. The German came to his feet confidently, ran forward and received Prentice's aimed shoe on the point of his kneecap. He was doubling up as his opponent crashed into him and rammed him against the rail. Prentice had used the natural tilt of the vessel to port to give him added momentum and now the German was half-spreadeagled over the side as the vessel went on dropping to port, lifting the German over the rail. Scooping his arm under the German's crooked legs he hoisted and the soldier went over the side head first into the heaving sea. Eberhay had seen the danger and had run forward with his pistol held by the barrel to club Prentice. He himself had earlier given the order that under no circumstances must there be shots fired which might alert the destroyer which now presented its stern to the *Hydra*. Eberhay was close to the lieutenant when he slipped on a wet patch and sprawled headlong on the deck. In front of the funnel he saw running men as he lifted his head. 'Volber!' he shouted and then dropped his head just in time to escape Prentice's aimed shoe. Volber and two other men were struggling with Prentice while Ford still fought on the deck with another Alpenkorps soldier as Eberhay looked quickly over the side. The seething waves had swallowed up the man who had gone overboard and there was no sign of him amid the churning crests. Eberhay had his back turned to Dietrich as the Abwehr man stooped to pick up the cigar he had dropped close to the raft. When he saw it was sodden he left it there, dropping into his pocket quickly the knife which had lain near the raft and which he had picked up on the pretext of stooping for the cigar.

In less than a minute both Prentice and Ford had been overpowered and were being taken along the deck with their arms pinioned behind them. Eberhay had warned Volber that they were wanted for questioning and that they must be looked after carefully, a necessary precaution after one of their comrades had been thrown overboard. Accidents could happen so easily and he didn't want Prentice tripped and thrown down the full length of the staircase. When he turned round, Dietrich was supporting his balance with a hand against a ventilator while he stared at the raft as though it might be alive.

'They almost got away,' were his first words.

'But they didn't . . .' Eberhay was unsure how to reply. The remark infuriated him since Dietrich seemed completely unconcerned that one of their men had just drowned, but it was also Dietrich who had first spotted the prisoners and called out a warning without any regard for his own safety - the prisoners could possibly have been armed.

'Three more minutes and they'd have been over the side,' the Abwehr man growled. He glared at Eberhay as though it were all his fault. 'And you wouldn't have dared open fire for fear you warned that destroyer.'

Eberhay rubbed his bruised hands with his silk handkerchief, almost lost balance again as the deck started to rise, then leant against the ventilator. The trend of Dietrich's remarks greatly disturbed him: he had heard that the Abwehr's chief, Canaris, had such a contempt for soldiers that he refused to allow any man who wore a military decoration to enter his office. It looked very much as though his aide shared his chief's views of the Wehrmacht. It had been a most unfortunate incident and the only officer present had been Eberhay himself. He tried flattery. 'You took a risk yourself going out into the open like that.'

'So far as I could see they had no guns. I am not interested in displays of courage, Major Eberhay,' he went on bitingly. 'My usefulness to the Reich lies in staying alive as long as I can. Considering what has happened I must have a word with Colonel Burckhardt immediately.' He looked across the Aegean in a westerly direction. 'There are certain things which must be cleared up before we reach the entrance to the Gulf of Zervos. Have you ever made this trip before? No? It will be an experience for you – going into the gulf through that narrow entrance on a night like this will be like entering the gates of hell.'

*

The destroyer had disappeared over the rim of the Aegean but the glass was continuing to fall rapidly, a point dramatised by the sway of the cabin lamp which caused two shadows on the wall to grow to enormous, distorted shapes and then shrink again as the *Hydra* briefly resumed an even keel. The shadows were those of Dietrich and Burckhardt who faced each other across a small table as they sat alone in the cabin. The watch on the colonel's wrist registered 2.30 a.m. and they were within thirty minutes' sailing time of the Gulf of Zervos.

'Now that you've insisted on seeing me alone,' Burckhardt began, 'what was the meaning of your remark in the companionway?'

'What remark?'

Perhaps it was because of some inner fury that Dietrich seemed to be deliberately insulting, his head back and staring at the ceiling as he made his abrupt reply. He watched the cigar smoke curling round the lamp so he didn't see Burckhardt's expression.

'You used the word "exactly" when I commented to Eberhay that the prisoners had been tied up.'

'Oh, that!' Dietrich was sprawled in his chair and his hat, much the worse for wear, was drying off on the table, but he still wore his leather coat. He looked at the colonel and the tone of his reply suggested that events had long ago overtaken that moment, so Burckhardt was clearly out of touch. 'The prisoners had cut their ropes, they had made their way down a long passage, one of them wearing Alpenkorps uniform ...' He was speaking with unusual rapidity like a man reciting an unnecessary catechism before he comes to the point, '... they went up the staircase nearest the stern, they went straight to a raft which had earlier been covered with canvas but was now uncovered.' He stopped for a moment, watching the colonel intently now. 'You agree?' he enquired quietly.

'Prentice wasn't wearing a uniform – only a coat.'

'But one of the soldiers in the cabins saw him pass wearing a cap as well. I heard that later.'

'Yes, well sufficient to pass for a uniform. So far I agree.'

'It doesn't strike you as peculiar – as significant?'

'What?'

Dietrich had the look of a man who is rapidly losing patience. He sat up straight and leaned forward, his shoulders hunched as he gazed grimly across the table. 'How did they get a knife to cut themselves free?'

'We haven't found that out yet.'

'How did they obtain an Alpenkorps coat and cap?'

'They might have picked one up in the companionway – kit is dumped there.'

'And coats and caps? I haven't seen any – and aren't those two things they normally keep close to them so they won't get mixed up with someone else's?'

'Possibly.' But Burckhardt knew there was a great deal of truth in this assertion: as yet he simply wasn't prepared to give an inch to someone who wasn't in the armed forces. Dietrich continued relentlessly with his deadly questions.

'How was it that with a guard permanently stationed outside the door at the other end of the companionway they chose to go to the door at the stern where there is no guard?'

It was on the tip of Burckhardt's tongue to say 'luck,' but the word stuck in his throat. Instead he said nothing and after a pause Dietrich put another question. 'How was it that the raft was uncovered and waiting for them – they were nowhere near the raft when I first spotted them? Who took the canvas off that raft?'

'Lieutenant Hahnemann.'

Burckhardt expected the frankness of his reply to surprise Dietrich but the Abwehr man simply nodded and looked serious, so serious that Burckhardt felt compelled to add something. 'I asked about that myself and Hahnemann explained that he had taken off the cover when the weather worsened in case we needed it in an emergency.'

'And he also speaks English, I understand?'

Burckhardt took his time before replying and when he did so his manner was deceptively calm. 'Yes, he does. Why?'

'Does either of the prisoners speak German?'

'Not so far as we know. You haven't answered my question, Herr Dietrich.'

'It's perfectly clear.' Dietrich was again speaking rapidly. 'Someone must have helped the prisoners – have helped to free them, must have provided the coat and cap, must have warned them to go to the staircase near the stern to avoid the guard on the other one, must have told them about the raft. And,' Dietrich leaned closer to the colonel, emphasising his words, 'if neither of the prisoners speak German, then it must be someone who could speak English to them – you can't possibly believe that all this was conveyed in sign language.'

Burckhardt sat very erect, his expression cold and distant. 'I find that a very ingenious suggestion – I also find it quite outrageous.' He hoped that he sounded convincing because the Abwehr man had simply put into words an appalling suspicion which had been growing in Burckhardt's mind for several hours. Dietrich's reply was so unexpected that the colonel was taken aback – instead of saying anything he took his hand out of his coat pocket and dropped something on the table which landed with a dull thud. One of the knives issued to the Alpenkorps.

'Where did you get that?' Burckhardt asked sharply.

'On the deck by the side of the raft where Prentice had dropped it.'

Dietrich sat back and smoked his cigar while he waited for his statement to sink in. Burckhardt picked up the knife and studied it before replacing the weapon on the table and getting up to pace round the cabin. 'You should have surrendered it to Major Eberhay,' he said eventually.

'Possibly, but it may be a good thing I didn't. I heard later that he had interrogated the prisoners. If so, he must speak English. Does he speak English, Colonel?'

'Fluently.' Burckhardt scarcely paused before replying, understanding only too well now why Dietrich had insisted on this interview alone with him. Still detesting this representative of the Abwehr, he also felt a shade of relief that there was one senior officer aboard he could discuss this nightmare with: He had been wise to heed his instinct that he had better not go too far with this strange man. All hell could be let loose over this, for him personally. But the paramount consideration was the security of the expedition. 'You realise that your accusation against a senior army officer is really outrageous,' he suggested mildly.

'I have made no accusation,' Dietrich told him bluntly. 'I have merely asked for facts – who speaks English among your unit? Does anyone else – other than Eberhay and Hahnemann?'

'No, they don't. Your theory is, of course, still only a theory.'

'Have you any other explanation to fit the known facts?' Dietrich had lifted his voice now as Burckhardt sat down again: the swaying of the cabin was making pacing difficult. 'I state quite openly that there is a traitor aboard. The question is – who is it?'

'We'll find out before the night is over. We have to.' Rising from the table, Burckhardt put on his peaked cap. 'I have a lot of things to attend to. I want to make sure that Greek, Grapos, is tied up, and then you'll find me on the bridge. Soon we'll be approaching the entrance and that may be difficult.' He left the cabin for the staircase leading to the lower deck and his mind was full of turmoil. A traitor on board, somewhere among his unit. The passage into the gulf coming so close, a passage he secretly feared. And beyond that, if they ever made the passage into the gulf, Italian mines floating somewhere in the night. At the foot of the staircase he looked quickly along the lower companionway and was relieved to see a guard standing outside the door leading to the hold. The guard snapped to attention, opened the steel door, and Burckhardt took one step forward on to the iron platform and stopped. Half-way down the iron step-ladder stood Hahnemann and from his sideways position Burckhardt couldn't be sure whether he was going down into the hold or was on his way up again. Near the foot of the step-ladder, lying on the floor with his back against a packing-case was Grapos, apparently asleep.

'I was just going down to check him.' Hahnemann looked up as he spoke and Burckhardt hurried down the ladder without replying. At the bottom he bent over the Greek's inert body and listened to the heavy breathing. Grapos snored slowly and ponderously like a pig. He bent lower to examine the bonds round the thick wrists, but these were half-concealed under the body. There was no point in waking him – he had merely felt that after the recent escape he had to see for himself that the prisoner was secure. He would go and check on Prentice and Ford and then make for the bridge. As he turned to mount the step-ladder he saw a huge figure standing in the open doorway at the top. Dietrich. The Abwehr man was staring down the ladder at Hahnemann with a curious expression on his face.

Burckhardt climbed the ladder with Hahnemann following and the three men went back to the upper deck. After the door had closed nothing moved inside the hold for several minutes. Then, satisfied that they had gone, Grapos changed position, sitting up and leaning against the packing-case. Holding his hands as far apart as possible, he resumed his task, rubbing the rope along the metal edge of the frame which held the case together. In less than an hour he should have freed himself.

4 · Sunday 3 a.m.

At 2.50 a.m. the *Hydra* was steaming into the eye of the storm as seas of unimaginable violence began to take hold of her. The hull shuddered under the impact of the seventy-mile-an-hour wind, the bows of the vessel climbed a rolling wall of water, a Niagara of spray burst in the air and was flung against the window of the bridge with hammering force, blinding their view for several seconds. To stay upright, Burckhardt gripped the rail tightly as he watched the mighty waves swarming in endless succession towards the ship from Cape Zervos, waves which seethed and heaved with a dizzying motion, advancing relentlessly as though bent on the ship's destruction. Close to the colonel stood his shadow, Dietrich, his hat jammed low over his head and an unlit cigar between his lips. A few feet in front of Burckhardt the wheel was held by Schnell, standing with his legs apart and braced, the strain showing in his stooped shoulders, while to his right Nopagos, his face lined and drawn, held on to the rail as he gazed fixedly ahead. Turning, he spoke quickly to Burckhardt, his manner so harsh that for a moment it seemed the Greek had once more resumed command of his own ship.

'We must wait till morning – if you continue you will wreck us on the rocks.'

'For the sake of your crew you must see that does not happen.'

Burckhardt answered decisively but his outwardly determined attitude did not reflect his thoughts. The view from the bridge was quite terrifying; although the moon was fading there was still sufficient light to see what lay before them as a series of menacing shadows, and to the north-east the cliffs of the peninsula soared up into the night towards the three thousand foot summit of Mount Zervos. As the *Hydra* straddled the crest of another giant roller Burckhardt was able briefly to see the entrance to the gulf, a gap between the shadows so frighteningly narrow that from a distance it seemed as though the hull of the ship might well scrape both sides of the bottleneck. The bows plunged downwards into a fresh trough, the view was lost, and Burckhardt comforted himself with the thought that distance across water at night was doubly deceptive. So when they came closer the entrance must widen, even comfortably so, if that was a word which could be used under such turbulent conditions. Schnell, who didn't understand a word of Greek, asked the colonel what Nopagos had said.

'He wants us to wait until morning. I have said no.'

Dietrich noted that Schnell made no reply to this and he suspected that the German naval officer secretly agreed with Nopagos, who was acting as pilot. But Burckhardt would continue on course, he was sure of this, and his assumption was correct. The colonel was in an impossible dilemma: he was compelled to maintain the pre-arranged timetable, to land the expedition at Katyra by dawn. Under no circumstances could there be any possibility of turning back or waiting – his key force had a vital role to play in a far more gigantic operation and play it they must, whatever happened. Or perish in the attempt. And as Burckhardt stared from the bridge it seemed highly likely that they might indeed perish – his staff and the two hundred Alpenkorps troops huddled below decks.

The men on the bridge wore life-jackets – a precaution which Nopagos had insisted on – and the troops below were also similarly protected. But to Dietrich, as he surveyed the way ahead, the precaution seemed futile. If they struck the cliffs the *Hydra* would be pounded to pieces and no one could hope to survive in the boiling waters which surrounded them. As the vessel climbed again, breasting a further crest, he saw with appalling clarity – even through the foam-flecked window of the bridge – the mouth of the gulf, a rock-bound narrows which would require skilful seamanship in the calmest of seas in broad daylight, but at three in the morning, at the height of an Aegean storm, Schnell was going to have to take the ship on a course which most Greek sailors would have pronounced suicidal. And the weather was definitely deteriorating.

Eberhay stood a few feet away to the Abwehr man's left, and he stood so quietly and inconspicuously, almost like a wraith, that once Dietrich had looked to see if he were still there. He was watching the grim spectacle with interest and it might have been assumed he was nerveless, but in that earlier glance Dietrich had noticed a gleam of sweat across the small man's forehead. He made his remark to the major, knowing that Burckhardt was bound to hear him. 'If the vessel founders we mustn't forget that Greek tied up in the hold.'

'The guard has his instructions,' Eberhay replied. 'In the event of an emergency he will bring Grapos on deck. I gave the order myself.'

Burckhardt pretended not to have heard the exchange but the muscles across his stomach tightened a shade and he cursed the Abwehr man silently. 'If the vessel founders . . .' '. . . in the event of an emergency.' The phrases pointed up dramatically the desperate course of action he was committed to and he found the reminders unpleasant. Despite the hardening experiences of war Burckhardt was now frightened as he realised that the storm was growing worse. The deck rocked under his feet, the engines throbbed with the agonised vibration of machinery strained to the limit, and the howl of the gale was rising to a shriek. If they weren't careful the ferry was going to slip out of control. He could feel the tension reacting across his shoulder-blades from standing erect in one position, but he remained standing like a statue, determined to give an example of fortitude, compelling himself to watch the rise and fall of the sea which was going up and down like a lift. Yes, conditions were much worse, dangerously so. Beyond the bridge the world was a series of shifting shadows, shallow mountain peaks of sea which were now soaring and surging high above the *Hydra*'s masthead as the ship sank into another trough. It was weird and nerve-shattering – to see the waves jostling all around and high above them, dark, sliding slopes of water which might overwhelm them at any moment. He had a horrible feeling that exactly this could happen – the sea closing over them as the ferry capsized and plunged down to the floor of the Aegean. Then, once more, the ship seemed to gather itself to mount wearily and falteringly yet another glassy slope as it dragged itself up out of the depths. At the very moment when he least wanted it, he heard Dietrich speaking again.

'Nopagos could be right – we may end up as a wreck on the rocks.'

'That is a chance we must take. Personally, I am confident that Schnell will take us through.' Burckhardt paused, struggling to control his sudden rage. He had purposely left out that remark of Nopagos when relaying what the Greek had said to Schnell, and it infuriated him that Dietrich should have repeated it for all to hear. But in spite of the immense pressure, the almost unbearable responsibility resting on his shoulders, Burckhardt's brain was still working and he had registered something he hadn't previously known.

'You understand Greek, then?' he asked abruptly.

'Perfectly. I speak it fluently – rather more fluently than yourself, incidentally.' Dietrich's tone of voice became scathing, a tone of voice which prickled the colonel's raw nerves. 'Why the devil do you think they chose me for this trip – one of the first qualifications, surely, is a mastery of Greek?'

'Any other languages?' It was just something to say and Burckhardt wasn't in the least interested in the reply.

'Yes, French. I don't anticipate being able to employ that particular talent on this voyage.' He spoke banteringly and his brief outburst seemed forgotten. This was another aspect of the Abwehr man's character which Burckhardt found so disconcerting: his moods changed with astonishing swiftness and kept you off-balance. He stiffened as Nopagos turned and spoke urgently, his eyes pleading.

'There is still time to change your mind – but you must decide now.'

'We are entering the gulf at the earliest possible moment. It is your duty to see that we make safe passage. For the sake of your crew, if for no other reason.'

Nopagos' manner altered. He stood up very straight and stared directly at the German with an authoritative expression. 'In that case we must change course. There is a dangerous cross-current from the east we must allow for if we are not to pile up on the rocks to the west. Tell your wheelsman . . .'

Burckhardt relayed the instructions automatically in German, instructions which he didn't understand completely and which he mistrusted. Nopagos had given the incredible order that they must steer straight for the cliffs of Zervos and the strangeness of the order raised an entirely fresh spectre in Burckhardt's already anxiety-laden mind. Quickly, he tried to resolve the fear before it was too late. Nopagos was undoubtedly a Greek patriot – his whole attitude had confirmed this to Burckhardt hours earlier – so to what lengths might he go to prevent the *Hydra* and its cargo of Alpenkorps troops ever reaching Katyra? Would he deliberately wreck his own vessel on those fearsome cliffs? He had a crew of his own countrymen aboard but would this prevent him from taking action which could only end in the death of every man aboard? Like Dietrich, Burckhardt was secretly under no illusion as to the chances of survival if the ship went down. If anything, they were less than they might have been ten minutes ago. It all depended on the inscrutable mind of one middle-aged Greek.

'There *is* a cross-current.' It was Dietrich who had spoken and now Burckhardt could feel the first signs of the ship heeling from starboard to port. The *Hydra*, its over-strained engines thumping heavily, began to move chaotically in the

churning seas, like a gyroscope out of control. Sick with
dread, Burckhardt watched Schnell struggling with the
wheel to keep the vessel on the nightmarish course Nopagos
had dictated, a course which seemed to have no direction at
all as the ferry wallowed amid the inferno of near-tidal high
waves rolling in all directions as the cross-current grew
stronger. Soon the ship was being driven two ways – forward
by the labouring engines and sideways by the powerful
current from the east. Then for several minutes they suffered
the illusion that they were making no progress – until the
illusion was shattered in a particularly terrifying manner.
Burckhardt had been under the impression that great bursts
of spray in the near-distance were the product of huge waves
colliding with each other and disintegrating, but as the spray
settled briefly he saw an immense shadow rising in the night
and knew that he was staring at the almost vertical rock face
of the towering cliffs which barred their way. The surf was
exploding at the base of the cliffs as the waves destroyed
themselves against the barrier. Horror-struck, he heard
Dietrich's voice close to his ear, a low rumble like a knell of
doom. 'I estimate we are six hundred metres from them . . .'
The *Hydra* reached the crest of a wave and now they were
near enough to see huge billows shattering against the awful
monolith of rock, sending up blurred spray which rose a good
hundred feet above the gyrating crests of the Aegean far
below. Burckhardt felt a constriction of the throat as he
gazed with fascination at the spectacle – the rock face rearing
upwards, the spurs at its base momentarily exposed as the sea
receded, the lift of the *Hydra*'s bows, so close now that with
their next fall it seemed they must ram down on that immovable rock base. And from the heaving bridge they could
hear a new, sinister sound – the boom of the sea as it drove
against the massive bastion of the headland. For the first
time Burckhardt felt compelled to speak, to voice a naviga-
tional question. He had to lift his voice so that Schnell, still
crouched over the wheel, could hear him above the shrieking
wind and the steady roar of sea breaking against the cliff face.

'What's gone wrong? We're nearly on top of Cape Zervos!'

Schnell made no reply, didn't even turn round as Burckhardt took a step forward, grabbing Nopagos tightly by the arm as he spoke harshly in Greek, trying to trap the man into an admission by the suddenness of his approach. 'We're too close, aren't we? You've done it deliberately . . .'

Nopagos stood perfectly still, his body frozen rigid under the German's grip. As he turned to gaze directly at the colonel, Hahnemann arrived on the bridge, slamming the door shut behind him and then waiting. Nopagos spoke with dignity. 'You think I would destroy my own men? Because you are a soldier you think you are the only one with responsibilities?' He looked down at the gloved hand which held his forearm. 'You are hurting me, Colonel. This is no moment to panic. You must leave it to Schnell – or hand over the wheel to me.' Burckhardt relaxed his grip, let go, his eyes still on the Greek's face. No hint of triumph, no suggestion of treachery in those steady eyes; only a touch of resignation. Burckhardt was unmoved by the suggestion that his nerve was going – it was immaterial to him at this moment what Nopagos thought so long as he got the truth out of the man. And he believed him. The tilt of the deck almost threw him clear across the bridge as the *Hydra* heeled over again, but the soldier who was guarding Nopagos saved him. Holding firmly on to the rail Burckhardt listened while Hahnemann reported that all was well below but more than half the unit was sea-sick. As Hahnemann spoke Burckhardt was waiting for the first grind and shudder as the ferry struck. The lieutenant completed his report, saluted, and left the bridge. He closed the door as water surged over the port side, enveloping him when the wave broke against the bridge, and for a moment Burckhardt thought he had gone, but when the flood subsided Hahnemann was still clinging to the rail and he took advantage of the respite to dash below.

The not unexpected news he had brought depressed Burckhardt: within two hours the unit had to go ashore and the landing might be opposed. For such an operation the troops should be in the peak of condition and already half their energy must have drained away under the impact of their experiences so far – and the voyage was not yet accomplished. In fact, the worst probably lay ahead. Suppressing a sigh, he turned to face the cliffs and saw only spray. A second later every man on the bridge was petrified and their expressions of hypnotised fear were etched on Burckhardt's mind – a long drawn-out grinding noise was heard and the ship shuddered. *She had struck!* The message flashed through his brain and then the engines, which had missed a beat, started up reluctantly, and he knew that it was this which had caused the diabolical sound and tremor. He caught Dietrich's eye and the Abwehr man nodded, as much as to say, yes, this is gruelling. Burckhardt turned to look ahead as the vessel climbed, the spray faded and the entrance to the gulf appeared again. Within minutes their position had changed radically and they were now lying close to the narrows and well clear of the Zervos cliffs. But within a matter of only a few more minutes an even graver crisis faced them.

*

The enormously powerful cross-current which had carried them clear of the cliffs now threatened to carry the *Hydra* to a new and equally total destruction. From the bridge Burckhardt could now see why Nopagos had advised the apparently suicidal course of steaming directly for the notorious cape – it was an attempt to take them close enough to the narrows to pass through the bottleneck before the cross-current swept them sideways beyond it. The Greek mainland to the west lay several miles away, but from its distant coast a chain of rocks stretched out across the gulf entrance, a chain which ended close enough to the cliffs of the Zervos peninsula to compress the entrance dangerously narrow. And the only navigable channel, Schnell had explained earlier, lay through the bottleneck, guarded by the last rock in the chain. Burckhardt was staring grimly at that rock as the ferry ploughed its way forward towards the entrance, half its engine-power neutralised by the insidious sideslip motion of the cross-current which, only a few minutes before their saviour, was fast becoming their most deadly enemy.

In size the rock was more like a small island, a pointed island which rose straight out of the sea to its peak, a saw-toothed giant against which a warship might well destroy itself at the first impact, whereas the ferry they were aboard was a little more fragile than a steel-plated cruiser. Mountainous waves were surging half-way up the rock's face and the bursting spray smothered its peak. It had the appearance of waiting for them.

'It is fortunate that we did not plan to scale the so-called cliff path,' Eberhay commented. He had said the first thing which came into his head to break the tension permeating the bridge like a disease. 'I hardly imagine it would have been a great success,' he went on lightly. 'There might have been some difficulty in disembarking the troops at the base of the cliff.'

'I don't believe there is a path,' Burckhardt replied. When the operation had been planned one of the experts had mentioned this path which he said climbed the apparently sheer face in a series of zigzag walks leading eventually to the summit close to the monastery. Superficially, it had seemed an attractive idea – Burckhardt could have taken his main objective soon after landing instead of going to the head of the gulf and then marching twenty miles back down the peninsula. From the monastery he could have sent out patrols to the north to occupy the peninsula from the heights – the operation would, in fact, have taken place in precisely the reverse direction from the one now contemplated. The operation had been revised to its present form when the planners had realised that the Greek ferry reached the cape in the early hours of the morning; the prospect of scaling the cliffs at night had been considered impracticable and the

ferry had to complete its run to preserve the appearance of
normality up to the last moment.

'Yes, there is a path,' Dietrich informed the colonel. 'It
links up the anchorite dwellings built into the cliff face. The
anchorites are hermit monks who spend all their lives in
isolation from their fellows – hence the extraordinary places
they live in.' He chuckled throatily. 'I have always thought
it must be similar to solitary confinement during a lifetime
in prison.'

'How do you know this?' Burckhardt was twisted round,
one hand still gripping the rail as the bridge swayed alarm-
ingly.

'Because I paid a visit to Zervos five years ago.' Dietrich
regarded the colonel ironically. 'Which is simply another of
my qualifications for being here. I travelled all over the
peninsula.'

'You went to the monastery?' Burckhardt put the question
casually but the information interested him intensely. He had
only one man among the two hundred aboard who knew
Zervos personally – Lieutenant Hahnemann – and he had
worried over this ever since the expedition had been planned.
Perhaps, after all, the Abwehr officer was going to prove
extremely useful during the dangerous hours ahead.

'Yes, I visited the monastery. Why?'

'I simply wondered how widespread your travels had been.
I understand there is no landing place along the peninsula
coast between the cape and Katyra at the head of the gulf.'

'There is Molos – twenty kilometres south of Katyra.'

'Yes, I know. It is a small fishing village – but has it access
to the interior?'

'It depends what you call access.' Dietrich was still
holding the cigar unlit in his mouth and he didn't bother to
remove it to reply to the colonel. 'There is a footpath which
goes up into the mountains but often it is washed away
during the winter.'

'I see.' Burckhardt replied as though this were news, but
he had heard this at the planning stage and it confirmed that

Dietrich did know the geography of the peninsula. 'There is a road south from Katyra, of course?'

'You know perfectly well there is, or I presume you would not be on board this ship. It is little more than a track and winds its way among the hills. You should have brought mules with you,' he told Burckhardt bluntly.

'We considered them – but it was hardly practicable to transfer animals from the *Rupescu* to this ferry.' Satisfied with Dietrich's replies he turned away, but the Abwehr man had the last word.

'All this is assuming that we ever penetrate that gulf. You see what is happening, don't you?'

Burckhardt, who had let his attention slip for the shortest period of time, looked ahead and stiffened. During the very brief interval while he had conversed with Dietrich, the *Hydra*, caught up in the main force of the cross-current, had been swept three-quarters of the way across the entrance and now he heard a fresh sound, a sound more muted than the breaking of the sea against the cape but no less sinister – the dull boom of the swaying Aegean against the base of the saw-tooth. They were very close to the narrows – close enough to see that there the water was quieter, although still it heaved and bubbled like a tidal race, but they were equally close to the saw-tooth. He looked away to starboard where the big rollers were rounding Cape Zervos and hurtling towards the ferry, a piling-up of the sea which had more than once shaken the vessel as though she were a toy ship. It was these mountainous rollers which posed Burckhardt's second nightmare. If a big one came just at the wrong moment as they were passing the saw-tooth . . . He noticed Schnell again turning his head to look to port, and Schnell's frequent glances in that direction worried him. The naval officer was clearly aware that they were engaged in a lethal race – to pass through the narrows before they piled up against the rock. There was no longer anything they could do except to hope. Everything seemed to conspire to screw up their tense nerves to an unbearable pitch – the engines were beating foggily as though on the verge of breaking down altogether; the vessel's movements were becoming laboured and had a discouraging, waterlogged feel; the cross-current seemed to be carrying them sideways faster than the bows of the ship moved forward. He heard Eberhay clear his throat and the sound alerted him, made him look again to port. They were about to enter the narrows but the saw-tooth was less than thirty metres from the hull. A wave broke on the rock's side and spray reached the apexed summit. Out of the corner of his eye Burckhardt caught a slight movement – Nopagos was staring in the opposite direction towards the cape as though transfixed.

Following his gaze, the colonel clenched his teeth and felt coldness like an affliction chill his spine. Another roller was coming, a roller more mountainous than any Burckhardt had seen. There must have been some accumulation of the waters, even an overtaking and merging of three giant waves to form the foam-crested colossus bearing down on them like an upheaval from the deep. All heads were turned in that direction now, even Schnell's before he dragged his gaze to for'ard by some supreme effort of will. The crest of the monster was well above funnel height. Hands gripped the rails tightly, bodies stood rigid with fright. Even Burckhardt took several steps back as Dietrich moved aside for him to brace his back against the rear wall. With the wood pressed against his shoulder-blades he stared incredulously at the appalling spectacle. The wave seemed to be climbing higher and higher, swallowing up more of the sea to swell itself to mammoth proportions. We'll be overwhelmed, Burckhardt thought, we'll never emerge from this: we'll plunge down to the floor of the gulf like a submarine out of control. God, had there been some frightful underwater upheaval, some shift in the earth's surface on the Aegean floor? The wave was within ten metres now. Half the wave's height would be clear over them . . . His hands locked on the rail, felt the greasy sweat inside his gloves, and then the *Hydra* tried to climb, to carry itself up the side of the monstrous wave – and instead was swept sideways. Lifted like a paper boat, it seemed no longer to move forward at all as the screw churned frantically inside the pounding sea. Eberhay lost his grip and was hurled bodily across the bridge where he collided with an Alpenkorps soldier. Bracing himself afresh, determined not to follow Eberhay, the colonel looked to port again. For a moment he saw nothing except the wave travelling westward, a shifting wobble of sea which shimmered his vision, then a window appeared in the water and his jaw muscles tautened. Just beyond the ship, it appeared, the saw-tooth was rushing towards them like the wall of a building toppling over on the port deck. He waited for the shuddering crash of hull disintegrating against immovable rock, the sinking sensation as the *Hydra* foundered.

Spray blinded the view. Unexpectedly he realised that the ferry was listing to starboard, was over the crest. Ahead lay the smoother water where the gulf was protected from the fury of the storm by the wall of the cape. He looked back through the window at the rear of the bridge in time to see the saw-tooth submerging under the surge of the sea, the spray bursting high above the summit as the whole rock was temporarily drowned under the immense fall of water. Then the rock began to reappear as water drained down its sides and Burckhardt's mind functioned again. *The rock was behind them.* They had moved inside the Gulf of Zervos.

Three minutes later he was about to leave the bridge, his mind concentrated on the peril of the Italian sea-mines, when Hahnemann reported that the unit's wireless set had been sabotaged.

*

'The Gestapo? Dietrich a member of the Gestapo? What the devil put that crazy idea into your head, Eberhay?'

Burckhardt stared grimly across the table at his second-in-command. It was a suggestion he could have done without at this stage of the operation as the *Hydra* proceeded steadily up

the gulf through the darkness. All its lights were ablaze to
preserve the appearance of normality and from the bridge a
powerful searchlight was beamed ahead as Schnell and
Nopagos strained their eyes for the first sight of the dreaded
mines. Inside the colonel's cabin Eberhay crossed his slim
legs and smiled faintly. The two men were alone and it had
seemed an ideal moment to voice his doubts. 'It is just a
feeling I had,' he explained, 'when I was talking to him on
deck some time ago.'

'Just a feeling!' Burckhardt was more annoyed than ever.
'No evidence – just a feeling. And why should Berlin
secretly put a Gestapo official on board this ship?' His voice
became more biting. 'You have a theory on that, I'm sure.'

'Yes, I have.' The little major, accustomed to the colonel's
moods, was unruffled. 'Since there appears to be a traitor on
board it could be someone the Gestapo has previously
suspected.'

'You mean Dietrich may have an idea who it is?'

'It would account for his presence on board – if my feeling
were correct.'

This new suggestion did nothing to soothe Burckhardt
who was now disturbed by a fresh anxiety: the presence of a
traitor inside his own unit was enough to give any German
commanding officer sleepless nights, but the thought that the
Gestapo had known of his existence earlier was a nightmare.
As colonel he could be held responsible for not detecting the
man over a long period of time. Were they all unconsciously
trying to drive him out of his mind – Dietrich with his
never-ending reminders of hazards, and now Eberhay with
his blasted theories? He was drumming his finger-tips lightly
on the table when the major carried the theory a shade
further. 'The sabotage of the wireless-set provides further
evidence that someone aboard is trying to hinder the expedition in every possible way . . .'

'I agree.' Dietrich spoke the words from the door he had
opened silently and Burckhardt's manner became icier as the
Abwehr man came inside and joined them at the table after

carefully closing the door. The sentry outside the cabin should have stopped him, of course, and the colonel reminded himself to deal with that later. But it was an interesting example of how the Abwehr man's powerful personality was dominating almost everyone aboard. A short while earlier Burckhardt had overheard an Alpenkorps soldier explaining to his cabin mates that the Abwehr officer had been sent personally by the Führer to watch over the operation, a suggestion which had not endeared him to the huge German who now sat at one end of the table holding his cigar while he spoke.

'Major Eberhay is, of course, correct. Someone aboard this Greek ferry is trying to prevent you from ever reaching your objective. In fact, we can identify him . . .'

'You know who this person is?' Burckhardt's tone was sharp as he received this uncomfortable echo of the major's recent words.

'I was going to say that we can identify him up to a point. He speaks English . . .' He turned to Eberhay and smiled without humour. 'Pardon me, but the fact is indisputable. He speaks English. He has sufficient freedom of action on board to steal an Alpenkorps knife, sentry coat and cap.' He paused, looking hard at Burckhardt. 'And he has the freedom of action to sabotage your wireless set. That I personally find most inconvenient – I wished to send a message to Berlin via your G.H.Q. in Bulgaria at the earliest possible moment. When would you have been able to break radio silence?'

'Not while we are on board,' Burckhardt replied evasively. 'But you may still be able to send your message later.'

Dietrich looked relieved, nodding as he lit his cigar. 'That is certain?'

'I cannot be sure yet when that will be.' He paused, conscious of a feeling that he was being too close-mouthed with this Abwehr officer. For all he knew he could be Admiral Canaris' right-hand man. 'We have a second wireless set in perfect condition,' he said briskly. 'Military signals will, of course, have priority, but you will be able to communicate with Bulgaria at a certain time after we have gone ashore.'

'The other set is permanently out of action?'

'Possibly not. Someone smashed the tuning coil but the wireless op. may be able to repair it in time.'

'It had been left unguarded?'

'No, not originally. But the man who was guarding it became sick and went to the lavatory. He was there for some time and because of his condition he didn't check the set immediately when he returned.'

'How can you smash up a tuning coil?'

Eberhay, who had seen the damaged set, explained this. 'Anything heavy would do the job – a pistol butt, or a rifle – anything. It could be done in less than a minute.'

'Why did Schnell keep to his cabin during the early part of the voyage?' asked Dietrich. The sudden switch in topic surprised both German officers and again it was Eberhay who replied. 'He made the same trip aboard the *Hydra* a fortnight ago to study the vessel and its route. Although he was disguised on that earlier trip we wanted to eliminate any risk that one of the crew might recognise him this time.'

'And he carried the weapons for use in taking over the vessel inside that cabin trunk which caused so much comment?'

'Yes!' It was Burckhardt who answered now, disliking the final qualification in Dietrich's question. 'Both wireless sets, incidentally, are now under heavy guard. And the seizure of this vessel went exactly according to plan.'

'I agree that that part of the operation was well-organised,' Dietrich said blandly with the underlying implication that the later stages had been little better than a dog's breakfast. 'I would like to ask where Lieutenant Hahnemann learned to speak English.' His manner had changed from one sentence to the next and now it was brusque and confident as though there was no doubt he would be answered.

'At Kiel University. He took a special crash course just

before the war. He has never been to England,' Burckhardt
added with equal brusqueness.

'But I have,' Eberhay informed Dietrich bluntly. 'I served
with the military attaché in London in 1938. I'm sure the
Abwehr files have this on record.'

Dietrich withdrew suddenly from the conversation. Sitting
back in his chair he regarded both men through his cigar
smoke as though something had just struck him. The German
officers had taken off their outer civilian coats and wore field-
grey Alpenkorps uniform: a tunic buttoned up to the neck,
trousers ankle-wrapped with puttees, and heavily-nailed
boots. The footgear, Dietrich thought, was an improvement
on the normal Wehrmacht jackboot he so disliked. Round
his waist each man wore a wide leather belt with a hip holster
slung on the left side and the Luger pistol set butt forward.
He remained motionless while someone hammered urgently
on the outside of the door and a moment later the knocking
was repeated. Burckhardt called out for them to come in and
Lieutenant Hahnemann appeared. The Abwehr man glanced
at him once and knew that a fresh emergency had arisen.
The lieutenant was standing stiffly but hardly able to control
his agitation.

'What is it?' Burckhardt asked quietly.

'One of the ten-kilogram demolition charges is missing –
and a time fuse.'

Dietrich had come to life suddenly, was standing up as he
fired the question, his great body overshadowing Hahnemann. 'That sounds like a large bomb?'

In his agitation Hahnemann replied immediately before
the colonel could say a word, addressing Dietrich directly.
'If it is placed in the right position it could destroy the
entire ship.'

*

'Something's upset their apple cart, all right.' Ford spoke
quietly as he stood alongside Prentice by the porthole. Their
cabin was being methodically searched by Alpenkorps

soldiers who prodded the bedding gingerly with short-bladed bayonets, opened cupboard doors as though expecting something to fall out, and peered cautiously under chair seats without moving them.

'They're nervy, too.' Prentice watched the searching process curiously and he thought he sensed a desperate urgency in their efforts, like men working against a clock. Near the door Sergeant Volber stood directing operations, although his main task, under orders from Eberhay, was to protect the prisoners. During the search more than one man glanced murderously at Prentice who was responsible for the death of one of their comrades, and Volber was present to exercise strict discipline. A moment later the sergeant spoke in German, and when Prentice failed to understand, he waved his Luger to indicate they must move to one side. A soldier who pointedly did not look at them opened the porthole, peered outside, then rubbed a hand round the outer rim as though seeking something which might be suspended there. Satisfied with his search, he closed the porthole and Volber motioned them to take up their former position.

'What the hell's going on?' Ford whispered.

'Don't know – but they're as jumpy as hens with a fox in the yard.' Prentice was glad of Volber's presence: all the Germans carried carbines,* as the technically-minded Ford insisted on calling them, and it had been known for a weapon to go off accidentally when aimed at a lethal spot. From the look on the faces of some of these hard-bitten youngsters a carbine could have discharged quite easily in his direction if Volber had omitted to attend the ceremony. Ford continued gazing out of the porthole where he could see on the mainland side of the gulf a chain of pinpoint lights crawling up the coast road to the north. He pressed his hand lightly on the lieutenant's arm.

'Look – must be our chaps across there.'

'I know, I've seen 'em.' Prentice hadn't relaxed his own

*Ford was referring to the Gewehr 98 K bolt-action carbine.

gaze from the interior of the cabin. He could feel the deep animosity radiating from the dozen men who went on turning the cabin inside out. One soldier walking past him chanced to let go of his carbine and Prentice had to move quickly. The metal-sheathed butt of the weapon thudded heavily on the cabin floor where a moment before his right foot had stood. If that butt had contacted, it could have crippled him. Volber called out sharply in German and was still barking vehemently when the soldier left the cabin.

'Sounds as though he's going on a charge. With any luck,' Ford added. 'You know, sir, I don't think they really like us.'

'Just be ready to do a quick tap-dance if the occasion arises,' Prentice told him and continued to stare at any man who caught his eye. Yes, Ford had been right: it was a damned queer situation. On board the *Hydra* there must be at least a company of well-trained German troops and some of them expected to operate at high altitudes – he had seen several pairs of skis inside one cabin when they had been taken along earlier for interrogation by that slip of a German officer who spoke English. Prentice had received a shock when Eberhay had first spoken to him but he had suppressed the look of surprise which had sprung to his face. And behind them, a few miles across the gulf through that porthole, they could see the hooded lights of traffic moving through the night along that vital mainland road to the north. Prentice had no doubt that those were the lights of Allied convoys driving up to the Alkiamon Line, completely ignorant of the fact that the ship whose lights they could see across the water was carrying a German spearhead aimed at Zervos. For by now Prentice had little doubt of the Alpenkorps objective – the Germans on board were on their way to seize that vital monastery observation post overlooking the road Ford was watching through the porthole.

'A whole load of people going on holiday,' Ford went on, 'I can see lights right up the coast.' This was his way of referring to the Allied convoys. There was no indication that Volber understood a word of English but Prentice, when he had first seen the moving lights, had cautiously referred to them in this innocent manner.

'What the blazes can this lot be looking for?' Prentice wondered out loud. 'And it bothers them. They're sweating.'

'They can melt away for all I care. What I can't make out is why they're still wearing their Mae Wests. It's as calm as the Serpentine outside now.' Ford's description of the gulf had an element of exaggeration because the *Hydra* was still steaming through a moderate swell, but contrasted with the seas off Cape Zervos it could indeed have been the Serpentine. The Aegean, one of the most unpredictable seas in the world, had subsided again.

'I told you, they were nervy,' Prentice replied. Inwardly, he assumed the wearing of Mae Wests was just another example of Teutonic discipline, but it was the object of the search which was nagging at his tired brain. Come to think of it, these lads didn't look as though they'd just got up in the morning. Which was a thought that gave him a certain amount of satisfaction: if they went on prowling round the ship like this they'd be exhausted before they ever got ashore. The soldiers were trooping out of the cabin when he went up to Volber. 'Speak with German who speaks Englische . . .' he began. It took him a pantomime of gestures to convey that he wished to talk to the little officer who had interviewed them earlier, and when Volber returned he came back with Lieutenant Hahnemann instead.

'What is it?' Hahnemann rapped out. There was tension here, too – tension and irritability in the manner and expression with which he regarded the two prisoners.

'What are you looking for? We might be able to help,' Prentice told him blithely.

The reaction was unexpectedly violent. Hahnemann took a step forward and his right hand rested close to his hip holster. It had been a mistake, Prentice realised at once. The Jerries were more at their nerve-ends than he had realised. He spoke quickly and tersely, letting a little indignation creep into his tone. 'I meant what I said. Why wouldn't I?

If I could tell you where it was – whatever you are looking for –.it would have saved us having the bedding bayoneted to bits.'

'You will stay here and not send for me again.' He turned away and then looked back. 'Why are you not wearing the life-jackets?'

'Because there isn't a storm any more.'

'You put them on now and they stay on. That is an order. For your safety,' he ended abruptly. They were left alone with the guard while they tied on their Mae Wests again. Prentice was relieved to see that it was the same guard, a thirty-year-old who sat some distance from them with his machine-pistol always aimed in their general direction. A sturdy-faced character, he had shown no exceptional signs of hostility although he was careful never to let them come within ten feet of where he sat.

'I'd still like to know what they were after,' said Ford as he sat down on a pile of massacred bedding. He looked up at Prentice. 'How much longer?'

'About an hour, if they're keeping to the ferry's schedule.' Prentice's watch registered 4.30 a.m. and the *Hydra* had been due to dock at Katyra at 5.30 a.m., a little before dawn. To keep awake he went over to the porthole again for another look at those tantalising hooded lights of the convoy moving along the coast road. Another hour. Nothing much could happen in that time.

*

The ten-kilogram composite demolition charge stood on the table. It was enclosed inside a black-painted zinc container about the size and shape of a deep attaché case and there was a web carrying-handle. Inset into the top face were two standard igniter sockets.

'Like that?' queried Dietrich.

'Its twin is hidden somewhere aboard this ship – with the difference that the clockwork time fuse has undoubtedly been attached and set in motion. Show him the fuse, Hahnemann.'

While Burckhardt waited, the engines of the ferry ticked over steadily, unpleasantly suggestive of the ticking of a time bomb. They were alone in the colonel's cabin with the exception of the temporary presence of Hahnemann who had brought in the demolition charge at the Abwehr man's request. As Dietrich had so unfortunately put it, he wanted to see what was going to blow him to kingdom come.

'The fuse,' said Hahnemann.

It was roughly shaped like an outsized egg-cup. Measuring a little over two inches across the top in diameter and six inches in overall depth, the casing was chocolate-brown Bakelite, and when Dietrich picked up the device Hahnemann showed him how it worked. The top was a hinged glass lid which had to be lifted to set the clock. Still holding the time fuse, he looked up at the lieutenant.

'And one of these is definitely missing with the charge?'

'Yes. They were in a rucksack at the bottom of the companionway stairs.'

'Not guarded?' Dietrich was looking down at the mechanism.

Hahnemann glanced at the colonel, who nodded. 'There was a mix-up of rucksacks. I'm sure it would never have happened if half the men hadn't been sea-sick. Corporal Schultz thought he had the rucksack with the charges inside with him in a cabin. It was only discovered later that he had someone else's while his own rucksack had been left outside.'

Dietrich ignored the explanation. 'Corporal Schultz is waiting in the passage? Good, I'd like to see him.'

Hahnemann went to the door and let inside a slim man in his late twenties who was clearly not at ease, and his embarrassment increased when he slipped on the polished floor. He glanced at the colonel as he saluted and Burckhardt merely told him to answer questions. He had already had a word with the negligent N.C.O.

'These fuses are totally reliable?' enquired Dietrich. The pink-faced corporal glanced at Hahnemann who told him briskly to answer the question. Schultz was uncertain how much to say and the colonel barked at him to get on with it.

'No, sir, not always,' Schultz began. And having begun he gained confidence and spoke rapidly. 'They have a habit when set of stopping for no reason at all. Then they can start up again of their own accord – again for no particular reason. We do know that they can be affected by jolting or vibrations. They're weird – I heard of one case where a fuse was set to detonate the charge in two days. It was put under a bridge during training and then the man who had put it there died in a motor crash. Everyone forgot about it.' He paused, his eyes on Dietrich who was staring at him fixedly. 'Two years later the bridge blew up. Yes, sir – two *years* later.'

'Thank you.' Dietrich returned the time fuse to Hahnemann who picked up the charge by the handle and left the cabin with Corporal Schultz.

'And where does that get us?' asked Burckhardt.

'It gets us into a worse state of nerves than we were before, I should have thought. You heard what he said?'

'Of course! Which point were you referring to?'

Dietrich clubbed one large fist and began drumming it slowly on the table. It took Burckhardt a moment to grasp that he was drumming in time with the beat of the *Hydra*'s engines. He pursed his lips uncomfortably as Dietrich rammed the point home verbally. 'Affected by jolting or vibrations,' he said.

'We shall not be on board much longer.' He hesitated. It must by now be patently obvious when they were going ashore to anyone who knew the *Hydra*'s timetable. 'Barely an hour. In the meantime the search continues and they may find it.'

'Colonel Burckhardt.' Dietrich was standing up now, his hat in his hand. 'This is likely to be the longest hour of your life. I think I'll go and help them try to find it. You never know – they say heaven protects the innocent.'

As he went along the companionway, hands thrust deep inside his coat pockets, he heard the frenzied clump of nailed boots everywhere. The boots rarely stayed still for more than a short time, as though their occupants were finding it impossible to keep in one place while they continued their frantic search for the missing demolition charge. Inside one cabin he found men with moist faces pushing aside a pile of dark brown hickory skis which could not possibly have concealed the charge. A soldier who didn't look a day over nineteen was peering behind a fire-extinguisher, another impossible hiding-place. There had been tension aboard the *Hydra* ever since the Alpenkorps had arrived, tension initially through the knowledge that at any minute they might be stopped by a British warship, tension because they were aboard the vessel of a country which Germany still officially treated as a neutral in the war. But the earlier tension brought on by the secrecy, by the storm, by the sabotage of a wireless set and the death of one of their men overboard – this tension had been serenity compared with the stark, livid tension which now gripped the *Hydra*'s illegal passengers.

It manifested itself in little ways. The lift of a rifle as Dietrich came round a corner. The kicking over of a bucket of sand by an Alpenkorps soldier hurrying past. The disorganised clump of those nailed boots on the ceiling when he was walking along the companionway of the lower deck. The sentry who guarded Grapos was still at his post, his back to the portholed steel door leading down to the hold where the Greek was imprisoned. Further along the companionway Dietrich looked inside the half-open door which led down to the engine-room. He had one foot on the iron platform when a rifle muzzle was thrust in his face, reminding him of the muzzle which Volber had thrust at him as he opened his cabin door when they had taken over the ship. But this time he withdrew swiftly – the muzzle had wobbled slightly. In that brief glimpse he had seen below at least half-a-dozen field-grey figures searching among the machinery while another man mounted guard over the chief engineer. The fear was a living mounting thing which he saw in men's faces as he climbed back to the top deck, faces damp, baggy-eyed and drawn with strain as they went on searching amid the ferry's complexities for something no larger than an attaché case. This is a formula for driving men mad, he was thinking as he went on climbing, for slowly shredding their nerves to pieces.

On the open deck it was quieter because there were fewer searchers: Burckhardt had given strict instructions that despite the gravity of the emergency only those men who could cover their uniforms with civilian coats were to be sent up here. Even now he was not prepared to risk a British motor-torpedo boat suddenly appearing and flashing its searchlight over the deck to illuminate men in German uniform. So far as Dietrich could see there were no more than a dozen, hatless men flitting in the shadows. But here again he heard the disjointed hurrying clump of those heavily-nailed boots pounding the wooden deck. It was quite dark now, the impenetrable pitch-blackness of the night before dawn, and a cold wind was blowing along the gulf. He leant against a ventilator to light his cigar and a soldier came round the side and cannoned into him. When he saw the silhouette of the hat against the match-flare he apologised and hurried away. Dietrich sighed. Again he had seen the lift of the rifle prior to recognition. He went to the stern and looked over the rail where the screw churned the sea a dirty white colour, stumbled over a piled loop of rope, and went back along the deck to the illuminated safety of the bridge. It was 4.45 a.m.

*

The ten-kilogram composite demolition charge swayed at the end of the rope. The vibrations of the ship's engines shuddered it in mid-sway and the rock of the ship's movements reproduced themselves in the sway itself. The charge thudded regularly against the metalwork as it continued its endless pendulum motion, but the sound of the thuds was camouflaged by the same engine beats which shook it. A man standing close by might not have heard those warning thuds as the charge dangled and swayed and shuddered. The clock was set and the mechanism was ticking, but the most vital sound – the ticking – was muffled by the larger noises. Occasionally the vessel plunged its bows a little deeper into the waters of the gulf and then the charge would strike the metal heavily, its rhythmic sway temporarily upset by the unexpected jolt. For a minute or more it would sway erratically, its pendulum balance disturbed, then it would recover its poise and resume the same even swing backwards and forwards with the regularity of a metronome. It was suspended a long way down the shaft, suspended from an Alpenkorps scabbard which still held its bayonet, a scabbard which had been jammed inside the shaft at an angle which might hold it there indefinitely. And as it went on swaying none of the hatless men who thumped along the open deck in growing desperation had, as yet, carefully examined the ventilator shaft amidships.

5 · Sunday 5 a.m.

The scuttering sound in the darkness of the hold was made by some small animal, probably a rat. Grapos had heard the furtive rustlings for some time as he sawed steadily at the rope and his wrists ached with the strain of being held in one position for so long. The trouble was that the metal edge of the packing-case frame was ragged only at certain points; he had to draw the tautened rope between his wrists backwards and forwards across a section about a foot in length. He rested occasionally for short periods, listening to the foot patter of the little passengers who shared the hold with him, checking the large face of his wrist-watch to make sure that he wasn't running short of time. He had to free himself and be clear of the hold well before 5.30 a.m. when the ferry docked at Katyra. The illuminated hands registered 4.55 a.m.

While he rested, he curled the fingers of his right hand inwards. His fingertips explored the frayed rope and there seemed to be only a few tenuous strands still imprisoning him. The discovery gave him fresh hope but still he waited: the next time he wanted the strength to finish the job, to climb that iron step-ladder and do what he must do. From where he sat near the foot of the ladder he could look up and see the porthole in the steel door at the top which led out into the lower-deck companionway. And at times, when the sentry had just received a visit from Hahnemann and knew he was safely alone for a while, Grapos could see the man's head as he leant back against the door to take the weight off his weary feet. It was important that the German should be occupying that position when he came to mount the step-ladder. And Grapos' alert brain had noticed something else important: when Burckhardt had visited him the steel door had opened smoothly and quietly on its well-oiled hinges. As he sat and waited a moment longer, his eyes fixed on that distant porthole above him, he wondered why they had turned out the lights. Had they left them on the sentry could have looked down through that porthole whenever the whim took him and Grapos would have been caught in the act of fraying the rope. He imagined that they had thought leaving him in the darkness would make escape more difficult, whereas for Grapos the contrary was the case. He took a deep breath, stiffened himself and began sawing furiously.

The rope snapped unexpectedly swiftly. It took him a moment to loosen the loops still round his wrists and to throw them away. Now for his feet. Pressing his broad back against the packing-case for support, he leaned forward and fiddled with knots he could only feel. They had tied him up well, but once his deft fingers undid the first knot he was soon able to free himself from the second rope. Still sitting, he rubbed the circulation back into his aching wrists and then stood up cautiously with one hand flat on top of the case. He felt cramped and bent, but as he exercised his legs by crooking and stretching them he felt the strength flowing back. He would need the strength and perfect muscular coordination for what he had to do. His last action was to lace his short powerful fingers between each other while he squeezed and flexed them. Those hands were going to be important, too.

His eyes were now well-accustomed to the darkness inside the hold and he could vaguely see the iron rail of the step-ladder going up to the door. The aspect which worried him most were his nailed boots – boots essential for the rough terrain of Zervos but hardly suitable for mounting iron treads silently. If he attempted to go up walking on the soles he might slip on the metalwork, so he decided to take longer and put a soundless approach before every other consideration. Gripping the cold rail, he lifted his right foot and put it down very carefully, only letting it take his full weight when he felt the tread under the boot. It was a painfully slow ascent and he was scarcely half-way up when he felt sweat on his forehead, a reaction from his anxiety rather than his exertion – his anxiety that the sentry would move away from the door. By the light in the companionway he could see the short-cut fair hair at the back of the neck and an inch of field grey collar. He was suddenly aware of a heavy silence in the hold – the rats were temporarily motionless as they listened to his deliberate tread slowly climbing closer to the platform, as though they instinctively sensed the tension and the danger. He went on climbing, and because the light shining through the porthole was stronger he could see now the embossed faces of the treads above where projections had been punched up out of the iron to make the treads less slippery. The neck of the sentry lifted away from the door and Grapos' hand froze on the rail. If the door opened now he was at least six treads below the platform. His hand relaxed as the neck leaned back again: he had merely shifted his balance to find a more comfortable position. Grapos started climbing again – close enough now to see that the door was firmly closed. It was the fear that they might have only closed the door on the latch, leaving a narrow gap through which sound could have carried, that had made his ascent up the ladder so cautious. With the steel door properly closed no sound inside the hold would ever reach the companionway, and this was a further element in what he planned to do. A great deal would depend on how the sentry was holding his rifle. He reached the wide platform which was surrounded by a slim rail and wiped his moist hands on the backs of his trousers. Hands which slipped at the wrong moment could cost him his life.

The door opened inwards and the opening process involved a turning handle. But before operating the handle Grapos would have liked to have some assurance that the companionway was occupied only by the sentry. He peered through the glass quickly in the gap between the sentry's neck and the porthole rim; the view was restricted and showed him only a few feet of empty passageway. He would have to risk it. If another Alpenkorps soldier appeared at the wrong moment he would be done for and that would be that.

The door was hinged on the right so he stood to the left of the opening edge as his hand rested on the steel lever and began to press downwards with infinite slowness and care. The slightest tremor of the door, the faintest squeak of the turning handle, would warn the sentry of his danger. Centimetre by centimetre the handle descended under Grapos' firm grip. Then it stopped. The door was now ready to open, to be pulled inwards over the platform. He had no idea of the weight of the steel slab, no idea of how much leverage would be required to do the trick. Some of these doors opened ponderously however much pressure was exerted – and a ponderous movement would be fatal. He had the lower part of his back pressed firmly into the rail, his feet placed a little apart to give better balance, his right hand flexed to let go of the handle at the earliest possible moment – providing the door moved swiftly. Taking in a deep breath, he was on the verge of pulling when the sentry stood away from the door. Still in view of the porthole window, he stood erect and stiffly. An officer had entered the companionway and was coming to see him. With a tremendous effort Grapos resisted the temptation to stay by the porthole window to see who was coming. Squeezing himself against the narrow section of wall between door and rail, he waited. A moment later a shock like a douche of icy water ran through him – *the turn-handle was pressed down in the open position and this could be seen from the outside.*

He held the handle fixed in that position because he dared not risk lifting it again – even the movement might be more than enough to attract the attention of the men in the companionway. And the unknown officer who had arrived was likely to be the same one who came to see him at intervals. If so, he would probably notice the handle. Grapos understood instantly that he was in an impossible position; if they came inside the first man would have his weapon ready, and even if that could be pushed aside the second man would be prepared. Gripping the handle, having no idea of what was happening beyond the steel door, conscious of the horrible stillness down on the floor of the hold where the rats were still silent, he waited. From where he stood he was able to see the elliptical shape of the porthole and suddenly the light on the platform was blurred. Startled, he took one step sideways and saw the neck of the sentry in its previous position. The officer must have walked straight past and gone away for him to take up his position of ease so quickly again. Grapos didn't hesitate: this might be his last chance.

Exerting all his strength, he hauled at the door. The slab opened without haste but smoothly, and as it swung on the noiseless hinges it gathered momentum and swept in a crescent over the platform. The sentry, his rifle looped loosely over one shoulder, lost his balance and stumbled backwards on to the platform as Grapos' hands locked round his shoulders and throat, stifling the shout which emerged only as a gurgle of cut-off breath. The German was still off-balance as Grapos careened him across the platform until his own back was against the rear of the half-open door. Under the pressure of Grapos' heave the door swung shut again as he bent his body backwards, his shoulder-blades against the steel, one hand ringed round the sentry's throat, the other arm pinioning his elbows. He had the German almost in his lap and his feet might have slipped but the nails under his boots engaged with the iron projections on the floor and held him. He was using his shoulders for leverage to hoist the sentry up and over the rail when the soldier broke loose, tearing himself free, swinging round to face his adversary as he backed up against the rail visible in the light from the porthole window. Then the German made a mistake. He thought he had time to unsling his rifle and aim it, but he had only half-completed the manoeuvre when Grapos, erect on his feet, lowered his head and charged the short space which divided them. The rail the sentry was backed against was waist-high for Grapos but only thigh-thigh for the taller German. The lowered head butted the sentry full in the stomach as he fumbled to free his rifle. Grapos felt the German's body collapse under his onslaught and he pushed harder, whipping out his hands to grab the rail on either side. The sentry fell over backwards and then his legs, trapped between the rail and Grapos' body, momentarily saved him. Realising what had happened, Grapos hung on to the rail and eased himself back quickly and was nearly kicked in the face as the upper part of the German's body dragged the legs clear off the platform. Hurtling down through the darkness into the hold he struck the floor thirty feet below with a breaking thud.

Grapos fumbled for the light switch by the door, turned it on, still holding the switch. The light blinded him for several seconds and then he saw the German spread-eagled face downwards on the wooden deck, his head turned to an angle impossible for a living man. By a matter of inches he had missed falling on a pile of cloth-covered bales which might have muffled his fall. Grapos switched off the lights, thought briefly of going down to pick up the rifle which lay a few feet beyond the dead German, then decided he hadn't the time. When he pulled open the door again the companion-way was deserted. He stepped out and shut it quickly. He had so little time – the first German familiar with this part of the ship who entered the passage would notice the absence of the sentry. He was running along the companionway and was close to the staircase which led up when he heard a door thud above him. Someone was about to come down the staircase. There were no lights behind the louvred upper half of the cabin door he stood close to so he went inside and closed the door. Footsteps, heavy-nailed footsteps, were advancing along the passage. One pair. Was this someone who would immediately notice that the soldier on guard ﹍ ﹍d vanished? The footsteps marched quickly, like a man on his way some-where definite. They were passing the closed door when Grapos felt a tingle at the back of his neck. Behind him in the darkened cabin he could hear quiet, steady breathing.

It had all happened so swiftly that the thought that there might be someone asleep inside the darkened cabin had never occurred to him. Perhaps subconsciously he had assumed that all the troops would be awake because of what he had seen when they had first transferred him to the hold. He had been knocked unconscious earlier while he slept in the saloon and only after the ship's seizure had he been taken to the hold. It was during this trip that he had seen cabins full of German soldiers fully dressed and clearly ready for anything. The breathing was becoming more laboured as the footsteps outside retreated into the distance without pausing at the door which led to the hold. The interrupted rhythm of the breathing warned Grapos that within a short time the man who lay asleep only a few feet away would wake up. Would the light from the companionway bring him to consciousness as the door was opened? Only a few seconds elapsed as Grapos' quick brain turned over that possibility and then a voice spoke out of the darkness in German. The man knew he was there. Grapos sensed it. He heard something heavy hit the floor. The German had sat up in his bunk. Grapos reached out and felt his hands slide over a buttoned tunic, reach an open collar. The soldier was starting to cry out, to struggle violently, his hands flailing over Grapos' shoulders as his own hands grasped the man's neck tightly and pushed him backwards and downwards. From a sharp crack Grapos assumed the man's head had struck the bunk wall but he was still fighting as he punched blindly. One blow grazed the edge of his jaw but Grapos was still holding on as he struggled in the darkness with a man he had never seen. Was there anyone else sharing the cabin? Had there been another man he must surely have roused himself by now however exhausted a sleep he had sunk into. The German's boot heels were hammering against the lower side of the bunk and the tattoo was a deafening sound. At any moment Grapos expected the door to be flung open, the lights to go on as Germans with guns came up behind him. Thrashing furiously sideways in a desperate attempt to release the grip on his throat, the unknown German lunged sideways so savagely that he smashed Grapos' knuckles against the woodwork. With a grunt of pain, Grapos let go,

felt the German coming up, lashed out blindly with his forearm, felt it contact the soldier's jaw. There was a second
sharp crack in the dark, a louder crack. The German went
limp under him.

Standing up unsteadily, one hand rested on the bunk for
support, Grapos waited for his breathing to return to normal
and then ran his hand up and down beside the door frame.
By accident he caught the switch and a light came on. The
Alpenkorps soldier sprawled on the bunk was dark-haired
and had an unpleasantly large jaw which gave him a brutal
look. He was fully-dressed in his uniform and his rifle lay on
a small table. Grapos was looking for signs which might
indicate the recent presence of another German who could
return to the cabin shortly, but the second bunk was made
up and unused. He picked up the rifle, examined it, ejected
the cartridges from the breech, worked the mechanism
several times and then reloaded it. Only last January a stall-
keeper in Istanbul who knew his interest in small arms had
offered to sell him a similar rifle. God knew how he had
obtained the gun but Grapos had spent some time in
examining it before returning the weapon as too expensive.
He spent another two minutes taking off the German's belt
with the ammunition pouches and fastening it round his own
waist. When he switched off the light and opened the door
there was no one in sight.

Grapos had very little hope that he could carry out the
long-distance plan which had formed in his mind while he
struggled to saw through the ropes in the hold. To have any
chance of success he must reach a certain hiding-place and
remain undiscovered for probably half an hour. Instinctively
he felt that it would be dangerous to linger in the obvious
places, but he had little doubt he would be intercepted on
the way. At least he was now armed. The real possibility of
eluding the Germans lay in his knowledge of a vessel he had
known for many years, and when he reached the staircase he
went behind it instead of upwards. A small door led to a
narrow passage which was also empty. Half-way along the

passage he opened another small door and climbed a crew staircase to the upper deck without meeting anyone. The open deck, he had foreseen, would be dangerous.

He was working his way along the port side, easing his body between the lifeboats and the outer rail, when he heard German being spoken near the starboard rail. Watching between two slung lifeboats, he saw the silhouettes of two soldiers searching inside a lifeboat opposite. Their activity meant nothing to him and as soon as they were standing with their backs turned he squeezed further along the deck until he reached the stern. The loop of rope was still there, neatly piled in a coil. Using his clasp-knife, he cut a generous length, attached one end firmly to the base of a rail's stanchion, pushed the coil back in place to hide the rope end, and then formed a loop of the other end which he dangled over the stern to check for length before attaching it round his waist. Glancing again along the quiet deck, he climbed over the side, the rifle slung diagonally across his back, then lowered himself a few feet, still hanging to the rail with one hand. With the other he looped part of the rope over a hook below him attached to the portion of the hull which curved inward under the stern. Then, without looking down to where the screw turned below, he lowered himself to the limit of the rope until he was dangling above the sea and partially concealed by the hull.

The stratagem didn't work as well as he had hoped. The rope looped round his waist had a tendency to haul the Alpenkorps belt high over his chest and the leather band which had fitted comfortably round his waist was constricting the upper part of his body. The sway of the rope and his generally encumbered position made it impossible to un-buckle the belt and re-fasten it so he ignored the inconvenience. At least he was out in the open, in a position where at the right moment he could haul himself back on deck and dive over the side closer to the funnel – and away from that churning screw. Despite his position of extreme discomfort, Grapos was not particularly aware of the early morning chill

which permeated the gulf – he was used to the sub-zero
temperatures which prevailed on Mount Zervos and he was
enjoying a certain satisfaction at his little success when two
Germans searching the deck leaned over the stern rail.

The satisfaction ebbed as Grapos realised he had made a
serious mistake. Normally on a voyage passengers near their
port of arrival were in their cabins, and the early risers had a
habit of clustering at the bows, the nearest point to their
destination, leaving the stern deserted. It was probably this
subconscious thought which had prompted him to choose
this hiding-place and only now did he grasp his appalling
danger. If one man leaned far enough over the stern he was
bound to see the figure dangling from its home-made cat's
cradle. And dealing with the problem would not pose any
difficulty – a few quick slashes with a sharp knife at the other
end of the rope . . . Grapos looked down to where the blades
of the screw sliced and beat the water into grey foam. Even
if he fell clear of that remorseless mincing machine the eddy
round it would suck him on to the screw's revolutions like a
whirlpool gyrating flotsam to its centre. The rifle was strapped
over his back in an inaccessible position and he had no means
of defending himself. With both hands wrapped round the
swaying rope he gazed upwards and saw the tip of an Alpenkorps boot perched on the lower rail only a few inches from
the rope coil. Above the slap and slosh of the revolving screw
Grapos heard faintly the sound of voices.

'I do not think we shall find the demolition charge,'
Corporal Schultz was saying. 'It is too small and the ship is
too large.'

'It must be somewhere. With the number of men we have
searching we may find it any minute.' Sergeant Volber was
feeling it necessary to preserve an attitude of confidence
which hardly corresponded with his thoughts.

'Then I hope I am not the man who finds it – the time fuse
may be set to detonate at any second.'

'Over the side is the answer – as soon as it is found it goes
into the water. For all we know it may not be on board –

whoever took it away may have thrown the charge overboard himself.'

'Then why take it in the first place?' demanded the pessimistic Schultz. He turned to leave the rail and stumbled over the coil of rope. With an oath he aimed his boot and sent the coil several feet along the deck. 'On ships people leave things lying about,' he grumbled. 'If the colonel were in charge he would have the place cleaned up.'

'But then he is in charge for this single voyage,' Volber pointed out. He leaned further out over the rail. 'What is that sticking out under the stern? Show your torch, a minute, Schultz.'

The corporal took out his pocket torch and fumbled at the switch with his gloved hands. In the process he dropped the torch and it rolled back along the deck towards the raft which had now been re-covered with the canvas sheeting. Cursing, he followed its path as it disappeared into the darkness. He thought he heard a slight bump as though something had impeded its progress and began feeling along the edge of the raft. Volber called out to him from the stern. 'Next time take off your glove, you idiot.' Schultz's fingers touched something, closed over the barrel of the torch. He called out that he had found it and hurried back to where Volber waited impatiently. He was taking off his glove when the sergeant reached out a hand.

'Give it to me! You are taking all night and we must continue the search. If Lieutenant Hahnemann finds you playing about like this you will be in even more trouble.'

'It was not my fault that the charge was stolen . . .' He broke off as Volber switched on the torch and directed the beam over the side. The long cone of light showed a short horizontal mast projecting from the stern while in the fading edge of the beam below the sea foamed greyly. Suspended from his rope, Grapos saw the light just miss his left shoulder and knew that the German above had only to angle his torch a few degrees to play the beam full on him. The light continued to shine downwards as though the holder of the torch was fascinated by the threshing water and now Grapos had carefully rested the soles of his boots against the vibrating hull to check the rope's sway. It was a difficult position to maintain and he was desperately afraid that in his attempt to conceal himself he might have achieved the opposite result – if the nailed boots slipped and scraped over the hull the sound was bound to be heard above. His calf muscles began to feel the strain quickly as the torch light continued to shine down on the water and the sound of the voices talking had gone. The absence of the voices grated on his wrought-up brain and he realised what could be happening: one of the Germans had spotted him and had gone to report his find to an officer while the man who held the torch pretended simply to be interested in the turning screw. So within minutes he might be given the choice of hauling himself back on deck or being shot. A graver fear struck him as the torchlight went on illuminating the water below – someone had gone to fetch a knife to cut the rope which supported him. It would be the easiest solution – to send him down on top of the screw where there would be no chance of his surviving to swim ashore. The grim possibilities were churning in his mind when he felt his left boot start to slip over the smooth hull.

His instinct was to drop both feet away from the ship, but he knew that this would instantly cause the rope to sway and carry him straight across the path of the beam. Tentatively, he tried stiffening his leg, but the boot was already slithering and it could only be a matter of seconds before it was completely out of control. In a last effort to hold his position he pressed harder with his right boot against the ship's surface and for a short time it worked. The other boot remained motionless as his full weight hinged on the pressure he was exerting on one foot. The torch beam lifted as a seagull flew into its glare and landed on the tip of the horizontal mast, another focus of attraction to keep the torch shining for longer. His legs were awkwardly splayed now and the strain extended up to his thighs so that he began to feel like a man stretched on the rack as the pain increased rapidly. Hung over the ship's side, legs stretched and hands clinging to the rope, his body arched at an angle of almost ninety degrees, the sound of the screw spinning below, Grapos was in as helpless a state as it is possible for a man to find himself in. The torch beam had just been switched off when he gave way. His legs splayed further apart as both boots scraped across the hull and made a grating rasp which was only half-muffled by the beat of the screw.

'What was that?'

Schultz asked the question as they were moving away from the stern. The sergeant paused, a few paces in front of the corporal, and there was irritation in his voice as he called back over his shoulder. 'I heard nothing – you may dislike the idea of searching for that demolition charge but you will get on with it now.' Volber had no particular liking for Schultz whom he suspected of avoiding risk at every possible opportunity. There was a malicious note in his final instruction. 'You will go at once to help with the search in the engine-room – the most likely hiding-place.'

The two men left the deck and at the stern the coil of rope sat in its new position, completely exposing the knotted end of another rope which could hardly fail to be seen with the first light of day.

*

'The Greek has escaped – I have instituted an immediate and intensive search of the ship.' Hahnemann reported the news to Burckhardt whom he had found on the bridge standing next to Dietrich. He waited nervously for the colonel's reaction, but Burckhardt, holding a pair of field-glasses, simply looked at him as he asked the question.

'How did it happen, Hahnemann? He was tied up in the hold and Private Kutzel was standing guard over him.'

'He must have freed himself in some way.' Hahnemann hesitated: the next item of news was bound to provoke an explosion. 'Kutzel is dead – I found him on the floor of the hold with his neck broken.'

'And his rifle?'

Dietrich smiled grimly to himself as he heard the question and he gave the colonel top marks for competence under stress. The weapon, of course, was vital, could make all the difference to the degree of menace posed by the escaped Greek.

'I found that on the floor close to his body . . .'

'Good. He shouldn't be difficult to round up. You said an "intensive" search, Hahnemann. How intensive? How many men?'

'Fifty, sir.' Hahnemann at least felt confident that he had organised the hunt for Grapos on a sufficiently massive scale, even though there was something else which he dreaded mentioning. He wished to heaven that the Abwehr man wasn't standing there with his hands behind his back, his great shoulders hunched forward as he took in every word the lieutenant was saying. The colonel's reaction gave him an unpleasant shock.

'Fifty? You mean you have taken fifty men off the search for the missing demolition charge?' Burckhardt was facing the unfortunate Hahnemann now, his hands on his hips as he went on bitingly. 'When will you get your priorities right? An explosive with a time fuse has been planted somewhere aboard this vessel, an explosive powerful enough to sink us in the middle of the gulf before we ever go ashore. That, since it appears you don't realise it, is a far greater risk than one unarmed Greek civilian who is probably gibbering with fright in some cupboard. You will tell off no more than twenty men to look for him – the other thirty must immediately resume the search for that demolition charge.'

'He is armed, sir – with a rifle . . .'

'You said you had found Kutzel's rifle.'

'That is correct, sir.' Hahnemann's rigid stance reflected the extent of his unhappiness as he went on stolidly. 'I think the Greek must have surprised Private Wasserman also when he was asleep in a cabin on the lower deck . . .'

'Asleep!' Burckhardt changed the direction of his attack:

what a soldier had been doing asleep during these vital hours was something he could enquire into later. Doubtless Wasserman had sneaked off into the cabin hoping no one would find him there. 'What has happened to Wasserman?'

'He's dead – strangled as far as we can tell. And his rifle and belt are missing so the Greek must have them.'

Burckhardt paused only briefly while he wished to God that the Abwehr man wasn't listening to all this, but he was still perfectly clear as to what must be done. 'You will still use only twenty men to hunt for the Greek. Issue a general warning that he's armed.'

'I have done that already, sir.'

'Then issue a special warning to those on the open deck – we don't want them starting to loose off at each other.' As Hahnemann hurried away he thought no, that would be the final disaster – to incur further casualties with the men shooting one another. Taking up a firmer stance, he stared ahead to where the searchlight beam shone down the gulf. It was 5.15 a.m. A quarter of an hour to disembarkation. Coldly, he catalogued in his mind the risks and setbacks which had bedevilled the expedition since he had come aboard the *Hydra*. A boatload of troops which had very nearly capsized during the transfer from the *Rupescu*; one soldier sent into the sea by the Englishman, Prentice; one wireless-set sabotaged by smashing the tuning-coil; the encounter with the destroyer which had almost proved fatal; a demolition charge of great explosive power planted somewhere in the bowels of the vessel; the escape of the armed Greek; and the death of two more Alpenkorps men during that escape. So three men out of two hundred were dead even before they set foot in Greece. Surely nothing more could happen during the remaining quarter of an hour? Although it was likely to be twenty-five or thirty minutes – they were behind schedule with this infernal ferry having to move more slowly because of the danger of mines – and Italian mines of all things. Schnell had insisted on the further reduction in speed to ensure that they sighted them in time. The irony of it was they hadn't seen a single mine since entering the gulf.

'I think I'll go and have a word with Major Eberhay – if I can find him.' Dietrich was already moving away and leaving the bridge to Burckhardt's relief – the large German seemed to dominate wherever he went, to hang over the ship like a prophet of disasters to come. Barely a minute later Sergeant Volber came on to the bridge and the colonel only had to take one look at his face to know it was not good news.

'What is it, Volber?' he rapped out sharply.

'We think Private Wolff may be missing, sir.'

Burckhardt instantly thought of the Greek who was prowling about somewhere with a loaded rifle. 'You *think*? Either Wolff is missing or he isn't? Which is it?'

'We don't know, sir.' Volber lacked Lieutenant Hahnemann's capacity for telling a complete account quickly, forestalling his commanding officer's questions so far as he could, and the sergeant's habit of replying without explaining was a foible Burckhardt found intensely irritating. He felt the blood going to his head as he forced himself to reply coldly.

'What the devil does that mean?'

'He hasn't been seen for a long time – I've asked several of the men and they all thought he was somewhere else. They're very scattered . . .'

'You've allowed your section to become scattered?'

'We're on the open deck and it takes time to check everyone in the dark . . .'

'Report to me as soon as you can whether he's definitely missing. Definitely, I said, Volber.'

The strain was telling everywhere, Burckhardt thought as the sergeant hurried away. Schnell was being over-cautious, the N.C.O.s were getting rattled, and the men were being steadily drained of their aggressive energies as they plodded round the ship searching for time-bombs and armed Greeks. And soon they would have to fight a campaign. Armed Greeks? The thought reminded him of a few vital questions he had to put to the captain. He took a step forward which placed him at Nopagos' elbow.

'The man called Grapos has escaped,' he said harshly. 'He has taken a rifle and ammunition – can he use them? Before you reply, remember that he is a civilian with no rights in war and I shall hold you responsible for the death of any of my men if you withhold information.'

Nopagos turned and stared at the German. His skin was lined and pouched with fatigue but he still held himself erect; what little responsibility he still held for his own vessel as its pilot would only cease when they docked at Katyra. He was tempted to tell Burckhardt to go to hell but he sensed something of the tremendous pressure the colonel was undergoing and it seemed senseless to take a risk when they had almost landed. 'He has been able to use a rifle since he was a boy,' he replied.

'But he has something to do with the monastery.' Burckhardt did not understand this at all and his mouth tightened as he held the Greek's eyes.

'He was a novice monk who had no vocation. When he left the monastery it was agreed that he should do odd jobs for them – like going to Istanbul on this ferry to bring back supplies of books and things like that. He has shot birds on the peninsula from an early age. Yes, he can use a rifle.'

'Well?'

'A marksman.' Nopagos gave this reply with a certain relish.

'His limp kept him out of the army?'

'It was his greatest regret. He would be an asset to any army in the world. Has he caused any trouble yet?'

'He has killed two of my men.'

'You see what I mean, then?' For a moment Nopagos thought he had gone too far. Burckhardt stiffened and a hint of fury came into his eyes and then faded as he regained control. He was careful to keep strict control as he put his next question.

'He knows this ship well?'

'Well enough to hide until we have reached Katyra as you have not found him now.' And with this last thrust Nopagos turned away and attended to his duties once more. But he was not able to resist asking a question which he carefully put in a polite tone. 'Have they found the time-bomb yet?'

'No.'

'So, there is still time.'

This simple comment stung Burckhardt more than anything Nopagos had said previously. He had given Eberhay orders to leave assembly for disembarkation until the last possible moment so they could keep on looking for that missing demolition charge – Burckhardt's greatest fear was that it would detonate just before they landed. He was thinking about this when Schnell, almost exhausted from his long hours over the wheel, straightened up as a soldier ran along outside the bridge and came in breathless. Burckhardt recognised him as one of the two men posted as lookouts as soon as they had passed through the narrows. In his anxiety to speak the man had trouble in getting out his message.

'Mines sighted, sir . . . on the port bow.'

*

They were out of their natural environment, Dietrich told himself as he walked slowly along the upper deck companionway, and this was demoralising them. A soldier emerged from a cabin, his weapon clutched tightly, and he jumped when he saw Dietrich. Fortunately the muzzle was pointed at the ceiling or the Abwehr man might have jumped as well. Half-way up the staircase two men on their way down hesitated as to whether to wait or push past him. Even a small decision like that was becoming difficult, and indecisions of that nature could be fatal once they were ashore. He found Eberhay at the top of the staircase giving Hahnemann disembarkation orders, and when the lieutenant left he launched into his attack.

'These men of yours don't like being cooped up in a confined space – one of them almost shot me a moment ago.'

'If you stayed on the bridge . . .' Eberhay began tactfully.

'I need to see what is happening – the Greek didn't stay below, I gather?'

'No, we have searched the lower deck thoroughly. If we had a little longer . . .'

'You'd discover both the Greek and the bomb. Anyone can do anything – given the time. It takes organisation and intuition to do things quickly.' Dietrich was in the worst of moods, towering over the small officer as he lit another cigar. 'The list of things which have gone wrong would fill a fifty-page report. In fact,' he informed Eberhay grimly, 'they may. Is that damaged wireless-set repaired?'

'No, not yet . . .'

'But you have another one. Well-guarded, I hope? I have to send a message at the earliest possible moment.'

'Two men are with it constantly . . .'

'And then there's the question of their being a traitor on board. You haven't forgotten that vital fact, I trust?' The Abwehr man's manner had become overbearing and so quietly ferocious that Eberhay was wondering how he could get away from him at once. The man had a strange hypnotic effect as he stared at you with unblinking eyes.

'We hoped you'd be able to help us there,' Eberhay replied smoothly. 'Espionage and treachery are more in your . . .'

'And you wonder why I have to go on prowling round this ship like a spectre? It's in the hope that I shall see something – something unusual and out of pattern. You must excuse me – I'm going out on deck.' He opened the door and slammed it shut behind him, leaving Eberhay to stare at the closed door for a few seconds before he ran down the staircase. Like a spectre – yes, that described the Abwehr man exactly. He had haunted the ship like a spectre, his huge shadow everywhere since they had come on board this cursed vessel.

On deck, Dietrich's temper seemed to be rising. As he had come through the doorway he had seen the silhouette of an Alpenkorps soldier by the ventilator amidships. Volber had swung round jumpily with his weapon as the door slammed shut and had jumped again as Dietrich's voice rang out along the deck where some of the searchers must have heard him. 'What the devil are you pointing that gun at me for? Don't you know me by now, for God's sake?'

'It was hard to see who it was . . .'

'Of course! I was only completely framed in the light from the door.' He advanced on Volber who instinctively backed a few paces along the deck. 'So naturally you couldn't possibly see who it was! Do I have to blow a whistle to let you know I'm coming?' He broke off abruptly and Volber escaped to issue a sharp order to the man who had been closest to the confrontation and who had witnessed his humiliation.

They had searched the lower deck thoroughly, so Eberhay had stated confidently, but with the Alpenkorps distributed throughout the ship this information had not reached everyone, and Corporal Schultz was among those unaware of this fact. A short time before he had obeyed Volber's order and had made his way down towards the engine-room. Not a very quick-thinking man, Schultz had been surprised to find the lower deck companionway in darkness but he had sensed nothing sinister as he fumbled round to find the switches and then gave up and began to feel his way along the darkened passage. He used the hand-rail to guide him and as he approached the hold where Grapos had been imprisoned he thought he heard a heavy thud nearby. He stood quite still in the blackness, not particularly alarmed because this was where the Greek had escaped from so he couldn't possibly be down there. Uncertain what to do, he waited a little longer listening to the throb of the engines and feeling a little faint from the hot airlessness of the lower depths of the ship. The heavy thudding was repeated and he felt sure now that it came from the hold. He could go back and report this to Sergeant Volber, but if it turned out that someone like Lieutenant Hahnemann was in the hold there would be an almighty row. Corporal Schultz was one of those soldiers who

feared any superior more than he feared the enemy, and
Colonel Burckhardt was always insisting that before they
reported anything they should come with a complete account.

Schultz was in the most agonising of situations – growing
a little worried about those secretive noises, wondering now
more than ever why the lights had been turned out, and yet
still apprehensive of making a fool of himself, of earning yet
another rebuke from the rough-tongued Volber. Holding on
to the rail gave him a feeling of security, so he went on
holding the rifle in his right hand while the left hand gripped
the rail as he crept along a few more feet of companionway.
If only he could see what was happening. The steel door to
the hold was slightly open – he could tell that by feel as his
hand left the interrupted section of rail and touched the
metal. Standing close to the porthole window he looked down
and saw the brief flash of a torch, but too late to catch a
glimpse of who was holding it. Had the lights failed on this
deck? Schultz's dull mind was taken up with three things –
the demolition charge with its time fuse ticking away somewhere aboard, the Greek who had escaped and who had
probably dived overboard, and his fear of more biting
criticism from Volber who never left him alone for long. A
wave of relief came over him. He'd got it! Someone was
bringing up supplies ready for the disembarkation – and the
lights had failed on this deck. He was walking quietly past
the partially open door when his curiosity got the better of
him: he really would have to see who was down there in the
hold or he'd wonder about it later.

He pulled open the door, being careful not to step inside.
There was probably an awful drop just beyond the opening.
The silence of the deep hold came up out of the darkness and
enveloped him like a smothering blanket. He was suddenly
frightened. He'd get away from here fast. He could report
this odd business as soon as he reached the engine-room;
there was bound to be an officer or senior N.C.O. there. As
he turned to continue along the companionway the butt of
his rifle banged against the wall and he jumped at the sound.

The silence which followed was so unbearable that he felt compelled to speak. 'Is there someone there?' The words came out as a hoarse croak and a few seconds later he felt a movement of the air. He backed away a little late. Something hard and heavy struck him on the side of the temples and he collapsed on the floor as his rifle clattered beside him. A shadow peered into the passage through the door which had now been opened wider. A stench of petrol fumes drifted upwards through the heavy air and percolated along the companionway. Without a sound the shadow withdrew back on to the platform. Something flared briefly as it fell through space, sputtered sparks as it landed on the wet floor below, and then a sheet of flame flared up vividly, illuminating the interior of the hold like an open blast-furnace so it became lighter than day. The flame leapt quickly over the petrol-soaked bales which had been placed up the step-ladder and within a minute the hold was ablaze, the fire had reached the platform and was exploring the darkened companionway, gradually illuminating it as someone went up the staircase at the far end.

6 · Sunday, Dawn

The explosion came at 5.45 a.m. as the *Hydra*, listing to port, her engines beating uncertainly, and with smoke billowing aft, began the ninety-degree turn which would take her inshore to the distant light of the Katyra landing-stage. They were almost there, Burckhardt reflected as he stood on the bridge behind Nopagos, but the last mile was likely to be the longest of the voyage. The dangers surrounding the expedition were now so overwhelming that his mind had reached the point where it could hardly take in any more – those damnable Italian mines were growing more numerous with every quarter-mile they glided forward; the fire in the main hold was spreading despite the desperate efforts to quench the flames; and they had still failed to locate the demolition charge which might detonate at any moment. Lifting his field-glasses to focus on the circle of mines ringing the vessel, he ignored the newcomers arriving on the already over-crowded bridge. Because of the risk of imminent disaster he had ordered the British prisoners to be brought up from their cabin.

'Are we abandoning ship?' Prentice asked quietly.

'No!' Hahnemann's reply was savagely emphatic as his hand guided the lieutenant by the elbow to the rear of the bridge. 'We shall be landing shortly.'

'Through that lot!' Ford sounded incredulous as he gazed over the colonel's shoulder along the searchlight beam which cut across the darkness. To port and starboard of the illuminated avenue at least four mines floated, metallic spheres which gleamed palely, their surfaces speckled with small shadows – the dreaded nozzles which caused instant detonation on contact. Burckhardt spoke briefly over his shoulder, instructing Hahnemann to tell them about the missing demolition charge; after all, they were soldiers, so they might as well know the position. With waning enthusiasm, Prentice and Ford listened to Hahnemann and were then pushed to the rear of the bridge, squeezed in between a press of uniformed Alpenkorps troops. Looking to his right, Prentice found he was huddled next to the large German civilian who had come aboard at Istanbul. On their way up from the cabin they had seen him in the distance climbing a staircase and Prentice had enquired who he was.

'Herr Dietrich is with the Abwehr,' Hahnemann had replied with a hint of respect in his voice. Prentice looked up curiously at the huge figure who stared back at him as he lit a fresh cigar with one elbow rested on the shoulder of the corporal next to him. A rum cove, this Dietrich, had been Prentice's reaction as he turned to listen to Ford who was keeping his voice down.

'How big did he say that demolition charge was? I couldn't catch all he said in this crush.'

'Ten kilograms. Is that bad?'

'It's not good, I can tell you that straight off. And if it's been dumped near the boilers and they go, too . . .'

He broke off as Burckhardt issued a stream of orders to Eberhay who had appeared at the door to the bridge and then hurried away when the colonel had finished speaking. They were close to the moment of disembarkation, which required disciplined control, and the little major was facing something like near-panic as the troops filed up the staircases. It was then that Prentice saw the Alpenkorps equipment which confirmed his worst fears: he had a glimpse of men with skis of hickory wood passing beyond the bridge. The skis were carried on their backs which also supported rucksacks – which could only mean they expected to be operating in the deep snows on Mount Zervos at the far end of the peninsula. The Alpenkorps' main objective was the natural observation post of the monastery which overlooked the mainland road carrying Allied supplies northward.

'Funny that bomb hasn't gone off already,' he remarked

lightly to Ford. He would have liked to feel that he was praying for the charge to detonate, but the truth was that he was sick with apprehension. 'Perhaps the chap who fixed it didn't know what he was doing,' he suggested.

'That's possible, sir. But their time fuses aren't all that reliable – a Jerry we had in the bag told me that. The damned things have a habit of conking out at the wrong moment.'

'You mean they become harmless?' Prentice tried to keep the hope out of his voice.

'Now I didn't say that, did I? Apparently they sometimes stop and then start up again. Vibrations can get them going again as easy as winking. The ship's engines are ideal for the purpose.'

'That's right, cheer us all up.' Prentice did not feel particularly reassured. Ford was an ammunition examiner who spent too much of his life fiddling with things which might go bang in his face at any second – including enemy explosives and equipment on which he was also something of an expert. But here on this German-held vessel he was displaying distinct signs of nervousness as he pulled at the lobe of one ear and kept looking round the bridge as though he expected it to disappear without warning.

'Fasten those straps at once!' Hahnemann had returned briefly to the bridge and had noticed that Ford's life-jacket was loose. Every man on the bridge wore his life-jacket and these cumbersome objects took up more space and further impeded movement. Prentice had the feeling that he would soon be lifted clear off the floor if anyone else crowded in on the bridge. He jerked his head round again to look through the rear window which gave a view along the deck towards the stern, a deck which was almost deserted since the order for uniformed troops to keep out of sight was still in force. Almost deserted, but not quite. Prentice's eyes narrowed as he watched oily black smoke from the fire below drift past a lamp near the starboard rail: by its light he saw a short, heavily-built man on the wrong side of the rail, a man who

carried a rifle over his back. Something about the shape and
the movement reminded him of the Greek civilian who had
also come aboard at Istanbul. Grapos, the captain had called
him. Smoke blurred the view and when it cleared the poised
figure was gone. He had dived over the side.

'Seen a ghost, sir?' Ford enquired.

'I've got a crick in my neck if you're referring to my
expression of almost unendurable agony.' Prentice felt sure
that at the last minute Dietrich had also glanced through that
window, but by then the smoke would have blotted out the
lonely figure. He was greatly relieved when the German said
nothing and continued quietly smoking the cigar which was
now adding to the growing foetid atmosphere inside the
packed bridge. So Grapos had made a dive for it and was
heading for the shore fast. Some people are lucky, he thought,
and then he remembered the mine-strewn waters the Greek
was swimming through at that very moment and he suppressed a shudder. Despite the number of men compressed
inside the confined space it was very silent on the bridge in
the intervals between Burckhardt giving sharp orders as
officers and N.C.O.s appeared at the door, a silence of
suppressed dread which hung over their still heads like a pall
as the engines slowly beat out their mechanical rhythm and
the *Hydra* continued to turn eastwards.

The bows of the vessel were now moving through drifts of
black smoke which were fogging visibility, yet a further
source of anxiety to Burckhardt, who had now left off his
civilian raincoat and was dressed in full uniform with the
Alpenkorps broad-brimmed cap set firmly on his head.
Nopagos stood like a man of wax, his eyes trying to bore
through the smoke-curtain at the earliest possible moment.
Schnell was crouched in a permanent stoop over the wheel,
glancing frequently to starboard where the nearest mine
bobbed gently less than fifty metres from the hull. At least,
he hoped that was the nearest mine. From his all-round
view at the rear, Prentice was looking from face to face,
noting the gleam of sweat on tightly drawn skin, the nervous

twitch of an eyelid, the hands which gripped rifles and machine-pistols so tensely that the knuckles were whitened. These men, all over the ship, were under the maximum possible pressure. They were going into action by dawn. They knew that the ship was slowly being burnt to the waterline by the fire, that the sea ahead was alive with mines, and that somewhere, perhaps under their feet, the time fuse was ticking down to zero. If someone had determined to bring well-nigh unbearable pressure on their morale they could scarcely have planned it better than this. But had someone planned it? The startling thought had just passed through Prentice's brain when he looked to his right again. Dietrich, outwardly the most composed man on the bridge, was still calmly smoking his cigar and looking down at Prentice as though assessing his character and qualities in an emergency.

'Not more than half an hour at the most.' Ford's voice was little more than a whisper, a whisper motivated more by a dislike of breaking the doom-like silence than by a wish not to be overheard.

'Less than that, I imagine. If we ever get there.' Prentice looked again at the landing-stage light which was visible and closer now the smoke had temporarily cleared. And there seemed to be light in the east on the far side of the peninsula. Hoisting his wrist upwards, he looked at his watch. Exactly 5.45 a.m. Schnell was turning the wheel to straighten course as Burckhardt transmitted an instruction he had received from Nopagos; Dietrich was studying the end of his cigar rather dubiously; a soldier was wiping moisture from his forehead; and Ford was looking round the bridge with quick darting glances when the explosion came.

The silence on the bridge was ruptured by a shattering roar. The *Hydra* shuddered from bows to stern as though struck by a mammoth blow and then wobbled. A wave was carried away from the ferry and swept towards the shore as it gathered up more water in its headlong flight from the vessel. For a few brief seconds it had been as light as day to starboard where a brilliant flash temporarily blinded those who had been looking in that direction. From beyond the open door of the bridge came a babble of panic-stricken voices and the sound of nailed boots scattering across the decks. Stark gibbering panic had seized the ship and on the packed bridge the hysterical murmuring was only silenced by Burckhardt thundering for quiet. He pushed aside Nopagos who had been leaning out of the window to starboard and leaned out himself. The sea appeared to have gone mad as it heaved and bubbled frothily. For a second Burckhardt thought that they had been struck by a torpedo and that a submarine was surfacing. Then the water began to settle. Schnell still held the ship on course, heading for the landing-stage which was coming closer and closer in the darkness, and he spoke without looking at the colonel. 'The mine was very close when it detonated.'

'It was a mine, just a mine, we have not been hit . . .' Hahnemann shouted out the news in German and then in English to stem the signs of panic.

'Well, if that doesn't start it ticking, nothing will,' Ford remarked grimly.

'It?' Prentice was still a little dazed with relief as well as shock.

'The demolition charge,' said Ford, whose mind was never far from explosives. 'If the time fuse mechanism had stopped only temporarily that thump was quite enough to get it moving again, believe you me.'

'I was under the impression that we had hit a mine,' Prentice told him icily. 'That's enough to be going on with, I should have thought.'

'Well, obviously we didn't – we're still steaming on course at the same speed. The mine just went off on its own accord rather too close for comfort.' He was having to lift his voice for Prentice to hear him above the shouts on deck as Burckhardt thrust his way roughly off the bridge and went out on deck himself.

'You mean they can be defective, too?'

'Frequently. They can go off without rhyme or reason. On the other hand something else may have bumped into it – although I can't imagine what.'

Prentice began to feel slightly ill. He could imagine what else might have bumped into that mine in its frantic efforts to reach the shore. He had a picture in his mind of Grapos diving overboard with that protruding rifle attached to his back, of him swimming among the mines and so easily forgetting the barrel projecting beyond his body. There would be nothing left of the poor devil now. Prentice didn't like to think of what explosive which could take out a ship's bottom might do to a single human being as it detonated within a few feet of the swimming body.

'I think that little bang has rattled them,' Ford remarked.

'It rattled me,' Prentice replied with feeling. He looked back through the rear window where there was a state of confusion on the deck below. Alpenkorps men in full uniform who had been huddled close to the rail were being sent under cover by Volber who was waving his arms like a man shepherding sheep back to the fold. Within a minute the deck was clear and the babble of voices beyond the open door had ceased when Burckhardt came back to take up his post behind Nopagos. But the damage had been done. Another heavy blow had been dealt at the morale of troops who, on land would have taken the explosion in their stride, but cooped up on the unfamiliar sea the experience was having an entirely different effect. Prentice thought he could see in the faces in front of him a little extra strain, a trace more tension as the cold light from the east died in the false dawn and the landing stage light at Katyra drew steadily closer.

Schnell was showing great skill as he steered the *Hydra* on the last stage of her perilous course, threading his way between a scatter of mines which floated in the path of the searchlight beam. An oppressive silence had fallen on the limping vessel as she moved through the dark water which was impenetrable beyond the beam, water supporting perhaps a hundred more mines for all Burckhardt could tell.

The men on the decks below were waiting – waiting for the final collision with a mine, waiting for the still-hidden demolition charge to detonate under them, waiting for the tension-fraught moment of the landing – although which of these hazards was uppermost in their strained minds it was impossible to guess. The engines ticked over monotonously as the ferry slipped towards a blurred shadow which was the coast.

Plagued by a dozen anxieties, Burckhardt maintained his outward appearance of calm confidence while inwardly he fretted at the damnably crawling progress of the vessel. He was already nearly thirty minutes behind his timetable and he was praying that the news of the general offensive launched at 5.45 a.m. was not yet on the air. It was unlikely – an hour or two should pass before the world read the reports of the German onslaught on Greece and Jugoslavia spearheaded by the Panzers and reinforced with airborne troops – and the peninsula was still devoid of Allied troops and wide open to his attack. The whole key to the operation was a swift dash back along the peninsula and the capture of the monastery before the Allies had time to recover their balance. Just so long as there really was nothing standing in his way – and that they were able to land safely. He felt the chill of the early morning air filtering through his uniform and braced himself to control a shiver as Dietrich appeared at his elbow.

'The inhabitants of Katyra are bound to have heard the mine explode,' the Abwehr man remarked.

'I realise that,' Burckhardt replied non-committally.

'So there is a serious risk that someone may have phoned through to Salonika.'

'We have attended to that, so once again you can put your mind at rest,' Burckhardt began ironically. Then he paused: they were so close to going ashore that really he was free to speak more openly. 'There is only a single telephone line out of the peninsula, Herr Dietrich, and that was cut several hours ago.'

'Good. But Salonika may wonder why the line has gone dead.'

'Last night's storm will account for that. In a way it was lucky – it has provided an explanation.'

'And you have transport waiting for you as well?' Dietrich enquired genially.

'There are mules on the peninsula. It was impossible to bring them with us but we shall find mules available. The planning has taken into account every possible contingency. As to transport, other arrangements have also been made . . .' Burckhardt trailed off vaguely and lifted his glasses, focusing on a mine which floated, so it seemed, only a few metres off the port bow. The vessel was already changing course to avoid the menace.

'And you expect no opposition?' Despite the atmosphere of suspense on the bridge Dietrich's manner was almost pleasant as he bowed his head to listen to the colonel's reply.

'None at all. There is no one to oppose us – except a handful of fishermen.'

'There are two policemen on the peninsula – or there were when I was last here.' Dietrich was very close to becoming jocular and good-humoured, a mood he shared with no one else on the silent bridge.

Burckhardt made a great effort to respond. 'I think we can manage if they appear. You come ashore with me, of course.'

'I had assumed that!' Dietrich stared round slowly as though he found it instructive to see the reactions of a company of soldiers about to go ashore into the unknown as dawn broke. He met stolid eyes, tightly-shut mouths, and once he caught Prentice's gaze as the lieutenant stared back at him curiously. 'I have my Luger,' he told Burckhardt amiably, 'just in case of trouble.'

'There is to be no shooting!' Burckhardt spoke sharply and for the first time he turned and looked directly at Dietrich. 'My men have strict orders to go ashore quietly. It will increase the element of surprise and their first task is to set up a road-block at the northern end of the village. The first troops ashore will see to that.'

'And when do you expect to take the monastery?'

'Who said we were interested in monasteries, Herr Dietrich? This is a war we are fighting, not a religious campaign.' And having delivered this rebuke the colonel turned away and devoted his whole attention to the lamp which was now so close that they could see it perched at the end of a stone jetty. Under the lamp stood two men, woken up doubtless by the explosion of the mine and anxious to hear what had happened. They're in for a surprise, Burckhardt was thinking as he saw the Abwehr man easing his way towards the door. I suppose he's checking up on our arrangements for the landing so he can put that in his report to Canaris. Still, with his knowledge of the peninsula he might come in useful yet. Burckhardt looked up as Hahnemann appeared in the doorway when Dietrich went outside.

'How bad is the fire?' the colonel asked crisply.

'It's continuing to spread rapidly – the lower deck companionway is full of flames. Have we much longer, sir?' Hahnemann spoke stiffly and Burckhardt read the traces of anxiety in his eyes. On land Lieutenant Hahnemann was the most reliable officer in the company but they were all off-balance on this vessel.

'Start withdrawing men from the fire-fighting and assemble them for disembarkation,' Burckhardt told him. 'What about the demolition charge?'

'No sign of it, sir. We are still searching . . .'

'Withdraw all men from the search except for those in the engine-room. And the Greek?'

'He hasn't been seen, sir – I took all the men who were hunting for him to check the fire as you ordered.'

Burckhardt removed the glove he had been wearing from his pistol hand and nodded. 'The Greek doesn't matter any more. Later the search can be continued by the men left to guard the ship – unless she burns to a cinder.' It was only a minor element in the meticulous plan – guarding the ship to make sure no one tried to take her across the gulf to warn the British. Burckhardt checked his watch. 5.55 a.m. Yes, they were thirty minutes late. It would be dawn just about the time they landed; already he could see faintly a low ridge silhouetted against a streak of cold grey light. The country-side in this part of the peninsula was hilly, with a single road to the south which wound its way between the hills until it reached the plateau. From there on the terrain became steadily worse, culminating in the grim wilderness of precipices and sheer ascents of the heights of Zervos.

'You will be responsible for the security of the British prisoners,' he told Sergeant Volber who had just entered the bridge to report that his section was ready for disembarkation. He had already decided that they would be taken half-way along the peninsula and then left there under guard. This obviated any possibility of their being captured and released by a Greek unit which might be sent to the peninsula from Salonika. The information they possessed as to the unit's strength was a little too valuable to share with the enemy. He glanced back at the two men who stared at him with expressionless faces.

'Looks as though they're going to make it,' Ford whispered, 'although I wouldn't bet a brass farthing on the outcome yet.'

'Looks as though *we* might make it,' Prentice corrected him drily. 'And frankly, I wish you hadn't said that – it's asking for that demolition thing to trip its whatnot.'

'There's time yet, sir,' Ford assured him.

Schnell was now having to conduct an awkward manoeuvre to evade a single mine floating dead ahead. He had to steer the vessel round the mine and then alter course afresh to bring the ship up against the side of the jetty. Burckhardt could see that the glowing lamp was a lantern fixed to the top of a low mast and underneath it a small group of figures was huddled. He sent several men off the bridge, ordered the rest to keep in the shadows and joined them. This last mine was causing further delay and he felt the impatience surging up:

he wanted to be off this damned Greek ferry, to get ashore and get on with it. And it was not only the timetable which made him curse that so inconveniently placed mine – that object so thoughtfully dropped by his allies was providing more time for the hidden demolition charge to detonate. He prayed to God that it wouldn't happen at the last moment, but a streak of pessimism in his nature made him fear the worst. In war, the chance happenings, the coincidences, were always bad ones. He had learned that in Finland where he had experienced the Winter War as assistant to the German military attaché in Helsinki when the Finns had fought the Russians to a ferocious standstill, in Norway where he had commanded . . . He spoke quickly in Greek as Nopagos moved to the starboard window. 'Stay by the wheel!'

'If they see me they will be reassured.' Nopagos remained by the window as he looked over his shoulder. His face was despondent and he looked as though he could hardly stand up: this was probably the last voyage of the *Hydra* and he was bringing home the most terrible cargo he had ever carried. 'I don't want any harm to come to them – if they start to run away . . .'

'My men have orders not to shoot.' Burckhardt hesitated. The fight had gone out of the captain and it gave a greater appearance of normality if he could be seen clearly on the bridge. 'You can stay there,' he said, 'but you are not to call out to them.'

Dawn was beginning to spread over the peninsula as Schnell edged his way round the solitary mine, and the bleak light showed a landscape still in the grip of winter. The olive trees on the scrub-covered hills were naked silhouettes and along the jetty a coating of frost glittered with the colour of *crème-de-menthe* over stones green with age. The little group under the lamp which glowed eerily in the half-light stood hunched up with their hands in their pockets and one man was stamping his feet on the stones. An appearance of absolute normality. Another ferry trip ending its voyage quietly as a matter of seagoing routine. Which was very satisfactory, Burckhardt was thinking. Near the end of the jetty, a primitive mole projecting straight out into the gulf, the beach was visible, a beach of rocks and stones. And behind the beach a high sea-wall stretched away into the distance. The Intelligence people had warned him about that unscalable sea-wall – had emphasised that the only entrance to the village was a gap in the wall at the end of the jetty where a causeway linked the mole with the road into Katyra. Burckhardt was looking beyond the wall now to the short line of two-storeyed houses which were shuttered and still like abandoned villas. The whole place had the look of a resort which is only open during the summer months. It was all going according to plan. They would land without any fuss, occupy the village, set up the road-block to the north, and within an hour the main body of the troops would be moving south into the heart of the peninsula. An officer Prentice had not seen before came on to the bridge to report and the colonel motioned him back into the shadows.

'Major Eberhay reports everything ready for disembarkation, sir.'

'Good. The wireless-set is being guarded by two men, I take it, Brandt?'

'Yes, sir. The major saw to it himself.'

'Tell him those civilians on the jetty are not to be brought on board because of the demolition charge. He can keep them on the beach and they can be escorted back into the village later.'

As Brandt left the bridge Burckhardt thought about the wireless-set. Until the sabotaged set was repaired it was their only means of communication with G.H.Q. to confirm that the reinforcements could be flown in. It was, in fact, one of the most vital pieces of equipment in the expedition. Without that he would be on his own and there could be the most appalling muddle when they arrived at the plateau. The vessel had almost circumnavigated the pestilential mine and was creeping in towards the jetty where the little group had shifted position. They were staring towards the stern and

Burckhardt knew they were looking at the smoke rising from the deck. He turned round and saw through the rear window a pall of blackness floating upwards. They'd see that from the mainland but he hoped it wouldn't cause too much comment. Prentice had moved nearer to the window and Burckhardt warned a guard that he mustn't get any closer. When he looked to starboard again the jetty was almost under the ship's hull.

The nudge from the rifle barrel warned Prentice that he had better keep still. The sight of the civilians standing innocently on the jetty wall bothered him and he had a feeling that something awful could happen. Ford had just said that the demolition charge had better do its stuff quickly if it was to catch the Germans and Prentice was almost hoping that this would happen. The jolt of the ship striking the jetty startled him and he waited for the charge to detonate.

*

The lower slopes of the hills were still in darkness as the gangway clattered on to the jetty. Major Eberhay was the first man ashore and a moment later Nopagos joined him, followed by a dozen Alpenkorps soldiers. These troops were unarmed, their collars neatly buttoned to the neck, and one man carried a plaque struck to commemorate the commencement of collaboration between Greek and German peoples. Only the space for the date was left blank. Drawn up in files of threes, they marched steadily along the jetty top in the direction of the causeway which led to Katyra. The plaque was for presentation to the mayor of Katyra. Outwardly, for the first few minutes, the disembarkation had the appearance of an arranged visit as the Alpenkorps paraded away into the distance. Only a band was absent to mark the occasion.*

'No resistance, please! We are overwhelmed!' It was Nopagos who delivered the urgent message to the group of

*The same technique was practised in Norway where the first unit of invading Germans ashore at Oslo was a brass band which played and marched through the capital to simulate a peaceful visit.

four men who stood stunned under the lamp as the troops passed them. It was not quite the message which Burckhardt had instructed him to deliver but it served the same effect. One man, larger and burlier than the others, took a step backwards as though to move away, but he was restrained by the leading soldier in the next section of troops leaving the ship. The German put a firm hand on the civilian's arm and ushered him back to the group which stared at the ferry as though hardly able to believe their eyes. The third file of men pouring off the vessel were heavily armed, their rucksacks on their backs, their rifles looped over their shoulders, and short bayonets sheathed in leather scabbards by their sides.

From the bridge Burckhardt watched the landing operation with approval and relief. It was all going according to plan. The leading section had already disappeared through the gap in the sea-wall and within minutes would reach their first objective – the mayor's house. It was light enough now to see the Greek flag fluttering in a breeze from a tower behind the wall. He checked his watch again as the file of armed troops began to cross the causeway. Half-way along the jetty the group of four Greeks was being hustled towards the beach while more troops marched past them. Yes, everything was going according to plan. A moment later the firing started.

The firing, which commenced immediately the Greek civilians were clear of the jetty, came at the worst possible moment for Burckhardt. The entire mole from gangway to causeway was dense with disembarking troops and the ski sections were filing off the ship. It was one of these men, encumbered with the skis over his back, who fell as the first shot rang out. Instantly, what had been an orderly disembarkation became a scene of chaos as the falling soldier crashed into his comrades and caused several to stumble. A second shot rang out and a second man on the jetty fell close to the first casualty. There was a danger of an imminent pile-up of men as the mole seethed with field-grey figures. Burckhardt swore and leaned over the bridge to look down at the open deck below where Hahnemann was issuing quick instructions, shouting to the men to clear the jetty and move inland. A third shot was fired and four men close together half-way along the jetty paused, then began to run towards the causeway, but as they ran one of their number sprawled lifelessly on the jetty floor. Burckhardt left the bridge and made for the open deck. At the top of the staircase Dietrich was staring across the peninsula and as Burckhardt ran past he noted a trivial detail: for the first time, so far as he could remember, the Abwehr man was no longer smoking a cigar. He was running down the staircase when he heard a fusillade of shots – the Alpenkorps were returning the fire, although what the God they thought they were shooting at Burckhardt had no idea. From his commanding position on the bridge he had been quite unable to locate the source of the attack.

At the bottom of the steps he noted a less trivial detail – the battalion wireless, the last set still in serviceable condition, was stowed against the wall with the flap opened back. An Alpenkorps soldier stood close by guarding the precious equipment. As soon as they had taken Katyra Burckhardt had to send the vital signal. *Phase One completed.* Despite the air of total confusion which now pervaded the vessel where men crouched low behind the rails or ran down the gangway urged on by Hahnemann, the colonel was still thinking clearly and a disturbing idea had entered his mind. Three shots, three casualties. That was the work of a marksman. It was quickly apparent that Hahnemann was disembarking the troops with all speed so Burckhardt, still concerned with his simple calculation, went swiftly back to the bridge where he could see what was happening. He arrived there in time to see more men hurrying along the jetty too close together as the firing continued. A man near the edge stopped as though struck by an invisible blow, tried to stagger forward a few steps, then plunged over the edge. He hit the water with a splash and when the body surfaced it floated motionlessly.

The fusillade continued for several minutes while the

Alpenkorps constantly disembarked and ran the gauntlet of the exposed jetty. During the firing Burckhardt ordered the two remaining guards on the bridge to take Prentice and Ford below ready for going ashore. Schnell had left earlier so now he was alone on the bridge as the fusillade ceased suddenly. He waited, turning his eyes now to the lower hill slopes still in the fading shadow of night. Hahnemann had carried out his order to cease fire abruptly and then hold fire for five minutes. Earlier, the colonel had assumed that those shots were coming from behind one of the shuttered windows, but so far he had seen nothing to confirm this. Half-a-dozen men were risking the jetty run again, their bodies crouched low as they ran past the huddled shapes lying on the stones. A single shot split the silence only broken by the thud of nailed boots on paved stone. One man fell. The others ran on, disappearing through the gap in the wall. On the bridge Burckhardt twisted his mouth grimly. He had seen it this time – the muzzle-flash in the hills to the south of the village. The marksman was indeed firing long-distance, and now he felt sure it was the work of one man. He left the bridge and Hahnemann met him at the foot of the staircase with news of the disaster.

'The second set is out of commission . . .'

'What!' Burckhardt was thunderstruck. He felt the blood rush to his head and paused before going on. 'How did it happen?'

'A bullet hit it – all the valves are smashed.'

A soldier was crouched over the set and he kept his head lowered as though afraid to face the colonel. Bending close to him, Burckhardt spoke very quietly. 'You were supposed to be guarding it, Dorff.'

'He could hardly have done anything,' Hahnemann interjected. 'He was by the rail firing off a few shots himself when it happened. He was never very far away from the set. It is just the most appalling bad luck, sir.'

'Bad luck, Hahnemann?' The colonel straightened up and stared at him. 'We have had one set sabotaged earlier in the voyage. Someone planted a demolition charge inside the vessel. Someone started a fire in the main hold. And someone, at the beginning, set free the British prisoners. Haven't you grasped it yet that some unknown person is making sure that bad luck does come our way?' He turned as Dietrich walked round a corner and stopped to look down at the wrecked set.

'More?' Dietrich asked bluntly.

'A bullet has smashed all the valves. The set is quite useless.' Burckhardt studied the Abwehr man for a moment. 'Herr Dietrich, I believe you possess a Luger. Would you mind showing it to me?'

Without a word Dietrich extracted the pistol from his pocket and handed it to the colonel. While Burckhardt was examining the weapon he stood with his hands deep inside his pockets as he gazed along the jetty where the last troops were hurrying towards the village. It was almost daylight now and the buildings behind the sea-wall showed up clearly in the pale sunshine. They had a decrepit, unpainted look and several tiles were missing from the shallow roofs which were a dull red colour. Once their walls had been brightly colour-washed but that had been a long time ago; now that the place could be seen properly in the dawn light it had shrunk from a shadowed village of some size to a tiny fishing hamlet of a few hundred people. Burckhardt had checked the gun, had found it fully-loaded with seven rounds. He sniffed briefly at the barrel and then returned it. 'Thank you.' He looked at Hahnemann, the other man who spoke English. Eberhay could not have been involved in the destruction of the wireless-set since he had been the first ashore. 'Hahnemann, let me see your pistol. Have you fired it recently?'

'No, sir.' He stared back at Burckhardt with no particular expression, knowing that the question had been pointless. Under no circumstances would it have made sense for him to use a hand-gun during the shooting. He waited while the colonel went through the same checks. Again, fully-loaded and no traces of recent use.

'Thank you, Hahnemann. We will go ashore. Tell Volber to bring the prisoners.'

Straightening his tunic, Burckhardt led the way on to Greek soil. Because of the *Hydra*'s list to port, the gangway was inclined at a steep angle, a detail he had overlooked, and he had to run down it on to the almost deserted jetty. Here again, he led the way, walking briskly but without undue haste, pausing to exchange a few words with two medical orderlies who were attending the casualties. One of them looked up and shook his head. Burckhardt resumed his even pace, knowing that men still aboard were watching him from the rails. Behind him came the Abwehr man, hands still inside his pockets, looking towards the south as he trailed the colonel, and behind him followed Prentice and Ford escorted by Volber and a private. At the end of the mole the colonel stopped and called down to Nopagos who was waiting with the other civilians on the beach. 'That Greek, Grapos, what other qualifications had he that you didn't tell me about?'

'He speaks English.'

Nopagos hadn't understood what the colonel was driving at and he saw the German stiffen. Burckhardt's reactions piled on top of one another. Was he being insolent? The question going through the colonel's head had been whether at some time Grapos might have undergone military service, perhaps before he contracted his limp. Grapos spoke English? As he walked on to the causeway Burckhardt tried to recall the sequence of events aboard the *Hydra*. Could Grapos have freed Prentice and Ford? He had been imprisoned in the hold at the time. Had he sabotaged both wireless-sets? Was he still on board? Then who was that marksman in the hills . . . Firmly, he pushed the riddle out of his thoughts as he went through the gap in the wall where a sentry had been posted. He saluted as the man jumped to attention.

Behind him Dietrich was taking his time about walking towards Katyra, dragging his feet until Volber and the prisoners caught up with him. He even stood quite still for a moment while he looked down at Nopagos, and when he continued along the causeway the prisoners and their escorts had passed and were a few paces in front of him. He appeared to be taking a great interest in the view to the south next, staring fixedly at the hills, and then he switched his attention to the sentry by the wall, noting the hand-grenade which hung from the soldier's belt. Finally, he looked back along the jetty to see if anyone else was close at hand. The gang-plank was empty and there was no sign of more troops coming ashore. He turned round and called out.

'Volber! I think you're wanted back at the ship.'

The sergeant gestured to the prisoners to halt. They had just passed through the gap and beyond a dusty track wound out of sight past a stone building into the main part of Katyra. Burckhardt had almost reached the bend and Dietrich's words had not been spoken loudly enough to reach him. The sentry looked puzzled and stared at the *Hydra* where a tall figure could be seen at the head of the gangway with its back turned.

'What is it, sir?' Volber took a few paces towards the Abwehr man and his expression was uncertain. In the distance, over his shoulder, the colonel disappeared round the curve in the road which was now empty. Prentice was standing with his hands on his hips while Ford stared pointedly at the soldier who stood a few paces away with his rifle at the ready.

'I think you're wanted back at the ship,' Dietrich repeated. 'I saw Hahnemann beckoning.'

Volber was in a quandary. He had received explicit orders from the colonel to escort the prisoners personally into the village and he had no inclination to vary from Burckhardt's command by so much as a centimetre. But Lieutenant Hahnemann was the officer who could, and did, make life arduous for him. So he compromised briefly, waiting to see whether the beckoning was repeated from the gangway. Dietrich remained where he was, apparently absorbed in the panorama across the gulf. If one ignored the huddled group on the jetty and overlooked the smoke drifting up from the

Hydra, which at times simply gave an impression that the funnel was emitting rather a lot of smoke, it was an extraordinarily peaceful scene. By early daylight the Aegean was an intense, deep cobalt with a backdrop of misty mountains on the mainland which seemed almost unreal. At the head of the lonely gulf, where the sun caught the water at a certain angle, the sea glittered like mercury, and on the nearby beach small waves, rippled by the breeze, slid gently forward and collapsed.

Volber stirred restlessly. 'I can't wait any longer, sir,' he ventured, and Dietrich nodded as though he understood. He followed the sergeant through the gap and stopped suddenly when he saw, to his right, that two Alpenkorps soldiers stationed behind the wall had been concealed from his view. As he appeared they were looking at the hills to the south, but now they lowered their field-glasses, hoisted their machine-pistols more firmly over their shoulders, and walked back to the gap to take one last look at the vessel which had brought them all the way from Istanbul. Apart from their uniforms and weapons, they might have been on a cross-country hike. Volber paused to have a word with them, making some joking reference to pleasure cruises, but Dietrich noticed that he was staring along the jetty in case Hahnemann appeared and started gesturing. Sighing out aloud, Prentice crossed on to the grass verge and sat down with his back to the wall where Ford joined him. Volber, standing in the middle of the gap with the other three soldiers, was about to reprimand him, when hell opened up on the gulf.

The reverberations of the detonation crashed round the hill-sides, roared out across the gulf like a cannonade, and sent a shock wave like a bombardment through the gap in the wall. The demolition charge had reached zero. Dietrich, half-protected by the wall, was still thrown sprawling on to the grass, and he thought he heard two explosions close together – the charge first, then the boilers going up. The full force of the shockwave had struck the four Alpenkorps soldiers and they lay scattered across the road. Only two men were trying to move feebly and one of them fell limp almost immediately as he lost consciousness. The sentry was bunched up against the outside of the wall in a strangely twisted position. As Dietrich lay on the grass, temporarily deafened by the roar, there was a stench of burning oil in his nostrils and Prentice and Ford, whose ears had been affected, heard debris clattering on the village rooftops like spent shrapnel from ack-ack guns.

For both of them the immensely strong sea-wall had muffled the blast. But Dietrich was recovering quickly. As he staggered to his feet Prentice began to move up behind him with a rock in his fist. The Abwehr man, unaware of what was happening behind him, fished the Luger out of his pocket, looked quickly up the road and along the jetty, and moved towards a soldier who was climbing to his feet in the centre of the road. Prentice, moving soundlessly on the grass, followed Dietrich as he lurched towards the soldier who had now brought himself to his knees and was shaking his head like a dog emerging from a river. He looked up as Dietrich brought the Luger barrel crashing down on his head. He was slumping to the ground when Dietrich tugged the loop of the machine-pistol free. Prentice stared in astonishment, the rock still poised in his hand, but when he saw the machine-pistol he moved forward again. The Abwehr man turned, knocked the unsteady fist aside and thrust the weapon into Prentice's hands. 'This will be more useful – if you can handle the damned thing.'

He had spoken in English and without waiting for Prentice's reaction he hauled another machine-pistol loose from an inert German, tossed it across to Ford, and then extracted spare magazines from the pockets of the two men on the ground. When he stood up he noticed that it was Ford who was familiar with the machine-pistol and shoved the magazines at him. 'Here – it looks as though they'd be more use to you. Now, we've got to get moving p.d.q. We go that way – along the wall to the south.'

'Who the devil are you?' Prentice demanded.

'Dietrich of the Abwehr.'

The reply was given ironically as the large man stared briefly along the jetty wall. The *Hydra* looked like a refugee from an Atlantic convoy. The funnel was bent at a surrealist angle and her bows were already settling in the shallow water. Around the hull men swam in the sea distractedly as a huge column of black smoke ascended into the clear sky like a gigantic signal which would be seen clear across the bay to the mainland. As he gazed at the wreckage a tongue of red flame flared up at the base of the distorted funnel. Soon the whole superstructure would be ablaze and would go on burning until the hulk was reduced to its waterline and the *Hydra* was a blackened shell. All Dietrich's efforts at preserving an appearance of normality had gone up with the demolition charge. 'I thought she'd never blow,' he said half to himself, and then he saw Nopagos clambering up on to the jetty. The shock wave must have blown straight over the heads of the group on the beach. He looked back towards the town and the road was still empty. 'They'll be coming soon,' he warned, 'so let's get to hell out of here.'

Prentice asked no more questions as Dietrich led them along the inner side of the wall towards the south, into the heart of the peninsula. As they started running, Dietrich's ears had become unstopped and his acute sense of hearing was functioning perfectly in the sudden quietness which succeeded the explosions. They were less than a hundred yards from the road, still making their way alongside the wall, when he branched off and ran behind a small stone outhouse, calling to the others to hurry. Ford had just followed Prentice behind the rear wall when three Germans came running down the road. They paused by the soldiers lying in the dust, then ran on towards the burning ship. Another two soldiers came up close behind them and also ran on to the jetty. Dietrich, who had kept watch from the corner of the wall, waited a half-minute more, and when no one else appeared he turned to Prentice.

'That should be the lot. Burckhardt won't spare any more men to come back and most of them were safely ashore, unfortunately. A bit further along this wall the ground dips and we'll be out of sight from the road. Don't look so dubious – I walked along here five years ago and I've a good memory for places. So let's get moving.'

'Who the devil are you?' Prentice repeated, and when the reply came without a trace of Teutonic accent the Scots burr was a little more pronounced.

'Me? I'm Ian Macomber.'

7 · Sunday 10 a.m.

By ten o'clock in the morning they had marched almost non-stop through punishing hill country which had caused them either to climb or descend most of the way, and they had still seen no trace of Grapos. It was Macomber who had urged them on mercilessly, insisting that they put as much ground as possible between themselves and the oncoming Germans before they rested. Several times Prentice had tried to talk and ask questions, but on each occasion the Scot, if that was his real ancestry, had brusquely told him to save his breath for the march. They followed a footpath which twisted and turned as its surface changed, sometimes sand, sometimes rock and often merely beaten earth. A path which led them past olive groves, over hilltops ringed with boulders, and down into scrub-infested valleys where the streams raced with swelling waters. But now they had reached a hilltop where Macomber consented to pause briefly because it gave a clear view back to the north where the road from Katyra came towards them in a series of bends and drops down the near-sides of hills dense with undergrowth.

'We can see them coming from here,' Macomber announced as he perched on a rounded boulder. 'And water is going to be our problem. There isn't much of it on the plateau.'

'This might help,' Ford suggested as he undid his coat and showed a pear-shaped water-bottle attached to his belt. 'I filched that off one of those knocked-out Jerries while you two pulled yourselves together.'

'Ford gets his priorities right,' Prentice remarked, and then stared hard at Macomber. 'Mind if I hear a little more about you now?'

Macomber took a swig from the water-bottle, handed it on

to Prentice and grinned faintly. 'I've spent the last fifteen months in the Balkans. Do you think that sounds cushy?'

'Depends what you were doing,' Prentice replied cautiously. 'What were you doing?'

'I'll tell you, then. I'm like Winston Churchill as far as ancestry goes – half-British and half-American. My mother was a New Yorker and my father came from Aberdeen. I spent a third of my early years in the States, another third in Scotland, and the rest of the time travelling round Europe with my parents. My father was a linguistics expert and I inherited his gift for languages.' There was no modesty in Macomber's tone but neither was he boasting: he was simply stating a fact. 'And that's where the trouble started,' he went on. 'Principally my languages are German, Greek and French – which comes in useful when you're in Roumania. because I had lung trouble before the war . . .'

'Lung trouble!' Prentice looked sceptical, remembering the tremendous pace the Scot had set up while they were making their dash up and down those endless hills.

'It's cured now – at least so a quack in Budapest assured me. He said it was the pure clean air from Siberia which blows across Hungary in winter that had done the trick. But that lung kept me out of the Forces in 1939, so the Ministry of Economic Warfare asked me to do a job for them. Get your head out of the way, Ford, I can't see that road.'

'What sort of a job?' Prentice asked casually. Without appearing to do so he was trying to check the Scot's story.

'Buying up strategic war materials the Jerries wanted. You'd never believe the funds I had at my disposal. I bought up everything I could lay my hands on and had it shipped out of the Balkans. I have an idea the bright boys foresaw the German *Drach nach Osten* and wanted to denude the place before Hitler arrived.'

'Sounds interesting,' was Prentice's only comment.

'You think so? Just sitting behind a desk and making out orders in quadruplicate for a few thousand gallons of oil or the odd few tons of copper – is that how you see it?'

'I didn't say so.'

'No, but you looked so!' He took out one of his remaining cigars. 'What I don't think you've quite grasped is that I had competitors, Jerry competitors, and they can play very rough, very rough indeed. When I'd survived two attempts to kill me – one in Györ and one in Budapest – I decided my luck was running out and the time had come to go underground, so I acquired some false papers and set up as a German.' He looked quizzically at Prentice over his cigar, put it back in his mouth and went on talking. 'Don't look so damned unbelieving – false papers can be obtained almost anywhere if you have the money, and I had a small fortune to play with.'

'You set up as Dietrich, then?'

'No, he came later. I called myself Hermann Wolff, and, you know, necessity really did turn out to be the mother of invention. I found myself mixing openly with the German community in Budapest, which in the beginning was simply excellent camouflage, but later when I ran out of stuff to buy up it gave our Ministry brains another idea, a diabolical idea.' He turned again to look over his shoulder at the hill behind, in the opposite direction from where the Germans must come, and this was a gesture he had repeated several times.

'Isn't that the wrong direction to fret over?' Prentice enquired. 'Or could they have got ahead of us on the road while we were doing our cross-country route march?'

'Old habits . . .' Dietrich spread a large hand. 'I've spent so many months looking over my shoulder – because the danger always comes from where you least expect it.' He shrugged and stared at Ford for a moment. 'When it comes, it comes.'

'A diabolical job, you were saying,' Prentice reminded him. As he listened he scanned the deserted countryside to the north where a dark smoke column from the burning *Hydra* was still climbing into the brilliant morning sky. They'd see that smoke as far away as Salonika, almost, if the weather visibility was as good across Macedonia. It seemed incredible that a whole German expedition was mustering itself somewhere beyond those hills for a forced march south to Mount Zervos. He heard every word Macomber said as he kept his eyes open for the slightest sign of movement.

'Yes, truly diabolical,' Macomber repeated. 'There were hardly any more strategic supplies I could lay my hands on, but there was a mass of stuff the Germans had bought up which still hadn't been shipped back to the Reich. It was lying around in warehouses and railway sidings, so the Ministry brainboxes said would I have a go at it? Very obliging they were, too – sent out an explosives man to teach me a trick or two about things that go bang in the night . . .' He paused, detecting a sudden freshening of interest from Ford, but when the ammunition examiner said nothing he continued. 'The trouble again was I was made to order for these sabotage jobs. I picked up information from the German community I was mixing with about what was where – and by then I was accepted in Budapest. We even used German explosives – like ten-kilogram demolition charges.'

'Why not British equipment?' queried Ford.

'Because I was operating in neutral territory and the Hungarian Government might not have taken too kindly to British time-bombs being planted inside their goods wagons. Those bombs don't always function according to the book and sometimes they don't function at all. Even when they do, the experts can often piece together a few vital bits and tell the type of bomb that was used and where it was made.' He glanced over his shoulder and grinned again. 'And don't ask me how we got hold of German explosives because that's a state secret.'

'You were pretty successful in passing yourself off as a German even in Hungary then?' Prentice suggested idly. He felt close to exhaustion but his mind was still sufficiently alert to go on checking Macomber's identity so far as he could.

'I knew the Reich well by the time war broke out. In peacetime I'd been a shipping broker – some of my business was with the Reich and I spent a lot of time in Germany before 1939 and sometimes, even then, it was convenient to pass for one of the *Herrenvolk*. The trick is to learn to think like them, to feel you are one of them – and that's something I had to work overtime at while we were on the *Hydra*. I may tell you that was the longest voyage of my life, and it took just twenty-four hours.'

'How did you fool the colonel? That must have taken some doing.'

'The ability to bluff big – nothing else. I took a leaf out of the dear Führer's book there: if you want to believe a lie, be sure it's a whopper. If I'd tried to pass myself off simply as a German civilian, I think they'd have restricted my movements, but the dreaded Abwehr was something quite a good deal different. I knew about the Abwehr when I went aboard the *Hydra* at Istanbul – in fact, I thought they had somebody on my tail ready to do an assassination act before I could get home . . .'

'You weren't put on that ship deliberately then?' Prentice found it difficult to keep the surprise out of his voice. Ford was emptying the machine-pistol while he tested the mechanism and then re-loaded.

'No, I'd finished with the Balkans and I was on my way to Athens to get a berth to Egypt. The Germans had occupied the whole area and it wasn't possible to operate any more with the key points swarming with their security chaps. I was coming on the direct Istanbul–Athens ferry, but that was cancelled at the last moment. When Burckhardt's lot took over the ship I wasn't completely surprised – the presence of several Germans on the passenger list was something I'd been thinking about ever since I got on board.'

'But why pretend you were the Abwehr?'

'Because I knew how they operated – months ago they'd sent men to Budapest to investigate the sabotage. But mainly because it's the one organisation inside Germany today which the armed forces get nervous about. Burckhardt was convinced I'd been put on the ship to check up on how he handled things – which gave me a psychological stranglehold over him from the outset.'

'You make it sound so damned easy.' There was a hint of admiration in Prentice's manner as he sat with his back propped against a boulder and waited, still listening for the slightest slip-up in Macomber's explanation.

'Oh, very easy – as easy as moving round inside Hungary and Roumania with top Abwehr agents on your tail. As easy as making frequent trips to wayside railway stations to collect suitcases left by someone you never see – suitcases containing demolition charges. As easy as lugging them across railway lines at two in the morning with engines shunting all over the place and guards with dogs looking for you.' Macomber's voice had risen to a low growl and once again Prentice, taken aback by the violence of the Scot's reaction to his innocent remark, thought he saw Dietrich, the Abwehr man, prowling the decks of the *Hydra* as she sailed through the night with her shipload of armed German troops. But Macomber hadn't finished yet as he glared at Prentice with an intensity of rage which was alarming. 'As easy as going back to your flat late in the evening and noticing that the lock has been tampered with – so you know that inside that darkened flat someone is waiting for you with a knife or a gun or whatever particular weapon they've decided will do the job quickly and quietly. Yes, Prentice, and it was easy on that ship we've just left, too – easy putting those wireless-sets out of action with two hundred troops all around you, easy coming into your cabin to cut your ropes to give you a chance to get clear and warn that destroyer . . .'

'I'm sorry – but you misread my remark.' Prentice lied a little, realising for the first time the tremendous pressure this man must have lived under for months, catching a glimpse of what it must have been like to go on living alone in the alien Balkans surrounded by enemies while he went on with his deadly work. He supposed that the outburst was the climax of God knew how much pent-up anxiety and living on the nerves endlessly, until it had seemed it must go on for ever. Macomber made no attempt to apologise for the outburst but he smiled wintrily as he smoked his cigar and started talking again.

'Planting the demolition charge was simpler than you might imagine. I just saw it lying with the fuses in a half-open rucksack and grabbed it. There was a little trouble in the dark on deck when I ran into a soldier, but a knowledge of unarmed combat can come in useful. Afterwards, I pitched him over the side like you did your chap . . .'

'You set the Alpenkorps on us when we were on deck!' Prentice had just remembered how Dietrich – Macomber – had called out and pointed when they were close to the raft. Ford, who was still holding his machine-pistol, raised the weapon a few inches so that it pointed at nothing in particular, but could quickly be aimed at Macomber. The Scot noticed the movement and laughed shortly and without humour.

'Of course I did! You'd already been spotted: I could see them running towards you from where I stood, but it was too good a chance to be missed of convincing Eberhay that I was what I pretended to be, and they were going to get you anyway. And now, Sergeant Ford, you can stop getting ready to level that gun at me.' He looked towards the road from Katyra and frowned, but if he saw something which disturbed him he made no comment as he rebuked them gently. 'I'm beginning to wonder why I risked my neck helping you to get away – it would have been safer to just make a run for it myself. I was going, too, in any case,' he told them bluntly, 'whether I could bring you along or not. The vital moment was when we'd just come ashore – I'd always foreseen that.'

'Why then?' asked Prentice quietly.

'Several reasons. Burckhardt's whole attention was taken up with the landing and capturing Katyra quickly. Later, he'd have more time to think, which is just what I didn't want him to have. Then there was the problem of the other wireless-set – I'd messed up the tuning coil with the butt of my Luger but I gathered they might be able to repair the thing. The moment they could wireless for confirmation of my identity I was finished. And,' he rubbed it in, 'you can thank whatever lucky star you were born under that the bomb didn't go off earlier – it must have stopped and then started again.'

'What time had you set it for?' Prentice was taking a great interest in the answer to this question and now he saw Ford looking over his shoulder towards the hill behind them. Macomber's fears were contagious.

'I set it to detonate at 3.30 a.m. while we were still well down the gulf.'

'Good God!'

A trace of the nervous reaction still smouldered inside Macomber and he didn't bother to put it too tactfully. 'I'm sure, Prentice, that by now you know there's a war on. There were two hundred German troops aboard who may yet do untold damage to the Allied cause – if I could sink them I was going to do it. And I still will, although how I haven't the slightest idea. You know they're heading for the monastery on Mount Zervos to set up an observation post, I take it?'

'I had an idea that was the objective. I agree we've got to get there first, if we can, but I can't quite see us forming the monks into a defensive battalion to hold off the Jerries. Is there any means of communication there we could use to get in touch with the mainland?'

'Not so far as I know apart from the telephone line to Salonika and that's been cut.' Macomber dropped the half-smoked cigar into the sand and carefully heeled it out of sight. 'But there's always something that can be done as long as you're there – that's something I've learned.' His expression became ferocious as he growled out the words. 'Whatever happens the Germans have got to be stopped from taking Zervos. Hell! If there's nothing else we'll have to set fire to the place to attract attention. There are British troops driving up that coast only a few miles across the gulf. Setting fire to the monastery may be the only solution!'

Prentice stared at the huge figure stooped forward over the boulder and realised that he meant what he said. Previously he had regarded Macomber as an enterprising civilian, with the accent on 'civilian,' but now he began to wonder whether the war he had fought in the Western Desert could compare with the shadowy, no-quarter struggle the Scot had waged inside the peace-time Balkans. He blinked to keep his eyes open as Macomber clasped both hands tightly and stared again at the road from Katyra with a dubious expression. It was over twenty-four hours since any of them had slept and the strain showed in their haggard faces; the brain was beginning to slow down, the reflexes to react sluggishly, and these were danger signals. He was about to speak when Macomber made the suggestion himself. 'I think three-quarters of an hour's sleep would help. And we may need every ounce of strength we can muster before the day is out but someone must keep watch.' He grinned, again without humour. 'So, if you two are sufficiently convinced of my bona-fides, I'll act as lookout while you get some kip.'

'No, I'll stand watch while you and Ford sleep,' Prentice said promptly. 'You've been through more than us, anyway,' he added quickly as the Scot gave him an old-fashioned look.

'Suit yourself,' was Macomber's terse reply. Dropping down off the boulder, he lay on the sand after casting one final look back at the hill behind. The hill looked dangerous was his last thought before he fell asleep.

*

Macomber was a man who, when he woke up, became instantly alert, all his faculties keyed up for immediate action. The trait had been sharpened during the war years and on waking he had developed another facility – the habit of never opening his eyes until he had listened for a few seconds. Lying on the sand with his back against the rock, he listened carefully to the sounds with his eyes still closed. The scrape of a boot over stone, which told him someone was moving nearby. The quick dull click of metal on metal, which was the movement of a rifle bolt. A coldness down his back was the physical reaction of his brain warning him of danger. Then a voice spoke. Prentice's.

'Don't move, Ford, whatever you do!'

Macomber's prone body was still relaxed and lifeless as he half-opened his eyes. Ford was sitting up on the sand, his suit crumpled, his right hand withdrawing from the machine-pistol which lay close by his side. He had a drugged look and had obviously just woken up. Macomber couldn't see Prentice but the thought flashed through his mind that the lieutenant must have dozed off and during those unguarded minutes a German patrol had arrived. Lying on his side, Macomber's hand was tucked inside his coat pocket where it had rested when he had fallen asleep, and now his fingers curled round the butt of the Luger. The problem was going to be to get in an upright position quickly enough. From the direction of Ford's startled gaze he calculated that the new-comers were stationed behind the boulder he was leant against. But how many of them? The boot scraped again and the shadow of a man fell across the sand in front of where he lay, the shadow of a man and a gun.

'Wait! For God's sake wait!' A note of desperation in Prentice's voice chilled Macomber. 'We can explain – don't shoot!'

The silhouette of the rifle barrel angled lower and Macomber guessed that it was now tilted downwards and aimed at him point-blank. He sensed that the slightest movement of his body would activate the shadow's trigger finger, and while he compelled himself to stay relaxed he felt the stickiness of his palm clutching the pistol butt. A strange tingling sensation sang along his nerves and his brain hung in a horrible state of prolonged suspension as every tiny detail seemed weirdly clear, a reaction which he had heard men experienced just before they died. The appalled expression on Ford's face, the mouth half-open and held like that as though in a condition of rictus. The wobble of the unknown man's silhouette as he shifted balance to the other foot to take the shock of the rifle's recoil. The flitting motion of some tiny insect hopping over the sand in the shade of the silhouette. Macomber's throat had gone so dry that he felt the most terrible compulsion to cough as a tickle crawled towards his throat.

'Do you understand any English at all?' Prentice again, his voice throaty with tension. 'We're on your . . .'

'Yes, I speak English.' A deep-chested voice with a rumbling timbre which sounded familiar. 'Why are you with the German?'

'Look, Grapos,' Prentice pleaded quickly, 'he's not a German. He's British. If you let him wake up and speak he'll talk to you in English as much as you want . . .'

'There are Germans who speak English.' Grapos' tone was unimpressed and savagely obstinate. 'I speak English but I am Greek. He has made you think he is English? We have very little time. He must be killed. Now!' The gun silhouette moved again as though the Greek was taking fresh aim and Macomber waited for the thud of the bullet, the last thing he would ever feel. And there was an urgency in Grapos' voice as well as in his words which filled the Scot with foreboding. There was some other danger coming very close, he felt sure of it, a danger the Greek was only too well aware of. Prentice was talking again and this time he was adopting an entirely different tactic, abandoning pleading as he spoke crisply as though he were giving a command.

'Look, I'm telling you, mate. His name is Macomber. Ian Macomber. He's a Scot – that's from the topside of my country – and he's the one who planted that bomb which nearly blew up all those Germans, only it didn't go off in time. He speaks fluent German – a damned sight more fluent German than you speak English. To help us get away he half-killed a Jerry – a German – in front of me. He grabbed a couple of German machine-pistols and gave them

to us. Since then he's led the way to where we are now
because he knows the country and we don't. And if that isn't
enough for you, you can go and dive in the sea again. So stop
aiming that gun at him and let him wake up and speak for
himself.'

'You are sure of these things?' Grapos sounded anything
but sure of what he had been listening to and the rifle was
still pointed down at the inert figure below.

'I'm perfectly sure!' In his vehemence Prentice, for a
moment, believed what he was saying. 'Don't you think I can
tell when I'm talking to one of my own countrymen?
Wouldn't you know when you were talking to a Greek even
if you'd heard that same man speaking good German earlier?'
Prentice deliberately lost his temper a little, and seeing the
look of doubt on Grapos' face he followed up quickly while
he had the Greek off-balance. 'And now, for Pete's sake, can
he get up and speak for himself? He must be awake now.'

'Yes . . . I . . . am . . . awake.' Macomber spoke slowly and
very clearly, resuming his normal manner of speech only
when he saw the shadow of the gun move away. 'So can I get
up and let you have another good look at me?'

'Yes, you may get up.' Grapos' boots scraped again as he
spoke and when Macomber climbed to his feet the villainous-
looking civilian was standing several paces beyond him with
his weapon still held so that it could cover Macomber with
only a fraction of movement. A German carbine, the Scot
noted. The one he had gone overboard with. The one he had
shot down the Alpenkorps men on the jetty with. Macomber's
hands hung loosely by his sides and he gazed at Grapos
without friendship as he asked the question with a single
word.

'Well?'

'You look like a German.'

'And you look like a bandit.'

The Greek's eyes flashed. The gun muzzle lifted and was
then lowered. He stared back grimly but with a certain
respect as he slapped his rifle butt once and then turned to

Prentice, ignoring Macomber as he spoke rapidly. 'There is trouble. German soldiers are coming up that hill on the other side . . .' He indicated the hill which had worried Macomber, the hill he had glanced back at so many times. 'When they come to the top they will see you here. We must go quickly.'

'Which way?' asked Prentice.

'That way.' He pointed towards the hill crest over which he had just warned them the Germans were advancing. Prentice took a step forward, stooped to pick up his machine-pistol, which he looped over his shoulder, and then shook his head uncomprehendingly.

'Grapos, you've just said the Germans are coming over that hill, so we'd better push off in some other direction.'

'No. They come this way – so we go this way. You will see. Come! We must hurry.'

'Half a minute!' Prentice was not convinced and his naturally sceptical mind was now wondering whether he could trust Grapos. 'We haven't seen any Germans come along the road down there and they'd have to do that to get over there . . .'

Macomber broke in quickly, relieved to see that Ford's common sense had automatically made him turn round and watch the empty hill crest while the others argued it out. 'Prentice, the Germans were confident they could get hold of mules in Katyra – not enough for all their men, I'm sure, but probably enough to send ahead an advance party. If Burckhardt acted quickly and sent out a patrol on mules in time, they could have passed along that road while we were moving across country. In which case some of them would be ahead of us – that was why I kept looking over my shoulder earlier.'

'Theophilous would supply them with mules,' said Grapos. He spat on the ground. 'Theophilous is at Katyra. He has German mother and Greek father, but he loves Germans. It is known for a long time. And Theophilous has mules . . .'

'And undoubtedly would know where to lay his hands on

others,' Macomber interjected. 'All right, assuming they're coming up that hill from the far side, where do we go?'

'We go down here and wait.'

'Wait . . . ?' Prentice still couldn't understand the Greek's plan but Grapos, without attempting to explain further, led the way down the flank of the hill which was fully exposed to anyone coming over the distant hill crest. From the summit of the hill where they had rested the view into the valley below had been obscured by an outcrop of rock, but as they descended through thick scrub which almost closed over the path they were able to see more clearly. A broad stream on its way to the sea ran along the narrow valley floor and at one point it was crossed by a series of stepping-stones which were barely above the water's surface. On the far bank, perhaps a hundred yards to the right of the primitive crossing point, Prentice caught a glimpse of the dusty track winding its way round the base of the hill towards Zervos. The hill crest, which reared above them now as a hard outline against the cloudless sky, was still deserted. What the devil was the Greek up to? He ran down the path and began talking as soon as he was within a few paces of Grapos who hurried downhill without looking back. 'Where are we going? I want to know.'

'To the pipe.' Grapos spoke over his shoulder without pausing, although he had begun to take a keen interest in the hill crest, staring frequently in that direction as he trotted downwards unevenly because of his limp.

'What pipe? What are you talking about?'

'The pipe takes the floods from the hill to the stream. It was built many years since to stop the waters rushing over the road. We go down the pipe. The Germans will not find us there.'

'How big is it, for heaven's sake?'

'It is big. I went down it when I was a boy.'

'You were smaller, then,' Prentice pointed out urgently. 'And they'll see us as soon as they come over that ridge.'

'That is why we hide. We are there.'

They were less than half-way down the hill when Grapos plunged into a deep gulley. The sides were lined with protruding rocks and it was deep enough to hide them from view completely. Prentice looked back as Ford and Macomber dropped into the ravine and then turned ahead to see Grapos on his hands and knees while he pulled at a clump of scrub with his bare hands. When Prentice reached him he had exposed the entrance to a large drain-pipe of crumbling concrete. The hole was at least three feet in diameter, a dark decrepit opening but large enough to crawl inside on hands and knees. Crouching beside Grapos, Prentice saw that it sloped down at an angle of about twenty degrees, so it should be navigable. Macomber and Ford were also bunched round the forbidding hole which was damp and smelled of decaying fungus, and the fact that there was no light at the end of the tunnel, no visible end at all, did nothing to increase their enthusiasm for the Greek's proposed escape route.

'Where does it come out?' demanded Macomber.

'By the stream. We cross by the stones.'

'And how long is it?'

'Not long.'

'How long is a piece of string?' Prentice muttered under his breath. 'Look, Grapos, we can't even be sure the Germans are coming in this direction. They could easily have changed their minds and be waiting for us further along that road.'

'They were coming up the hill. You will see. We can see from here.' Grapos climbed out of the end of the gulley and stood behind a dense grove of undergrowth which was taller than a man's height. In places there were gaps in the vegetation which formed natural windows and when the others joined him they found they had a clear view of the hill beyond. Without much expectation of seeing anything, Prentice stared through a tracery of bare twigs, and it came as a shock when he saw figures against the skyline. There were six of them, well spread out, and they started to descend the slope in a semi-circle with the two in the middle maintaining a higher altitude than those on the flanks. Which was

correct procedure, Prentice was thinking – the two men in
the centre had better observation and could give covering
fire to the men below if necessary. He recognised at once the
field-grey uniforms and the distinctive caps of the Alpenkorps.

'Why should they choose this area for their patrol?'
Macomber wondered out loud.

'Because Theophilous will have told them about the path,'
Grapos informed him promptly. 'There are two main ways
from Katyra to Zervos – the road and the path. They have
come over the road by mule and when they do not find you
they turn back – to trap you on the path.' He stared blankly
at the Scot while he pulled at a tip of his straggled moustache
and his continuing distrust of Macomber was only too
obvious.

'They could seal us off inside that pipe with only one man
at each end,' Macomber persisted.

'When they reach the stream and cross it, we go into the
pipe. They come up this hill and we pass under them.'

'Sounds feasible,' Prentice commented. 'If it works.'
Turning round, he renewed his observation of the patrol
which was descending the hill slope rapidly; already they had
covered more ground that he would have expected and he
reminded himself that these six oncoming Germans were
highly-trained Alpenkorps troops, men whose natural
habitat was wild, untracked countryside, and who were now
operating under ideal conditions. The fatal mistake would be
to underestimate them and the only advantage he possessed
was the company of two men who knew the peninsula. A
disturbing thought struck him and he asked Grapos a
question quickly. 'I suppose there's no risk that this chap,
Theophilous, might have told them about the pipe, too?'

The Greek snorted contemptuously. 'He is not a man who
ever walks or hunts – he would be frightened that he gets
lost. We wait. When they cross the stream we go into the
pipe.'

Macomber had moved close to Prentice as he gazed

through the dense thicket and he was frowning as though there were something he didn't understand. For a few minutes he watched the patrol, clambering over rocks, sometimes disappearing up to waist-height in undergrowth, but always maintaining their careful formation as they came closer to the stream, then he voiced his doubt. 'I don't like it – Burckhardt is using his men too wastefully.'

'What are you getting at?' snapped Prentice. Still without sleep, he could feel the strain telling and he knew he was trigger-tempered, but Macomber's remark implied that he might have overlooked a crucial point.

'Burckhardt has two hundred men at his disposal to take and hold Zervos. At least he had two hundred when he left the *Rupescu*, he told me. He lost four while on board the *Hydra* . . .'

'Four?'

'Yes, four. There was the man you threw overboard. Grapos killed two more while escaping, and I put one over the side when I was carrying that demolition charge up on deck. His bayonet and scabbard came in useful, by the way – I used them to support the charge inside the ventilator shaft. That's two per cent of his force without adding in those who died on the jetty and when the ship blew up. Yet he feels he can spare another six men to look for us. Does it suggest something to you, Prentice? Something alarming?'

'It suggests he feels he still has enough left to take care of a few monks.' Prentice was having trouble thinking straight. What on earth was the persistent Scot driving at now?

'It suggests to me that he expects heavy reinforcements in the very near future, which isn't a happy thought.'

'You mean by sea? Another boatload in broad daylight?'

'I doubt that. They may use some entirely different method this time.' Macomber found himself looking upwards. The sky was clear blue as far as the eye could see, its only occupants a flock of seagulls sailing high up in the sunlight as they flew away in the direction of Katyra. 'He wouldn't expend a patrol of six men just looking for us unless he was confident more help was on the way,' he repeated obstinately.

'Just what we need at the moment, a Job's comforter,' Prentice muttered irritably. The Alpenkorps were half-way down the hill and they had begun to converge inwards towards the stepping-stones, although as a target they were still spread out over a considerable distance. Keeping his voice down, Macomber had now turned to question Grapos.

'You know the monastery well?'

'I lived there for two years.'

'Is there any other means of communication whatsoever apart from the telephone which has been cut?'

'When they want things, they phone to Katyra. Sometimes they phone Salonika.'

'There is, of course, no wireless transmitter for emergencies?'

'No, nothing like that.'

Grapos was staring through the thicket as he replied without looking in Macomber's direction, and his replies were grudging, but the Scot appeared not to notice his reticence as he pressed on as though interrogating the Greek. 'You mean there is no other way . . . are you listening to me? Good.' Grapos looked at Macomber directly and the brown eyes which looked back were compelling him to concentrate, to remember. 'Is there no other way at all whereby the Abbot can send a message if the phone breaks down?'

'Only the pigeons.'

'Pigeons?' Macomber's voice was sharp. 'You mean he keeps carrier pigeons? Where do they go to when released?'

'To Livai on the other side of the gulf.'

'On the mainland, you mean?'

'Yes. Livai is near Olympus and there are more monks there.'

'God in heaven!' said Macomber, unconsciously repeating the German phrase in English. He was so astounded by the information that for several minutes he said nothing more while the German patrol continued its descent to the edge of the stream. Even when they crossed they displayed good military caution, only one man moving over the stones at a time until they had all reached the bank below where Grapos and his group waited. As the last man landed on the near-side bank the Greek grunted and moved towards the mouth of the hole. Prentice had earlier noticed that they were standing in a natural water catchment area; above where they stood three small ravines converged into the gulley and he guessed that during bad weather a minor flood must pour into the pipe. A drift of heavy cloud had appeared in the sky and it was coming their way as he followed Grapos. Once again the unpredictable Aegean weather was changing and he prayed there wouldn't be a cloudburst while they were inside that unsavoury-looking pipe. The Greek was on all fours, about to enter the mouth, when he fumbled under his coat, extracted a knife from his jacket pocket, flicked it to eject the blade, then held it upright. The five-inch blade retracted of its own accord. He was putting it into his coat pocket for easier access when Ford rapped out his question. 'Where did you get that?'

Grapos looked over his shoulder and glared at the sergeant. For a moment it seemed as though he wasn't going to reply and then he answered resentfully. 'It is just a knife. My knife.' Ford glanced at Prentice who had immediately detected the note of suspicion in the sergeant's voice and told Grapos to wait a minute. 'It's a German knife,' Ford explained. 'A parachutist's gravity knife. What the hell is he doing with a thing like that?'

'We have to go into the tunnel,' Grapos reminded them sullenly.

'We have to know about that knife, first,' Prentice replied briskly. 'Where did you get it? Come on – I want to know.'

The German patrol must already have started advancing up the hill towards them but the possession of this strange weapon bothered Prentice and he was determined to get an explanation before they followed the Greek inside the pipe. For precious seconds it seemed like deadlock as the three men stared down at the Greek who gazed back at them with a hostile expression. Then he shrugged his broad shoulders, adjusted the rifle he had previously looped diagonally across his back, and addressed Prentice. 'I took it from the German I shot.'

'You were miles away in the hills when you fired on the jetty,' Prentice protested. 'Just a minute, do you mean one of those Jerries on the boat?'

'No. The man I shot over there.' He made a gesture forwards to the hill the Alpenkorps patrol had just descended. 'There were seven men when I saw them. I shot the man who was to the right and he fell from a rock into the bushes. They did not find him and when they had gone I took the knife.'

'You mean you've alerted this lot! They know someone is close because you've already shot one of the patrol?' Prentice was appalled. He had accepted the Greek's stratagem for evading the Alpenkorps because he had been confident they were only searching hopefully. Now those six highly-trained men below *knew* they were stalking someone who couldn't be far away, which meant they would be in a state of total alert.

'Yes,' Grapos confirmed, 'one is shot. When we go through the pipe they will not know we are on the other side . . .'

'So that's it!' Macomber stepped forward and gripped the Greek by the shoulder. 'You want us to go through the pipe and then open fire on them from the other side?'

'We have to kill Germans,' Grapos replied simply. 'When I go to join the army they say I am no good because of my limp. When I have killed many Germans I go to Athens and tell them – then I join the army.'

'Grapos!' Macomber spoke with low intensity. 'We have to get to the monastery before the Germans – in the hope that we can send a message to the mainland in time, or do something to upset them. If the Germans do take the monastery half a division won't shift them – maybe not even a division.

Our job is to reach the monastery – to keep out of the way of any Germans we meet on the way, not to fight them.'

'Not fight!' Grapos was outraged. He looked up at Prentice. 'You are a British officer. I was told that when they wanted to know if I knew you. You agree with what this man is saying – this man who pretended he was a German?'

'Macomber's right,' Prentice said quietly. 'We want to get there and the only way we can do that is to dodge them – there are too many to fight. We may achieve a lot more by keeping out of their way.'

'Because it is you who say this.' Grapos glared in Macomber's direction and started crawling down the pipe which left less than a foot's clearance above his arched back. At the lieutenant's suggestion, Macomber followed the Greek into the insalubrious hole and the clearance above his back was barely six inches. Prentice, who had decided to bring up the rear, sent Ford down next, took one last look at the gulley to make sure the surface hadn't retained traces of footprints, then went inside himself with his machine-pistol over his back and a fervent hope that the Greek wouldn't start quarrelling with the Scot in this situation. Further along the pipe Macomber was already finding his great bulk a distinct handicap as he crawled behind Grapos. He had only to lift himself a few inches and he found his back scraping the curved concrete; his contracted elbows grazed the sides of the pipe and his knees were slithering on a film of slime at the base of the pipe as he accelerated his awkward movements to keep up with the Greek's phenomenal rate of progress. The downward slope of the pipe helped him to keep up a certain speed but he was beginning to dislike the feeling of being shut in as he went on shuffling forward through the total darkness beyond the mouth of the pipe.

Within two minutes he found himself taking great heaving breaths and this was no place for deep breathing – as he penetrated deeper inside the buried pipe the damp smell changed to an oppressive airlessness and the place seemed bereft of oxygen. How the broad-bodied Grapos managed to keep up such a killing pace he couldn't imagine and gradually the sensation of being entombed grew. He had expected his eyes to become accustomed to the darkness but it was still pitch-black and the only sound was the noise of scuffling feet and knees some distance behind him, a sound which reminded him of rats he had once heard scuttering inside a derelict warehouse. He plodded on, hands stretching out into the unknown followed by the haul of his knees over the scum-like surface of the pipe which he now realised had been embedded in the ground for God knew how long; his hands told him this because frequently the surface of the pipe wall flaked off at his touch and more than once a large piece came away and clattered grittily on the floor. It was badly in need of running repairs but he imagined that when something was built on Zervos it was hopefully expected to last for ever. Nightmare possibilities began to invade his mind – supposing the far end was blocked? The only similar culvert pipe he could remember had been barred at the exit end by an iron grille to prevent small boys swimming in the river from investigating its interior. Grapos had been this way before years ago, but there was no reason why such a grille should not have been fixed more recently. At a rough guess the pipe must be a quarter of a mile long – so what would be the position if the exit were closed? He could never hope to turn round in this confined space and their only hope would be a slow, endless crawl backwards and uphill, a prospect he contemplated with no great relish.

As they went on and on the angle of the pipe dipped more steeply, Macomber remembered that the hill slope dropped sharply when it approached the stream. He began to have a horrible feeling that they had taken the wrong decision – that they should never have entered this Stygian cylinder which might be their grave. For a brief second he paused to wipe the gathering sweat off his forehead and then ploughed on, his wrists aching under the weight they had to bear, the palms of his hands sore and tender with groping over the

gritty concrete, the pain increasing across his back and down
his thighs. When the hell were they going to get out of this
blasted tunnel Grapos had led them into so confidently?
There had to be a bend soon because only a bend would
explain why there was still no light ahead. Unless the tunnel
exit was completely blocked: that certainly would account for
the continuing state of darkness they were crawling down
through. It might also account for the worsening difficulty in
breathing.

Macomber was having great trouble in regulating the
intake of air now as he shuffled downwards blindly and
automatically. But if the exit were stopped up they would be
descending into a region of foul and foetid air where breathing
might become well-nigh impossible. His great fear now was
that they would discover the grim truth too late – that by the
time they knew there was no way out they would have
degenerated into such a weakened state that they would
never be able to summon up the strength needed for the
return trip. Years later when they excavated the pipe they
would find . . . He killed the macabre thought and concentrated on keeping going, hands first, then that dreadful,
wearying haul forward of the knees which it was becoming an
agony to move. His head was vibrating gently and frequently
he blinked as brief lights flashed in front of his eyes. He was
aware of feeling warmer and he couldn't be sure whether this
was an illusion or a symptom warning that something was
going wrong with his system. He had moved forward
mechanically for so long that his heart jumped with the shock
when his outstretched hand touched something hard. The
sole of Grapos' stationary boot. Was there a crisis? Had the
Greek collapsed on the floor of the tunnel under the murderous physical strain? He called out. 'Grapos . . .' Because of
the silence which had lasted so long he found he was unconsciously whispering as he called again. 'Something
wrong, Grapos?'

The voice which came back out of the darkness was hoarse
and breathless. 'We are at the bend. I can see the light at the

bottom. When we arrive, you wait inside the pipe. You do not come out until I tell you.'

'All right. You're doing fine.'

Grapos grunted and began heaving himself forward again, on his stomach now because he found this an easier way to progress as the pipe angled downhill more precipitately. Macomber was about to follow when he felt a hand touch his own foot and he called back over his shoulder. 'Nearly there, Ford. We can see the end of the tunnel. Pass it on.' There was a considerable element of exaggeration in his statement but it seemed a reasonable moment to send back a cheerful message. As he rounded the bend, Macomber was able to appreciate the extent of his exaggerated optimism: the pipe was angled downwards at an increasingly nerve-wracking pitch and the blur of light in the distance was little larger than a sixpence. They were probably barely half-way down the hill slope. He was easing himself round the bend when his right knee contacted a particularly slippery patch and before he knew what was happening he lost balance and crashed heavily against the tunnel wall. He felt it crumble under his impact and a large piece of concrete slithered into his thigh followed by a shower of loosened earth. In places the damned thing was little thicker than paper. Calling back to warn the others, he crawled forward again with a sensation of moving down a chute. The brief pause had hindered rather than helped – his knees were wobbling badly and he expected at any moment to keel into the wall for a second time. When the accident happened it was so unexpected, so unforeseeable and bizarre, that it took away Macomber's breath. He had just caught up with Grapos and was within inches of his rearmost boot when the uncanny silence inside the tunnel was shattered by a ripping, cracking sound. Little more than a foot beyond Grapos' head the tunnel roof splintered, caved in and exposed a small hole – and thrust down through the hole was an Alpenkorps boot with a leg showing to the knee.

Macomber froze as Grapos lay rigid, his face inches away

from the point where one of the Alpenkorps patrol had trodden through the rotting roof of the ancient pipe. Sufficient light percolated through the small aperture for him to see the pattern of large nails on the sole of the boot. Scarcely daring to breathe, he watched the leg withdrawing. For a few seconds it was held fast by the smallness of the hole when the boot tried to free itself, then it disappeared upwards, leaving the small aperture with ragged concrete edges. It was an incredible stroke of bad luck, but no more incredible than when two men on different sides creep up to the same corner of a building from opposite directions, an incident which Macomber himself had experienced in Sofia. Still on all fours, Macomber prayed that the others behind him would lie still, that they had realised something had happened, that they would understand the desperate need for preserving total silence.

Grapos was still lying motionless on the tunnel floor, unable to reach the rifle looped over his back and having the sense not to attempt that dangerous manoeuvre. With agonising slowness the Scot eased his tender knees forward a few more inches, wondering whether the hole was large enough for the invisible German to peer down and see Grapos, but he doubted whether that was possible. The Greek should be just far enough from the hole to go undetected. But how bright would that Alpenkorps man be? Would it occur to him to investigate the pipe, to kick in a little more of the crumbling roof? Originally, the pipe must have been laid just under the earth's surface, but over the years the rain had probably washed away some of the protecting soil until only a thin layer had remained. He found it an uncanny feeling to be lying there cooped up inside the narrow space, buried just underneath the hill slope and knowing that not three feet above them there was probably a German standing, undecided what to do about this phenomenon. Or had he gone away and climbed further up the hill over their heads, cursing the pipe and not giving it another thought? He would have his orders to maintain the line of the sweep and German discipline gave little scope for personal initiative. But these were Alpine troops, men very different in training and background from the average breed of Wehrmacht footslogger. Their training taught them to use their heads, to think for themselves.

All these rattling thoughts passed through Macomber's brain as four men lay absolutely still inside the pipe while two of them – Prentice and Ford – had even less idea of what was happening because they had been further back. All they knew was that the wriggling, advancing worm of feet and heads had unaccountably stopped after that weird breaking sound had travelled back up the tunnel. Instinct alone, or perhaps a telepathic sense of emergency, prevented them from calling out to ask what had gone wrong. Macomber felt the boots resting against his knuckles begin to wriggle and he understood the signal – Grapos wished to move back a little further away from the hole. To avoid the risk of two men's movements, Macomber simply perched both hands a little higher up the tunnel wall and the legs wriggled back underneath his own hoisted body, then stopped moving. He had made no sound during his short passage backwards but Macomber wished to heaven that he knew what had caused the Greek to retract that short distance. Was it in anticipation of something? The next moment he had confirmation that he had guessed correctly – a heavy instrument was hammered against the ragged rim of the aperture. Fragments clattered on the floor of the pipe and then the steel-plated butt of a rifle came half-way inside the pipe as a piece collapsed unexpectedly. The German was enlarging the hole to get a better view.

Macomber felt Grapos' body tense and then relax almost immediately – he had been about to seize the rifle butt and jerk it downwards out of the unseen hand holding it. Had the Alpenkorps man been alone it would have been a worthwhile action, but Grapos had remembered in time that the German was not alone on the hill slope. Grimly, Macomber waited for the hammering to be resumed, for the hole to be enlarged to a point where they must be seen, but as the seconds passed the hammering was not resumed and there was an unnerving stillness beyond the aperture. Apparently the soldier was now satisfied that it was simply a deserted culvert and he had continued uphill with the sweep. Or was this too comforting an explanation of the lack of activity above that tell-tale hole? Had he, in fact, seen Grapos? Probably not – Grapos had moved further up the tunnel just in time. The complacent thought had hardly passed through Macomber's head when he realised how fatally he had been wrong, realised that the German was still standing there just above them and that this was a man who was going to make sure of the business with very little expenditure of effort. The expenditure of a single hand-grenade, in fact.

The stick-like object fell through the hole and landed on the floor of the pipe. Macomber knew at once that they were going to die, that the grenade would detonate under perfect conditions. Inside that confined space the blast would be enormous with only a fraction escaping through the aperture; the main part of the explosion would be concentrated and funnelled along the pipe in a searing wave of bursting gases which would tear them to pieces. Prentice at the rear might just survive – survive with ruptured ear-drums as the hellish noise roared over him. Macomber felt Grapos stir under him and knew what he was trying to do, but the Greek was sprawled along the floor in a near-helpless position and he would never manage it in time. The Scot's hand closed over the grenade as he pivoted, taking his whole weight on his left hand to give him hoisting room. Gripping the throwing-handle and knowing that he held death in his fist, he looked upwards, calculated in a split-second and then jerked his hand, praying that the missile wouldn't catch the rim of the hole and come bouncing down again. The grenade sailed up through the aperture's centre and vanished as Macomber instinctively huddled over Grapos who now lay perfectly still. The detonation echoed back to the prone men as a hard thump like the thud of a rubber hammer against an oak door.

Macomber let out his breath and then nearly fell over as Grapos scrambled out from underneath him, half-stood up, pushed his head through the hole and heaved with his shoulders to force his way through the fractured rim.

What the devil was he up to now? The manoeuvre took Macomber completely by surprise. Was the Greek on the German side, was he taking this last chance to get out of the tunnel and reach his friends? Still standing in a half-crouched position with his head and shoulders only above the rim, Grapos was doing something frantically with his hands and arms. Below him Macomber held the Luger aimed at the lower part of his body while he tried to work out what Grapos was trying to do. He waited a whole minute and then the Greek lowered himself back inside the tunnel, pausing on his knees to reach up outside the hole while he hauled clumps of vegetation over the aperture. His hands were streaked with blood and when Macomber caught a glimpse of the prickly undergrowth he understood – he had been clawing and arranging a screen of vegetation to conceal the hole from the rest of the Alpenkorps patrol. Grapos sagged into an awkward sitting position and wiped his streaked hands carefully underneath his coat while he took in great gasping breaths of air. When he could speak he looked at Macomber and his former mistrust had gone as he dragged out the words. 'The German is dead – the bomb must have landed at his feet. He is alone . . . the others will come and will think the bomb went off by accident . . . with luck. If they do not see the hole . . .'

'You covered it completely?'

'I think so. If they search they will find it – but why should they do that if they think the bomb exploded by mistake? They will see it is not in his belt.'

'Thanks,' Macomber said simply. 'Think you can make it to the end of the tunnel? Good. And now you'd better be extra damned careful how you emerge.'

'I will manage.' Grapos wiped hair away from his face and stared at the Scot. 'And thank you – that bomb came within centimetres of my nose – if it exploded here I would have no head now . . .'

'Get moving – those Germans will be here any minute now.'

In spite of their cramped state the four men made speedier progress down the last stretch of the tunnel and then waited at the bottom until Grapos signalled that all was clear. Like the Alpenkorps, they crossed the stepping-stones singly, and in less than five minutes they came out from the undergrowth on to the deserted road to Zervos. Grapos grinned as he hoisted his rifle over his shoulder prior to leading the way. 'It will be good from now,' he informed them. 'We are in front of the Germans.'

'I wouldn't count on that,' Macomber replied sharply. 'I've got a nasty idea something very peculiar is going to happen between here and Zervos.'

The advance guard of the Alpenkorps was in sight and since they were mounted on mules it could only be a matter of time before they overtook anyone moving on foot. Perched on the crag which hung over the road a hundred feet below, Macomber closed the Monokular glass which Prentice had returned to him and looked down at the roadside where Grapos waited for the oxen-carts coming from Zervos. It had been agreed that it would be better if he questioned the peasants riding on the carts alone and the three of them – Macomber, Prentice and Ford – had climbed up from the road to keep out of sight. For the Scot this had been a welcome opportunity to see a long distance back over the way they had come, although the view could have been more encouraging.

'I hope Grapos isn't going to take all day arguing the toss with those peasants,' Prentice said irritably. Lack of sleep was making it increasingly difficult to keep his eyes open and now it was only will-power which sustained his movements. The trouble was that he had missed even the short rest the others had enjoyed before Grapos had appeared on the hilltop.

'He may get some news from them – or at least find out where we can get some food,' Macomber pointed out.

'I couldn't eat a thing. And that lot following us hasn't put any edge on my appetite either.'

'It shouldn't take them too long to get here,' observed Ford. 'They'll drive those mules till they drop – and mules don't drop all that quickly.'

Macomber forced his sagging shoulders upright and began speaking rapidly. It was clear that Prentice was in such a low state that a few minutes of pessimistic conversation might be more than enough to sap his remaining resistance, so he deliberately instilled a rough vigour into his voice. 'We're standing on a good lookout point to check the geography of the area so you know what lies ahead of us. It's about ten miles from Katyra to the plateau and the plateau itself is about six miles long. Then there's about another four miles from the far end of the plateau up to Zervos. That last four miles is pretty appalling – you climb up a winding road from the plateau which zigzags all over the place – so if we can conscript some mules for ourselves, we'd better do it. Grapos may manage to fix that up – I gather he knows just about everyone on the peninsula.'

'You mean we have another ten miles to do before we get to the monastery?' Prentice started to sit down on a rock and then remained standing; he had the feeling that if he relaxed he might never get up again. 'I don't see us getting there today,' he said firmly.

'Burckhardt will get there today – I'm sure that's the key to his whole timetable. And if you look over there I rather think you'll see Mount Zervos in a minute.'

From their elevated position at the top of the crag they had a panoramic view over the peninsula and to east and west the Aegean was in view, still a brilliant blue across the gulf where they could see the mountains on the mainland above the vital road the Allies were using. The surface of the water glittered in the sunlight and when Macomber had scanned it with his glass he thought he could make out small dark specks amid the calm cobalt, the specks of Italian mines floating in the gulf. The mainland was still half-shrouded in mist but here and there the sunlight caught the tiny square of white-ness which must be the wall of a building. To the north a dark column of smoke still hung in the sky from the burning *Hydra*, but the plume was less well-defined now and less smoke drifted upwards to maintain its density. And it was in that same direction where a distant file of men on mules advanced towards the crag at a seemingly snail's pace, a file which was telescoping as the head of the file went down inside a dip in the white streak of road.

To the south a fleet of heavy clouds drifted low over the peninsula, but the clouds were thinning rapidly as they continued out across the gulf beyond Cape Zervos and, as Macomber had predicted, the mountain slowly emerged from the clouds like a massive volcanic cone, a cone whose slopes were white with snow to the triangular-shaped summit. Prentice stood watching the mountain appear with a sense of awe – had they really a dog's chance in hell of scaling that giant and reaching the strategically vital monastery before the Germans took it? Borrowing Macomber's glass again, he focused and saw that the clouds had never really covered the peak; they had smothered the plateau and intervened between the mountain and the view from the north. So the met. men had been right – Zervos was hardly ever obscured by the weather and once Burckhardt was established up there he would have a continuous view of the supply road. Prentice felt temporarily overwhelmed – overwhelmed by what was at stake and by the apparently insuperable problem of arriving on Zervos in time.

'It's not so good to the east, though,' Macomber warned them soberly. 'At this time of year the weather comes from that direction and I don't like the look of what's on the way.'

To the east the sea was still visible, a grey ruffled sea rapidly disappearing under a fresh formation of dense cloud banks which had a heavy swollen look. There was very little doubt that extremely dirty weather was coming, heading for the section of the peninsula they would have to cross. To take his mind off it, Prentice stared again southwards where the mountain was now fully exposed to its base, and when Macomber told him to focus on a certain spot he thought he saw a tiny rectangle of rock perched close to the sea. 'If you're looking at the right place,' the Scot told him, 'that's the monastery. It's pretty high up, as you'll see.'

'Pretty high. Well above the snow-line, in fact.'

Perhaps a mile further on from the crag the last remnants of cloud were now clearing from the edge of the plateau which rose abruptly from the foothills like a wall. Again Macomber pointed out a certain spot and Prentice found the road which climbed up to the tableland. On the eastern side of the plateau a wisp of smoke eddied into the sky as it was caught by a strong wind and there appeared to be a huddle of buildings under the smoke. 'That's the village of Elatia,' Macomber explained in reply to Prentice's question. 'We shan't go near that – a spur track runs off the main road to reach it.'

'Main road? Some main road!' Prentice handed back the glass and looked down to where the oxen-carts had stopped below while Grapos talked to several peasants who had gathered round him. At one moment Grapos gestured vigorously towards Katyra and Prentice guessed that he was warning them about the approaching Germans. Shortly afterwards something like panic gripped the gathering. Three of the four oxen-carts filled up with the peasants and began to leave the road to drive straight across the fields which stretched away from the base of the hill. One wagon got stuck as its wheels caught in the ditch and the shouts of the passengers urging the beasts to make greater efforts echoed up to the crag. The fourth cart, empty, remained standing in the road as Grapos stared up at the crag and waved both arms furiously to summon them down. As they started their descent Macomber took one last look north-wards and saw the tail of the Alpenkorps column sliding out of view. When it emerged in sight again it would be that much closer to the crag and to Mount Zervos.

*

'The news is bad – very bad,' Grapos greeted them. 'The Germans attacked my country and Jugoslavia at 5.45 this morning. They say the forts at Rupel have held the first attack.'

'They said the Maginot Line would hold all attacks,' Prentice muttered under his breath. 'Why have they left this wagon?' he asked out aloud. Grapos had turned the cart round so that now it faced away from the Alpenkorps.

'For us! They are going into the fields to escape the Germans so that it did not matter that they knew you were here. With this we can save our strength and some of us can sleep. I know where we can get food and clothes.' He looked at Ford and Prentice. 'With those clothes you would freeze to death on Zervos.'

'Any other news, Grapos?' Macomber enquired brusquely. 'And how do your friends know about the German offensive? The telephone line was going to be cut.'

'It has been cut since last night. They heard the news on the wireless.' Grapos' manner had become openly hostile as though he resented the question, and Prentice thought Oh, Lord, those two are at it again! 'I tell you the truth,' the Greek added vehemently.

'Of course you do,' Macomber replied, completely un-ruffled. 'But I deal in facts and I like to know the details. Where can we get the food and the clothes?'

'At a house where the road climbs. We must go . . .'

'Just a minute! You know this family well?'

'There is no family. There is one man and I have known him many years. He would be in the army fighting but he is old. And he has no German mother – if that would really worry you, Mr Macomber.'

'Then let's get moving. This will be a chance for you to get some rest, Prentice. Make the most of it. I have an idea it may be the last chance you'll get!'

The inside of the oxen-cart was carpeted with straw and Prentice, who sprawled full-length after bunching up the straw into a makeshift palliasse, had fallen asleep almost before the cumbersome vehicle started moving. Grapos held the long whip which signalled the animals that it was time to work again and they began lurching forward over the dusty road at a laboured pace across a small plain. The foothills continued on their right, hiding the gulf from them, but they became lower as the wall of the plateau crawled towards them with infinite slowness. It would have been at least as quick to march on foot but Macomber felt that Prentice must recuperate even though the Alpenkorps on mules must inevitably close the gap between them, and the cart provided a means of rest for all four men. Even Macomber sensed that it was crucial to conserve their energies for what might lie in front of them, but the slow-motion pace of the cart irritated him almost beyond endurance. The wagon was drawn by two long-horned oxen which plodded along sedately as the ancient wagon creaked and groaned as though it might fall apart at any moment. They were coming close to the wall of the plateau when Ford asked Macomber his wry question. 'Anything worrying you – anything in particular, I meant?'

'Well, this ox-cart for one thing. It's not exactly the Orient Express.' He stared ahead as Grapos, who stood between them, glared in his direction. 'For another thing, I can't work out how we're going to communicate with the mainland forces in time to warn them of what is happening here. In time,' he repeated. 'Once Burckhardt has established himself on the heights no one will ever shift him – the place, the position, everything, makes it a natural fortress. But the thing which bothers me most of all is the size of his force – I'm absolutely certain that he's expecting massive reinforcements.'

'Hard to see how – unless they sneaked in by sea again. Could they land somewhere over there?' Ford pointed towards the eastern coastline which was still clear, although out over the Aegean the clouds were continuing to mass.

'There's no way inland. The cliffs go on until they reach the delta area in the north. But I can't see them risking a sea-going expedition twice – and this one in broad daylight. They can't be expecting to break through from Salonika in time or else they wouldn't have sent Burckhardt in the first place . . .' Macomber trailed off and stared ahead as he put himself in the colonel's position and tried to imagine his next move. Ford was standing with his back to the way they were going so he could watch the road behind but so far it stretched away emptily as far as he could see. When they reached the base of the plateau wall Grapos took them inside a single-storey stone house concealed by a grove of cypresses and there the owner, a man in his seventies, divided among them the meal he had just prepared for himself. The food was strange and strong-tasting and consisted of balls of meat rolled inside the leaves of some unidentifiable vegetable. He offered to cook more but Macomber said they had no time and they ate with relish food they would normally have rejected as inedible.

Macomber was keeping watch by himself just beyond the cypresses while he drank *ouzo* from a large glass when he saw them coming. His Monokular brought them closer – Alpenkorps on mules, a file which extended back into the distance and which was a far more formidable force than he had imagined from his earlier sight of them. He ran back into the house to find Prentice and Ford trying on two ancient sheepskin coats the owner was providing and then exploded when the lieutenant started to write the man's name in a notebook so they could send him payment later. 'Prentice, you may have just signed that man's death warrant! If the Germans catch us and find that . . .'

'Of course! I must be half-asleep,' the lieutenant replied apologetically. He went to a stone sink and began setting fire to the page prior to washing away the embers. The room was stone-paved and stone-walled. A hideous place to spend seventy years of one's life.

'And we have about half a minute to clear out of here,' Macomber rapped out.

'I'm just burning a death-warrant, as you so aptly pointed out.' Prentice had recovered his normal composure after the sleep in the cart and there was a faint smile on his face when he stared back at the large Scot. 'How close would you say?'

'Two miles. Maybe less.'

'Close enough, I agree. We'll have to hike it up to the top of that plateau. I hope you can walk faster than a mule, Ford.' He dropped the blackened paper into the sink and poured a stone jugful of water over the mess, pushing it down the drain with his finger. 'There's no way up except the road, I suppose?'

'No other way,' Grapos told him.

'Right! The road it is!' He turned to the old man. 'Tell him he has our grateful thanks for his hospitality. I rather fancy it would be a mistake to offer money for the food?'

'A mistake,' Grapos agreed abruptly. He was looking through the open doorway towards the road and hoisted his rifle higher as he moved towards it.

'Tell him also,' Prentice went on, 'that when the Germans arrive and ask about us, he's to say he saw us get off the wagon we'd obviously stolen and run up the hill. If he tells them something they're more likely to leave him alone. Tell him also to wash up three of those plates and glasses and just leave his own dirty. They'll be looking for things like that. And don't forget the thanks.' He waited while Grapos poured out a stream of Greek and the old man kept shaking his head as though it were nothing, and he was relieved to see as they left that the old man was already starting to wash the dirty plates.

When Macomber looked back as they started to climb the hill, the line of mounted troops was already appreciably closer and he knew that they must hide soon or be captured. With the Scot in the lead they ascended the winding road at a slow trot, but long before the top they were slowing down badly. The gradient was steep and wound its way between huge boulders which seemed on the verge of toppling down the rugged incline. Groves of bare olive groves studded the hill slope and the frequent twists in the road soon hid them from the plain below, which had the advantage of hiding them from the Alpenkorps mule train, but had the disadvantage of preventing them seeing how close their pursuers were drawing. Cover was what they needed, Macomber was telling himself, and he was tempted to leave the road altogether and hide on the hill slope, but this would mean throwing in the sponge: the Alpenkorps would ride past and continue on to Zervos. I'm damned if I'm giving up as easily as that, he thought, after surviving that voyage from Istanbul.

'I'd say we have another thirty minutes left – at the outside,' Prentice called up to him.

'At the outside,' Macomber agreed. Thirty minutes before the leading Alpenkorps troops overhauled them. It was beginning to get a bit desperate and he was pinning all his hopes on seeing a chance to escape when they reached that plateau which stretched six miles to the base of the mountain. This was one area where he had very little idea of the topography because when he had travelled this way five years before it had been drenched in mist while they drove over the tableland. The stitch in his side was getting worse as he forced his legs to keep up the route-march pace and each thud of his boots on the road pounded up his side like a sledgehammer. To counter the pain he stooped forward a little, cursing inwardly as Prentice caught up with him.

'Take it easy, Mac, you'll kill yourself. You're streaming with sweat.'

'Time is running out – we had a head start on them and we've lost it. We'll have to make a quick decision when we reach the top.' The effort of speaking was a major strain but he was damned if he was going to give up. Keep moving, you'll work it off! Prentice was walking alongside him and this gave him a pacemaker to keep up with. He forced himself to resist the impulse to look at the ground because this brought on greater fatigue. Straightening up, he stared at the ridge they were approaching. Was this the rim of the plateau at long last? He had thought so hopefully with three lower ridges and had been disappointed each time. In his state of extreme exertion the unseen plateau above was now taking on the character of a promised land, a haven where there must be some salvation from the relentless Alpenkorps coming up behind.

He was hardly aware of the landscape they were passing as the pain grew worse and pulled at him like a steel wire contracting inside his body. Boulders, olive groves, clumps of shrubbery moved past in a blur as he fixed his eyes on that wobbling ridge moving down towards them as they turned another bend and then another. Despite his robot-like condition he was conscious that the air was cooler, that a breeze was growing stronger, and this gave him fresh hope that they were close to the head of the tortuous road which went on and on forever – another bend, another stretch of white dust, another bend . . .

'Must be nearly there – with this wind,' Prentice commented.

Macomber only grunted and stared upwards. Was he breaking the grip of the stitch? It seemed a little less agonising, a little less inclined to screw up his muscles into complex knots. It left him quite suddenly and with the realisation that he had conquered it he began to take long loping strides which Prentice could hardly keep up with. He wiped his face dry as he walked and then accelerated his pace, feeling a sense of triumph as he saw only sky beyond the lowering ridge. They were almost there! Revived by the small quantity of food and the wine he began moving faster still as the gradient of the road lessened, leaving Prentice behind in his anxiety to catch his first glimpse of the plateau. There must be no hesitation here – they must decide swiftly what they were going to do and do it. There might even be a convenient farm at the top. With a lot of luck there might even be bicycles – he had seen men cycling when he had visited Katyra before the war. A cycle should be a match for a mule. They needed some form of transport which would take them the six miles across the plateau, something which would put them well ahead of that blasted mule train of Burckhardt's. He put on a spurt, came over the top and the plateau lay before him.

The disappointment was so crushing that he stood quite still until Prentice reached him. A classic tableland spread out into the distance, an area of flatness devoid of any form of cover for several miles. In fact, he could hardly have imagined a region less suited for them to escape the Alpenkorps. The road was a surprise, too: a highway of recently-laid tar which ran straight across to the mountain, the land greenish on one side and brownish on the other. They must have started the highway from the peninsula tip, a highway which in due course would be extended to Katyra.

'Not quite what we're in the market for,' Prentice remarked.

'It might as well be the sea for all the good it is to us.' Macomber glanced over his shoulder. 'How's the Greek?'

'Had a bit of trouble with his limp coming up. Ford stayed back to keep him company. What's exciting them now, I wonder?'

Ford and Grapos had appeared but they were standing together on an outcrop of rock a short distance from the road as they waved their hands with a beckoning motion. Prentice left Macomber gazing bleakly at the plateau and went back to the outcrop. The ground he scrambled up was dry and gritty, which confirmed that the storm of the night before must have blown itself out somewhere near Cape Zervos. And there was a trace of excitement in Ford's voice as he called down. 'Hurry up or you'll miss it.'

'Miss what?'

The sun which shone on the back of Prentice's neck as he hauled himself up on to the rock had no warmth in it and the coldness of the light breeze was a reminder that they were approaching a zone of low temperature. Standing beside Grapos, he adjusted his sheepskin coat. It was too big and flopped off the shoulders; Ford, who was wearing another coat belonging to the same man, fitted far more comfortably inside his sheepskin. Had the Greek possessed a third coat? The thought had never struck Prentice during the flurry to get away from the house. Following the line of Ford's pointed arm he could see the roof of that house now, its faded red tiles so levelled by the height that it looked flat-roofed. And only a few yards beyond the cypresses the head of the Alpenkorps column was approaching the foot of the hill road. 'There they come,' said Ford, 'the first of the many.'

'You're sure they are the first? There may be more of them already coming up the hill.'

'No, sir. You and Macomber were in such a perishing hurry to get up here I don't imagine you ever looked back – but we caught sight of them more than once and that's the head of the column.'

Prentice was surprised. Earlier he had been startled to find German troops in front of them when they came over the hilltop near the pipe, and now he was surprised at how long it had taken them to reach this point since he had glanced back when they rushed out of the house below. But they had been travelling over a flat plain and distance could be very deceptive. He waited for two or three men to turn aside and enter the house, but the column went straight past and vanished as it began to mount the hill road. The wagon had been left behind the cypresses, which also concealed the house, and the Alpenkorps were going to ride up the hill without ever realising its existence. With a feeling of relief he jumped down from the platform and hurried back to where Macomber still stood, stood like a man of stone as he gazed upwards, his hands inside his coat pockets, the expression on his face so grim that it recalled the Abwehr man, Dietrich.

'What's the matter?' asked Prentice. He tilted his head. 'What's that – I can hear something?'

'The reinforcements – Burckhardt's reinforcements. By God, I expected something but I hadn't expected this. They must have half the Wehrmacht up there coming in.'

The sky to the north-east was still clear, more than clear enough for them to see the huge aerial armada which was descending on Zervos. The steady purr of their engines grew louder as they flew over the peninsula at a height of less than a thousand feet and they were close enough already for Macomber to see that they were three-engined machines with an iron cross on the fuselage and the swastika on the tail. 'Transport planes,' Ford said in his ear. 'They'll very likely have parachutists aboard.' In the distance, flying even lower, came more planes and these were towing other machines with different silhouettes. Macomber was focusing his glass on them as Prentice spoke.

'The Alpenkorps have just started to come up the hill behind us.'

'They'll take Zervos before nightfall. There's nothing to stop them,' said Macomber.

'Unless this airborne crowd is heading for the mainland,' Ford suggested without much conviction.

Macomber stared through the glass, holding his head tilted back as the planes flew in closer. The aircraft towing other machines were losing height rapidly while the transport planes circled above the plateau, their engines a muted roar. There were no Allied fighters to intercept them, of course, although a flight of Messerschmitts had now appeared: the bulk of the over-strained R.A.F. was supporting the Greek war in Albania and even these formations were few and far between. With a feeling of appalled helplessness they watched the aerial fleet droning casually over the plateau like a flying circus putting on a show before an invited audience, although the only audience to watch this display of Luft-waffe air power was the group of four men on the plateau rim. There were probably between twenty and thirty planes, but it was the thought of what they might contain which frightened Prentice. 'Those machines they're towing are gliders,' said Ford. He saw Macomber nod in confirmation and now the shadows of the planes were flitting over the level surface of the plateau, a perfect landing ground for putting down an airborne force. A moment later a cluster of black dots sprayed from one of the transport machines and the dots became cones as the parachutists floated downwards. A machine detached itself from its powered carrier and the gliders started to come in to land.

*

The four men were retreating from the plateau in the faint hope of hiding themselves on the hillside above the road when Macomber called out. 'Wait a minute, Prentice! Something's going wrong with this one.' A glider detached from its powered transport was wobbling unstably as it headed for the earth and had the appearance of being out of control as it descended towards the rim of the plateau close to where Macomber waited. An ugly, ungainly beast, it was twin-tailed and the fuselage was squat, suggesting great carrying capacity.

Half a mile along the road more parachutists were floating down over the brownish ground which seemed to be the main landing area and the sunlight caught their tilting cones – white for parachutists and various colours for the 'chutes supporting supply containers. Only one transport plane had attempted a landing to the left of the road and the machine was propped at a dangerous angle with the nose well down and its tail angled in the air. On the other side of the road two transports had already touched down safely and a third was just coming in.

'That plane on the left will be in trouble,' Prentice said tersely. 'It's marshland on that side.'

'How do you know that?' Macomber asked quickly.

'Because I persuaded the pilot to make a detour and fly over here on our way to Istanbul. We'd been discussing Zervos before I left Athens and I wanted to see what the place looked like. He told me that the green area was marshy . . .'

'Those transport machines are JU 52/3s,' Ford interjected professionally. 'I've heard they can carry mountain guns . . .'

'This is hardly a good time to start cataloguing German equipment,' Prentice snapped. 'I say we'd better get out of here – and fast.'

'And this brute of a glider coming towards us is a Gotha unless I'm very much mistaken,' Ford continued, and then found he was alone as the others ran back towards the boulders and scrub at the top of the hill. As he followed them he could hear the whine of the wind rising and the steady beat-beat of more transports coming in. Ford, who had a fatalistic streak in his make-up had little doubt that this was the end of the line; they would spend the rest of the war in some German prison camp, unless they were shot in the process of being captured. He was close to the first boulders when the machine-pistol slipped off his shoulder and he had to turn back to pick it up.

The huge Gotha assault cargo glider was flying down at an unpleasantly acute angle less than a hundred yards away. If it wasn't very lucky it was going to miss the rim of the plateau and go crashing down on to the plain below. Fascinated by the spectacle of the imminent disaster he stayed out in the open, remembering how his sister had once told him that when the first German bombers came high over London in broad daylight people had stood in the streets watching instead of fleeing for the shelters. Macomber seemed similarly affected, because now he came out from behind the rocks and stood close to Ford as the massive glider swooped down, tried to level out at the last moment, and then thudded into the soft earth a bare hundred feet away.

'For God's sake get under cover, you idiots!' Prentice shouted from behind them. Ford, the spell broken, turned to go, but Macomber still waited as he gazed at the machine. The shock of landing had righted the fuselage and now the whole of the nose of the aircraft was lifting back like an immense hood. A soldier stood near the entrance as the aperture yawned larger, exposing a vehicle like a large car which waited to emerge. The German was moving unsteadily as he climbed behind the driver's seat and he paused to wipe something which might have been blood from his forehead. The engine started up and the vehicle began to move slowly out of the nose with a rattling sound as the driver slumped over the wheel as though he could hardly hold himself up. There was little doubt that he had been badly knocked about by the crash-landing. Prentice, who had come out from cover with Grapos, spoke over the Scot's shoulder. 'If we could just grab that . . .'

'Exactly what I was thinking, but there are bound to be more men inside.'

Ford grabbed his arm and his voice reflected a rare excitement for the phlegmatic sergeant. 'It's a bloody half-track! Look!'

The clanking sound grew louder as the vehicle came out with painful slowness and the dazed driver remained still unaware of their proximity. Capless, he was wearing the uniform of the Alpenkorps, but it was the vehicle itself which Macomber was staring at as he put his hand inside his coat pocket and began to move forward purposefully over the grass. A long vehicle without any roof, its body was painted a drab olive-grey and at the front it was supported by two normal wheels, but there were no wheels at the rear; instead it was held up by two large caterpillar tracks. As Ford had said, a half-track – half-tank, half-car. The grinding of the tracks was muffled as they moved down on to the grass and now the driver lifted his head to see where he was going and saw Macomber standing a few feet away. The Scot spoke swiftly, rapping out the words in German.

'Brake! Colonel Burckhardt is here. He needs this vehicle at once!'

The driver reacted automatically to the command in German, braked, then stared hard at the man who had given the order. His eyes travelled over the Scot's shoulder to where Prentice and Ford were moving forward while Grapos watched the road behind. As he made a sudden movement to reach something Macomber pulled out the Luger and struck him across the temples. He had the door open and was hauling the soldier out before he had sagged to the floor while Prentice and Ford ran to either side of the open mouth of the glider. Heaving the driver out on to the grass with one hand while the other still retained the Luger, he looked up as another German soldier appeared at the open nose, his rifle at the ready. Two shots were fired within the fraction of a second. The first, fired by the soldier, struck Ford. The second, fired by Macomber, entered the German's body as Prentice ran round the back of the vehicle, arriving at the moment when the Alpenkorps man slumped down in the space between the rear of the tracks.

'Heads down!' It was Prentice who shouted as he snatched a grenade dangling from the fallen German's belt. The grenade sailed into the interior of the glider and detonated near the back. A moment earlier Macomber had caught a glimpse of movement from inside the plane, but when he raised his head after the thumping explosion there was no further sign of activity aboard the Gotha. Ford was holding on to the side of the tracks, stooped forward on his knees, but he was trying to clamber up as Prentice and Macomber reached him. The passage of the bullet was marked by a neat tear on the right sleeve of his sheepskin coat. Prentice had an arm round his chest and was helping him to his feet as he snapped at Macomber.

'Leave it! I can manage him. You'll have to try and drive this blasted thing – they'll be on to us in a minute.'

Ford was upright now, one arm clutching Prentice round the waist for support as he clambered inside a cut-out aperture which was the rear-door of the half-track. He spoke through his teeth to Macomber. 'Drives like a car . . . any car . . . the tracks move with the wheels.' Macomber was turning to go to the front when he saw the distinctive Alpenkorps cap on the head of the soldier slumped between the tracks. He scooped it off and rammed it down over his own head as Grapos arrived, running at a shuffling jog-trot with his rifle between his hands.

'The mules are here,' he gasped out. 'Coming over the hill quickly. I think the first man . . .'

'Get in, for God's sake.'

Prentice had successfully manoeuvred Ford into one of the benches behind the two front seats and Macomber was behind the wheel as Grapos climbed aboard. Brake, clutch-pedal, gear-lever – it *looked* like an ordinary car. Ford told Prentice to shut up a minute and leaned forward. 'An ordinary car, Macomber, that's all it is – for driving, anyway.' He

sagged back against the bench seat as Prentice twisted his
handkerchief into a makeshift tourniquet ready to tie it
round the sergeant's arm and then the vehicle began moving
forward over the grass towards the road. The tracks clanked
gently as they revolved over the field and the vehicle had a
feeling of great stability.

Macomber was concentrating on three things at once –
primarily on getting to know how this queer monster worked,
but also he was keeping an eye on the hilltop over which the
Alpenkorps might stream at any moment, and with what little
attention he had left he cast quick glances to the south where
the road ran past the landing zone. The sky was littered with
a fresh wave of falling parachutists and another transport
plane had just come to a halt after a bumpy landing. Dammit,
he said to himself and speeded up. The half-track reached
the road at the moment when the leading Alpenkorps soldier
crested the rise on his mule.

Hahnemann! Macomber felt certain it was the German
lieutenant on that animal. He must have been hurled overboard into the sea when the *Hydra* blew up, must have been
one of those men swimming in the water. The thought
darted through his brain as it all became a kaleidoscope and
he reacted with pure instinct. Two more men on mules
appearing behind Hahnemann. Parachutists hitting the
earth, their 'chutes landing and pulling sideways. A giant
glider cruising in to land on the brownish area. The steady
throb of planes' engines overhead mingling with the urgent
shouts of the men on the mules. Still feeling like a man towing
a caravan, he turned the wheel and the half-track climbed on
to the road. As its great metal tracks ground their teeth into
the hard tar they set up a jarring vibration sound and the
unexpected barrage of noise panicked the mules. There was
more shouting, frantic now as the animals headed across the
hilltop, threading their way nimbly among the boulders and
away from that strange machine. Macomber completed his
turn, hunched his shoulders, pressed his foot down, and the
half-track began to build up speed as the wheels spun and

the tracks churned round faster and faster, half-deafening its passengers with the pounding beat of metal on tar.

'How fast can it go?' shouted the Scot.

'Twenty . . . thirty . . . forty. Fifty would be pushing it.' Ford had his arm out of the sleeve now and was taking off the right side of his jacket as he replied. There were three rows of bench seats across the vehicle behind the front seats and Grapos occupied the rear position. He had aimed his rifle at Hahnemann but the half-track had lurched at the wrong moment, almost throwing him off, and he hadn't fired a shot. Now there was no target – the mules and their riders were lost somewhere inside the tangle of boulders. He swore colourfully in Greek when Macomber shouted over his shoulder for him to get down on the floor out of sight – Grapos was rather too distinctive a figure for his liking at the moment.

Ahead more transport planes were droning in the sky as they waited their moment to come down, and already the plateau to the right of the road had the look of a disorganised military tattoo. So far there were no troops close to the road but a few hundred yards away parachutists were grappling with the supply containers and a number of men were already armed with machine-pistols. Several looked up as the half-track roared past and their uniform was very different from that of the Alpenkorps, so different that they might have belonged to another army. They wore pot-shaped helmets not dissimilar to diving helmets, smocks camouflaged with mottled dark green and brown, and overall trousers which gave them a deceptively clumsy appearance, but there was nothing clumsy about their movements as they began to form up in sections. Macomber, having got the feel of the vehicle, was now sitting very erect so his Alpenkorps cap was prominently on view and frequently he drove with one hand while he waved with the other to the men assembling in the field, a performance which Prentice witnessed with some trepidation. It was typical of Macomber, he was thinking, to carry the bluff to its utmost limit.

'Look out!'

Prentice shrieked out the warning. Like Macomber, all his attention had been fixed on the airborne force's landing area and it was only by chance that he glanced to the left. A Gotha assault glider released from its tow-rope was coming in to land from the east. It was already flying very low, perhaps twenty feet above the ground, flying on a course which would take it directly across the road just ahead of the speeding half-track. Prentice guessed that the pilot was desperately trying to maintain flight long enough to take his machine beyond the marshland area and it was horribly clear that the two very different forms of transport were headed on a collision course. Macomber had time to slow down but nearby a drawn-up section of parachutists was marching steadily towards the road. If he slowed, stopped, they'd get a damn' good look at who was inside the vehicle and they had machine-pistols looped over their shoulders. Without hesitation he accelerated and it became a race towards destruction.

His shoulders hunched again, he watched road and oncoming glider. It was an uncomfortably fine calculation – known speed of half-track against estimated speed of glider, with the added element of the plane's angle of descent. The half-track was now thundering down the road, which had begun to slope, at a pace which alarmed Prentice, the tracks rotating madly under increasing tension as the moving metal smashed its way forward with a rattling cannonade of sound. Across the green field the glider grew larger as it maintained its course unerringly and lost more height. He must be mad, Prentice was thinking. Macomber's going to try and beat the bloody thing, to sneak past ahead of it! The glider was so close now that he wanted to close his eyes, to look away, but he felt a terrible compulsion to stare at the oncoming machine which now seemed enormous.

'We won't make it,' said Ford who had now become aware of what was happening, and Ford was good at this sort of hair's-breadth calculation. Prentice would have felt even less happy had he known that exactly the same thought was pressing down on Macomber, and now it was too late to think of reducing speed. The converging projectiles were so close that he would probably smash into the tail of the glider as it passed. The only answer was a little more speed.

The downward gradient of the road was increasing as he pressed his foot harder and prayed – prayed against two catastrophes. He had heard somewhere that if you drive a tracked vehicle too fast a caterpillar could break loose, freeing itself from the small wheels over which it revolved and leave the vehicle altogether. If that happened at the speed they were moving at now there would be very little hope of survival, and certainly all hope of escaping the Germans and reaching Zervos would be gone. Grimly, he kept his foot down, his mind totally concentrated on the straight road ahead, the tortured gyrations of the over- strained tracks, and that huge drifting shape about to move across his bows. Prentice had one arm steadying Ford while the other hand gripped the side of the vehicle as the glider lost more height and now cruised forward barely six feet above the plateau and less than fifty yards from the road. Grapos, lying resentfully on the floor with his feet under a bench and his back against the rear of the vehicle, had the shock of his life when he looked up and saw the bulk of the Gotha loom up. The half-track raced forward, Grapos involuntarily ducked, and the Gotha passed over the rear of the vehicle, landing a short distance beyond the road.

Prentice sagged against the back of the bench and stared at the back of the huge Scot, his lips moving soundlessly. Macomber was already slowing down to a safer speed, expecting some uncomplimentary comment from his passengers, but the occupants of the bench were stunned, so he was saved an argument. In the distance a transport plane was stationary close to the road and Macomber whistled under his breath when he saw something which looked like a part of a field-gun coming down a ramp through a large opening in the fuselage. 'How is Ford?' he called out over his shoulder.

'Ford is surviving,' Ford replied.

'The bullet grazed him,' amplified Prentice who was now fixing the tourniquet to his final satisfaction. 'He's lost a bit of blood and he looks like Banquo's ghost but the fresh air will probably tone him up a treat.'

'There's a plane ahead with something coming out – better try and identify it so we know what we're up against.'

'We can see what we're up against,' Prentice told him bluntly. 'The cream of the Wehrmacht. And I suppose you've seen there are more half-tracks over to the right? Another one's on its way out of that Gotha which just missed us.'

'Pity.' Macomber made his voice sound genuinely regretful. 'If we'd brought down that glider we'd have inconvenienced Colonel Burckhardt.'

'We'd have inconvenienced ourselves as well.'

'Do you think we're nearly clear of them?' asked Ford and there was a note of anxiety in his voice.

'Not much ahead as far as I can see. Why?' Macomber had detected the anxious note and was wondering what had struck the technically-minded Ford.

'Because we've been lucky so far – it's wireless communication that worries me. If the Alpenkorps who came over the hill can send a message ahead we may have a reception committee waiting for us.'

It was a point which had worried Prentice but he hadn't seen any point in raising new problems at this particular juncture. So far they had got away with their audacious dash along the fringe of the assembly area, and this didn't entirely surprise him: the Germans had just landed on enemy territory and were taken up with carrying out a certain vital routine – collection of weapons from the supply containers, the unloading of heavy equipment from the gliders and transport planes, and the assembling of the men into their units. They had no reason, when their attention was so

divided, to see anything strange in one of their own recently-
landed half-tracks speeding along the road to Zervos. But
wireless communication was a different matter.

'We may be lucky,' said Macomber. 'I made a mess of both
Burckhardt's wireless-sets and if he hasn't got that tuning
coil fixed he'll have to wait until he finds one with this airborne mob. Now, watch it, Ford.'

He had been travelling at little more than twenty miles an
hour to give the tracks a rest but now he began to build up
speed again as they approached the transport plane which
had landed little more than a hundred yards from the road.
Men were scurrying round the machine and he saw beyond
it another plane which had been hidden from view. Close to
the aircraft stood a complete field-piece. Ford twisted sideways on the bench as they roared past and this time, to
Prentice's relief, the Scot did not attempt his cheerful
waving act. The planes were receding behind them when
Ford spoke.

'They're 75-mm mountain guns – just what they need
where they're going. And I saw several 8-cm. mortars. This
lot is really going places.'

'Some of the half-tracks will haul the mountain guns?'
Prentice enquired.

'Yes, that's it. And they'll carry troops aboard as well.
They've landed a beautiful heavy-nosed spearhead for the
job.'

'Why send Burckhardt's expedition at all?' Macomber
asked.

'That's very necessary,' Prentice explained, 'for a variety
of reasons. First, if they hadn't had this patch of clear
weather the airborne force could never have landed at all and
then Burckhardt would have had to do the whole job himself.
Second, I can see now that it was vital for them to land men
at Katyra to seal off the peninsula . . .'

'And third,' interjected Ford, 'there's a limit to how much
a glider or transport can carry. You can have heavy stuff –
the mountain guns, the half-tracks – or you can have men,

but you can't have both. So it's my bet Burckhardt's expedition is bringing in a sizable portion of the manpower while the airborne fleet brings in the heavy stuff. Together, it makes up a beautifully balanced force.'

'That's the second time you've used the word "beautiful," ' Prentice complained. 'Frankly, I can't see one damned thing that's beautiful in what's coming to us.'

'Just a professional observation, sir,' Ford explained blandly.

'I think we've left them behind,' Macomber called out. 'It looks as though those two planes landed closest to Zervos.'

The road stretched away across the plateau and still ran straight as a Roman road, a perfect highway for the advance of the German invaders. They were much closer to the mountain now but it no longer rose from its base with majestic symmetry; a heavy cloud bank from the east was drifting across the lower slopes and the peak had a lop-sided look. The disturbed Aegean was no longer visible from the plateau and another formation of low cloud was gradually obliterating the tableland itself. The road was sloping upwards as it climbed towards the mountain wall and Macomber could feel a distinct drop in temperature as the wind grew stronger. The worsening of the weather was a development he viewed with some disenchantment; his photographic memory for places vividly recalled that murderous stretch of road further on which zigzagged up the flank of the mountain, a road twisting and turning over precipitous drops as it ascended into the wilderness. During his previous visit to Zervos, he remembered, at several points he had been forced to back his car to the edge of fearful brinks as he took spine-tingling corners in two turns. At least Burckhardt's tracked spearhead wouldn't be able to do a Le Mans over that course, but the trouble was he would have to take the half-track up the same road. The gradient was increasing more steeply as Prentice called out to him.

'How are we off for petrol?'

'We had a hundred litres – a full tank – when we started, so that's the least of our problems.'

'The pilot of the glider would insist on a full tank before he took off,' Ford pointed out helpfully. 'That minimises the risk of something going wrong during the flight – an explosion, even.'

Prentice groaned half-audibly. 'And talking about trouble, I don't much like the look of that dirty weather blowing up from the east.'

'Is the Greek still on the floor?' Macomber asked. 'He can get up now if he is and give us his opinion – a met. forecast, in fact.'

Prentice glanced round and lifted his eyes to heaven. Grapos was sprawled on his side with the rifle cuddled in his arms and he was fast asleep. How anyone could kip down on top of those vibrating tracks passed Prentice's comprehension. 'The Greek,' he announced in a loud voice, 'is in dreamland.'

'Well, wake him up,' Macomber commanded brutally.

Disturbed from his slumber, Grapos sat on the bench behind Prentice who put the question about the coming weather to him. He stared across the plateau, pulling absently at one corner of his moustache and then feeling the stubble on his chin. Then he stared ahead to where the mountain was fast losing itself behind the vaporous pall which was drifting across the plateau in front of them. As he watched, the mountain disappeared. 'It is bad,' he said. 'It is very bad. The worst. There will be much snow within the hour.'

'Exactly what makes you predict that?' Macomber called back to him sharply.

'It is from the east. The clouds are low. They are like a cow with calf – swollen with snow . . .'

'First time I've heard of cows with snow inside them,' Prentice commented in an effort to lighten the pall Grapos himself was spreading over them. But the Greek was not to be put off by unseemly levity.

'The sea has gone from the plateau – that is another sign. The top of the mountain has gone – another sign. As we climb it will get worse and worse. It will be very cold and there will be a big fall of snow.'

'Thank you,' said Prentice, 'you're fired! We'll get another met. forecaster from the B.B.C.'

'You ask me – I tell you. There may be landslides on the mountain. There will be ice on the road . . .'

'And the sea shall rise up and encompass us, so we'd better find a Noah's Ark,' said Prentice in a kind of frenzy. 'For Pete's sake, man, we asked you for a weather forecast – not a gypsy's warning of doom. Now can it!' And he looks a bit like a gypsy, the old brigand, he thought as Grapos glared at him resentfully and then gazed stolidly ahead as though drawing their attention to the appalling prospect which lay before them. 'That answer your question, Macomber?' he called out.

'I think so. Further outlook unsettled.'

It was the reference to ice on the road which most disturbed the Scot. He would have to take this cumbersome half-track up a route which, five years before, a car had found difficulty in negotiating in good weather, because during that trip only the plateau had been blotted out by low cloud. It would make it equally hazardous for Burckhardt, of course, so it really depended on which way you looked at the problem, but Macomber was going to be in front with the Germans coming up behind. He changed gear as the gradient increased again and now they were moving at little more than twenty miles an hour when Prentice asked if he could borrow the Monokular glass. He kept it for only a short time and then handed it back as he spoke.

'You were right, the outlook is unsettled – behind us. A half-track is coming after us like a bat out of hell. It could be Hahnemann aboard, but I'm only guessing, of course.'

'How many men?' Macomber was already trying to coax a fraction more speed out of the vehicle.

'Three or four. I couldn't be sure. He's on the flat at the

moment so he'll have to slow down when he starts coming up.' Ford and Grapos twisted round on their benches and saw in the distance the half-track coming towards them at speed. Macomber was watching what appeared to be the crest of the hill they were climbing and beyond it the cloud hid the base of the mountain which must be very close. He would have to out-drive Hahnemann up that devilish road: the snag was he would soon be slowed down by the mist while the German could drive full-tilt up to this point, thus narrowing the gap between them to almost zero. The weather was certainly not their friend at the moment. He drove up steadily, reached the crest, and immediately the road turned and dropped into a dip between dry-stone walls where it turned again. The oxen were massed at the bend.

There were three Greek peasants with the animals which had accumulated at this point, and they were shouting their heads off and flailing the beasts with birches made of slim stems. So far as Macomber could see as he drove down towards them their efforts were only adding to the confusion and the road was well and truly blocked. With the thought of that other half-track tearing towards them, he pulled up his own vehicle inches from the chaos of animals and drovers. 'Sort them out, Grapos! Get them moving and damned quickly! They can shove them on to that bit of grass by the next bend till we get past. Then tell them to block the road again.' He waited while Grapos got out of the vehicle and began shouting at the drovers, who, at first, simply shouted back. An ox rested its horned head on the side of the half-track and stared at Ford with interest. Grapos continued his shouting and gesticulating match with the drovers and Prentice felt his temper going. A minute later the animals were still milling round the vehicle and Grapos was still conducting his verbal war with his countrymen. Something snapped inside Macomber. He stood up, pulled out his Luger and fired it over the heads of men and beasts. The animals panicked and began to trot off down the road, followed by the drovers who penned them into the grassy area while the half-track grumbled past them.

'You told them to block the road again?' Macomber shouted back to Grapos who had resumed his seat on the bench.

'I told them the Germans were coming and they must make them wait.'

Macomber swore violently to himself: the mention of Germans to the drovers would undoubtedly frighten them so much that they would simply keep their animals penned up off the road at that point until the second half-track had passed. They had closed the road to him and they would open it to the others, he felt sure. He had to do something drastic to increase the gap between the two vehicles. The road was straightening out once more as it descended a hill between high earthen banks, so he put his foot down. The half-track built up speed rapidly under the pressure of his foot and he felt a coldness on his face as the road flew away under him. The mist was floating aimlessly and as it drifted to and fro he caught glimpses of the mountain wall rising up like an immense fortress bastion. Here and there pinnacles of rock spurred upwards and then vanished as the mist closed in again. Glancing at the speedometer, he saw that they were moving at the equivalent of fifty miles an hour and he was well aware that only the weight and stability of the racing tracks was holding them on the road. When the mist parted again momentarily he saw a stone bridge at the bottom and the old route came back to him: beyond the bridge the road veered left and then started its fierce climb up the mountain-side. Within only a minute or two he would be reduced to crawling pace as he attempted the first acute bend and the realisation of this fact made him exert a trifle more foot pressure.

Behind him Ford was white-faced with the aftermath of his wound, but Prentice was white-faced at the speed they were travelling. Grapos had sunk to the floor again to wedge himself in against the side of the vehicle and Ford leaned forward briefly, then braced his back against the bench again. The high earthen bank slid past them in a blur, the sound of the pounding tracks confined inside the sunken road was like the noise from a stamping mill and the revolving metal was developing a disconnected sound. The bridge below appeared again, much closer this time, and Macomber relaxed his foot pressure a little. It was at this moment when the left-hand track, unable to bear the strain any longer, slipped its cogwheels, parted company with the vehicle altogether, and skittered past them down the road as an intact ring.

The half-track, supported now by only two wheels and the remaining caterpillar, slewed to the right and crashed against the earthen bank with shattering impact. Foreseeing the collision, Macomber steered to the left, expecting at any second that the massive vehicle would turn over and pin the occupants under its weight. The vehicle bounced smartly off the bank and a flurry of earth minced up by the single revolving track showered over them as he reduced speed, steering to the right as the other bank rushed towards them. But the speed was too great to correct the course again and for a second time they cannoned into the right-hand bank as the spinning track which had freed itself catapulted down the road, hit the bridge wall, bounced over it and vanished.

The second impact of half-track against bank was more brutal than the first and the wheel nearly leapt out of his hands, which would have brought on final disaster, but somehow he maintained his grip as the vehicle shuddered violently, wobbled uncertainly, still holding its equilibrium as more earth burst in the air and rained back over them. He had steered to the left again but there was an agonising, drawn-out moment when it seemed that the surviving track had become trapped as it rotated furiously against the bank. The churning metal rasped over rocks embedded inside the bank, a hellish sound which lasted only seconds but seemed to go on for ever, and then the half-track leapt forward again down the natural gradient while Macomber wrestled desperately to keep control, to lose more speed without tipping them over sideways while the right-angled bridge rushed up to them. At the last moment he avoided colliding with the bank to the left and reduced speed still further, feeling the half-track tipping backwards and sideways under him at the very moment when he realised the brake wasn't working. A slight rise in the road elevated the intact track and their balance was momentarily corrected as he lost more speed and then they began to move faster under the natural momentum of the vehicle so that he knew that they could never hope to negotiate the sharp bend as without hope of success he tried to work the useless brake.

'Jump!' he shouted.

The dry-stone wall of the bridge came straight at him like a moving thing and then met the front of the half-track. Macomber automatically switched off the engine as a jarring sound of collapsing metal hit his ear-drums and the wall disintegrated. The stones tumbled backwards over the edge and the vehicle nose pushed its way through to hang down over the brink; below he had brief sight of rushing water which carried along half-submerged floats of greenish ice. At the moment of impact he had braced himself rigidly and had just prevented his body from being impaled on the wheel, but not without receiving a sharp blow in the chest. Everything blurred as he stood up and turned to see the others dropping through the left-hand doorway which was now canted close to the road surface. The sideways and backward tilt of the wrecked half-track was making it difficult for him to get clear quickly and he had the oddest feeling that he was still moving forward when Prentice shouted from the roadway. 'For God's sake hurry, Mac – the damned thing's on the move again!'

So it wasn't an illusion of his dazed brain – under the impulse of some weird mechanical defect the intact caterpillar was still revolving slowly as it pushed the wrecked vehicle further over the drop. He was scrambling towards the rear aperture when he changed his mind and made his way between two benches to the side. Lifting one leg to climb over, he felt the tilted floor rise under him suddenly as it became level again and the unexpected movement threw him backwards. His head had struck the other side and he lay there half-stunned while the track went on revolving

wearily, sliding the remnants closer and closer to the brink
through the breach in the wall. Vaguely conscious that
Prentice was standing over him, hauling at his shoulders, he
forced his legs to function, dragging himself to his feet and
stumbling forward between the benches again. His hands
clenched the side for support and he saw that the half-track
was already half-way through the breach. Hoisting one leg
over he felt Prentice shove hard and he went over the side
and crashed into the waiting Grapos as Prentice followed
him into the road. He went down on his knees into the road
but Grapos prevented him sprawling and he held on to the
Greek's shoulders to pull himself upright. The rear of the
half-track paused inside the breach as the caterpillar ground
to a halt and then the front weight suspended in mid-air
dragged it down. It fell into the river with a great splash and
when they looked over the battered wall only the tip of the
upended track showed above the surface of the river.

'I'm sorry to see that go,' said Prentice, breathing heavily.
'It means we're back to footslogging again.'

'Where to?' asked Macomber. He was talking in a fuddled
way and leaned against the undamaged section of wall to wait
for his heart-beats to slow down. 'Hahnemann will be up the
road, right behind us soon, and he's not on foot, the road's
useless, why did I lose that vehicle . . .'

'Take it easy,' Prentice began, but the Scot turned on him
and flared up.

'Leave me a minute, can't you? Hahnemann's on the way,
the only way through to Zervos.' Macomber straightened up
from the wall and Prentice watched anxiously as he started
pacing up and down the bridge, stamping his feet hard on the
ground as he thrust his hands deep inside his coat pockets to
help brace himself erect. At one moment he took out the
Luger pistol and reminded them out loud that there were
only six rounds left as though to impress the fact on his own
mind. His large face was whiter than Ford's had been
immediately after the German had shot him, and Prentice
wondered whether, after his immense efforts, the Scot was on

the verge of collapse. But as he paced backwards and forwards, taking in deep breaths of the cold air, the colour came
back into his face and his whole body seemed to stiffen up.
'They'll be here in a minute,' he said suddenly in a harsh
domineering voice, 'so we'd better get off this bridge.'

'Give yourself a bit longer,' Prentice urged, 'it may pay
dividends in the long run.'

Macomber looked at his watch. It was exactly two o'clock
in the afternoon and the silence of the mountain hanging
over them in the mist was like a weight pressing down, a
silence broken only by the gush of the torrent below and the
stamp of his boots on the hard ground. Ford had been sitting
on a pile of rocks but now he, too, started to wander round
the bridge as though spurred into life by the Scot's display of
physical effort. Prentice thought the sergeant was looking
better despite their recent experiences and Grapos, now fully
awake after his sleep in the back of the half-track, looked
ferociously alert as he occasionally slapped the butt of his
rifle and looked with interest up the road they had descended.
He's hoping to have a go at Hahnemann and Co. when they
arrive, he told himself. Macomber was standing in the centre
of the bridge, facing the direction where the enemy would
appear, when he spoke in a normal voice. 'Is there any other
route to the monastery from here, Grapos?'

'There is one other way, yes. I have been thinking of it, but
it is difficult. Very difficult.' He looked dubiously at Ford.
'We would arrive there before the Germans,' he added.

'Even in their half-tracks?'

'They will have trouble with the road because of the ice.
They will come up to Zervos slowly or go over the edge . . .'

He stopped speaking as Macomber turned his head sideways to listen more carefully. There it was – above the gush
of the water he could hear the sound of an approaching
engine, the laboured grind of the caterpillars as another half-
track came cautiously down the road above. Without a word,
Grapos looped his rifle over his shoulder and hurried across
the bridge. For once, and without persuasion, he had decided

that the vital task was to reach Zervos before the Germans if that could possibly be managed. Macomber went after him, followed by Prentice and Ford.

Immediately he had crossed the bridge he turned down a winding path to the right which descended to the bank of the river. A small mill-race had developed round the almost-submerged half-track and they had just reached the bank when they heard Hahnemann's vehicle coming. 'Hurry!' Macomber called out to Grapos in front of him, 'they mustn't see which way we've gone.' He had the hope that if only they could cover enough ground they would vanish inside the mist before the Germans spotted them, but the hope died as they began to ascend close to the mountain wall. The path was paved with worn rocks buried in the earth and they had climbed perhaps a hundred feet when Macomber heard the half-track slow down and then stop with its engine still ticking over.

He looked back and then down the rock-strewn slope which slid away to the river. Prentice and Ford were close behind and already the drifting mist was beginning to fog the silhouette of the bridge below. The half-track was stopped on the bridge near the breach in the wall and there were four passengers who wore the Alpenkorps cap. One of them stood in the breach with his hands on his hips and he was clearly gazing down at the submerged vehicle. So long as they weren't seen, Macomber thought, that tip of wreckage was the perfect alibi: Hahnemann would assume that they had all perished in the accident and that their bodies were now floating in the river on their way to the Aegean. He would have liked to suggest stopping for a short time to avoid any risk of their movements attracting the attention of the Germans below, but they were still uncomfortably within rifle range so he kept quiet and plodded on uphill after Grapos who, despite his limp, was climbing the difficult path with the sure-footedness of a mountain goat. The rifle shot shattered his fresh hopes.

The sound echoed along the mountain wall in a disconcerting manner, ricocheting hollowly from one rock face to another. As Macomber swung round, Grapos turned, raised his rifle, took aim, fired. The Scot doubted whether he had scored a hit since the mist was swirling over the bridge and a moment later the Germans were hidden from view. The main thing was that they had spotted the men on the path and there was little doubt that within a few minutes they would be hurrying up the mountain after them.

'We'll have to move fast now,' he called out to Grapos.

'Why not wait and pot them off?' suggested Prentice. 'It's four against four.'

'Because of that! Listen!'

The halted briefly and the sound of at least two more half-tracks grinding down the hill towards the bridge travelled up to them. From what Macomber had learned about the capacity of these vehicles the reinforcements could be anything up to another twenty men, so flight was the only answer. They followed Grapos along the path which climbed gradually higher and at times, when the mist thinned briefly, Macomber caught sight of a rock wall coming closer from the far side of the river. They were travelling inside a canyon whose walls were drawing closer together. After a few minutes, to his surprise, the path began to descend and the mountain wall on their left receded. What kind of a route to Zervos could possibly be quicker for men on foot as opposed to men aboard tracked vehicles? He had an uneasy feeling that they should have enquired a little more closely about this phantom route of Grapos because now he remembered that on his previous visit the Abbot of the monastery had told him that there was only one way up to Zervos and that was by road.

'Is it like this all the way?' he called out to the Greek whose stocky figure was almost lost in the mist ahead.

'No! You will see!'

They crossed a shale slope where the path had almost vanished and then they began climbing steeply and straight towards the mountain, the loose stones slithering away under their feet so treacherously that several times Macomber looked back to see how Ford was faring. The sergeant was trudging ahead of Prentice and he came steadily upwards, waving his hand once when he saw he was being observed. In spite of the cold dampness which clung to his face, Macomber had a feeling that the sun might soon break through and this bothered him because it would improve the observation of the men he was sure were following them. And they were making far too much noise in an atmosphere where sound could travel long distances. The fall of their feet was a sharp cracking sound on the shale and frequently they disturbed the substance and sent it rattling down the slope. When he looked up again Grapos had halted on an area of level ground and less than a hundred yards behind it the mountain wall reared up vertically.

'We are here,' Grapos announced. 'We will rest and then begin.'

'Begin what?'

Without replying, Grapos waited for Prentice and Ford to join them, and then sat on a flat-topped rock where he could view the slope below with his rifle across his lap. The habit of secrecy which the Greek liked to indulge in had begun to irk Macomber considerably, particularly since his novel ideas for escape routes were more than likely to be hazardous. Near the edge of the platform were several large boulders and Macomber leaned against one of these while he explained to Prentice and Ford that Grapos considered this a suitable moment to rest.

'With Hahnemann and his pals probably close on our heels!' Prentice exploded. 'We ought to keep moving non-stop.'

'Leave him for a minute. I've noticed his obstinate moods don't last for long,' Macomber replied, keeping his voice low. 'And a few minutes' rest might be a good idea – heaven knows what he has in store for us this time.'

'Oh, no! Not another treat like that pipe!'

'He's got something up his sleeve. Haven't you noticed he

chews the end of his moustache when he's feeling very satisfied with himself? He's chewing away like blazes now.'

'Well, let's hope it chokes him. I like to know where we're going and . . .'

'Don't fret,' Macomber suggested mildly. 'The mist's clearing so we may get a chance to see whether Hahnemann really is on our tracks.'

Macomber glanced over his shoulder and saw that the mist was also moving away from the mountain wall which, he could now see, was not the uninterrupted rampart of rock he had taken it for. At one point the towering face was split by a narrow gulch which ran back into a pocket of mist higher up; a slender thread of whiteness showed where a stream spiralled down the gulch on its way to the river below. So that's Grapos' secret entrance, Macomber told himself. If the Jerries are in the vicinity I can't see them missing that unless the mist closes in again. He waited a minute or two longer and then went over to Grapos who scrambled off the boulder as he approached. A long way down the shale slope the mist had dispersed suddenly as the yellowish sun filtered through and by its light he saw three men climbing the path. He ducked back out of sight, wondering whether Grapos had moved off the boulder in time, but he doubted it. His voice was sharp and demanding as he asked the question. 'Quick! Where do we go?'

'We go up – inside the mountain.'

*

Ignoring the narrow gulch, Grapos led them at a slow trot straight for the face of the mountain. As they came closer Macomber saw that several needle-shaped pinnacles rose up out of the ground just in front of the wall, pinnacles which had long ago been left as solitary spires when the softer ground had been eroded away. It was towards one of these pinnacles that Grapos was heading and when Macomber followed him behind the strange edifice the Greek was disappearing through a dark fissure in the mountain face.

Making sure that Prentice and Ford were close, he took out his pocket torch and followed Grapos inside the cavern.

The cold hit him at once, the clammy freezing cold of air trapped underground in a place which never saw the light of day. Walking ahead of Grapos, he shone the torch over a floor of moist rock until the beam was swallowed up by the shadows beyond. Down the centre of the cavern ran a trickle of water confined inside a crevice, and the running water made a quiet bubbling sound which echoed eerily. He shone his torch upwards and the light was lost in more shadows which showed no trace of a roof in sight. 'You really know this way?' he asked Grapos sharply. 'We don't want to find ourselves walking up a dead-end.'

'Dead-end?'

'No way out – a place that doesn't lead anywhere?'

'Then why should we come here?'

'That's what I'm trying to find out, Grapos! If those Germans come up behind us we'd be trapped.'

'No!' Grapos' whiskered face shook vehemently in the torchlight. 'We go up through the mountain. We come out near the monastery. Come!'

Grapos moved deeper into the cavern and Macomber was obliged to follow to light the way. Behind him, Prentice switched on his own torch and swivelled it round unenthusiastically as they felt the floor beginning to slope upwards under their feet. 'You know, Ford, I'm beginning to wonder if this is such a good idea already. I never was one for cathedrals and this place reminds me of a huge underground cathedral.'

'It probably is a good place to say our prayers,' Ford replied non-committally.

As they went deeper inside the mountain the walls of the cavern closed in and appeared on either side of Macomber's torch beam. He had the impression that it was narrowing before it came to an end, and when he flashed the light briefly upwards the ribbed rock of the vault hung over his head, perhaps three feet above. Directing the torch ahead, he saw a rock face which, for one awful moment he thought was solid, and then the light penetrated an aperture like a large doorway and beyond it a tunnel climbed at an angle of about twenty degrees. He paused at the entrance, bringing the single file behind him to a halt with Grapos at his elbow. The tunnel was not quite roofed over: the curving rock failed to join in the centre where a crevasse continued upwards a greater distance than his torch could reach. It looked as though at some time long ago a fault had fractured the interior of the mountain and the presence of the trickle of water which also came down the tunnel floor was partially reassuring: the water probably originated at the top of the mountain so there must be some way in – and therefore some way out. But only partially reassuring since the water might easily be entering the mountain through some cavity no larger than a man's fist.

'You're absolutely sure that you know the way?' he asked the Greek again.

'We go up and up and up. Then we reach the monastery.'

Prentice directed his own torch up the tunnel. 'It's not exactly Aladdin's cave, is it?'

'But then we're not hunting for buried treasure,' Macomber reminded him and began to ascend the tunnel. He found he had to tread carefully because the floor surface was damp and the upward slope didn't make walking any easier. His broad shoulders just missed brushing the rock walls and he had the feeling that the whole weight of the mountain was pressing down on him as the tunnel started to curve to the right. That probably made sense because the road Burckhardt's forces would use went up the mountainside to their left and later turned westward to reach the monastery. And that's one thing we're short of, he was thinking – a compass. The silence inside the mountain was oppressive, the only sounds the shuffle of their feet and the trickling of water. He was aware already of a further drop in temperature sufficient for him to pull up his coat collar and the cold seemed to infiltrate his clothes. This was certainly no place to pause for a breather. They had been climbing steadily for some time when he stopped suddenly, flashing his torch back down the wall on the right. He had very nearly walked past without ever seeing it – another opening in the wall, another tunnel of impenetrable blackness which also sloped upwards.

'You're sure we don't go up that one?' he asked Grapos.

'No – straight up . . .' The Greek pointed confidently ahead while he pulled his rifle more firmly over his shoulder.

'This I don't like,' Prentice called out from behind Ford. 'How the hell can you be so sure? Look, if we get so far and we can't get any further, we could get lost on the way down again if we took the wrong turning here.' He pulled out a notebook, told Ford to hold his torch, and scribbled something in it. 'I'm going to make a rough chart of this place, then we can't go wrong.'

'The side tunnel goes up,' Macomber pointed out. 'We'd know we had to keep on down . . .'

'I'm still keeping a record,' Prentice replied obstinately. 'This isn't the sort of place where you can stop and ask someone the way.'

They went on climbing and the tunnel widened, but still curved to the right, towards the west. It was becoming extremely cold and there seemed to be less air, or possibly the air was more rarefied. Macomber was experiencing a slight dizzy sensation as he trudged upwards, and frequently he had to rub the window of his torch to wipe away condensation. If the Greek was leading them into a dead-end it was going to be a hellish long way back. He held the torch at a lower angle to see where he was putting his feet because the tunnel floor was no longer smooth rock; at intervals it was littered with loose stones which shifted under his tread. He was trying to decide what had altered in the sounds they were making when Prentice called out urgently.

'Look! Another side tunnel!'

This one, Macomber had to agree, was a more dangerous proposition: it ran off from the left-hand wall and, when viewed from above, there could easily be confusion as to which was the right route if they had to descend again. The side tunnel also sloped downwards, so its direction of incline would be no guide. He waited while the lieutenant wrote in his notebook, extracted his case, found that he had only two cigars left and decided to hoard them for later.

'We could have missed more tunnels on that side,' Prentice warned. 'It begins to look as though the whole damned place is one huge honeycomb – and it beats me how Grapos can be so sure we're going the right way.'

'We go up . . .' began the Greek.

'Yes, I know,' Macomber interrupted him brusquely. 'We go up and up and then get out at the top. It's as simple as that, so let's get on with it.' He started climbing again, then stopped to call down to Prentice. 'You're at the rear, so you watch for tunnels on the left and I'll keep a sharp eye on the right-hand wall.' The lieutenant had a point, he thought, as he went on climbing; they could have missed a few side tunnels on the way up, especially after the tunnel they were ascending had widened, which raised two interesting possibilities. If they did have to retrace their steps they might well be confronted with a junction of a side passage with the main tunnel where they couldn't be sure which was the right course to take. The second, even more alarming possibility, was the question whether Grapos could really know his way clear through the mountain under such conditions. He had only climbed a few more steps before his torch shone on a new passage leading away through the rock wall. He waited while Prentice recorded its existence and then resumed his climb.

A few minutes later he had to wait again as Prentice called out that he had found another one on the left. He looked at Grapos, who merely nodded his head in an upwards direction. As they waited, Macomber realised why the sounds inside the tunnel had changed; rather than a change it was the absence of a sound, the sound of trickling water. He shone his torch down on the crevice which now ran close to the left-hand wall and a reflection of the light gleamed dully.

He put his foot over the crevice, felt the sole slide, and pressed hard. The trickle was solid ice.

Only a short distance beyond this point the tunnel began to widen as Macomber changed the torch to his left hand and flexed his fingers to get the circulation moving again. Because the temperature had been dropping gradually as they ascended he hadn't realised how the cold was creeping into his body, but now his hand was dead from holding the torch and he had the odd feeling that everything – his pace, his reflexes, his thinking processes – was slowing down. It was taking too much effort to move his limbs, to lift his legs as he went on climbing, and his feet were like leaden weights. The sudden realisation of their lethargic state frightened him as he dimly understood the effect of the insidiously penetrating cold. Prentice's call from the rear confirmed his worst suspicions. 'What say we rest for a bit?'

'No!' Macomber's reaction was violent. He swung round and beamed the torch down the tunnel. 'We keep moving, do you hear? Keep moving until we're out of the mountain!'

'All right. Keep your shirt on.'

Prentice's protest was feeble and he spoke wearily as though he hardly cared whether he argued or not. But it was by the light of the beam that Macomber saw how far gone they were. Ford was standing limply with sagging shoulders and his face had a glazed expression, while behind him Prentice blinked in the light, pouchy-eyed and with his face drawn and haggard. He mumbled something about getting that damned light out of his eyes and then the beam was switched to Grapos. The Greek showed less signs of wear but Macomber thought his eyes moved less alertly and some of the aggression seemed to have gone out of his personality. Turning away, the Scot forced himself to climb a little faster in the hope of forcing the others to exertion which might revive them a little. In less than a minute they were inside the cavern.

'God! What a place!' Prentice mouthed the words as

Macomber swivelled the torch. The light travelled slowly, passing over rugged walls of dark rock twisted and contorted by some ancient upheaval, or weathered to this primeval state by the passage of thousands of years, rock coated with a white glitter which might have been frost. Walking across to the nearest wall, Prentice ran a finger over it and saw the whiteness dissolve. From the roof of the cavern long luminous daggers were suspended, glacial daggers which could have been stalactites had they been larger, but which were icicles without any sign of dripping at their extremities – a clear indication of the intense sub-zero temperatures inside the huge cavern. Macomber had noticed the slowness of Prentice's movements as he had walked over to the wall, had observed that Ford and Grapos were standing like statues as though they were dreaming. At the back of his mind a warning bell rang faintly while the pain behind his eyes and under his cheekbones grew stronger, a deadening ache which was a symptom of the lethal numbing process sapping their will-power. His feet felt attached to the floor and he had an almost irresistible urge to rest for a while, for just a few minutes . . .

Summoning up a last spark of resistance, he began stamping his frozen feet hard and the ground crackled where a layer of ice was forming over the cavern's floor. The others were ignoring him as they stared lifelessly round the walls and no one took any interest when he flashed his torch towards the rear and saw a continuation of the tunnel curving away to the left. A change of direction. But what roused Macomber to drastic action was the sight of Ford sinking wearily to a sitting position on a patch of ice. Prentice drifted towards him, but whether he was going to join the sergeant or to warn him, the Scot had no idea. This final indication of surrender galvanised him into action. He took two steps forward and kicked Ford in the side.

'Get on your feet, man! Go on, get up and get moving! Or have all the guts run out of you?'

'What the hell are you . . .' Prentice turned on the Scot

dangerously, but he was cut short by a blistering stream of abuse.

'What kind of soldiers do you think you are? You've got the guts of a hyena. Do you think the Alpenkorps would give up in these conditions . . .'

'Who said a bloody word about giving up?' stormed Prentice.

'You did – the lot of you – with your attitude! Can we have a rest, please? You were whining away back there in the tunnel and now your precious sergeant thinks it's time to give up the ghost just because he's a bit cold. And you let him! You're his officer and you let him get away with it! You're not fit to command mules, let alone men . . .'

'When you've quite finished,' Prentice broke in savagely as Ford clambered to his feet.

'Finished! You're the ones who are finished! What guts you ever had you've left behind in the tunnel. You're dead on your feet, Prentice, and in a place like this that means you're dead! The lot of you. That Greek peasant hasn't enough grit left to pull his rifle trigger if he saw a German coming up the tunnel now . . .'

'You believe that?' Grapos had slipped the rifle from his shoulder and was holding it diagonally across the front of his body. His eyes glittered as he stared at Macomber and for a long moment Prentice thought there was going to be a tragedy inside the cavern. Macomber was standing fully erect now, his head thrust forward so that he was the very image of the man they had known as Dietrich.

'That's better,' he told Grapos brutally. 'And you want to keep that rifle where you can use it. Now, come on!' Without waiting for their reaction he turned away and headed for the next section of the tunnel. He was close to the entrance when, in his haste, he slipped on the ice. He had the devil of a job recovering his balance, but he managed it, and in the glimpse he had back into the cavern he saw the others moving towards him in single file. Grapos was grinning at his near-accident. That's better, he thought, as he plunged inside the tunnel, they've woken up now – there's nothing like a little hatred to stir men's blood. With a bit of encouragement they'll hate my guts until we're out of this and that should keep us going.

He felt better himself for his outburst and the pain in his head and face was less bothersome. As Grapos had said, they must keep going, up and up and up. He climbed the tunnel as rapidly as he could force his legs to move and when he looked back the others, urged on by their bitter resentment at the man in the lead, were close behind him. It was only a short time later that the suspicion that they were being followed, that the German patrol might be close behind them, struck him like a blow in the chest.

*

They hadn't come to a halt quickly enough for Macomber's liking, and when they listened they heard nothing. No sound disturbed the tomb-like silence of the mountain now that the water trickle was frozen, but the silence itself was almost a sound. 'Hear anything just now?' he asked in a whisper.

'No.' Grapos looked at him searchingly. 'But you did?'

'I thought so.' He stared at Prentice who was watching him over Ford's shoulder. 'What about you? You were furthest back – did you hear anything?'

'No, but I've gone a bit deaf – it must be the altitude or being inside this place. You're sure you're not imagining things? It must be a good place for that.'

'I don't think so. I thought I heard a rattling sound – like a machine-pistol falling on the rock. Someone else could have slipped on that ice.'

'We'd better keep moving then – you can step up the pace if you like. All right, Ford?'

'I'll keep up with him, don't worry!' There was a vehemence in Ford's voice, a fresh vigour in Prentice's, which Macomber found heartening, but his manner was still overbearing when he spoke again.

'We'll go up a bit higher. I'm going to hold up my hand so

you can see it – when I drop it, stop instantly, and this time I mean instantly.'

The tunnel was winding as it climbed now, and the fissure over their heads had closed when they entered the cavern below, so they were completely sealed inside this section. Macomber thought the gradient was less steep, but the ice was more prevalent and here it coated the walls so that the torch beam reflected back in a greenish glow and their distorted shapes were vaguely mirrored on the curved walls. He dropped his hand suddenly and they all stopped at once, Prentice in mid-stride. The distant sound came weirdly but clearly up through the mountain from behind and then stopped after a few seconds – the distinctive sound of heavily-nailed boots clumping upwards.

Macomber smiled grimly and nodded to Prentice. Then he waited. It was Hahnemann with his patrol, all right, but how far back were they? It was impossible to estimate distance by the degree of sound inside a natural echo chamber like this. But they couldn't be all that far behind – he felt pretty sure that the deep-freeze cavern would swallow up noise from the tunnel beyond it. So they had probably just entered this same tunnel. And Hahnemann knew that his target was ahead of him because he had halted his patrol the moment the sounds above him had stopped. And he was still waiting, somewhere further down the tunnel. Macomber fancied that he could see the German lieutenant standing quite still, his head cocked to one side, just as he himself was standing, while two opposing minds tried to work out the next move. He was tempted to wait in the hope that the German would lose patience and continue his climb up the tunnel, but Hahnemann would be too fly for that. Somehow they had to evade them or wipe them out. Macomber could have wished for one of those side passages now which would have made a useful ambush point, but he had no idea how many men might be trailing up behind them. There had been at least two more half-tracks coming down the hill. They had seen only three men advancing up the shale slope but the mist could have concealed any number of reinforcements. Ford and Prentice were bunched close to the Greek when Macomber bent his head and whispered very softly, 'Do you think we can get out and leave them behind?'

'It will be difficult. I think not.'

'Why?'

'The way out is difficult.'

Macomber bent his face closer. 'Grapos, what is this way out? I want to know. Now, this very minute! We haven't time for any more of your vagaries.'

'There is a hole.' Grapos ran both hands up and down close to each other.

'What sort of a hole?' He had an inspiration. 'Look, suppose you're coming into the mountain from the top – what's it like? Try to describe it to me. Is the end of the tunnel just under it? Stop shaking your head, man, and tell me.'

Grapos thought hard and during the time there was no sound from the tunnel below. Hahnemann was waiting for them to move up so that the sound of their footsteps would muffle his own progress. 'Over a long time,' Grapos began, 'the rain makes holes in some rocks. The hole is made deeper by little stones and they make it very deep and wide until a man can go down . . .'

'Pothole,' said Prentice. 'God! That's all we needed.'

Macomber was taken aback. He had assumed that the tunnels eventually led up to some crevasse in the mountain's surface which they could scramble up. This sounded disastrous, quite disastrous. The reaction must have shown in his face because the Greek spoke again reassuringly. 'I have climbed down. I have climbed up. Both ways.'

'When did you last do either – go up or down?' Prentice asked casually.

'Nineteen-twenty. When they said I was no good as monk.

'Twenty years ago!' Prentice whistled soundlessly through his teeth and purposely looked at the tunnel wall. He felt as though he could have hit the Greek. Macomber's face was like stone. He knew a little about potholes. A friend of his had potholed and he remembered his explaining that sometimes they disappeared over a period of years; if a storm sent a cascade of water down a hillside it could carry a rock inside a pothole, a rock which might become jammed inside. Later sediment would pour down and accumulate round the rock until the hole was firmly plugged. A development which might easily have taken place over twenty years, he thought. It was clear now that Grapos had known the inside of the mountain as a youth and hadn't tried the hazardous route since. He looked at the Greek who was staring down at the ground as though working something out. When he looked up again, Grapos was smiling devilishly. 'We can do something with the Germans! Go up!' He gestured confidently up the tunnel and without a word Macomber began climbing again. There had been too much whispering already and he could only hope that Grapos, with his native cunning, had devised an idea that would work.

The floor of the tunnel was sloping more shallowly and soon it became level as it went on twisting round corners like a mine shaft hollowed out by drunken men. The bitterly cold air was bringing on the pain again and he was having difficulty in breathing as it took hold of his lungs. Once, he stumbled and had to reach out a hand to the wall for support. The ice-coated rock was slippery and he withdrew his hand quickly. He was almost inside the rock chamber before he realised that the air was moving, a slow ice-cold draught which made his eyes water. But moving air meant they were somewhere near the exit.

'Stand there! Don't move!'

Grapos held Macomber's arm and the Scot played his torch over a chamber which was much smaller than either of the two caverns they had passed through previously. The roof hung only a few feet above his head and was canted lower towards the left. The floor was covered with snow and a thin crust had formed where it was beginning to freeze solid. Something ethereal drifted through the torch beam and a second later another snowflake floated down inside the chamber. Macomber tilted the light and it shone upwards inside a dark funnel which ascended vertically and then vanished round a bend. The exit. The mouth of the chimney opened at a point where the roof was no more than five feet above the floor. Grapos had been right – they were nicely trapped. Clambering up inside the chimney was not likely to be a speedy process and the Germans would undoubtedly arrive before the last man was clear. They could then fire point-blank up the funnel at whoever was still in sight. Prentice peered over his shoulder as he spoke. 'How far up there, Grapos?'

'Not far.'

'I know. Just four or five hundred feet. Shin up it in a couple of minutes.'

'We must hurry,' said the Greek, ignoring Prentice's thrust. 'They will be here soon. Shine the torch to the hole.'

Macomber was elevating the torch again, but Grapos had meant something else and he grasped Macomber's arm and guided the light to the far side of the chamber. Macomber saw another tunnel opening, an end to the snow, and a thin shadow of blackness between the rim of the crusted snow and the entrance beyond. 'We go that way?' he asked. Grapos shook his head and took out a cartridge from his pocket. He threw the missile carelessly and it just missed the edge of the snow, landing beyond it in the shadowed area. Macomber waited for the clatter of its impact on the rock floor beyond and heard nothing, nothing at all. The shadow was a crevasse of enormous depth. He shivered inwardly as he thought that he might have walked across the snow to the tunnel entrance. 'Now,' said Grapos, 'we hide and wait.'

'We may as well shoot it out here,' snapped Prentice. 'Then we'll know they're not on our tails.'

'We don't know how many of them . . .' Macomber began, but Grapos interrupted him excitedly.

'Please!' This time he looked to Macomber for support. 'There is another way. No shooting – there may be falls.'

'I think he means landslides,' Macomber explained quickly. 'He's frightened that the reverberation of shots might start something off. It could block the chimney and then we're finished.'

'What other way?' Prentice demanded sceptically.

'Please! You hide. Over there.' He began taking careful steps towards the precipice and then looked back. 'You must keep on the light for me. Please!' He was taking careful steps in the snow now as though he expected it to collapse under him at any moment. His prominent footprints traced a clear path towards the shadowed area. When he was close to the edge of the snow Macomber held his breath: if he overdid it by only a few inches . . . Taking his weight on one leg, Grapos delicately impressed a final footprint in the snow close to the brink, then he retreated, stepping back inside the prints he had already made. Had he carried out a similar stratagem years ago when the police had been after him for some minor misdemeanour, Macomber wondered, tracing his steps in the snow over some field and then retracing them as he had done just now? He had the feeling that this was not the first time Grapos had played this trick, although this time its purpose was truly lethal. To increase the illusion that they had crossed the snow and gone inside the tunnel he took off his Alpenkorps cap and threw it. The cap landed close to the final footprint.

There was no natural hiding-place as Grapos had confidently indicated, but they were able to huddle themselves inside a shallow rock alcove in the right-hand wall of the chamber. Macomber had expected Grapos to join them and he was alarmed to see the Greek hauling himself up inside the chimney mouth with the rifle looped over his shoulder. Which wasn't a good idea because the Germans might easily spot him there. Prentice had another valid objection. 'If we're not damned careful,' he whispered, 'we'll be shooting at each other. He's parked himself directly opposite us.'

'I hope there won't be any shooting,' Macomber told him. 'Grapos is genuinely frightened of a landslide and he's lived in this part of the world all his life. You're not keen on being buried alive, I take it?'

'I'm not keen on being buried in any way.'

The knowledgeable Ford cleared his throat quietly. 'I have heard that in some areas the slightest vibration has been enough to start off a landslide.'

Macomber settled down to a long wait. He had switched off the torch and the chamber was in darkness with not a trace of daylight filtering through from the chimney. He glanced at his watch and the illuminated hands registered 2.57 p.m. The glance reminded him of a risk he had overlooked and he took off the watch and put it inside his pocket. He had just completed this precaution when he heard them coming.

The light he had expected, because they had to have some form of illumination to bring them so high up inside the mountain, but the lack of sound in their approach and their prompt arrival startled him. He could hear no more than a faint padding sound instead of the rasp of nailed boots on rock which he had anticipated. Had they removed their footgear to facilitate a silent approach? It seemed impossible, considering the low temperature. And because of the freezing conditions under which they waited he almost welcomed the early end to their suspense; whatever happened now they would escape drifting off into the sleep of death which was the most terrible hazard in sub-zero temperatures.

He was close enough to Prentice to feel the lieutenant tense as the strange, sinister padding sound came closer and closer. It was almost like the cautious approach of a hostile animal which scents danger. The light grew stronger as it penetrated deeper inside the chamber, a beam more powerful than that thrown by a hand torch, which increased enormously the chance that they would be seen. Macomber thought he understood now why the Germans had trailed behind them when they were coming up inside the mountain: before entering the lowest cavern Hahnemann had sent back for some form of illumination. The padding sound stopped suddenly as the beam continued to shine inside the chamber. He heard the intake of Ford's breath, felt something hard brush his sleeve. The sergeant had elevated his machine-pistol. The nerve-wracking silence continued as muscles stayed rigid and feet rejected the impulse to shift into a more comfortable stance. What the devil were the Germans waiting for? Had Hahnemann sensed the danger of an ambush? If so, why was the light still beamed steadily through the entrance? Macomber was leaning against the cold rock wall and he could feel the iciness seeping through his clothes without daring to move: the silence was so complete that even the faintest sound – the scrape of leather over rock, the creak of a shoe – would confirm the patrol's suspicions. He could imagine them standing there, waiting a few yards down the tunnel, rifles at the ready, bayonets in scabbards at their sides, grenades dangling from their belts . . . God, he'd forgotten that! If one of the patrol hurled a grenade and it detonated inside the cavern! Grapos had been worried enough about a few rifle shots – but the detonation of a grenade . . .

The more Macomber considered the possibility the greater seemed its likelihood. If Hahnemann became convinced that they were waiting for him there was one unbeatable tactic he could adopt – retreat a short way back down the tunnel and throw several grenades inside the cavern. The explosive power of two or three German grenades inside the rock walls of the small chamber would be devastating. Grapos' supposed bear-trap for the patrol would turn into a death-trap for those already waiting in the cavern. Straining his ears, he listened for the slightest hint of any sound – a footfall on rock, the scratch of a button against the tunnel wall, the unguarded clearing of a throat. But he heard only the endless silence which baffled and frightened him. He wished desperately to warn Prentice and Ford of what might be coming, but there was no way of indicating the danger to them. And for how long could Grapos hang suspended inside that chimney without changing position? He was holding the Luger motionless in his right hand and nearly dropped it when light flooded the chamber.

Hahnemann himself was holding the powerful lamp which brought up a dazzling light from the snow, but it also threw massive shadows which concealed parts of the chamber. The three hidden men stood at the edge of one of these shadows, so that it would take only the merest twitch of the German's wrist to illuminate them. Close behind the lieutenant an Alpenkorps soldier waited with a machine-pistol at waist level, still looped over his shoulder to steady it, and the muzzle was aimed across the chamber where the light shone on the tunnel entrance. The boots of both men were muffled by scarves tied round them. The beam dropped, showing up more clearly the footprints and the cap Macomber had thrown, and was then raised again to shine a short distance inside the tunnel beyond the snow. A third Alpenkorps man appeared at the shoulder of the second as Macomber felt the first throat tickles which warned him of the coming sneeze.

'Stay exactly where you are – we may hear something yet.'

Hahnemann had spoken quietly but Macomber heard the words clearly, and he had also seen the brief inclination of the lieutenant's head as though he were going to glance to his right and had then changed his mind at the last moment. As if to concentrate his hearing powers, Hahnemann turned out the lamp and they were once more plunged into darkness, a darkness which seemed temporarily blinded by the glare of the lamp. Macomber was still leant against the wall, his back slowly congealing into a block of ice as he grappled with two problems. The impulse to sneeze and that brief inclination of the German's head before the lamp went out. He used the fingers of his left hand to squeeze his nostrils tight while he breathed through his half-open mouth, swallowing several times to make liquid which might ease the tickling sensation. His eyes watered with the effort and now his whole throat was contracting as it became one vast irritation He let go of his nostrils and grabbed at his throat, squeezing and massaging it roughly. The irritation remained but the desire to sneeze was temporarily quenched. He couldn't make up his mind how long the process of quieting himself down had taken and this also worried him. Had Hahnemann caught sight of them out of the corner of his eye, instinctively started to turn his head, and then stopped himself in time? He went over the sequence of events again.

The German had inclined his head a little. A moment later he had spoken. 'Stay exactly where you are – we may hear something yet.' Then the lamp had gone out. It seemed terrifyingly obvious now. He had spotted them. He had had the presence of mind not to show it. The clever swine had manoeuvred things so that he could re-position his men. A gentle tug on the sleeve in the dark would move each man into the correct place, and the muffled feet would help them to do it soundlessly if they took great care and had a little luck. What next? Macomber thought he knew the answer to that one – a concentrated burst of machine-pistol fire sprayed over the right-hand chamber wall. Or he might use the grenades. Macomber felt himself checkmated, fatally out-manoeuvred. This was the penalty for trying to out-guess trained soldiers: Prentice had been right – they should have attempted to set up an ambush.

The lamp came on again so unexpectedly that he was momentarily blinded even though it was aimed across the chamber and up the tunnel. Hahnemann's voice was crisp and confident. 'They must have moved faster – we'll have to hurry! Hans, keep close behind and have your machine-pistol ready. When we overtake them I'll dodge to the left – to the left, remember – and you empty your magazine.' He led the way into the chamber, marching across the snow with a soldier at his heels while the third man followed a little further behind. Then, half-way across the snow, he stopped, and Macomber, his body locked rigid, watched the German beam his lamp further along the tunnel, raising it high so he could see as far up the sloping passage as possible. Something caught his attention and he gave the impression that he was uncertain as to whether to proceed in this direction. The soldiers behind him had also halted and one of them was looking towards where Grapos still hung suspended inside the chimney, but he was peering into a shadow and his own night vision must still be affected by the light blaze. The Luger in Macomber's hand felt like an iron weight and his throat was becoming horribly irritable as he refrained from even swallowing, pressing his teeth together in a final attempt to keep himself under control. Then Hahnemann walked forward.

He was near the tunnel entrance with the Alpenkorps soldier close behind when the lamp he held swerved violently, briefly shining directly upwards on the roof. The lamp swerved again and Hahnemann cried out as he plunged forward, feeling the ground melt under him. He half-saved himself by turning as the rearmost soldier switched on his own lamp, and he still had one foot on the edge of the abyss as his hand shot out and grabbed the shoulder of the man behind him. By the light of the second lamp Macomber saw a flurry of legs and a topple of shadows on the wall as the two Germans struggled to regain balance, one of them shouting as they keeled over, a shout which was swallowed up inside the abyss as they sheered down out of sight. The surviving German stood perfectly still a foot away from where the edge of the snow had a crumpled, ragged look. He was still standing in this petrified state, holding the lamp beamed downwards, calling out 'Hans!' in a voice which clearly expected no answer, when Grapos dropped down out of the chimney. He came up off the snow with his rifle extended like a lance as the German began turning and lunged it forward viciously. The muzzle caught the soldier in the side with all Grapos' strength behind it. The German let out a choked yelp, slipped on the snow and then followed his lamp into the chasm.

Why was there no more snow drifting down through the chimney? It was a question which never left Macomber as he continued the treacherous ascent up the first leg of the ice-coated funnel. When they first entered the chamber below they had seen snow-flakes floating down from the mouth of the chimney, but he could not recall having seen any further sign that somewhere in the world above it was snowing. The obvious explanation was that it had stopped snowing, but Macomber was less than ever inclined to accept the easy answer. Since their escape from Katyra bad luck had hounded them: they had run into a German patrol; the half-track had been destroyed at the very moment when they needed it most; and Hahnemann had found his way inside the mountain. Macomber saw no reason to assume that their bad luck had run its course – on the contrary, he could not shake off the feeling that it was mounting to a crescendo.

'All right up there?' Prentice called out from the bowels of the earth, or so it seemed as his voice spiralled eerily up the chimney.

'Not more than another couple of miles,' Macomber shouted back.

'If you get stuck, send us a telegram.'

'If that happens I'll send down a rock,' Macomber growled.

Close below him Ford waited while he fractured more ice off the walls with the butt of his Luger. It was a thin layer of ice which responded quickly to his hammering by flaking off and rattling down the slope of the wall – a minor hazard for those beneath who simply kept their heads down when they heard him thumping. But it took extra time and he was not at all happy about the freezing temperature which still persisted inside the funnel. Once the varnish of ice was removed there were footholds and toeholds which could be used – crevices in the rugged surface which alone made it possible to ascend the curving funnel. The narrow diameter of the hole was claustrophobic, giving a greater feeling of being sealed inside the mountain than they had experienced before, but here again it was helpful. With a firm foothold he was able to lean back against the other side of the funnel to give him a safer balance, but this involved chipping away the ice from two sides before he dare proceed higher. So the ascent was not insuperably difficult, but it was painstaking and dangerous: if he failed to remove all the ice from a ledge and then used it as a foothold, there was a grave risk that he would slip, go down, crash into the next man below, unhinge Ford from his perch, and cause a chain reaction of disaster sending them perhaps twenty feet to the floor of the chamber below. And the disaster could have a sting in its tail – they would land on the slippery snow only a few paces from the brink of the abyss.

'Any sign of daylight yet?' Prentice called up. He was bringing up the rear, climbing below Grapos who had relapsed into a sullen mood when Macomber had refused to let him lead the ascent. The Greek knew the way but he was impetuous.

'Too early yet. Keep your heads down!' Macomber attacked the next deposit of ice above his head. He had phrased that reply carefully since there was no point in lowering morale until he knew the worst. His great fear was that there had been some recent blockage which would account for the lack of falling snow; possibly one of Grapos' landslides which might have closed over the exit. Pressing his back against the wall behind him, he shifted his right foot to a ledge higher up and a moment later the other foot slid free of its crevice and he began to drop out of control. He stiffened his back and felt that begin to slither downwards over a patch of hard ice. He was going straight down. Instinctively knowing that only his back could save him, he pressed harder and the ice under his shoulder-blades cracked, but now it was meeting a fresh layer and he felt his back swivelling round inside the tunnel like the turning of a cork in a bottle. Then the left shoulder-blade met a protruding spur of rock which served as a wedge as it bit deep into his coat. The sudden pain made him grunt but he had stopped sliding.

'All right, Mac?' Prentice called up anxiously. He had seen the erratic swivel of the torch Macomber held in his left hand.

'Give me a minute,' Macomber growled.

The sickness welled and he forced it back. He had an awful conviction that the pain was going to make him faint – the pain in his shoulder-blade and his right foot which was still trapped in the ledge above and turned at an unnatural angle. While the foot remained firmly lodged inside the upper ledge his body had rotated through an angle of between ten and twenty degrees and he was praying to God that the ankle wasn't broken. To overcome the waves of dizziness rolling over his brain he started moving, locating by the light of his torch a secure hold for the left foot and then exerting his back and his hands to return himself round the funnel to a position where he could release the trapped right foot. The torch was now tucked back inside his coat pocket so he couldn't see what he was doing until Prentice shone his own light up the funnel, a feeble illumination because the lieutenant was part way beyond the curve of the chimney below. And that was another thing – what he had taken to be a short bend was developing into a continuous curve.

He reached a position of stability where he could draw his right boot clear of the ledge. It hung in space while he fumbled for his torch and a few seconds' relief was succeeded by a stabbing pain in the ankle. With his torch lit again, he worked the suspended foot and found that it moved – that he was able to lift and drop it again. When he had it settled inside a convenient ledge the pain stabbed again. This was going to be tricky. 'I'm still in one piece,' he called out and then started thudding the pistol butt into the ice above. From now on he attacked the ice more viciously, flailing at large areas before he attempted a fresh ascent, and he found that this reduced the danger of slipping even though it showered a rain of broken crystals on the men waiting patiently below. It couldn't be helped; it was the only way he could hope to make it. The narrowing of the funnel brought on his next fear.

The curve of the chimney was levelling out and his torch was showing a small platform of rock beyond when he felt the chimney wall pressing against his shoulders on both sides. He had a momentary spasm of panic – he wouldn't be able to squeeze through. Probably because of his extreme state of fatigue it was his worst moment since they had entered the mountain – the thought that when they were so close to the exit his own girth would make it impossible for him to escape. Pushing the hideous thought to the back of his mind, he took a deep breath and heaved savagely upwards. His body travelled a short distance and then became completely jammed inside the narrow opening, his face barely a foot away from the rock platform which was covered in snow. He swore viciously. He was stuck with his arms above the encircling collar of the funnel, his shoulders trapped by the collar, and with only one foot resting on a ledge below – held like a cork rammed inside the neck of a bottle. A tremble of pure fear addled his brain and he had a crazy urge to start screaming his head off. The reaction so shocked him that he clamped his teeth together and made no further effort while he fought to bring himself back to normal. To hell with those below – they'd have to wait. He was plugging the chimney anyway.

The margin for escape he needed was very little, perhaps only the cloth thickness of his heavy coat. Crossing his arms, he used the fingers of opposite hands to try and squeeze up the shoulder padding clear of the tunnel. The torch he had laid on the snow and it remained on the crusted surface. God, it was cold! Yet he was bathed in sweat with his exertions or with the spasm of fear. Taking another deep breath, he heaved his body upwards and stayed fast, caught tighter than ever. The rock had a constricting, crushing feel which blotted out the pain in his shoulder-blade and ankle and he couldn't suppress the idea that he was permanently trapped. He thought someone was calling out to him from below but his body muffled the sound and he had an illogical urge to shout back at them for God's sake, wait! He breathed deeply again, but this time without trying to loosen himself, concentrating on asserting his will-power. The fresh air was helping, air so cold that it seemed like liquid ice, but it was a wonderful reviver. He had been like an animal caught in a trap which threshes wildly about without using its cunning. And when he did get loose he'd need every ounce of strength he could muster to lead the way up the next shaft. At least he was now considering the possibility of getting loose. He began to wriggle gently instead of forcing his way up through sheer rock, shifting his muscles in different directions like a man slipping a wrist through a handcuff. When he hoisted himself again cautiously he found he was free.

He crawled on to the snow-covered platform like a dog on all fours, feeling the crunch of the substance under his knees, and then he gazed up the shaft which wasn't there. He was inside a small pit of rock with the rim no more than five feet above him, looking up at grey swollen clouds which were so low they might have been barely a tree's height away. They had made it. They had emerged from the mountain. He was clambering to his feet, eager to see what lay beyond the rim, when the snow began to fall, heavy, slow-moving flakes which coated his shoulders as he rested his hands on the rock edge and looked over the top.

They had emerged into a pocket of wilderness at high altitude. Prentice's heart sank as he stood beside Macomber a few yards beyond the rim of the pit, a depression which swiftly overtook his mood of temporary exhilaration at coming out of the mountain alive. They were standing in a natural basin and the snow-covered slopes swept up above them on all sides, slopes now roofed in by the cloud ceiling which drifted over the surrounding ridges and filtered smokily down towards the four men, so that the lieutenant had the impression of being inside a cauldron, a cauldron which bubbled at the edges. There was something majestic and frightening about the seething sky which might at any moment roll down inside the basin and smother them, and he had a feeling that they might be the only four men left on the face of the earth. It began snowing more heavily, forming a white cap on Macomber's bare head, when Prentice asked the question. 'Where the devil is it, Grapos?'

'Where is what?'

Prentice exploded. 'The monastery, Mount Zervos, the lake – everything you described to us earlier.'

'Over there.' The Greek waved a hand beyond the pit, beyond the ridge which had disappeared, beyond the clouds so far as Prentice could make out.

'How far?' he asked tersely.

'Not far . . .'

'How far is not far?' Prentice had seized the Greek's arm as his temper snapped at his eternal vagueness. 'Half a kilometre, one, two?'

'Two, maybe three.'

'God! I thought you said we came out of the mountain and we were there! You gave us the impression your ruddy hole was perched on its doorstep . . .' He stopped as he heard Macomber swear briefly under his breath. In German. This had happened before – and quite recently – when the Scot had been climbing the chimney. The subconscious relapse into the German language was beginning to worry Prentice and for the first time since they had reached the plateau suspicion stirred at the back of his mind. 'You even think in German, don't you?' he said lightly.

'When you're impersonating another race you have to do exactly that if you're going to have a dog's chance in hell of getting away with it.' He wiped snow off his head and then brushed his hands. 'I remember I did the same thing when we were leaving Istanbul – I'd got myself so much into the way of thinking I was German that I made an uncomplimentary comparison between the Turkish port and Hamburg. And that was thinking to myself, not saying it out loud . . .'

Again he's half-convinced me, Prentice thought, but only half. The large brown eyes stared back at him as though endeavouring to read his mind, the Scot's left shoulder sagging as he took the weight off his injured right ankle. While they had rested inside the pit to recover a little strength a conversation had taken place which kept running through Prentice's brain. Macomber, with his back rested against the pit wall as he sat on the snow, had lit one of his remaining cigars while Prentice checked his ankle. 'I can't feel anything broken,' he had reported, 'but it's swelling up.'

'I can stand on it, so I can walk,' Macomber had replied roughly. 'But we're likely to have two limping men on this trip from now on. And before I forget, I think I'll ditch this.' He had balanced the Luger in his hand. 'I can't say I'm too keen on firing this after what it's been through down there.' When he lobbed it back inside the chimney they had heard its clattering passage down the interior of the funnel.

'You may need that yet,' Ford remarked. 'Now you've left yourself with only your fists.'

'Think so?' Macomber produced another Luger from his other pocket. 'In the Balkans I found it useful to keep one in the bedroom and the other in the kitchen. The two places an assassin thinks he can catch you off-balance. It stands to reason, I suppose – when you're in bed or bent over the stove. A Polish underground chap told me that. And Burckhardt never tumbled to the fact that I was carrying two pistols. Fortunately. When he found someone had put a bullet in his other wireless-set during the landing he asked to see my gun – and Hahnemann's, because he spoke English – so I showed him the one that's just gone down the hole.' He indicated the pistol he was holding before he put it away. 'This one did the job.'

'You took a chance there.'

'No, I gave myself a chance. As soon as Burckhardt opened up communication with his G.H.Q. I knew I was done for. It's simply a question of calculating the odds.' He watched Prentice over his cigar smoke, his eyes very alert. 'You two just happened to be aboard the *Hydra* during this particular trip?'

'I've told you before we were.'

'So you did.' Macomber had laughed shortly. 'I'll have to take a course of Pelmanism to sharpen up my memory.' But Prentice believed that Macomber had a longer memory than that and he couldn't shake off the feeling that the Scot had deliberately chosen a moment when he might be off guard to repeat his earlier query. With the huge figure standing by his side now as the clouds moved deeper into the basin, Prentice was beset by a growing feeling of uncertainty which he couldn't completely account for. He had heard, of course, that men fluent in another language thought and even dreamt in that tongue. And yet . . .

'Which way, Grapos?' Macomber asked abruptly. 'It's time we got moving and this time we don't stop – not for anything – until we've reached the monastery. And we move as fast as we can.' He glared at both Prentice and Ford. 'This stuff is getting worse and it may have snowed on the other side of the mountain earlier – in which case Burckhardt could have made slow progress.'

'In half-tracks?' Prentice replied sceptically.

'In half-tracks which have to negotiate one of the worst roads in Europe – a road covered with ice and which winds all over the place.' He turned to the Greek again. 'I said, which way, Grapos, for God's sake.'

'That way is to Zervos.'

The Greek set off in the direction he had indicated through the falling snow and the others followed. Prentice had seen a blurred ridge where the hand had pointed, but already it was enveloped by a white curtain as they trudged uphill, their feet sinking ankle-deep into snow which had not yet hardened, their heads bent to avoid the worst of the wetness and cold on their faces, so the snow began to build up on their crouched backs until very soon they were dragging themselves upwards out of the basin, leaving behind deep footprints which began to disappear before they had moved a dozen paces beyond. It was less cold than it had been inside the mountain, but temperature is a question of degree and their resistance was lower, so that for all of them the conditions seemed no improvement on what they had endured earlier. Grapos, despite his short legs and his limp, soon out-distanced them and was then trailed by Prentice, who passed Macomber. The Scot was having trouble with his ankle and, as he had anticipated, he was limping, hauling rather than lifting his right leg through the entangling snow. The low temperature seemed to anaesthetise the pain but it did nothing to increase his mobility and he was sweating again with the endless physical exertion involved in coping with his foot, levering his bulk up the increasingly steep slope, trying to brush his bare head comparatively free of snow before it hardened, and keeping Prentice in sight through the dense curtain of snow.

As they climbed higher a further inconvenience began to trouble them. The wind. Near the floor of the basin they had been shielded from the malignance of this particular element, but the higher they climbed the more they experienced its rising strength. It was coming from the east, a wind originat-

ing in the grim wastelands of the Turkish plateau, and now
it was razor-edged, cutting into their already battered faces
with a raw intensity which took their breath away as it
created flurries higher up still on the ridges, flurries like
white whirlpools which blew the snow in all directions at
once. Macomber was getting glimpses of these fierce-looking
flurries as the wind blew gaps in the snow, and through the
gaps he also made out that they were climbing a minor ridge
out of the basin with a gulley below where the snow settled
more peaceably. He was having trouble with his breathing,
trying to bring his lungs back to normal as he trudged on,
when he saw that Prentice had stopped ahead of him, and
his numbed fingers automatically tightened over the second
Luger inside his pocket. As he came closer he saw Grapos
coming back through the snow, and one hand was held up
urgently warning them to stop immediately. Something had
gone wrong: the Greek had encountered something unexpected. Macomber looked back and saw Ford close behind,
stooped forward under a back congealed with hardening
snow. When he looked ahead Prentice had also turned and
was coming towards him with his machine-pistol unlooped
from his shoulder. Grapos followed, his rifle ready in his
hands.

'What is it?' Macomber demanded.

'Grapos spotted something at the top of the ridge further
up. The snow cleared for just long enough for him to see
what we nearly walked into blindly . . .'

'What?' Macomber repeated impatiently. 'Get to it, man.'

'On the top there's a lookout armed with a machine-gun.'

*

Burckhardt had arrived, had occupied the monastery, had, of
course, with his half-tracks, overtaken and outdistanced them
while they were still locked up inside the mountain; he had
even had the time to set up outposts at the approaches to the
monastery. This had been Prentice's forbidding conclusion
when Grapos had brought his news. While a blast of wind

had briefly cleared the ridge above, the Greek had clearly seen it – the silhouette of a crouching man, a blurred silhouette of a figure crouched over a machine-gun. Then the snow had closed in again, blotting him from view.

They had decided at once on the only possible tactic. Since the route led over that ridge they must tackle the outpost which barred their way. A long diversion – at least six kilometres Grapos had estimated – was unthinkable in such weather conditions. So, because he knew the terrain, they had accepted the Greek's simple plan: to go down into the gulley and then move along its bed until they reached the point where they could approach the outpost from below under cover of the hill slope. Grapos was to leave the gulley at its head where he could cross the ridge behind a crag and then circle up on the post from the rear while the others tackled the lookout from the side. In theory, it seemed eminently workable, but Prentice began to worry as soon as the Greek vanished ahead in the snow. With Macomber and Ford close behind he calculated that he was only half-way to his objective whereas Grapos, who had little further in the way of distance to cover, was already rapidly outpacing them. He checked his watch. 4.17 p.m. The arrangement was that they would all reach the outpost at exactly 4.30 p.m.

Five minutes later Prentice was cursing under his breath as he stumbled forward over ice-sheened stones and frozen water; the sides of the gulley were too steep for a man to keep his footing walking parallel to the gulley and the glacial watercourse was slowing him down badly. Both Macomber and Ford had fallen behind and the lieutenant, on his own, had decided he must make the assault up the slope without them. His nagging fear was that the Greek would reach the outpost alone, a post which might easily be manned by several Germans, and he still hadn't come to the point where the gulley turned sharply to the right, the point where Grapos had said he must ascend straight up the slope. He was moving blindly through the falling snow when the slope sheered up in front instead of at his side: he had reached the turning-point. The thought of one man tackling that post on his own impelled Prentice to even greater efforts, to force his aching legs and punished feet to move even faster as he left the gulley and started to climb the slope.

He went up mechanically, teeth clenched, looking up through the blinding curtain of snow as he hauled himself up past icy spurs of rock, threaded his way round boulders, and then tried to get back on course again, frightened that he would arrive on the ridge too low down and in the sights of that machine-gun if visibility cleared for a moment. Once, he slipped on a patch of ice, falling to his knees, but he was up again instantly, hardly aware of the bruising force of the fall which had hammered his kneecaps. Knowing that he was going to be late, he tried to accelerate his progress and went up the slope in a frenzy of effort, exploiting to the full his light weight and leanness of frame while the blood pounded in his ears and his legs threatened to give way under him. The wind was buffeting him savagely now, at times almost throwing him off-balance, but its mounting viciousness told him something – he was coming close to the spine of the ridge, to the moment when he would know whether he had gone fatally off course and was arriving too far down. And this was the moment when he should proceed more cautiously for fear that a clatter of stones dislodged by his feet might warn them he was close, that he existed, even above the howl of the wind which was rising to a shriek. The thoughts tumbled through his keyed-up brain while his nerves and muscles took him mechanically up the treacherous slope, spurred on by the dreadful lack of minutes to get there in time.

At one point he arrived on a small level area, a shelf on the slope where the snow in turmoil rushed wildly at him, so that for vital seconds he lost his sense of direction totally, not knowing which way was up and which down, and only the sight of a large blurred figure toiling up from below sent him on a correct course in the opposite direction: Macomber was overtaking him. He took several steps upwards and then paused to wipe snow and ice crystals off his watch-face. 4.30 p.m. Grapos would be attacking at any second, might already have done so. Forgetting all caution, he went straight up the slope, vaguely aware that the snow was thinning as the wind scoured the hill ferociously, his ears tuned for the sound that would tell him he was too late. A short burst of machine-gun fire.

He very nearly ran into the outpost, but seeing a fogged shadow behind the swirling snow, he pulled up. A few yards above him rose a low wall of stone, a shambles of a wall with no mortar to bind the stones together, a wall about four feet high. He was directly under the post and there was no human sound on the wind-ravaged ridge. Dropping quietly to the ground, he unlooped the machine-pistol and eased his way forward, holding the weapon in one hand. The scream of the wind was deafening and snow had lashed his face, stinging his skin as though with red-hot particles. At least that berserk wail of the elements would drown the noise of his body dragging over the snow. He couldn't see any sign of the lookout, but his head was close to the ground and the wall served as a screen. Prentice squirmed round on his belly through an angle of forty-five degrees and hauled himself along the base of the wall towards the rear of the post, the direction from which Grapos would appear. With every foot he dragged himself forward the howl of the wind increased as it rose to tempest force; exposed here on the summit of the ridge the full fury of the bitter east wind whipped at his face and befuddled his vision with eddies of powdered snow so that his eyes were narrowed to slits as he approached the end of the side wall. Prentice knew exactly what he was going to do: he was going to come in from the rear of the post himself, banking on the hope that the German, singular or plural, would have their heads down against the onslaught of the storm and that one burst should do the trick. He reached the end of the wall and peered carefully round the corner, his eyes almost at ground level. Only a scurry of snow swept round to meet him full in the face, gritty snow like a sandstorm in the Western Desert. He put his left hand on the ice-cold ground to lever himself up and Grapos came through the wind and the snow.

The Greek was moving forward in a crouch with his rifle held out in front. He had come within six feet of the post before Prentice was even aware that he was there – a tribute to his makeshift camouflage. As he came forward he looked down, a brief glance, at the prone lieutenant. His rifle wavered for a fraction of a second, a second which seemed an eternity to Prentice who recognised the reflex as the instant before firing. Then the rifle steadied, maintaining its previous aim. Prentice jumped up as Grapos reached the post, saw the figure of a soldier crouched over a gun aimed out over the ridge, a soldier whose head was protected with a khaki-coloured balaclava. Just one man, thank God! Facing away from them, he was coated with snow like a tree bowed under its own weight, so concentrated on his watch over the ground below the ridge that he hadn't stirred in the few seconds between Prentice jumping up and Grapos moving forward. The Greek's rifle was within inches of the hunched, snow-rimed back when Grapos paused, the rifle still extended, his legs slightly apart as though braced for the recoil.

Prentice, dazed with his exertions and the sudden appearance of Grapos, took all this in while his brain tried to send him a message which he hadn't yet co-related. The crouched soldier's body masked his own weapon as the wind blew the snow clear off the summit and at that moment Grapos acted, pressing the muzzle of his rifle into the man's back as though prodding a sack. Prentice stared in amazement. Nothing had happened – the man hadn't moved, hadn't reacted to the prod in any way. Grapos prodded harder. The motionless figure remained still, as though resenting this treatment, then swayed over sideways and collapsed stiffly into the small enclave inside the walls. He turned over as he fell and ended up on his back with his side close to the wall and his face staring up at the snow which was now falling less thickly, while beyond the ridge the massive shape of Mount Zervos began to emerge. The staring face had a rigid look, the skin an unnatural bluish tinge. Prentice stared down, his mind chilled and perplexed. The poor devil had frozen to death at his post, and the lieutenant recalled the slow insidious way the numbness had crept inside his own body while they had stood in the icicled cavern deep down in the mountain. The freezing-to-death process could steal over a man without his ever realising it was happening. They had been stalking a corpse, a frozen-stiff corpse.

But his horrified surprise at the man's condition was a minor reaction compared to his belated recognition of the uniform the soldier wore and the make of the machine-gun he had died over, a weapon which still stood mounted in position, the barrel encased in ice and frozen snow so that it had the appearance of a glass gun. The British were already on Zervos.

The monastery was in sight. The snow-storm had faded as impetuously as it had blown up and Mount Zervos, massive above the vagaries of the weather, was fully exposed to view. Standing in front of the outpost walls, Macomber saw that it was as he had remembered it – the huge bluff shouldered out from the mountain, hanging over the sea on one side while the other plunged sheer to the lake below. The walls of the monastery rose vertically from the lip of the bluff; four windowed slabs like giant watch-towers linked together by battlemented walls. They seemed to grow up out of the rocky bluff as they sheered upwards and were silhouetted against the sea with the mainland beyond, the most remote and ascetic hermitage in all Europe – and the ultimate objective of Colonel Burckhardt.

The sea was grey and choppy but comparatively calm as the storm crossed the gulf a little to the north, leaving a clear view from the monastery across the strait. Macomber doubted whether the snow had even reached the bluff this time – its ceiling had been just a few hundred feet below the eminence. He looked again to the east where a hill slope curved down to the far end of the frozen lake, the point where, Grapos had just told him, the road from Katyra left the mountain zig-zag to run round the lake shore below them prior to its final ascent to the monastery.

'They haven't arrived yet,' said Prentice. 'That snow would show up half-track trails and it's undisturbed.'

'The snow we have had might cover the marks,' Grapos pointed out, 'but they have not come.'

'Could you put that just a little bit clearer?' Macomber rumbled.

'They have not come because they could not pass that.'

He was pointing below the ridge where an immense mass of
snow was heaped up against the lower slope. 'The road is
under there,' he explained. Macomber gazed down and was
inclined to agree with him: this was drift snow, anything up
to thirty feet deep probably, snow which had been blown
there recently by the high wind and which would strangle
any sort of powered vehicle attempting to drive through it.
And the frozen surface of the lake was undisturbed, even
supposing it was thick enough to support half-tracks and
mountain guns. Without knowing of the lake's existence one
might have thought it simply an exceptionally level area
enclosed within the amphitheatre formed by the hill slopes
and the sheer walls of the mountain and the bluff. While the
wind raked his face, Macomber studied it more closely and
found he could see wavelets of snow where the wind had
blown it and then dropped it in small ridges. Using his
Monokular, he thought he could see in the lens the dull
gleam of patches of hard ice where the snow had been blown
clear. He was looking at a battlefield, he thought, or what
would soon be a battlefield: the British army was on Zervos
and Burckhardt's force was coming up the mountain.

'He's been dead an hour or two at least.'

It was Ford's voice which spoke behind him and when
Macomber turned the sergeant was inside the post's walls –
a shelter for sheep in bad weather, Macomber imagined. As
Ford handled his unpleasant task he appeared to be turning
over a waxwork figure rather than a human being. The lapels
of the greatcoat were like metal and one of them broke off as
he worked his hand inside. The hand came out with a brown,
cloth-covered folder, a British army pay-book which he gave
to Prentice. The lieutenant fingered open the cover and
looked up at Macomber. 'He's Private Leslie Smith. Number
19479205. Middlesex Regiment.'

'You knew our troops were on the way?' Macomber asked
sharply.

'No. When I was last in Athens they were still nattering
about it – and getting nowhere. Some Greek official in their

war ministry wouldn't give us permission to send anyone.'
He paused, startled by his own frankness, but he was still
half-stunned by his first sight of the British uniform. 'Of
course, that was almost a week ago,' he went on quickly.
'I've been in Turkey since then and they probably got agree-
ment for us to land here after I'd left.'

'I see.' Macomber sounded strangely unconvinced and
Prentice sensed a fluttering at the back of his own mind as he
looked down again inside the pit. The weapon Private Smith
had crouched over so vigilantly was a Lewis gun and the
circular magazine was so laden with snow which had turned
to ice that its distinctive shape was scarcely recognisable. He
saw Macomber brushing more snow out of his hair and
hesitated, but the living had first priority, so he told Ford to
rescue the balaclava. With difficulty the sergeant peeled off
the woollen helmet, tearing it round the edges, and handed it
wordlessly to the Scot. Macomber rammed it down over his
large head and brushed snow off his gloves. Standing there
with the wind blowing round him, upright despite his
groggy ankle, Prentice thought he looked like an Arctic
explorer.

'We must get moving as fast as we can go,' Macomber
growled. 'If they have warning of what is coming, it may help.
You can send someone back later to deal with your friend.'
He stamped his left foot several times on the iron-hard
ground; the right one would have to stay frozen. 'I want to
be there . . .' he pointed across the lake to the towering
monastery, 'within fifteen minutes.'

'That's damned impossible . . .' Prentice began, but Grapos
had already shouldered his rifle and was leading the way
downhill with Macomber plodding close behind. The route
lay along the edge of another spine which descended from the
main ridge towards the lake shore. And marching downhill
Macomber seemed able to thrash forward through the snow
as though his limp didn't exist, keeping so close to the heels
of the Greek that Grapos felt compelled to step up the pace
of their descent. The lake rose to meet them and the heights

of Zervos climbed above them as the two handicapped men plunged furiously down the slope at such a speed that Prentice and Ford found themselves breathing heavily to keep up. In spite of his gruelling experiences, the bitter cold, and his lack of sleep, the Scot seemed to have reserved one great burst of energy for the final lap. They passed the end of the great snow drift which had obliterated the road on their left and saw its continuation on their right, a section of snow-covered highway which disappeared round the seaward side of the bluff where it ascended to the monastery.

Near the bottom of the long ridge Macomber overtook Grapos and hurried past him, his face moist with the exertion of the tremendous spurt he was putting on, dragging himself partially sideways like a crab to counter the limp. He only stopped when he had crossed the road and reached the lake shore. Behind him Prentice was still hurrying down the ridge, hopefully anticipating a reprieve from the freezing wind at a lower altitude, but if anything had changed it was for the worse – the wind blew more bitterly across the ice-bound water and the temperature was lower than ever, possibly because of its passage over the half-mile long sheet of snow-drifted ice. Looking back along the invisible road, Macomber pointed to the immense drifts which filled the area between hillside and lake shore. 'Burckhardt can never get through there.'

'So they come this way – over the lake.'

Grapos spoke with conviction and, as if to prove his point, he walked out over the lake. His boots made a dull, stomping sound as he crossed the frozen water, and when he was many yards from the road he stopped and stamped his boot down hard several times. Macomber followed him for a short distance, breaking off frozen grasses as he walked and behind him the grasses scattered on the ice like pine needles. He had little doubt that a man could march clear across the lake in its present condition, probably even drive a vehicle safely over its surface. Here was, as Grapos had predicted, Burckhardt's road to Zervos.

The wind whined eerily across the frozen desolation and he could hear the faint rustle of snow being carried over the ice. He paused and then veered to take a short cut to where the road vanished behind the bluff, walking over the ice along the straight side of the arc formed by the road. He walked alike a man possessed, his expression as grim as any Dietrich had ever assumed, his head bowed against the wind and tucked down inside the snow-stiffened collar of his coat, hearing behind him the muffled thump of feet on ice as the others followed him. When he reached the shore he increased his pace, even though now he was moving up the slope of the road. During that passage over the ice something had clicked inside his ankle and it felt firmer, less likely to give way under him at any second. When Prentice, who had run a short way through the snow, caught up with him and shouted breathlessly, he refused to slacken pace.

'Look there – out at sea!'

They were under the hanging bluff now and the soaring rock face loomed over them like a threat, but on the other side of the road, to the west, the ground was falling away endlessly towards the sea which seemed a mile below. They were, Macomber saw, climbing directly above Cape Zervos – the saw-toothed rock at the end of the shipwrecking chain extending from the mainland told him this. And in the distance to the south a lean grey vessel was approaching with smoke streaming from its stack and a clear wake to stern. A British destroyer was heading for the peninsula.

'It may be coming here,' Prentice panted, unable to keep the excitement out of his voice.

'And it may be going on to Katyra,' Macomber replied bleakly. He sounded supremely uninterested as he kept up the same treadmill pace even though the road was climbing steeply, and Prentice dropped back to speak to Grapos. To their right the road edge was becoming a precipice while on the other side the overhang of the bluff leaned towards them, so that now they felt compressed between the rock face and the bottomless brink. Macomber glanced up once as the road veered to the east and far above his head he saw a spur of white at the lip of a crevice which severed the bluff. It was a tongue of ice where a waterfall had frozen solid during the sub-zero temperatures of night. A dozen paces down the road the lieutenant was talking to Grapos.

'I heard there was some sort of path up the nose of Cape Zervos. Is there? It didn't look possible from the little I saw when we were on board.'

'There is a path, yes. A path for goats. Once there was a landing-place at the bottom, a jetty. But it has not been used for many years.'

'If there's a jetty then presumably men could climb this so-called path for goats?'

'I have been up it and I have been down it. The lonely monks live in the cliff face by themselves . . .'

'Hermit monks, you mean?'

'Probably. They have machines which lowered the stones to make the houses . . .'

'Pulleys, you mean? Wheels with cables round them?'

'Something like that, yes. Why?'

'Nothing, I was just wondering.' Prentice stared out to sea where the destroyer was gradually coming closer. From its present course it could be heading for the narrows, prior to steaming up the gulf, but it would be a while before he could be sure. He looked up the road and Macomber was disappearing inside a trail of cloud creeping over the road.

The cloud was not large but its vaporous mist seriously fogged visibility at a moment when the road was narrowing. Macomber was acutely aware of that precipice on the right as he felt the ice-cold drizzle on his face and he instinctively moved towards the rock face, hardly able to see where he was going as the road continued to veer to the east. He had a second of sheer panic when the ground disappeared under his feet and then he stumbled into the ditch which ran immediately under the bluff. His outstretched hands slapped hard against moist clammy rock, but the brief pain was a form of near-ecstasy – his brain had signalled that he was going over the brink and down to the Aegean. With a tang of salt air in his nostrils and the drizzle spraying his face and coating his balaclava, he fumbled his way upwards, knowing it would be wiser to halt until the cloud had passed but impelled on by a feeling of terrible urgency he couldn't completely account for. Water was starting to run down the snow-packed road, making the ground slippery and difficult to grip. Once, he slithered out of control and again he swerved to the left and ended up in the ditch where ice crumbled under his impact. Clambering to his feet he went on up through the sodden mist, feeling his clothes grow heavier as the dampness penetrated and clung to him. He was cold and shivering and had never felt more miserable; it was as though the elements in their malice were flinging at him one final ordeal to break his spirit within sight of his goal, and as he ploughed his way carefully upwards he thought he could hear a dull booming sound.

For a moment he wondered whether it was the boom of the sea on Cape Zervos nearly three thousand feet below, but then realised that the sound would never carry up to these heights. Was it simply a noise inside his fevered head? Was his mind at long last caving in under the frightful strain? The mist began to thin and he had the impression that the sun was trying to break through. Or was this another hallucination? The muffled booming had a certain rhythm and sounded like a large bell tolling. The vapour thinned still further and another ten paces took him out of the top of the cloud and into the sunlight, the cold bright sunlight of winter. He could hear the sound quite clearly now as the great bell of Zervos rang and echoed and re-echoed round the heights like a tocsin of doom.

The road ran straight ahead to the monastery which lay less than two hundred yards away, but Macomber turned off the road to his left and crossed a low rise at the seaward end of the bluff. Unless his sense of direction had failed him completely he should get a view down over the frozen lake from the top of the rise. With his clothes adhering to his body in one sodden mass, he felt a tremor of excitement as he climbed rapidly, hearing someone call out behind him and knowing that Grapos had also emerged from the cloud. It was floating out over the gulf now, almost clearing the bluff, a frothy drift he could look down on as though from a plane. The view came suddenly. His head breasted the rise, saw a widespread cloud bank covering the plateau in the distance and the lake spread out so far below that he could hardly credit they had come up so far so fast. The lake was as they had seen it from below, although the perspective had changed, and there was only one detail added to the frozen panorama. Round the flank of the snow-covered slope where Grapos had pointed a small dark bug-like object was crawling forward. The first half-track had arrived.

He went back quickly down the rise, the mournful tolling of the bell in his ears as he watched the destroyer heading steadily for the peninsula. For a brief moment something flashed on the vessel and he thought it might be signalling, but it was only a flash of sunlight which had reflected from it. Returning to the road where Grapos waited with Prentice and Ford, he heard the pealing of the bell take on a deeper, more urgent note, and then it broke off in mid-peal and the unexpected onset of silence was strange.

'There is something wrong . . .' the Greek burst out.

'He says the tolling of the bell is the wrong tune or something,' Prentice explained. Macomber, who was tone-deaf, had noticed nothing positive, but it had sounded a weird, disorganised cacophony even to his unmusical ear.

'Never is the bell rung like that,' Grapos went on vehemently. 'It was a signal, a warning. Something terrible is wrong at the monastery. I tell you. I know!'

They stared along the short stretch of road where there was no sign of life. The towers and the wall which linked them were much lower on this side and beyond the wall-top in one place Macomber saw the greenish shell of a dome which, he remembered, was the church. With Prentice in the lead, they began to walk towards the ancient gatehouse which stood in the centre of the wall, a tumbledown wooden structure which appeared to lean back against the wall for support.

The gates under the archway were open and beyond they had a glimpse of deserted courtyard. A spur track led off from the road to the right, curved out beyond the end of the monastery and, so far as Macomber could see, came to a full stop where the bluff merged with the mountain. Perhaps in summer there was a track which came down on the far side of the lake. Mount Zervos, its summit rising immediately above the bluff, was bathed in sunlight, a stark triangle of whiteness which glittered where the light caught snow crystals. A mere few hundred feet above the bluff, it seemed as aloof and remote as Everest.

'Isn't there someone usually about?' Prentice asked irritably.

'You see them reading on the terraces,' replied Grapos who walked by his side, 'but there is no one there.' Prentice assumed he was referring to the wooden box-like structures attached to the stone walls three or four storeys up. They protruded from the walls like giant dovecotes or porches at the fronts of houses, and each box had tall shutters which led out to a small balcony. No sign of anyone up there.

'Maybe they keep under cover in cold weather,' he surmised.

'But there is no one at the entrance,' Grapos objected. He had unlooped his rifle and now his eyes were everywhere, scanning the wall-top, searching the balconies, staring through the archway and then looking quickly up to the wall-top again as though he hoped to catch someone off guard. It was a bit queer, Prentice was thinking, and yet someone had been tolling that bell. He looked curiously up at the gatehouse where a roofed-in, railed passage ran the full width of the place on the first floor. It was empty. He paused at the entrance, a space wide enough to admit a large wagon, looking through it to a vast stone-paved courtyard with a single plane tree in the centre. Before entering with the machine-pistol at the ready, he glanced back. Ford was close behind but Macomber lingered at least a dozen paces away, as though now he had reached their objective he was oddly reluctant to enter. Prentice shrugged and marched firmly forward under the arch and across the yard.

It was even larger than he had imagined and was over-looked on all sides by windows and balconied walks running round the inner walls on each floor. As they walked across the worn stones he stifled the illogical feeling that they were horribly exposed, that anyone could shoot them in the back from those windows behind them. The four great towers and the high wall which looked down on the lake on the far side were ahead as they passed a stone well and skirted the domed church. The place was the size of a small village, almost large enough to accommodate a small army. But what the devil had happened to all the monks?

'I think we should go,' said Grapos. 'I have a feeling.'

'Well, nurse it,' snapped Prentice.

He reached the far wall and stopped close to where a stone ramp led up into an arcaded walk. Had he heard something behind that shuttered door at the top of the ramp? Could the monks have locked themselves in, scared by the new arrivals? It was possible – after all, they were carrying guns. He went up the ramp quietly and was close to the door when a voice spoke through the louvres.

'Don't shoot, old boy. We happen to be on your side.'

The shutter opened cautiously as though to give Prentice time to adjust himself and was then opened fully. A uniformed figure stood in the doorway, a man of about thirty-five who was lean-faced and freshly-shaven. The three pips on either shoulder shone brightly and identified him as a British army captain. His Sam Browne belt was highly polished and his whole appearance made the crumpled, unshaven Prentice feel unbearably scruffy. Behind the captain stood a sergeant holding a Lee Enfield rifle and the shoulder flashes of the Middlesex Regiment on his tunic were smartly new. He grinned without speaking at Ford as the captain spoke.

'Glad I heard you speak a bit of our lingo. I'm Brown.'

'Lieutenant Prentice,' Prentice replied, and then felt he must add something. 'Excuse the limp civvy get-up, but it's rather a long story. You know the Jerries are on the way, I hope?'

'God, no! Look, you'd better get in here, the lot of you, and then we can talk. What kept you?'

'Kept us?' Prentice felt dazed as he entered a large stone-floored room which was half in darkness. The windows at the back had the shutters firmly closed and the only light was coming in through the open doorway. Captain Brown hastened to remedy this by opening the front shutters as Ford and Grapos filed inside the room followed by Macomber who had taken off his balaclava and stuffed it inside his pocket. Ford was going to speak to the sergeant but he had moved to the rear of the room and was still holding his rifle casually. The butt plate looked brand-new and hadn't a scratch on it so far as Prentice could see. 'What kept us?' he repeated. 'I'm afraid I don't follow that.'

Brown looked perplexed and his dark eyes stared hard at the lieutenant's chin, then he smiled blandly. 'We're waiting for reinforcements from Katyra so we assumed you were some sort of guide.' His tone changed. 'Aren't you?'

'No, and there's a whole German army coming up the mountain. It's due to get here any time now.'

Macomber, who had shown no eagerness to be introduced, was walking round the back of the table where a half-opened can of bully beef lay next to some papers. The captain's stick lay on a side table. The Scot stopped behind the table with his hands in his pockets, glanced at the sergeant, and then down at the papers again briefly before he resumed his slow stroll. A British soldier appeared at the open door, received a nod from Brown, and took up a position where he could see inside the room. A moment later something poked open a closed shutter at the rear of the room. A Lee Enfield held by another soldier. Brown called out to him. 'It's all right, Perkins. Friends have arrived.' It's another confirmation, Prentice thought, that Brown isn't sure of us yet. He's a careful cove and I haven't even shown him any form of identification.

'Look, sir,' he began. 'Can I ask you how many men you have up here.'

'You can ask, old boy,' Brown told him familiarly, 'but I'm not at all sure I'm going to tell you. What's all this hocus-pocus about a German army being on our doorfront. Eh?'

The shutter at the rear of the room rattled. Out of the corner of his eye Prentice caught a blur of movement from the direction where Macomber was standing, a movement he hadn't time to see fully before the voice spoke a brutal, urgent command.

'Prentice! If you move, I'll shoot! That applies to you, Ford, as well.' He said something quickly in Greek to Grapos and then relapsed into German, addressing Brown. 'Take their guns off them and be damned quick about it. We haven't all day and you've wasted time already. I'm Dietrich of the Abwehr – I've travelled with these men all the way from Katyra to get what information I could out of them.' He held the Luger levelled at Prentice's chest and was standing with his shoulders hunched forward, the largest man in the room. Brown took the weapons off the three men and handed them to his sergeant, speaking rapidly in German.

'Keep them covered! Watch the Greek especially.'

The soldier in the doorway held his rifle aimed inside the room and his comrade beyond the rear window had his rifle pointed at Grapos. Brown's sergeant had had the three men covered within a split second of Dietrich's shouted command. They were being marched from the room when Prentice glanced over his shoulder. Dietrich had immediately slipped his pistol inside his coat at the first opportunity as though he disliked firearms, and he was standing with his hands clasped behind his back as Prentice glared at him with loathing. This, then, was the real Dietrich, a senior officer in the Abwehr.

*

'. . . so it was a necessary manoeuvre,' Dietrich explained to Captain Braun as they walked the monastic arcade on the sixth floor. 'It seemed too much of a coincidence that two British soldiers disguised as civilians should be aboard the *Hydra* on that particular voyage. I suspected that they were part of an advance force sent to take over Zervos – but I'm convinced now that they just happened to be travelling back from Istanbul.'

'Remarkable,' said Braun politely. Already he was looking forward to the moment when Burckhardt would arrive to take the Abwehr man off his hands; within a matter of minutes Dietrich was imposing his domineering personality, putting to Braun loaded questions which implied a doubt as to whether the captain was really up to it.

'How many men have you?' he demanded abruptly.

'Six – including one at an outpost overlooking the road . . .'

'Five, you mean. That man is dead. Frozen to death . . .' He rumbled on over Braun's protestation of surprise. 'You're not exactly an army, are you, Braun?'

'We had to come by car yesterday, as you know. There were seven of us – one man dropped off near Katyra to cut the phone wire and contact our Greek collaborator who was organising a supply of mules. We were supposed to be replacement staff for the embassy in Athens from our legation in Salonika and more than seven would have aroused suspicion. As it was, we needed three cars to bring the equipment as well. We left late in the afternoon from Salonika and then turned off to the peninsula after dark . . .'

'And dressed yourselves in British uniforms when you were near here to effect a surprise entry?'

'Exactly. We were worried about the Abbot's carrier pigeons – if he had been able to send a message to the mainland . . .' He shook his head. 'It doesn't bear thinking about. They were surprised when we arrived, but since the British are their allies they let us in and that was that.'

'Where have you posted your five men?' Dietrich had

stopped by a window and was looking down into the courtyard. The tone of his question suggested grave doubts as to
Braun's capability. The captain answered stiffly, guessing
that the answer would be reported back to the people in
Berlin.

'One is on the balcony of the gatehouse . . .'

'He let us through without challenge.'

'But he saw your arrival and you would not have left that
room downstairs alive.'

'Possibly not. Go on. There is a British destroyer approaching, you know.'

'We have observed it. We have the measures to deal with
it. Another man is on the ground floor guarding the refectory
at the far end.' He made a gesture. 'The monks are locked up
in there. One man is guarding the prisoners on the floor
below, as you have seen. And the other two are on the roof
where we are going. I think my arrangements are adequate,
considering the size of my force,' he ended icily as Dietrich
resumed his walk along the arcade.

'We all do our best,' Dietrich replied enigmatically. Near
the end of the corridor he paused before an open door. The
room inside was very large, old rugs hung from the walls,
and the windows overlooked the lake. 'What is this room?'

'The Abbot's quarters. I have requisitioned them for my
temporary headquarters.' Braun indicated some papers on a
large desk behind one of the tall windows. 'And now we will
go up to the observation post.'

'Who was tolling that damned bell when we arrived?'

Braun's expression changed and his lips twisted. Blast the
swine! He would put his finger on the single mistake,
on something he had conveniently wished to forget. As they
reached the end of the corridor he explained curtly that the
Abbot had pretended to be ill and had then made straight for
the bell-tower. Opening a small studded door, Braun went up
a dark spiral of steps which led up to the roof of the tower
closest to the sea. At the top he rapped with his pistol butt
in a certain way on the underside of a closed trap-door.

Dietrich heard a bolt withdrawing and followed Braun up through the opened trap on to a stone roof surrounded by a waist-high wall.

An icy breeze flowed over his face which made him almost feel dizzy, a reaction which was intensified by the vastness of the view. To the south and west a grey ruffle of sea; to the north the gulf under a heavy sky; beyond the eastern wall a precipitous drop to the amphitheatre spread out below. He gave a grunt of satisfaction, his first display of this emotion, when he saw tiny figures spreading out across the ice from the furthest shore of the lake. There was even a half-track a short distance from the shore where Burckhardt's force was assembling as a stream of troops came round the corner from the mountain road below. The colonel was testing the ice prior to sending his army over the frozen lake.

'We should be all right,' was his only comment. 'Unless that causes trouble.' He pointed to the south-west where the British destroyer was closing the cape at high speed. No doubt any more that its objective was not Katyra.

'This is likely to cause the destroyer trouble,' replied Braun. He was pointing at a short, squat-barrelled mortar set up on its tripod with the ugly barrel aimed out over the sea. Close by snub-nosed shells half-covered with canvas waited to service the weapon. 'As soon as they come within range,' Braun continued, 'and meanwhile we proceed with our task of observation.'

The rooftop was well-organised, Dietrich had to admit to himself. Two soldiers, both in British uniform and one a corporal, stood by the wall facing out over the gulf. The corporal was crouched as he pressed his eye to a powerful field telescope also mounted on a tripod, while the other man, his rifle slung, held a notebook and a pencil. He began making notes as the man behind the telescope spoke rapidly. A few feet behind them a wireless-set with the antenna mast fully extended stood on the stone-paved floor. Braun was already observing and recording the movement of Allied formations up the mainland road.

'You have any suggestions?' he asked Dietrich with apparent politeness.

The Abwehr man made no reply and focused his Monokular glass on the incoming warship. Her deck was crammed with troops and he fancied he recognised the individualistic hats the Australians wore. Australians and some Kiwis probably. A well-aimed mortar bomb would make a nice mess on those decks. Braun invited him to take a look through the large telescope when it was available, but Dietrich glanced at his watch and shook his head. There was something he wished to see to immediately. He had a word with the corporal who had left his telescope while the other man began working with a code book prior to transmitting the information, talking to him briefly about his home town, Munich, then he turned to Braun. 'There was some mention of a path up from the cape – I want to interrogate the Greek about that at once.'

'Even if they land,' Braun protested, 'they will never survive. Colonel Burckhardt will have arrived – his men will wait for the Englanders at the top of the cliff and fire down on them. It will be a massacre . . .' He trailed off. The Abwehr man hardly appeared to be listening as he cupped his hands against the breeze to light his remaining cigar.

'I said I wish to interrogate the Greek,' he repeated, his eyes holding Braun's as he lifted his head. 'I need you to inform the guard of my request.'

Braun hesitated, looked at the destroyer, remembered that promotions were sometimes decided on or vetoed in strange quarters, and then decided to play for safety. 'We shall have to hurry,' he said coldly. Behind his back the corporal winked at the private, a reaction which Dietrich did not fail to notice. Evidently the stiff-necked Braun was none too popular with his men.

'I thought I made it clear,' Dietrich said mildly, 'that I'm in a hurry myself.'

He followed the captain down through the trap-door and heard the bolt shoot home as the lid closed over his head. In his annoyance Braun went down the spiralling steps as quickly as he could. He had disappeared round a curve when Dietrich took the cigar out of his mouth and pressed the lighted tip against the wall in the darkness. Sparks flared as he went down, still holding the cigar hard against the stone. At the bottom of the staircase he closed the door carefully and wandered after Braun who was walking ahead of him along the corridor. As he had anticipated, the captain slowed down and waited for him, and then they began walking alongside each other without speaking as they made their way towards the main staircase at the far end of the corridor. They were close to the Abbot's quarters when Dietrich stopped. 'I'll catch you up – my cigar's gone out.' He put his hand in his pocket for a box of matches. Braun shrugged and started to walk forward again. He was level with the open door when Dietrich came up behind him. He was within a foot of the captain when he raised the hand holding the Luger by the barrel and brought the butt down with a tremendous thud on the back of Braun's head.

*

Dietrich was smoking his cigar as he passed the sentry on the third floor who was standing outside the locked room which held the prisoners. Taking the cigar out of his mouth, he turned and walked back again slowly with his right hand inside his coat pocket. He halted five or six feet away from the soldier who stood at ease with his Lee Enfield, the same man who had waited outside the doorway of the room below where they had first met Braun.

'Don't you normally come to attention in the presence of an officer?' Dietrich enquired softly.

The guard, a dull-looking twenty-year-old, had a moment of bewilderment and then snapped to attention. Manoeuvring the British rifle for the exercise, he fumbled it a little, and an expression of disapproval crossed Dietrich's face as he stared hard at the man. 'I thought so,' he went on in the same soft tone of voice, 'I recognise you from the files. You're Hollinger.' He pulled out the Luger and aimed the pistol. 'Be very careful, Hollinger. Rest your rifle against that wall.'

'I'm Schmidt . . .' The guard was stupefied and still stood rigidly to attention.

'Unfortunately for you, I have an excellent memory for faces, Hollinger. I won't tell you again. Put your rifle carefully against the wall. That's better. Now, turn round, we're going to see Captain Braun . . .' Schmidt was facing the other way when Dietrich clubbed him with great force to allow for the British army forage cap. The German sagged against the wall and Dietrich grabbed the rifle as it started to topple. Bending over the collapsed body, he searched desperately through the pockets and found the key under a packet of Player's army issue cigarettes: the Germans were nothing if not thorough. He had the packet in his hand when he inserted the key, threw open the door and went inside. Grapos' violent charge from the wall he had been pressed against knocked him off balance and then Ford was trying to choke the life out of him. 'For God's sake get them off me, Prentice!' he snarled. 'Burckhardt's arrived and . . .' The lieutenant had darted into the corridor and now he returned with the Lee Enfield which he levelled at Macomber. The Scot heard the click of the safety catch being released as he spoke.

'Leave him a minute! Just make one mistake, Dietrich, and I'll put a bullet in your hide with the greatest of pleasure.'

'Use your bloody head, Prentice!' Macomber leant against the wall as the others released him and his manner was anything but apologetic. 'I've just knocked out the guard and let you out, haven't I? There's only four of them left here now and we've got to . . .'

'Not so fast!' Prentice broke in sharply. 'I've seen the guard outside . . .' He turned to the sergeant. 'Ford, drag him in here quick. Give him a hand, Grapos. Now, Dietrich-Macomber, or whatever your name is . . .'

'It's Macomber and always has been. Look, there's no time left for explanations . . .'

'There is, you know. Why did you hold us up down there?'

'To save your stupid lives!' Macomber was beside himself with cold fury at the delay. 'They were going to shoot us down at any second – they were all round us, just waiting for the signal from Braun.'

'I can see that now. But how the hell did you catch on so quick?' Prentice was still holding the rifle aimed as Ford and Grapos hauled the unconscious Schmidt inside the room, still trying to make up his mind about Macomber.

'The brand-new uniforms, for a start. Buttons and belts highly polished, a rifle butt without a scratch. They must have used some of the hoard they captured off us at Dunkirk. They even have British cigarettes – I was going to give you some.' Opening his fist, he showed the crumpled pack. 'But the map half-folded on the table confirmed it – the map of Zervos peninsula.'

Prentice frowned uncertainly. 'What's strange about that?'

'All the wording was in German!' Macomber exploded. 'And there was a Luger pistol underneath it,' he added for good measure. 'In case you still don't believe me, I've just knocked out Braun – the one you know as Captain Brown – and he's stuffed under a table in the Abbot's room on the floor above. We can look at him on the way . . .'

'On the way where?'

'To the tower. They've got an observation post up there.' He squared his shoulders and used his foot to stub out the smoking cigar which had been knocked out of his mouth when he entered. 'And they have a mortar which they say they're going to use to attack that destroyer when it gets close enough.' He looked at Ford. 'Is that really possible? A mortar against a destroyer?'

'If it's an 8-cm. job like those we saw where they were landing, yes. They'll have to be excellent shots but just one bomb down the stack and into the boiler room . . . Well, you saw what happened to the *Hydra*. If they drop one behind a gun-shield or land one close to . . .'

'All right, Ford!' Prentice snapped. 'This isn't quite the time for a dissertation on high-explosive . . .'

'And the decks of that ship are packed with troops,' Macomber went on. 'Now, let's work it out quickly. There are two men on the tower – that's where I'll have to come in because they know me.' He looked at Grapos. 'There's another man outside the refectory door on the ground floor where they've locked up the monks, and one more supposed to be on that gatehouse balcony although I didn't see him when we arrived.'

'He'd probably rushed back to alert the others,' Prentice pointed out. 'That's why Braun had his reception committee ready and waiting. Can you deal with the Jerry in the gatehouse, Grapos?'

'I deal with both – they are a long way from each other. No,' he shook his head as Prentice glanced down at the rifle, wondering whether to hand it over to him, 'you keep that. I use this. The Germans do not search well.' He bent down, lifted a trouser leg, and withdrew from his sock the parachutist's knife Ford had spotted just before they had entered the pipe. Macomber felt a little cold as he realised the Greek could so easily have used this weapon when he had entered the room. At the doorway, Ford, on his own initiative, was keeping a watch on the corridor as the Greek balanced the knife, flicked out the blade, balanced it again and then whipped it back over his shoulder. The knife sped through the open doorway past the alarmed sergeant's head and twanged as it bit deep into a narrow window frame on the far side of the corridor. 'Yes,' Grapos repeated judiciously, 'I use that. It is quiet.'

'Use what you like,' replied Prentice, 'but for God's sake keep it quiet. We don't want to warn those Jerries on the tower roof before Macomber's worked the oracle.' He turned to the Scot. 'Exactly how are you going to work this particular oracle, Mac?'

'I haven't the slightest idea,' said Macomber, and walked out of the door as Grapos shuffled along the corridor in the opposite direction. 'The first thing,' he continued as Prentice joined him, 'is for me to get up on the tower roof. They have a very solid trap-door which they keep bolted down. I'll try and delay them closing it and divert their attention while you and Ford follow me up. That tower is the key to everything – it dominates the whole monastery, they're about to open fire on the destroyer, and it overlooks Burckhardt's forces.' As they reached the main staircase he broke into a run, taking the steps two at a time, and then hurried back along the sixth floor corridor as Prentice caught him up. 'If we ever get the chance that mortar might just come in useful.' He glanced back to Ford who was close behind. 'Do you know how to operate the thing?'

'If it's the 8-cm., yes.'

'That door at the end leads up a dark spiral staircase to the trap-door. You'd better keep a few steps down – if they see you coming they'll slam the lid shut and that will be that.'

'You may get caught up there on your own,' Prentice warned.

'I'll just have to take my chance on that. Good, here we are. Now, remember, keep well back. I'll be talking in German and I want you to listen carefully – when I use the word "Deutschland" come up those steps like a bat out of hell.'

Macomber paused outside the closed door, brushed off his coat quickly where dirt covered it from Grapos' onslaught, ran his fingers through his hair and straightened his tie. Anyone would imagine I was going in to dinner, he thought, then he opened the door, listened for a few seconds, and started to mount the steps. With Ford behind him, Prentice followed, taking care to keep out of sight as the Scot neared the top. He heard Macomber stop, rap on the underside of the lid in a certain way, and then there was a rattling sound as the bolt was withdrawn.

*

It went wrong at once. The trap-door opened slowly as Macomber pushed his head upwards, anxious to see – and to be seen. The wireless op. was removing his headphones as he completed a transmission. The angle of the mortar barrel had been changed. The canvas had been pulled clear of the piled bombs. The corporal was out of sight: he would be lifting the trap-door for Macomber to come up on the roof. The Scot mounted the last few steps and was already talking as he turned round, then he stopped as the trap slammed shut and the corporal, on his knees, thrust home the bolt. The pistol he held aimed was very steady.

'What the devil are you up to?' Macomber demanded.

'Where is Captain Braun, please?'

'Down in his room. I left him there,' Macomber replied truthfully.

'I had expected him to return here at once.' The corporal was standing now but he still held the pistol aimed at Macomber's middle and there was no uncertainty in his manner.

'I imagine he answers to his own expectations rather than to yours. I'm going to have to report this, you know.' Outwardly, Macomber was cold and controlled, but as he had come on to the roof he had seen far below men tentatively moving out on to the ice and the guns had been unlimbered from the half-tracks prior to their journey across the lake.

'I have my orders,' the corporal replied, unperturbed by the suggestion of reprisals. 'And they include the instruction that no one is allowed up here in the captain's absence.' He paused and his eyes were shrewd, but he put the next question with a shade too much effort at casualness. 'Did Captain Braun give you permission to come up here on your own?'

'No. I came up by myself to see what was going on. Nothing as far as I can see, except a pedantic adherence to instructions when you have other things to do I should have thought.' Macomber took a chance. He deliberately turned his back on the gun and walked over to the far corner where he stood staring out to sea. The corporal hesitated, but the other soldier who was now gazing at the oncoming destroyer through field-glasses spoke and turned his mind to other things.

'In a minute, I would say.' His lips worked soundlessly as he peered through the glasses and Macomber guessed he was working on some theoretical calculation. 'In a minute or two at the outside.' He was referring to when the destroyer would come within distant range and he laid the heavy glasses on the wall-top near the Scot as he went to the piled bombs in readiness. It was an extraordinary situation, Macomber thought: the British destroyer loaded with troops and racing hopelessly to reach the cape in time, while on the other side of the monastery a small German army drew itself up for the march which would take it to its final objective. The Germans should win, of course – they could arrive on the heights in a fraction of the time it would take the destroyer to land its men who would then have to toil up that terrible path. Apparently still absorbed by the scene out at sea, he did a natural thing, reaching out for the heavy glasses as though about to use them.

He was well aware that the corporal was still keeping a curious eye on him insofar as his work permitted; at the moment he was knelt by the mortar while he made a fine adjustment to the angle of fire, but the pistol was laid on the stones close to his hand. Within less than two minutes the first mortar bomb would be away, soaring out over the sea towards that troop-crammed warship. If the first shot was a lucky hit he dreaded to think of the havoc which would be caused on those crowded decks. I've less than a hundred-and-twenty seconds, he told himself, and whatever I do must be exactly right first time, because there won't be a second chance. He had rejected any idea of reaching inside his coat pocket for the Luger – the corporal, if that was his real rank, was intelligent and quick-thinking: his instant slamming down of the trap even though no one else had been in sight proved that. And he was still mighty suspicious of the man he supposed to be an Abwehr officer. The soldier had a bomb he had taken from the pile cradled in his arms and he placed it gently on the folded canvas beside the mortar. Straightening up, he watched the corporal fiddling with the mortar's mechanism, realised he had a few moments to spare, and went back to the wall to bend down and look through the telescope pointed at the mainland. It was a slim enough opportunity, the short time while he was distracted by what he saw inside the lens, but Macomber grabbed it instantly.

Lifting the heavy field-glasses, he moved silently towards the corporal who was bent over the mortar, but his pale shadow on the stones gave him away and the corporal looked up. Macomber was towering over the corporal, the glasses raised high for a smashing downward blow, when the German, displaying great agility, scampered backwards, his hand closing over the butt of the pistol as he leapt to his feet. Too late, Macomber realised that his reflexes had slowed down. He followed the German, who was quick-witted enough to realise he had no time to aim and fire, so he used the pistol barrel as a club and the Scot ran straight on to it. The sweeping gunsight raked the bridge of his nose, filling his eyes with tears which blurred his vision. The field-glasses slipped through his fingers and he knew he had lost the crucial advantage of those vital few seconds when the other man was distracted. He could still see the corporal as a vague shadow as he lashed out, a violent kick with his boot which caught the German a terrible blow on the kneecap. The blurred shadow stooped under the pain and Macomber stumbled forward, still hardly able to see what was happening. Instinctively, acting on pure blind reflex, he lifted his hands, linked them, and brought the coupled hands down with all his strength on the back of the corporal's exposed neck. The force of the blow sent a shudder up his own arms as the German leaned forward and collapsed on the stones, his body hiding the pistol he was still holding.

Wiping his eyes to clear the water, still half-groggy with the searing pain, Macomber saw the wireless operator on his knees while he tugged furiously to free something caught under the canvas which cushioned the bomb. It came free as

Macomber reached him. The German, still on his knees, swung round with the machine-pistol in his hands as the Scot grasped the end of the muzzle in mid-swing. Instead of pulling, which the German expected, he pushed viciously and the soldier lost balance, letting go of the weapon as he fell over backwards, but his elbows saved him. Hardly able to see what was happening, Macomber made a mistake – he thought he had enough time to get a proper grip on the weapon. He was still fumbling when the German was on his feet and at his throat, and the sheer momentum of his charge carried Macomber back against the waist-high tower wall. He couldn't even attempt to use the gun which was compressed between their bodies as they grappled fiercely but with little effect until Macomber began to feel himself being pressed back remorselessly over the brink. The soldier was a few inches shorter but he was powerfully-built and ten years younger, and the Scot was very close to the end of his physical resources. With the gun penned between them, the German had both hands locked tightly round Macomber's throat and now, as his head pounded with the pain from the blow on the sensitive bridge of his nose, he felt his air supply going. A momentary sense of panic gripped him as he felt himself going over the drop, the rim of the wall hard against the small of his back and acting as a fulcrum for the German to lever him into the depths.

Knowing that he was winning, the soldier forgot about the gun, squeezing his hands tighter as Macomber's face changed colour. The Scot's hands were still gripping the weapon and he managed to force it loose sideways, but he still couldn't use it. Had the German ignored the freed weapon and continued his pressure he would have sent Macomber over the edge within seconds, but he saw the gun come loose and released his right hand to grab for it, confident that his adversary was done for. And Macomber was half-stupefied – the German was holding his throat with only one hand but he had quickly inserted his thumb on the Scot's windpipe and his victim began to choke. Get rid of the gun! The message raced through Macomber's brain and he jerked feebly but with just sufficient force to snatch it out of the hand holding the dangling strap. He let go and the machine-pistol disappeared over the edge.

As the thumb pressure increased reddish lights sputtered in front of his eyes and he felt his last remaining strength ebbing away. This was it. Nothing else left. His right hand fluttered, felt hair at the moment when the German's nailed boot ground against his tender ankle. Pain shrieked up his leg like an electric shock and he was seized with a spasm of blind fury which sent fresh adrenalin through his veins. He grabbed a large handful of hair, clawed his hand, twisted it and dragged it sideways with all the energy he could muster, hauling at the hair as though to tear it out by the roots. The thumb pressure slackened, was released. Macomber sucked in a gasping lungful of cold mountain air, knowing that within seconds the brawny German would recover. Releasing the hair, he clawed his hand again and, as the soldier's face reappeared, he struck. The savagery of the onslaught unnerved the German and he propelled himself backwards away from the wall to save his face, catching the heel of his boot on an uplifted stone. He was fighting to restore his balance when he gave a yelp of fright and threw himself sideways, missing by inches the pile of fused bombs. A hazard for both of them, Macomber reminded himself as he used his legs and the lower part of his body to launch himself clear of the wall.

He could see clearly now but he was staggering like a drunken man as the German escaped the bombs and crashed into the mounted telescope. The contraption toppled heavily and broke in two – the barrel leaving the tripod to roll over the stones until it was stopped by the far wall, crossing the closed trap-door during its course. Someone was thudding heavily on the underside as though trying desperately to crack the bolt, but Macomber knew there was no chance of reaching it to draw the bolt: the German barred the way. He was trying to tug the Luger out of his pocket where it was caught up in the cloth when the soldier stooped and grabbed the loose tripod with both hands. It was a heavy metallic instrument and the Scot was still trying to free the Luger which was upside down inside the pocket when the German came at him. A vicious swipe from the tripod missed him by inches as he dodged and then the continuing flail of the club missed the piled bombs by centimetres as it almost shaved the noses. The German lifted the tripod for another blow as Macomber reached him, forgetting his Luger as the instrument began to descend. He grabbed the German close to his elevated wrists and they swayed within a foot of the bomb pile as the soldier tried to bring the tripod down and Macomber fought to keep it up. The Scot's nails stabbed into the other's wrists and the German felt his grip going. When he had to let go he endeavoured to drop it on Macomber's head but the tripod grazed his back and clattered to the stones. To save his head, Macomber had ducked, and now he rammed his lowered head forward, catching the soldier off guard. He felt the German keeling backwards and then a foot tripped Macomber and brought him to his knees with a jar that ran right through him. He was on all fours when he realised that the wall had half-saved his opponent. As the German slapped his hands on the wall-top to break his momentum a hand whipped round his right ankle and lifted. He made his last mistake. Still off balance, tilted back over the wall, he lifted his other foot to kick Macomber in the face, which brought both feet off the ground. The Scot hoisted as high as he could, no more than a few inches, but a little more of the German's weight was now poised over the brink than over the roof. The held foot jerked upwards out of Macomber's grasp as the soldier was propelled outwards and his scream came up as a fading wail as he plunged into space. Macomber hauled himself painfully to his feet and peered over, too late to see the spread-eagled figure swallowed up by the snow hundreds of feet below.

For no logical reason he pulled the Luger free from his coat and then used the wall for support until he was close to the trap-door. He pulled back the bolt but he left them to open it and when the lid lifted it was raised by Ford. Prentice stood above him with the Lee Enfield pointed at Macomber and a few steps down Grapos waited. The lieutenant came on to the roof and glanced round at the shambles – the broken telescope, the crumpled German corporal, the wireless-set which had been knocked over at some stage of the struggle. 'I thought there were two,' he said crisply.

'One went over the side . . . you'd better look down here quick.' Macomber was still holding on to the wall for support and he felt sick when he stared down at the lake. 'Burckhardt's nearly here,' he went on. 'Can you use that mortar, Ford?'

'It is an 8-cm. Yes. You stopped them lobbing stuff at our chaps, thank God.'

'We need the stuff lobbing elsewhere and pretty damned quick. The Aussies on that destroyer need time to land and come up the cliff path. I don't think they're going to get it.'

Prentice looped the rifle over his shoulder and gazed down with his hands resting on the wall. Burckhardt had moved quickly while Macomber was engaged in his struggle with the Germans: his force was already arrayed and moving far out on to the lake, so that as the lieutenant looked down from his crow's nest vantage point he had the sensation of watching a diorama in a war museum. Six half-tracks, spread out widely over the ice like toy models, led the advance, followed by Alpenkorps and parachutists en masse on foot. Further back more half-tracks crawled forward and each of the weird vehicles carried only its driver – to minimise casualties if the ice broke at any point Burckhardt had sensibly emptied the half-tracks of all superfluous passengers. Several light ack-ack guns and 75-mm. mountain howitzers, unlimbered from the half-tracks which had hauled them up the mountain road, were being drawn bodily over the ice, two men to a gun, and Prentice noticed that round all the vehicles and guns there were unoccupied areas of frozen lake – the men on foot were understandably nervous of the weight this equipment was imposing on the lake's surface. The impression of looking down on a scale model was heightened by the heavy silence which had fallen over the mountain as the wind dropped and no sound of the advancing army reached the watchers on the tower. Prentice looked round as Ford, with Grapos' aid, dragged the 8-cm. mortar into a new position behind the wall facing the lake.

'Any hope at all, Ford?'

'It depends,' replied the sergeant cautiously as he straightened up and stared out over the lake with his hands on his hips. The phlegmatic Ford, on whom everything hinged, seemed the calmest man on the roof as he took his time, turning his face sideways briefly to gauge the strength of the fading breeze, screwing up his eyes as he estimated distances and trajectories. While he made his calculations, Prentice crossed to the other side of the roof and was just in time to see the destroyer coming in close. It had altered course decisively and was steaming direct for the cape; within a few minutes it would have vanished under the lee of the bluff prior to commencing landing operations. The lieutenant called out a question to Grapos.

'How long do you reckon it would take a man to come up that cliff path?'

'Three or four hours. It depends on the man.'

Prentice was looking through the Monokular which Macomber had handed him. 'They're Aussies and probably some Kiwis, so they'll come up bloody fast.'

'Once Burckhardt's crossed the lake he'll be up here inside of thirty minutes,' said Macomber abruptly. 'What the hell is Ford playing at?'

'Leave him be.' Prentice had lowered his voice. 'He's like this – you can't hurry him but he knows what he's doing.'

'Just so long as he doesn't do it too late,' the Scot growled. 'And I suppose you've seen the lake isn't the only problem?'

Prentice nodded as he went back to the opposite wall. In

spite of the fact that he confidently expected the monastery to be in Braun's hands, Colonel Burckhardt was proving himself an excellent tactician and was leaving nothing to chance: the greater portion of his force was assembled on the lake, but beyond the distant shore two straggled lines of dots were ascending the lower slopes of Mount Zervos itself as the ski troops made for the monastery by a different route. Watching those two lines climbing higher, Prentice thought he could guess at that route. The southern shore of the lake was made impassable by a cliff which rose vertically from the ice's edge, but ski troops could ascend to a certain height from the eastern shore and then move westward over the mountain's flank above the cliff-top, following a route which he was pretty sure terminated at the beginning of the spur road running round the back of the monastery. The snow-bound mountain had an overloaded look above the cliff and Grapos, who had followed the lieutenant's gaze, spoke grimly.

'They will need care and luck up there.'

'Why?'

'The thaw is coming – the time for the mountain to move.'

'You mean avalanches?'

'Maybe. Each four or five years, the mountain comes alive. The last time was in nineteen hundred and thirty-six . . .'

'Avalanches don't happen to order,' Macomber broke in impatiently. 'And we'll need more than luck to halt this lot in their tracks.' He glanced savagely towards where Ford was examining a bomb he held cradled in his arms. The sergeant had the appearance of studying a theoretical exercise on a target range, so deliberate were his movements as he replaced the bomb on the canvas and then crouched down beside the mortar to make another adjustment to the angle. The Germans were about to take Zervos and this lunatic was fiddling around as though time meant nothing. Unable to give any directions or take any decisions, Macomber was enduring a fever of impatience and frustration as the half-tracks crawled steadily forward like mechanical bugs –

bugs which were now almost two-thirds of the distance across the lake. And even from the height where he stood he thought he could at last hear a faint purring sound travelling up through the still mountain air, the purr of engines and caterpillar tracks grinding over the ice. To give himself something to do, he focused his glass on a compact open car which was driving through the lines of men slowly as it reached a position mid-way between the distant lake shore and the leading half-tracks. Burckhardt would be inside that car, Macomber was thinking, and the colonel must have upwards of five hundred men on the lake and up the flank of the mountain.

'A Kubelwagen,' remarked Ford, who was now standing beside him. 'The car, I mean. Looks like a squashed bucket close up. They'd bring that in by glider.'

Macomber struggled grimly for control, biting back the anger he would have liked to unleash on the sergeant. Ford may have sensed something of his feelings because he looked up with a faint smile as he went on.

'I'm waiting for them all to get well out on the lake. No good half-doing the job. It shouldn't be more than a minute or two at the most.'

'There are also the ski troops coming across the mountain,' Macomber said tightly.

'One thing at a time, sir. That's my motto.'

Macomber thrust both hands fiercely inside his pockets, and inside the left one his fingers encountered a small hard object. He extracted a single cigar which must have dropped out of his case and lit it quickly to soothe his strung-up nerves. The first few puffs revived his flagging energy and his mood changed at once. Feeling he had displayed a certain amount of bad temper, he joked with Prentice. 'I've gone over to the enemy – I've developed a real liking for Jerry cigars.'

'No accounting for tastes.' Prentice was in the direct line of fire as the smoke drifted over him. 'I haven't liked to mention it earlier, but those things have the stench of old seaweed.'

'They're probably made of just that,' the Scot told him cheerfully. 'Everything in Germany these days is pretty ersatz. Except for the Wehrmacht,' he added, indicating what lay below with the cigar. The Kubelwagen was moving closer to the front line, halting frequently for a few seconds, presumably while Burckhardt had a word with his troops. The six half-tracks in front were now three-quarters of the way across the lake and within minutes they would have reached firm ground. Ford had his head bent forward as he watched them and spoke to Prentice at the same time.

'I'll need your help, sir, I'm thinking. I want to observe and I can't do that and load at the same time. So, you've just volunteered . . .'

'For God's sake,' Prentice exploded, 'I'll need a little tuition, won't I?'

'No, and I don't want you thinking about it too much. There are only three basic things to remember – don't put the bomb down nose first, or else we can all say goodbye; slide it in, don't push; and keep your hands out of the way afterwards if you want to hang on to them. Come on, I'll show you with the first one and then you're on your own – I'll be by the wall.'

Thirty bombs, Macomber noted. He had been counting the pile and it didn't seem many, not nearly enough. He was puffing rapidly as he went to the corner where Ford told him not to move from. Grapos was sent to another corner while the sergeant, who had been demonstrating to Prentice what he must do, ran to the wall for a last look down. Nodding to himself, he went back to the mortar, hoisted the first bomb and held it ready for feeding into the barrel. It was at this moment that Macomber noticed the faint trails in the snow on the nearside of the lake, trails which reached the shore and then curved back towards the lake's centre. Earlier Burckhardt must have sent a single half-track over the full length of the ice to test its stability before risking his whole force. The entire German strength was now mustered over the lake or up on the mountain and Macomber found himself clenching his cigar tightly as he waited for the first bomb to go away.

It was fired a few seconds later, soaring out over the wall and diminishing almost instantly in size as it described an arc and landed on the ice some distance ahead of the leading half-tracks. Macomber watched its fall, feet wide apart as when he had played Dietrich, hands clasped behind his back. Nothing happened. He thought he saw a brief spurt of snow where the projectile hit. Then nothing. His eyes met Ford's as the sergeant pressed his hands flat on the wall, taking up his position of observation while Prentice lifted another bomb and stood by the mortar.

'It didn't go off,' said Macomber.

'I thought not. A dud. Let's hope the whole batch isn't. I hear there's quite a lot of sabotage in German factories.' Looking over his shoulder at Prentice, Ford gave the order. 'Fire!' The second bomb was away, vanishing to a pinhead. It landed close to the dud, followed by the sound of its detonation. To Macomber's bitter disappointment the ice remained intact. Was it too thick for penetration? In his state of extreme fatigue his hopes hadn't been too high from the beginning. 'Fire!' Ford had rushed to the mortar to make a fractional adjustment to the angle of the barrel before returning to the wall and giving the order. The third bomb sped through its parabola, curved in its descent. It landed close to the leading half-tracks and the distant thump echoed back to the tower as snow flew in the air with the burst of the bomb. An area of black shadow fissured across the lake as the ice cracked and disintegrated and water opened up under three half-tracks. 'Fire!' The fourth bomb spread the fracturing process as the three half-tracks disappeared almost simultaneously. One moment they were there and then they were gone as a new lake spread, a lake of ice-cold water. Over fifty metres deep, Grapos had informed Macomber in reply to an earlier question while they had waited for Ford to complete his preparations. So those half-tracks were now settling one hundred and fifty feet below the lake's surface.

'Fire!' Ford had made a further minor adjustment before he rushed back to the wall, his head thrust forward as he scanned the whole lake. At this stage even Macomber, who could see what was happening, had not grasped the magnitude of the plan Ford had devised for the destruction of the entire German forces.

The fifth bomb sped out over the wall, almost too fast for the eye to follow, descended, struck the lake in the middle of the three surviving half-tracks closest to Zervos. Another spray of snow flashed upwards, another thump reached the distant tower, and then a huge area of ice cracked. Macomber gazed with astonishment as a sheet of ice became a temporary island separated from the rest of the frozen lake, a sheet supporting the three half-tracks and a group of Alpenkorps gathered behind them. The island's existence was momentary. The sheet fissured in all directions, broke up and sank. Through his Monokular glass Macomber saw one half-track at the outer edge of the ice go down, wheels first, the tracks tilting upwards into the air, and then the whole vehicle slid out of sight under the ink-dark water which had appeared. The chance of a single man surviving in those sub-zero waters was nil. 'Fire!' The next bomb landed further to the right, just reaching the ragged rim of the still-intact ice, detonating while still above the water-line. Figures beyond the rim were thrown into confusion, some falling and some scattering in a hopeless search for safety. The whole ordered array on the lake was beginning to change, to falter, to break up into a vast disorganised chaos as Ford increased the attack, frequently adjusting direction or angle or both.

'Fire!' This bomb travelled much further, the zenith of its parabola far higher above the lake, the descent point more distant. With the forgotten cigar still between his lips, Macomber rammed the Monokular into his eye, aiming it at the Kubelwagen. He heard the thump and saw the snow dust at almost the same moment – dust which rose immediately behind Burckhardt's vehicle. The whiteness surrounding the car dissolved, became pitch-black water, and as the vehicle went straight down Macomber saw there were still four people inside. Burckhardt was drowning, surrounded by his own troops. The fresh area of sinking ice stretched out towards the monastery road, tilting as men on top of it ran in all directions trying to escape. Macomber saw one man run straight off the edge into the water and as he took the glass away from his eye the ice sheet went under. A huge channel of dark water, perhaps a hundred yards wide, separated the frozen area of the lake from the road on the western shore which led up to the monastery.

'Fire!' Ford had again made an adjustment and Macomber saw that the mortar's barrel was pointed at an extreme angle. The bomb coursed out over the lake, became a tiny dark speck against the whiteness below, and landed close to the distant eastern shore on the far side of the troops. The thump was fainter. A fresh channel of water opened up, starting at the shoreline and spreading inwards towards the centre as three more bombs landed and black dots scurried over the diminishing white surface. Two mountain guns vanished. A half-track driving to the rear to escape the cannonade drove straight over the edge. More than a third of the attacking force on the frozen lake had disappeared and for the first time Macomber grasped the painstaking cleverness of Ford's plan. He had quartered the lake systematically in his mind and was destroying it section by section in such a way that he could inflict the maximum amount of damage, commencing with the vital section near the road up to the monastery, working backwards, and then over-leaping to destroy the ice near the far shore. His ultimate objective was to compress the surviving Wehrmacht force on a huge island of ice caught between water to east and west, the snow-drifted road to the north, and the sheer cliff wall of Mount Zervos to the south.

'Fire!' The bomb landed uselessly in clear water. 'Fire!' Macomber's glass was focused just beyond the most recent dropping point and he saw two puffs of snow as the bomb bounced across the ice and detonated in the midst of a crowd of German troops fleeing towards the cliffs. At this point some of the more quick-thinking Alpenkorps were escaping. Using their climbing ropes, they had begun to scale the precipitous cliff face, realising that only suspended in air would they be safe from the rain of missiles pouring down on them. Ford was now turning his attention to the section of frozen lake which bordered the snow-drifted road. A large number of troops and a mountain gun were heading for the drift zone when the falling bombs began to shatter their escape route, driving them back on to the huge remaining sheet of ice which covered perhaps a third of the lake. 'Fire!' Macomber removed the Monokular and dropped it into his pocket. The fatigue of staring through his glass made him rub his eyes and then dab them with his handkerchief, and all the time the bombardment was continuing as Ford concentrated on the huge island of ice covered with marooned Germans. 'Fire!' 'Fire!' 'Fire . . .!' Macomber had lost count of the number of bombs Prentice had slipped into the barrel, but he was aware that the rate was increasing as Ford built up the barrage and Prentice, wiping his hands frequently on his trousers for fear of dropping a bomb, fed the mortar with fresh ammunition.

When Macomber looked out across the wall again he was astounded at the change of scene. The lake, which had so recently been a white plain, was now a dark sheet spattered with what, from that height, looked like slivers of snow, but which were really large spars of floating ice. The central island had almost disappeared and there was only a handful of men still marooned on a small patch of whiteness which Ford had surrounded with five fountainheads of spurting water. Five misses. The next bomb landed dead centre on the remaining floe and fragmented it. Perhaps a dozen Alpenkorps men still clung to the cliff face which they were slowly ascending, but the invasion force on the lake had been annihilated.

'Like a target range,' Ford said. 'Unique.'

'Not quite,' Macomber reminded him quietly. 'There was also Austerlitz.*'

There were three bombs left on the tower roof when Grapos took hold of Ford's arm and pointed. Unlike the others, whose whole attention had been concentrated on the lake below, the Greek had been watching with increasing anxiety the ski-troops' progress. They had now climbed the slope to a point well above the cliff-top and were coming forward in a line which curled over the flank of the mountain. The leading man was less than a quarter of a mile away as he sped closer towards the rear of the monastery.

'You make avalanche,' Grapos said urgently. 'Where the dark hole is . . .'

'He means that hollow in shadow,' Prentice interjected. 'Why there?' Ford was already shifting the mortar's position and then changing the angle of fire as the Greek went on talking, and there was no deliberation in his movements as he struggled to bring the weapon to bear before it was too late.

'Because,' Grapos explained, 'that is where the Austrian ski man started the avalanche five years since. We had warned him not to go – but he laughed at us. I was standing on this roof watching him. He came down over that hole and the avalanche begins. The mountain comes alive.'

'Better try it, Ford,' said Prentice wearily. 'It's a gamble but it's the only one we've got. If that lot gets through there's more than enough of them to make a mess of the Australians if they're posted above them.'

'No offence meant, but I'd like to handle this myself. I can see them coming this time.'

'You're welcome,' replied Prentice. His arms were stiff and aching with the continuous lifting of the bombs and now that he had paused he didn't trust himself to handle any more. The reaction was setting in and he felt he might collapse on the roof at any moment. To hold himself up he went to a

* At Austerlitz Napoleon destroyed a Russian army by firing at a frozen lake and drowning the enemy crossing the ice.

corner and leant against the wall close to Macomber. The Scot was looking through his glass at the hollow which lay perhaps a hundred feet above the advancing line of Alpenkorps, and he saw the first bomb hit the snow some distance above the hollow.

'Damn!' It was the first display of emotion Ford had shown since they had begun firing the mortar. The shot was wide and he knew it was his fault – he hadn't taken enough care over the initial preparation in his anxiety to do something quickly. And there were no bombs this time to waste on ranging shots. He adjusted the angle and picked up the second bomb. Macomber saw this one land below the hollow, close enough to the Alpenkorps column to encourage a sudden swerve in the line which was well spread – the section leader had not overlooked the lesson of what had happened on the lake, and had spaced out his column so that it would have taken a hail of bombs from a dozen mortars to cause many casualties. Ford bit his lip. Too low this time. And only one more to go. But he kept his nerve: the first two shots had bracketed the target above and below, so now he must drop one mid-way between the two points. He adjusted the barrel very carefully, took a deep breath, then fed in the final bomb. It hit the mountain a short way above the hollow.

The four men on the tower were very quiet and stood perfectly still while they waited. Behind them the mortar barrel gaped at the sky, as harmless now as a piece of old scrap iron, something they might as well tip over the wall so that at least the Alpenkorps would never use it. It was imagination, but the Scot fancied he could hear the faint swish of oncoming skis as he stood with his eyes fixed on Mount Zervos. He blinked and looked again, unsure whether his eyes had played him a trick. He had been watching the hollow but now he transferred his gaze higher up the mountain to a point near the summit where something had caught his attention. Was there a gentle ripple of movement, so gentle that the eye would never have noticed it but for their fading hopes? There seemed to be a trembling, a hazy wobble close to the peak. Slowly, like the rolling back of a sheet, the snow began to move in a long wave, the wave stretching the full width of the slope as it surged downwards, gathering height as it swallowed up more snow. And now Macomber could hear something – a faint growl which gradually grew in strength and deepened to a sinister rumble as he saw fresh signs of something terrible happening. The slope was shifting downwards at increasing velocity, a moving slope at least a mile wide as the wave mounted higher, picked up momentum and thundered down on the Germans like a mounting tidal wave. The mountain had come alive.

Macomber understood Grapos' words as he watched the whole slope seething and rolling down on a terrifying scale as Mount Zervos erupted sideways, the wave curling at the crest as the snow slide roared forward, the rumble now a tremendous sound in their dazed ears, a sound like the eruption of a major volcano blowing its lava flow up from the interior of the earth. The Alpenkorps tried to scatter at the last moment as the mountain bore down on them, and for a brief second in time they were like a disturbed nest of ants scurrying away from catastrophe. Then the wave reached them, sweeping over the broken line from end to end, engulfing them, burying them, carrying them down the slope and over the cliff face as the wave cascaded like a vast waterfall down the precipice and washed away the men still ascending its face. Prentice shouted his frantic warning as the wave reached the cliff-top – the leading skier, not yet overwhelmed by the avalanche, had stopped, unlooped his rifle from his back, and was taking aim at the roof of the tower. Macomber, his gaze fixed on the cliff-top, heard the shout too late. He was dropping to the floor when the bullet thudded into him and when he sprawled across the stones he was unconscious.

*

The calendar on the wall registered Monday, April 14. The

window framed a view of Athens rooftops. The feet pushing up the sheets at the end of the hospital bed suggested the accommodation was too small or the occupant too large.

'We'll get a bigger bed for you in Alex.,' Prentice assured the Scot as he sat down. 'It should be all right in Egypt – the dragomen out there are almost as big as you are. They're flying you out soon, by the way.'

'When my shoulder's mended, remind me to punch you on the jaw for that remark,' Macomber growled. 'Now, what happened after the destroyer brought me out?'

'They took you down that cliff path strapped to a stretcher,' Prentice said thoughtfully. 'Pity you hadn't been conscious – the view going down must have been quite something . . .'

'I said what happened!'

'Keep your shirt on – the one you're not wearing. The Aussies and Kiwis went up that cliff path like demons. They occupied the monastery and another lot dragged up dismantled twenty-five pounders – God knows how. They held the place while our chaps came back down the coast road unscathed. Our people over here guessed something was wrong on Zervos when the *Hydra* blew up . . .' He paused. 'You've heard we're back in business, I suppose? There's another retreat on the go.'

'I dragged it out of the nursing orderly. He seemed to think the news might send my blood pressure up – what sent it up was getting him to talk . . .'

'And talking isn't allowed much now, I gather. Wilson said if the Jerries had been on Zervos there'd have been a massacre when our lot started coming back down the coast on the other side of the gulf . . .' Prentice went on talking for a short time and then, satisfied that Macomber was a good deal stronger than he'd feared, he took his leave with a mischievous expression on his face. 'I'd better push off now – there's a chap who's anxious to see you. A Captain Brown.' He paused when he saw the look on the Scot's face. 'This one really does spell his name B-R-O-W-N. I know you've seen the Intelligence people but he wants to see you about something quite different. He's only just arrived, doesn't know much about you, and he's very admin., so treat him gently – like you treat everyone.'

'What is it about?' Macomber demanded suspiciously.

''Bye for now. I'll send him in.'

Macomber sat up straighter in bed, pounding a pillow into submission. His rising irritation was making him feel better already and he glared savagely at Captain Brown as the officer came in breezily.

'Are we improving, I hope?'

'We were.'

Brown was a slim man in his late thirties. He wore a bristly moustache which Macomber took an instant dislike to, wavy brown hair, and his uniform was spotless. His complexion was white, so he wasn't out of the desert; he was probably fresh out of Whitehall. He sat down carefully, propped a large form pinned to a board on his knee, and smiled encouragingly.

'You're a civilian of military age. Rather unusual out here, and that's why you concern me.'

'Don't let it get you down.'

Brown looked confused. He smiled palely. 'I meant you come within my jurisdiction. I gather you came out of the Balkans recently – you must have travelled with Legation staff.'

'Something like that.'

'I hear the Germans treat them surprisingly well – all the courtesies observed and all that.'

'Naturally.'

'So it may come as a bit of a shock to hear that you're probably eligible for military service.'

'You don't happen to have a packet of German cigars on you?' Macomber enquired.

'No, I don't.' Brown's manner stiffened and then he remembered he was addressing a patient. 'I don't smoke at all. You've gone a bit reddish since I arrived.'

'Blood pressure.'

Brown rose at once. 'Perhaps I shouldn't have mentioned the military bit at this stage. I'll come back later.' He patted the bed genially. 'Look, old chap, there's not a thing to worry yourself about – we'll make a soldier of you yet.'